# TWENTY-FIVE HUNDRED HISTORICAL WOODWIND INSTRUMENTS

An Inventory of the Major Collections

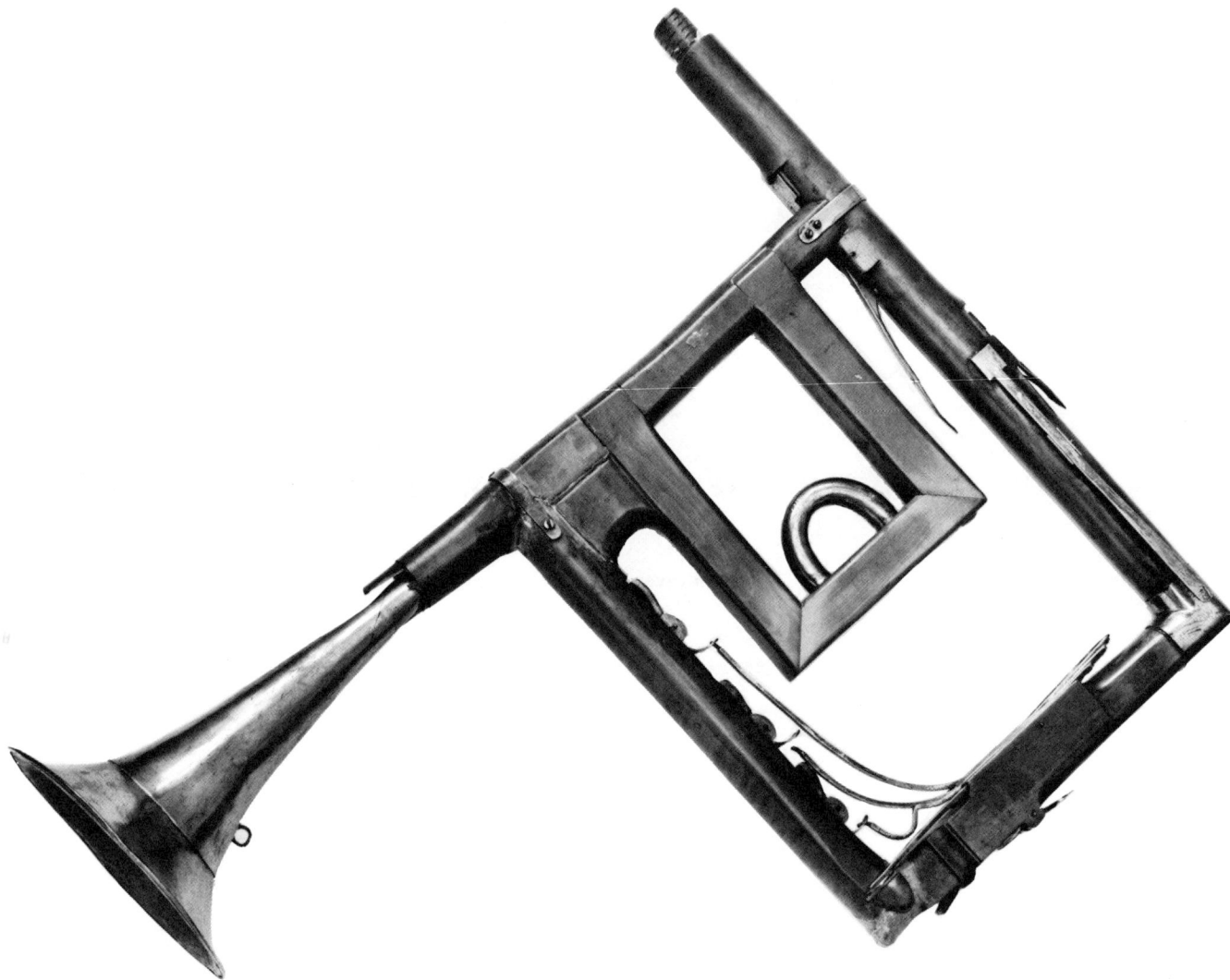

Basset horn, by Johann Georg Eisenmenger, Mannheim. See Plate V, center of the book, for further details.

# TWENTY-FIVE HUNDRED HISTORICAL WOODWIND INSTRUMENTS

## An Inventory of the Major Collections

I·C·DENNER

by

Phillip T. Young

*PENDRAGON PRESS*     New York, N.Y.

*To the memory of*

*JOSEF MARX*

*Also by Phillip T. Young*

Lichtenwanger, Hoover, Higbee, and Young, *A Survey of Musical Instrument Collections in the United States and Canada,* Ann Arbor 1974

Phillip T. Young, *The Look of Music, Rare Musical Instruments 1500 - 1900,* Vancouver 1980

**Library of Congress Cataloging in Publication Data**

Young, Phillip T.
  Twentyfive hundred historical woodwind instruments.

  Bibliography: p.
  Include index.
    1. Woodwind instruments——Catalogs and collections.
I. Title.  II. Title: Twenty five hundred historical
woodwind instruments.  III. Title: 2500 historical
woodwind instruments.
ML462.Y69      788' .05'075          81—17724
ISBN 0—918728—17—7                  AACR2

# TABLE OF CONTENTS

# PREFACE

I needed this book for my own work, and since no one else had it under way, I decided to do it myself. I began collecting such data almost twenty years ago and only much later thought of it becoming a book. Now it has been my principal research activity for several years. I confess that I have both amused myself and found grim encouragement in the possibility that this might be the last such compilation done without computer assistance.

The Galpin Society *Journal* had published inventories of instruments by Bressan, the Stanesbys, Gedney, Collier, Hale, and the Schucharts, among others, and in 1967 published my own inventory of instruments by Johann Christoph and Jacob Denner. Even *I* found it difficult thereafter to keep up with or even to find a logical place to record the additions and amplifications that trickled in. The Galpin Society *Journal* reported specific changes on its 'Current Register of Historic Instruments' page, but otherwise could not spare precious space for entire revisions of such lists. The successive editors of *GSJ*, the late Eric Halfpenny and both earlier and more recently Anthony Baines, encouraged me to work toward a book and generously gave me permission to update the inventories already published. Dr. Maurice Byrne has kindly allowed me to revise and republish his lists in the Galpin Society *Journal,* to which it will be seen that I have been able to add relatively little.

One of my first stimuli was the vague statement in Grove's Dictionary, 5th edition, that "more than fifty" Denner instruments had survived; I knew that *I* had seen nearly that many on a single tour of principal European collections in 1964. Surely there must be others. Indeed, when the Denner inventory appeared in 1967 it listed 67 instruments vs. 123 recorded here. I am certain that a further edition of this book will be necessary not only through my further work but by reader contributions, more numerous that much sooner by publication of this book now, holes and all.

I have hoped it would be a useful reference book, but I also think there will be those who actually sit down to *read* it, discovering as I have on almost any page a new characteristic or apparent preference or idiosyncracy of a maker that had not been clear before. I have not always called attention to each such point in recognition of the pleasure of discovery for one's self and awareness that fresh perspective will often permit varied conclusions. Debated at length were the respective merits of vertical columns of data vs. a short paragraph devoted to each instrument, the latter format used in *GSJ XXXI* in my inventory of instruments by six Dresden and Leipzig makers. There are advantages in each system of organization, but I think the present format using columns, with many footnotes for overflow, is a happy solution.

WHY INVENTORIES AT ALL?

In my opinion, it is simply impossible to overstate the importance to us all of Lyndesay Langwill's *Index of Musical Wind Instrument Makers.* At the same time, the lists of instruments under every maker's name in Langwill's *Index* were never intended to be complete listings, of course, and by now are clogged with stale information and uncorrected errors. Where can one go to find a list of surviving Hotteterre instruments, for example? (A very *important* example.) How many flutes made by Boehm himself or saxophones by Adolphe Sax still exist? Are oboes *made* by Guillaume Triebert himself stamped with any distinguishing mark from his sons' oboes?

Even if we had fat, decisive, regularly updated catalogues of the major collections, inventories devoted to individual makers would have special value. We may count ourselves blessed by the appearance within a few years of each other of two volumes (string and brass, respectively) of an excellent new catalogue of the Berlin Musikinstrumenten Museum, a complete catalogue of the Bachhaus Collection in Eisenach by the brilliant Herbert Heyde, and several volumes (winds by Heyde and various keyboard volumes by his colleague, Hubert Henkel) of a new catalogue of the Leipzig Musikinstrumenten Museum. Fortunately, all these are *models* of what instrument catalogues should be. Now available is the first volume (brass) of John Henry van der Meer's long-awaited catalogue of instruments in the Germanisches Nationalmuseum, Nürnberg, a major catalogue beyond question, thanks to its author himself and to the quality of the collection he has assembled.

Beyond that, the picture is very bleak indeed. I know of no new catalogue planned (the previous catalogue's publication date is in parentheses) in Brussels (1893-1912), Paris (1884-1903), Frankfurt (1927), New York's Metropolitan Museum (1902), the Smithsonian (1927), and Stockholm (1928). The Hague Gemeente Museum and Vienna's Neue

Burg Museum have apparently suspended publication of further volumes after producing a single volume each (brass and keyboards, respectively, in 1970 and 1966). In any event, inventories give us not only some of the more important data we might learn from a museum catalogue but in a form that makes comparison and synthesis notably easier and perhaps more productive, therefore.

It has been necessary of course to omit data that would be useful to many readers. Overall length of specimens is given where known, but is of limited use; overall length of air column would be better, but I have not found it practicable to make accurate measurements of such elbows and turns as are encountered in many brass instruments, for example. Overall lengths are normally with the longer or longest alternate joint, except as noted. *Beware:* instruments' measurements change to a remarkable degree. Even overall length can vary as much as 3 to 5 millimeters from week to week, using the same rule. My own measurements are used, of course, whenever they differ from those given in catalogues and other books.

The number of pieces, joints, or sections of which the fully assembled instrument is comprised, is a useful point in descriptions of flutes and clarinets if less so with oboes and bassoons. The sole reason I use the word 'piece,' as in '3 pc,' incidentally, is that it abbreviated more compactly than 'section.' It will amuse some (the book can stand this) that I have troubled to record whether a key spring is attached to the underside of the key (SATK) or to the wood (SATW) or ivory (SATI).

This minor detail can be valuable in determining which keys might be later replacements, and then, how much later. There will be instances, for example, where a ten-keyed oboe has its c' and e♭' springs attached to the body, three other keys' springs riveted to the keys themselves, and five keys on posts and axles with needle springs. If not necessarily conclusive, this raises some questions at least. It has seemed that 'SATW' would be an easier abbreviation to recall than just 'W' by itself. The column headed 'Pitch' will disturb many readers. Letters are not precise but are intended as a rough guide. Often they are the Museum's deduction rather than mine.

Finally, a blank space means that the datum is not yet known. If an instrument is known to be unmounted, it will be so specified. A blank space means that it is not known whether it is mounted or not. Three dashes (———) means the information will not be available, ever.

I hope that readers will inundate me with reports of further instruments that should be added to this inventory and with further details of those that are already listed. All such contributions will be acknowledged, by letter if time permits, and certainly in any subsequent edition as well. Such help is earnestly solicited.

*P. T. Y.*

School of Music
University of Victoria
Victoria, B.C. V8W 2Y2
Canada

February, 1982

# ACKNOWLEDGEMENTS

This book has been made possible by several institutions with which I have been fortunate to be associated. While a member of the faculty of The Taft School, Watertown, Connecticut, I was given my first five-key boxwood clarinet by a colleague, was encouraged to mount a loan exhibition of early American woodwinds at the School—the largest such exhibition to that date, and was eventually awarded its Farwell Fellowship to visit the more important European instrument collections. From that exhibition and that European tour came the first data that would become this book. At Taft I was also encouraged to undertake graduate study at the School of Music, Yale University, which resulted in a master's thesis devoted to Asa Hopkins of Fluteville, Connecticut, one of the first American woodwind makers. When I later joined the School of Music faculty, it resulted as well in a close association with the Yale Collection of Musical Instruments.

The University of Victoria granted me study leave in 1975-76 to live in Munich from whence to gather data for this project. I was assisted then and have been repeatedly before and since by travel grants from the University. In 1977 I was invited by the Vancouver Centennial Museum to plan and to select all specimens for an international loan exhibition of instruments, *The Look of Music*, that took place in Vancouver from November 1980 through March 1981. While traveling in North America and Europe for the Museum, I was able to add significantly to the manuscript.

So important and unbelievably generous has been the help given by many, many people that I must try to list them individually however likely it is that a few will be accidentally omitted. It has touched and pleased me enormously that among those most patient and eager to help are some of the most admired, busiest performers on early instruments: Michel Piguet, Nikolaus Harnoncourt, Frans Brüggen, William Waterhouse, Bruce Haynes, Paul Hailperin, Konrad Ruhland, Piet Honingh, and Hans Rudolf Stadler, to name a few. Robert Kessler of Pendragon Press has been generous with expertise exceeded only by his patience and good humor. Closer to home, and especially in translating from other languages, I have been given generous help by my friends and colleagues Gordana Lazarevich, Hana Komorous, Elisabeth Duschnitz, Jesse Read, Anthony Booker, Nicholas V. Galichenko, and especially my wife, Catherine.

To the last named, special thanks for special patience and more.

## INDIVIDUAL ACKNOWLEDGEMENTS

Dr. Richard Abel, Doylestown
Florence Abondance, Paris
Clifford Allanson, Delmar, New York
Øystein Angen, Trondheim
Dr. Anthony Baines, Oxford
Dr. Sigrid Barton, Zurich
Philip Bate, London
Nicholas Benn, Meopham
Dr. Alfred Berner, Berlin
Ludwig Böhm, Munich
David D. Boyden, Berkeley
Alfredo Bernardini, Rome
Josiane Bran-Ricci, Paris
Susan Brombaugh, New Haven

Frans Brüggen, Amsterdam
Willi Burger, Zurich
Ernst W. Buser, Binningen
Sand Dalton, Orcas Island
Henk de Wit, Jr., Amsterdam
René de Maeyer, Brussels
Ilse Domizlaff, Eisenach
Dr. Robert E. Eliason, Dearborn
Dr. Ernst Emsheimer, Stockholm
Thomas Eschler, Rothenbach
Hans Fabini, Munich
Adolf Gebhard, Biebrich
Dr. Brigitte Geiser Bachmann, Bern
Ernst Gewinner, Markneukirchen

Dr. Henrik Glahn, Copenhagen
Paul Hailperin, Zell-Riedichen
Malou Haine, Brussels
The late Eric Halfpenny, Ilford
Dr. Nikolaus Harnoncourt, Vienna
Pastor Günter Hart, Peine
Christa Hartl, Passau
The late Dr. Kurt Haselhorst, Munich
Bruce Haynes, Dedemsvaart
Peter Hedrick, Ithaca
Dr. Karl Heller, Darmstadt
Friedmann Hellwig, Nürnberg
Dr. Hubert Henkel, Leipzig
Dr. Herbert Heyde, Leipzig

*Acknowledgements*

Dale Higbee, Salisbury
Renate Hildebrand, Basel
Dr. Georg Himmelheber, Munich
Piet Honingh, Haarlem
Cynthia Adams Hoover, Washington
Helmut Hoyler, Cologne
Heikki Hyvonen, Helsinki
Dr. Gisela Jaacks, Hamburg
Dr. Friedrich Jakob, Männedorf
Corneille F. Janssen, Assen
The late Will Jansen, Nieuw Loosdrecht
Jean Jenkins, London
Hanna Jordan, Markneukirchen
Berol Kaiser-Reka, Frankfurt-am-Oder
Cary Karp, Stockholm
Marcario Santiago Kastner, Lisbon
Jindřich Keller, Prague
James Kennedy, Victoria
Ignace de Keyser, Brussels
Jerome Kohl, Seattle
Dr. Henryk Kondziela, Poznan
Rudolf Komorous, Victoria
Greta Kraus, Haslemere
Dr. Dieter Krickeberg, Berlin
Barbara Lambert, Boston
Lyndesay G. Langwill, Edinburgh
Dr. André P. Larson, Vermillion
Robert A. Lehman, New York
Dr. Simon Lewin, Leningrad
Laurence Libin, New York
William Lichtenwanger, Maryland
G. Littmann. Kassel
Richard Lottridge, Madison

Dr. Victor Luithlen, Vienna
The late Josef Marx, New York
Hans-Jörg Maucksch, Göttingen
William Maynard, Massapequa Park
Rosario Mazzeo, Carmel
Ursula Menzel, Bucheberg
Dr. Hermann Moeck, Celle
Jeremy Montagu, Oxford
Mette Müller, Copenhagen
Dr. Walter Nef, Basel
Dr. Ekkehart Nickel, Schwabach
John Norris, Great Yarmouth
R.W. Payne, Oklahoma City
Michel Piguet, Basel
Lanny Pollet, Victoria
Wolfgang Rauch, Berlin
Jesse Read, Victoria
Richard Rephann, New Haven
Nicholas Renouf, New Haven
E.A.K. Ridley, London
Dorothy & Robert Rosenbaum, Scarsdale
Dr. Richard Roth, Rheinfelden
Dr. Konrad Ruhland, Niederalteich
Dr. Konrad Sasse, Halle
Dr. Manfred Hermann Schmid, Munich
Dr. Maria Schmidt, Cologne
Dr. Margot Seidenberg, Zürich
Frederick R. Selch, New York
Michael Seyfrit, Washington
Nicholas J. Shackleton, Cambridge

Robert Sheldon, Washington
David Shorey, Cranberry Island
John Shortridge, Rockport
Alois Sittinger, Munich
Hans Rudolf Stalder, Zumikon
Hans Ulrich Staeps, Vienna
Warren Steel, Ann Arbor
Dr. Gerhard Stradner, Vienna
Dr. Walter Thoene, Berlin
Fritz Thomas, Munich
Walter Thut, Zürich
Jacques Tilmans, Brussels
Dr. John Henry van der Meer, Nürnberg
Stuart-Morgan Vance, Louisville
Karl Ventzke, Düren
Dr. Volker v. Volckhamer, Harburg
Dr. Clemens von Gleich, The Hague
Dr. Robert A. Warner, Ann Arbor
William Waterhouse, London
Rainer Weber, Bayerbach
Dr. Kurt Wegerer, Vienna
Elizabeth P. Wells, London
Wolfgang Wenke, Eisenach
Christan Widmer-Ritter, Burgdorf
Dr. Brigitte Wied, Linz
Narcissa Williamson, Boston
Dr. Wolfgang Willms, Aachen
Michael Zadro, New Paltz
The late Dr. Helmut Zeraschi, Leipzig
Frau J. Zimmermann, Düren

# HOW TO USE THIS BOOK

The book is organized alphabetically by makers' last name, and under each maker's name the instruments are listed in the following order, basically the common top-to-bottom order as found in orchestral scores:

|              |                  |
|--------------|------------------|
| recorders:   | soprano          |
|              | alto             |
|              | tenor            |
|              | bass             |
| piccolos     |                  |
| flutes       | sopranos         |
|              | low flutes       |
| oboes        | soprano          |
|              | d'amore          |
|              | tenor            |
|              | English horns    |
|              | baritone or bass |
| clarinets    | soprano          |
|              | basset horns     |
|              | alto             |
|              | tenor            |
|              | bass             |
|              | d'amour          |
| bassoons     | fagottini        |
|              | usual (bass)     |
|              | contrabassoons   |

Other woodwinds such as saxophones, Heckelphones, musettes, racketts, shawms, and the various flageolets, flutes d'accord, galoubets, czakans, and walking-stick instruments, etc., are inserted at what seem appropriate places in the above basic order. Brasswinds follow in those few instances when the maker made both.

The typical listing ideally includes the following data about each specimen, listed in columns under the several headings:

Left to Right:

*Young Number:* under each general type, consecutive numbering

*Number of keys and key metal:* the principal means of organization, fewest keys increasing to most keys within each general type.

*City where now located, owner, inventory number:* some abbreviation necessary, but more detailed versions may often be found in Appendix A: Museums and Collections Represented.

*Pitch:* soprano, tenor, etc., if not given in heading, and/or in E, Bb, F, etc.

*Number of pieces:* how many sections make up the completely assembled instrument, irrespective of alternate upper joints, any missing sections, etc.

*Height/length:* overall length in centimeters, not including reed or staple. Angular and sickle-form instruments are measures from mouthpiece tip, along the outer side, to the bell rim, and are therefore only approximations. Parentheses around a given height indicate that the length is innacurate, usually because one section is missing or is a replacement.

*Body and mounts:* the material of which the body is formed; unless *unmounted*, what further material is used for decorative and/or structural rings.

*Flaps:* the shape of that broad portion of the key that covers a sound hole: round, square, trapezoid, and/or one of the shapes shown in Appendix D.

*Springs attached to:* either to the wood of the body (SATW), underside of key (SATK), or if the body is ivory (SATI). Significance is discussed in the Preface.

*Finger holes doubled:* counting from the top (near the mouth), various finger holes may be doubled. Nos. 3 and 4 are most common, 7 infrequently.

*Tuning holes:* double-reed instruments may have one, two, or as many as four "tuning holes" in their bells.

*Additional details:* whatever has not been compressed into one of the above.

*Illustrated in:* the most important sources of such photographs are found in Appendix B: Bibliography and Sources of Illustrations of Specific Instruments. Each entry has its abbreviation, which is given (often with specific page number) under this heading, e.g. "Schröeder Hamburg" or "JJ-GT-BR".

On the pages devoted to certain makers, the above order and even the headings themselves have been altered in the interest of better organization. Examples are Papalini, Mayrhofer, Hans Rauch von Schratt, and Claude Rafi. Such modification is obvious where it occurs. I am uncomfortable with the heading "Young number" but it does permit such precise identification as, for example, "Grundmann oboe, Young no.4" and "Delusse contrebass oboe, Young no. 1."

# LIST OF PLATES

*Plates are located between pages 84 and 85*

Plate I — Two bass recorders by Hans Rauch von Schratt (...1535...) from the Bayerisches Nationalmuseum, Munich.
Above: Great bass, No. Mu 180
Below: Quintbass, No. Mu 174

Plate II — Three close-ups of the above.

Plate III — Two oboes by Hendrik Richters from the Gemeente Museum, The Hague.
Above: No. Ea 7-X-1952
Below: No. Ea 584-1933

Plate IV — Basset horn, by Johann Georg Eisenmenger, Mannheim, No. Mu. 128, Bayerisches Nationalmuseum, Munich. (also frontispiece.)

Plate V — Four bassoons by Heinrich Grenser, Dresden, from the Gemeente Museum, The Hague. Each instrument is reproduced with the front view on the top and rear view on the bottom. This plate covers two pages.

Plate VI — Four bassoons from the collection of William Waterhouse, London. The makers are (1) F.G.A. Kirst, (2) Kaspar Tauber, (3) Thomas Stanesby, Sr., and (4) Stanesby, Jr. Three of the bass joints are intentionally reversed to show keys.

Plate VII — Three early American instruments, ca. 1810
Top: bassoon, John Meacham, Jr., Hartford, from the Collection of Prof. Richard Lottridge, Madison, Wisconsin. 4 brass keys.
Middle: bass clarinet, "Invented and Made by George Catlin, Hartford, Con." from the Henry Ford Museum, Dearborn, Michigan, No. 77.68.1, 6 brass keys.
Bottom: bassoon, Catlin Bliss, Hartford, from the Collection of Greenfield Village and the Henry Ford Museum, Dearborn, Michigan, No. 77.68.2, 6 brass keys.

Plate VIII — Two Hotteterre instruments from the Collection of Frans Brüggen, Amsterdam.
Oboe: 2 silver keys, boxwood, ivory mounts.
Tenor recorder: (anchor) 1 silver key, grenadilla, ivory mounts.

Plate IX — Three oboes from the Musikinstrumenten Museum, Leipzig.
Top: No. 1327, Fornari, Venice (undated), ivory keys, one a long c' for LH 4
Middle: No. 1312, Rippert (undated), 2 silver keys, boxwood with ivory mounts
Bottom: No. 1328, Fornari, Venice (dated 1792), 2 brass keys, ivory with brass mounts

Plate X — Two pommers from the Historisches Museum, Frankfurt am Main.
Top: Alto pommer, Johann Christoph Denner, No. X-436, 1 brass key
Bottom: Discant pommer, Jakob Denner, No. 437, 1 brass key (the entire key is exposed to view, not covered by a fontanelle).

Plate XI — Two clarinets from the Musée Instrumental, Brussels.
Top: J.B. Willems, No. 2573
Bottom: Thomas Boekhout, No. 2561

Plate XII — Bass flute by Joannes Maria Anciutti, Milan, dated 1739, Kunsthistorisches Museum, Vienna, No. GdM 371.

Plate XIII — Contrebasse oboe, Christoph Delusse, from the Musée Instrumental, Conservatoire National Superieur de Musique, Paris, Nos. E. 150 and C. 459, over 6' high!

| Young No. | No. Keys and Metal | City, Owner, No. | Pitch | No. Pcs. | Length | Body, Mounts | Flaps | SAT | Holes Dbld. | Tuning Holes | Additional Data | Ill. Source |
|---|---|---|---|---|---|---|---|---|---|---|---|---|

## AMLINGUE

### PICCOLO
| 1. | 1 silver | Cambridge: V. Law | | | | ebony, ivory | | | | | | |

### FLUTES
| 1. | 1 silver | Brussels 3277 | C | 4 | 62.3 | boxw, ivory | Sq | SATK | | 1 upper jt. | No register. | |
| 2. | 1 | Quito, Ecuador 3422 | | 4 | 60.0 | boxw, ivory | | | | 1 upper jt. | | |

### OBOES
| 1. | | Halsingborg, per Langwill | | | | | | | | | | |

### CLARINETS
| 1. | 5 brass | Paris C. 530 | F | 6 | | boxw, ivory | | | | | | |
| 2. | 5 brass | Paris C. 526, E. 396 | Eb | 6 | | boxw, ivory | Sq | SATK | | | 6th key (c#) added on posts and axle. | |
| 3. | 5 brass | Paris C. 531 | | 5 | | boxw | | | | | | |
| 4. | 5 brass | Paris C. 532, E 203 | | 5 | | boxw | Sq | | | | Keys in knobs. | |
| 5. | 5 brass | Boston MFA 38.1750 | Bb | 6 | 67.5 | ebony, ivory | Sq | SATK | | | 2 upper joints, 2 middle joints, 2 bbls, 2 mthpcs | |
| 6. | 5 | Geneva, Ernst | | | | | | | | | | |
| 7. | 5 | Leipzig 1475 | | 5 | as is 59.8 | boxw, horn | Sq | SATK | | | Keys in knobs. Mthpc missing; bbl, upper jt, lower jt, long bell | |
| 8. | 5 brass | Leningrad 500 | | 4 | 53.7 | boxw, horn | | | | | | |
| 9. | 6 brass | Paris C. 534 | Bb | | | | | | | | 1 silver key added later. | |
| 10. | 7 silver | Paris. C. 535 | | | 61.0 | wood, ivory | | | | | | |

### BASSOONS
| 1. | 7 brass | Oxford: Bate 303 | | | 130.2 | maple, brass | | | | | Keys sunk into body. Wing joint not original | |
| 2. | 5 brass | Boston: Casedesus 69 | | | 127.5 | maple, brass | (V) | SATK | | | Crook missing. | |

| Young No. | No. Keys and Metal | City, Owner, No. | Pitch | No. Pcs. | Length | Body, Mounts | Flaps | SAT | Holes Dbld. | Tuning Holes | Additional Data | Ill. Source |
|---|---|---|---|---|---|---|---|---|---|---|---|---|

## ANCIUTI

ANCIUTI

*Dated*

### RECORDER, SOPRANO

| | | | | | | | | | | | | |
|---|---|---|---|---|---|---|---|---|---|---|---|---|
| 1. | | xBerlin 470 | 1733 | 2 | 24.5 | boxw, unmtd | | | | | Sachs: 2 pc but in 3-pc form. | |

### RECORDER, ALTO

| | | | | | | | | | | | | |
|---|---|---|---|---|---|---|---|---|---|---|---|---|
| 1. | | London V&A 20/5 | 1740 | | 47.5 | ivory, unmtd | | | | | Body octagonal in cross section. | Ill Baines cat., Fig. 117 |
| 2. | | Rome: sold 1978[1] | 1729 | | | boxw, unmtd | | | | | per A. Bernardini | |

### RECORDER, PITCH UNDETERMINED

| | | | | | | | | | | | | |
|---|---|---|---|---|---|---|---|---|---|---|---|---|
| 1. | | Vienna Harnoncourt | 1717 | | | | | | | | | |

### FLUTE

| | | | | | | | | | | | | |
|---|---|---|---|---|---|---|---|---|---|---|---|---|
| 1. | 1 silver | Milan Castello Sforzesco 320 | 1725 | | 59.9 | ivory, silver | Trap | | 3 upper joints | | A. Bernardini says is unstamped, probably not by Anciuti. | Ill Gallini cat. (1963), Tav 87 |

### BASS FLUTE

| | | | | | | | | | | | | |
|---|---|---|---|---|---|---|---|---|---|---|---|---|
| 1. | 1 brass | Vienna GdM 371 | 1739 | | 80.5 | boxw, ivory | | | | | Mouthhole in brass U-bend, sharply raised tone holes. | Ill. this book, Pl. XII |

### DOUBLE FLUTES (FLUTES D'ACCORD)

| | | | | | | | | | | | | |
|---|---|---|---|---|---|---|---|---|---|---|---|---|
| 1. | 0 keys | Paris C. 416 | 1722 | 1 | 25.58 | ivory, unmtd | | | | | All holes with inner lid closing them half way. | |
| 2. | 0 keys | London Kneller Hall No. 21 | | | 25.0 | boxw | | | | | | EAMI 440 |
| 3. | 0 keys | Venice, Cons. B. Marcello | 1712 | | | boxw | | | | | | |
| 4. | x0 keys | xLeipzig 1150 | 1713 | | 26.5 | boxw | | | | | | |

### OBOES

| | | | | | | | | | | | | |
|---|---|---|---|---|---|---|---|---|---|---|---|---|
| 1. | 2 silver | Paris C. 472, E. 107 | undated | | 56.35 | ivory, unmtd | oct. | | 3&4 dbl | 2 th | | |
| 2. | 2 brass | Rome, Mus.d.S.M. 909 | 1709 | | | boxw, unmtd, | oval C ro E♭ | | 3&4 dbl | 2 th | | |
| 3. | 3 brass | London V&A 23/2 | undated | | 54.5 | ivory, brass | ro | | 3&4 dbl | 2 th | | Ill. Baines cat., Fig. 126 |
| 4. | 3 brass | Berlin 5079 | 1721 | | 54.8 | boxw, horn | ro E♭, trap C | | 3&4 dbl | 2 th | | |
| 5. | 3 brass | Paris C. 1111 | 1719 | | 55.4 | boxw, unmtd | | | | | | |
| 6. | 3 | Rome, Mus.d.S.M.1094 | 1738 | | | boxw, brass | oval C 2xE♭ ro | | | | straight, unadorned body, possibly experimental model? | |
| 7. | 3? | Rome, Mus.d.S.M.1368 | 1718 | | | ebony, ivory | oval C 2xE♭ sq. | | 3&4 dbl | 2 th | Acanthus foliage carving on body. | |

[1]by Early Music Shop, Rome

| Young No. | No. Keys and Metal | City, Owner, No. | Pitch | No. Pcs. | Length | Body, Mounts Flaps | SAT | Holes Dbld. | Tuning Holes | Additional Data | Ill. Source |
|---|---|---|---|---|---|---|---|---|---|---|---|

**ANCIUTI** *(cont.)*

### CONTRABASSOON

| | | | | | | | | | | | |
|---|---|---|---|---|---|---|---|---|---|---|---|
| 1. | 9 brass | Salzburg 15/18 (G. 209) | 1732 | | 210.0 | maple, brass | | | | Keys suspect? | Ill. Birsak cat., cover & Taf.X. Jansen, fig.26 |

# BIZEY

### RECORDERS, ALTO

| | | | | | | | | | | | |
|---|---|---|---|---|---|---|---|---|---|---|---|
| 1. | 1 brass | Washington: DCM 1055 | F | 3 pc | 52.5 | boxw? | | | | | |

### RECORDER, TENOR

| | | | | | | | | | | | |
|---|---|---|---|---|---|---|---|---|---|---|---|
| 1. | 1 brass | Leningrad 404 | | 3 pc | 67.4 | boxw, ivory | Sq | | | 1 brass key on hole 7, hinged from lower end, sq cp in middle | LOM 66 |

### FLUTES

| | | | | | | | | | | | |
|---|---|---|---|---|---|---|---|---|---|---|---|
| 1. | 1 brass | Nürnberg GNM MIR 282 | C | 4 pc | 61.7 | boxw, ivory | Sq (A) | SATK | | cyl ft | Ill. Bowers, AMIS 3, p 36 |
| 2. | 1 silver | Oxford: Bate 1 | C | 4 pc | 57.9[1] | ivory | Sq | SATK 2 up jts | | cyl ft. 3 keys added | |
| 3. | 1 silver | Oxford: Bate 106 | C | 4 pc | 58.0[1] | boxw, ivory | Sq | SATW | | cyl ft | Ill. Bowers, AMIS 3, p 37 |
| 4. | 1 silver | Edinburgh: Rendall Coll. | C | 4 pc | 61.6 | ivory, silver | Sq | | | | GS Exhib. 1968, No. 44. |
| 5. | 1 silver | Hague Ea 462-1933 | C | 4 pc | 62.0 | boxw, ivory | Sq | | | cyl ft. "Attributed to Bizey." Unmarked. | Ill. Hague 1974 Exhib. cat., p. 14 |
| 6. | 1 silver | Paris C. 439, E. 598 | C | 4 pc | 62.0 | ivory | Sq (C) | SATI 2 up jts | | cyl ft | EAMI 469 |
| 7. | 1 silver | Haslemere: Dolmetsch 69 | C | 4 pc | 65.0 | ivory, silver | Sq | 1 up jt | | | |
| 8. | | Turin: S. Balestracci | | | | boxw, ivory | | | | | |

### BASS FLUTE

| | | | | | | | | | | | |
|---|---|---|---|---|---|---|---|---|---|---|---|
| 1. | 5 brass [2] | Linz 17 | G | 4 pc [3] | 99.5 | boxw, brass | Ro | | | Copy Vienna KHM | ill. Schlosser, Taf. LI |

### OBOES

| | | | | | | | | | | | |
|---|---|---|---|---|---|---|---|---|---|---|---|
| 1. | x3 | xBerlin 2935 | C | 3 pc | 60.5 | boxw, horn | | | | | |
| 2. | 2 silver | Brussels 424 | C | 3 pc | 60.1 | boxw, wide ivory | Sq | SATW 3&4 dbl | 2 th | | |
| 3. | 2 brass | Oxford: Bate 201 | C | 3 pc | 60.0 | maple?, unmtd | Sq | SATW 3&4 dbl | 2 th | | |
| 4. | 2 brass | Paris C. 1112 | C | 3 pc | 57.64 | boxw, ivory | Sq Eb, ro C | SATW 3&4 dbl | 2 th | Wooden reed cap. Bell missing. | |
| 5. | 2 | Basel: Michel Piguet | C | 3 pc | | | | 3&4 dbl | | | |

---

[1] Speaking length, from center of embouchure to end of foot jt, not overall length.

[2] Hole 1, 3, 4 & 6 keys are hinged at one end, flap in center, touch at other end. Eb key is usual design.

[3] Fourth piece is U-shaped, wood with brass U, includes mouthhole.

| Young No. | No. Keys and Metal | City, Owner, No. | Pitch | No. Pcs. | Length | Body, Mounts | Flaps | SAT | Holes Dbld. | Tuning Holes | Additional Data | Ill. Source |
|---|---|---|---|---|---|---|---|---|---|---|---|---|
| **BIZEY** *(cont.)* | | | | | | | | | | | | **BIZEY** *(cont.)* |
| MEZZO OBOE | | | | | | | | | | | | |
| 1. | 2 silver | Boston MFA 17.1910 | A | 3 pc | 61.7 | boxw, ivory | Sq E♭, oval C | SATW | 3 & 4 dbl | 2 th | | Ill. and full description, Bessaraboff. pl IV. |
| TENOR OBOE | | | | | | | | | | | | |
| 1. | 2 brass | Paris E. 2351 | F | 3 pc | 73.2 | boxw, ivory | Sq E♭, ro C | SATW | 3 & 4 dbl | 0 th | | Ill. JJ-GT-BR no. 99 LOM 92 |
| BASS OBOE | | | | | | | | | | | | |
| 1. | 2 brass | Paris C. 494, E. 642 | | 5 pc | 81.75 | boxw? unmtd | Sq E♭, (V)C | SATW | 0 dbl | 1 th | 4 pcs. plus crook | EAMI 548[1], LOM 96 |
| RACKETTS | | | | | | | | | | | | |
| 1. | 3 brass | Munich: BNM Mu 126 | | | 23.0 | maple | (V) | SATW | | | Keys in brass saddles. Restored by R. Weber. Gold-tooled, black leather over body. | LOM 106 |
| 2. | | Paris | | | | | | | | | W. Waterhouse says not Rozet but Bizey. | |
| BASSOON | | | | | | | | | | | | |
| 1. | 4 brass | Bonn BH (Zimmermann 113) | C | | 125.1 | maple, brass | (V) | SATW | | | Keys in brass saddles. No decorative bell ring. Keys: Bb, D, F, G♯. | |

# TH. BOEHM
**TH. BOEHM**

| Young No. | No. Keys and Metal | City, Owner, No. | Pitch | No. Pcs. | Length | Body, Mounts | Flaps | SAT | Holes Dbld. | Tuning Holes | Additional Data | Ill. Source |
|---|---|---|---|---|---|---|---|---|---|---|---|---|
| FLUTES MADE BEFORE THE 1832 MODEL | | | | | | | | | | | | |
| 1. | 9 silver | Nürnberg MIR 314 | C | | 67.2 | ebony, silver | | | | | "old system," no rings, conical bore. | |
| 2. | 8? brass | Washington: DCM 631 | C | | (41.3) | boxw, ivory | | | | | Head, bbl, and upper jt only; the rest lost. 3 brass keys, probably originally 8. | |
| 3. | 9 silver | Washington: DCM 975 | C | | 67.0 | cocus, silver | | | | | | Ill. Girard The Flute; Ill. Gilliam & Lichtenwanger checklist; LOM 220 |
| 4. | | Munich Stadtmuseum 79-13 | | | | boxw | | | | | | |
| 5. | | Stuttgart: G. Braun | | | | boxw | | | | | | |
| 1832 MODEL FLUTES | | | | | | | | | | | | |
| 1. | silver | Oxford: Bate 166 | | | 65.8 | boxw, silver | | | | | | ill. Baines WITH Pl.XXVI; LOM 221 |
| 2. | silver | London: Horniman 11a | C | | 67.4 | cocus, silver | | | | | c. 1840. | EAMI 486 |

[1] Bate, *The Oboe* has full description & ill.

| Young No. | No. Keys and Metal | City, Owner, No. | Pitch | No. Pcs. | Length | Body, Mounts Flaps | SAT | Holes Dbld. | Tuning Holes | Additional Data | Ill. Source |
|---|---|---|---|---|---|---|---|---|---|---|---|
| **TH. BOEHM** *(cont.)* | | | | | | | | | | | **TH. BOEHM** *(cont.)* |

## 1832 MODEL FLUTES *(cont.)*

| Young No. | No. Keys and Metal | City, Owner, No. | Pitch | No. Pcs. | Length | Body, Mounts Flaps | SAT | Holes Dbld. | Tuning Holes | Additional Data | Ill. Source |
|---|---|---|---|---|---|---|---|---|---|---|---|
| 3. | silver | London: Horniman 11b | C | | 65.9 | cocus, silver | | | | c. 1840 | |
| 4. | | Washington: DCM 471 | | | | brass | | | | Not a flute, a jig used by Boehm to determine the location of 1832 model tone holes. | |
| 5. | silver | Washington: DCM 974 | C | | 65.3 | cocus, silver | | | | Open g♯. | |
| 6. | silver | Washington: DCM 1056 | C | | 67.5 | rosew, silver | | | | Open g♯. | |
| 7. | brass | Eisenach I-133 | C | | 65.6 | grena, brass | | | | Brille keys. 1832-1833. | Ill. Heyde Eisenach, p 225 |
| 8. | G.silv. | Munich: Deutsches Mus 24760 | C | | 64.8 | grena, German silver | | | | Open g♯. c. 1840 | |
| 9. | silver | Munich: Stadtmuseum 79-18 | C | | 66.95 | cocus, silver | | | | Open g♯. | |
| 10. | silver | Nürnberg MIR 327 | C | | 66.9 | ebony, silver | | | | Open g♯. | LOM 222 |
| 11. | | Leningrad 2220 | | | 65.5 | cocus? ivory | | | | 3 sections. Might it be pre-1832? | |
| 12. | | Nürnberg MIR 331 | | | | grena | | | | | |
| 13. | | Sollentuna: J. Brinckmann | | | | ebony | | | | | |

## 1847 MODEL FLUTES

| Young No. | Boehm's serial no. | City, Owner, No. | Pitch | No. Pcs. | Length | Body, Mounts Flaps | SAT | Holes Dbld. | Tuning Holes | Additional Data | Ill. Source |
|---|---|---|---|---|---|---|---|---|---|---|---|
| 1. | No. 1 | Washington: DCM 652 | C | | 63.5 | brass, silver | | | | 2 pcs, brass with wooden tube at embouchure. 1847 | LOM 223 |
| 2. | No. 2 | Washington: DCM 470 | C | | 62.5 | nick pl brass | | | | Silver ring keys. Open g♯. Nickel pl brass w ivory tube at embouchure. 2 pcs. 1847 | |
| 3. | No. 4 | Washington: DCM 305 | G | | 86.3 | silver | | | | Open g♯. Schlief key. 1847-62 | Ill. Gilliam-Lichtenwanger checklist. |
| 4. | No. 5 | Nürnberg MI 414 | C | | 64.5 | G silver | | | | Closed key covers | |
| 5. | No. 7 | Munich: Deutsches Mus 21785 | C | | 64.4 | silver, ivory | | | | Open g♯. Silver with ivory embouch & crutch. 1848. | |
| 6. | No. 14 | Washington: DCM 1237 | C | | 70.6 | silver | | | | Open g♯. Richard Carte bought this from Boehm in 1848. | Ill. Gilliam-Lichtenwanger checklist. Also EAMI 491. |
| 7. | No. 19 | Washington: DCM 99 | C | | 66.3 | silver | | | | Keys mounted on far side. Open g♮. 2 head joints. First Boehm flute brought to America. | |
| 8. | No. 21 | Washington: DCM 653 | C | | 63.1 | silver, ivory | | | | Ivory embouchure. Open g♯. Belonged to Knierer, once Boehm's flute pupil. | |
| 9. | No. 24 | Munich: Stadtmuseum 81-1 | | | | G silver | | | | | |
| 10. | No. 27 | Lahr/Schwarzwald J. Hammig | | | | G silver | | | | | |

## TH. BOEHM *(cont.)*

### 1847 MODEL FLUTES *(cont.)*

| Young No. | No. Keys and Metal | City, Owner, No. | Pitch | No. Pcs. | Length | Body, Mounts Flaps | SAT | Holes Dbld. | Tuning Holes | Additional Data | Ill. Source |
|---|---|---|---|---|---|---|---|---|---|---|---|
| 11. | No. 29 | Munich: Deutsches Mus 38068 | C | | 63.6 | G silv, ivory | | | | Ivory embouchure; Open g♮. Two piece. 1848 | |
| 12. | No. 30 | Oklahoma: R.W.Payne | | | 60.3 | silver, gold | | | | 1850 | |
| 13. | No. 38 | Washington: DCM 1398 | C | | 63.0 | silver, gold | | | | Keys on far side. Open g♮. 1849 | |
| 14. | No. 41 | Brussels 1084 | C | | | silver, gold | | | | Cap frozen on tenon, so can't assemble. 3 pieces. | |
| 15. | No. 52 | Weiblingen: P. Thalheimer | | | | silver | | | | | |
| 16. | No. 54 | Munich: Otto Eckart | | | | silver | | | | | |
| 17. | No. 57 | Washington: DCM 782 | C | | 62.4 | silver, gold | | | | Orig like DCM 653, but Dr. Miller says keys redesigned & new. 1851 | |
| 18. | No. 60 | Bonn BH (Zimmermann 82) | C | | 63.4 | G silver | | | | Open g♮. Three piece. 1851 | |
| 19. | No. 73 | Markneukirchen 1083 | | | | G. silver | | | | | |
| 20. | No. 89 | Ann Arbor: G. Stout | | | | silver | | | | | |
| 21. | | Berlin 4950 | C | | 63.8 | | | | | c. 1853 | |
| 22. | | Washington: DCM 197 | C | | 65.5 | grena, silver | | | | Open g♮. Experimental model with unique style clutches. c. 1860 | |
| 23. | | Washington: DCM 771 | C | | 66.9 | cocus, silver | | | | Dorus g♮. | |
| 24. | | Washington: DCM 875 | C | | 65.9 | grena, silver | | | | Open g♮. | |
| 25. | | Washington: DCM 1236 | C | | 65.0 | silver | | | | Open g♮. Rack & pinion tuning adjustment. Maybe not by B?[1] | |
| 26. | | Oxford: Bate 150 | C | | 62.0 | silver, gold | | | | "Rather unusual model." c. 1860. | Ill. Bate Flute, pl 8f. LOM 224. |
| 27. | | Scarsdale: D. & R. Rosenbaum | | | | | | | | | |
| 28. | | Nürnberg MI 413 loaned by Karl Ventzke | C | | 64.0 | silver | | | | Closed key covers | |
| 29. | | New Orleans: J. Swain | | | | silver | | | | Said to have serial No. "4" | |
| 30. | | Munich: H. Prager | | | | silver | | | | | |
| 31. | | Munich: H. Prager | | | | silver | | | | | |

[1]Stamped "Th. Boehm/Munchen/Rudall&Rose/Pattentees/ Southampton Gt Strand/London"

| Young No. | No. Keys and Metal | City, Owner, No. | Pitch | No. Pcs. | Length | Body, Mounts Flaps | SAT | Holes Dbld. | Tuning Holes | Additional Data | Ill. Source |
|---|---|---|---|---|---|---|---|---|---|---|---|
| **TH. BOEHM** *(cont.)* | | | | | | | | | | | |
| **PICCOLO** | | | | | | | | | | | |
| 1. | | Leipzig 3389 | C | | 29.1 | G silver, ebony | | | | 1858-61. | Ill. Heyde Leipzig, tafel 15 |
| **ALTO FLUTE** | | | | | | | | | | | |
| 1. | silver | Eisenach I-135 | G | | 87.5 | silver, gold | | | | Closed key covers. 1858-61. | Key schematic, Heyde Eisenach, p 21. |
| **OBOE** | | | | | | | | | | | |
| 1. | brass | Leipzig 1331 | | 2 pc | 60.4 | rosew, brass | | | | I could not find any kind of maker's stamp on this specimen | |

## BOEHM & GREVE

| Young No. | No. Keys and Metal | City, Owner, No. | Pitch | No. Pcs. | Length | Body, Mounts Flaps | SAT | Holes Dbld. | Tuning Holes | Additional Data | Ill. Source |
|---|---|---|---|---|---|---|---|---|---|---|---|
| **FLUTES MADE BEFORE THE 1832 MODEL** | | | | | | | | | | | |
| 1. | 9 silver | Washington: DCM 240 | C | | 66.8 | cocus, silver | | | | Boehm's 1829 system | Ill. DCM's *The Flute & Flute Playing* |
| 2. | 8 brass | Washington: DCM 657 | C | | 66.2 | boxw, ivory | | | | | |
| 3. | 8 brass | Amsterdam: Frans Brüggen | C | | 66.5 | boxw, ivory | | | | | |
| 4. | 8 brass | Forest Hills, N.Y.: Moskovitz | C | | 68.6 | fruitw, ivory | | | | | |
| **1832 MODEL FLUTES** | | | | | | | | | | | |
| 1. | | Berlin 4850 | C | | 65.8 | ebony? cocus? silver | | | | c. 1835. foot to c' | Ill. Otto 1965 handbook, p 139 |
| 2. | | Brunswick 89 | C | | 66.0 | grena, German silver | | | | c. 1840. 3 pc | |
| 3. | | Washington: DCM 654 | C | | 66.1 | boxw, brass | | | | before 1838 | Ill. Girard *Flute*; ill. Gilliam-Lichtenwanger checklist |
| 4. | | Nürnberg MI 412 | C | | 68.5 | ebony, silver | | | | c. 1840. loaned by Karl Ventzke | |
| 5. | | Bremen, per Langwill | | | | | | | | | |
| 6. | | Munich: H. Prager | | | | wood | | | | | |

## BOEHM & MENDLER

| Young No. | No. Keys and Metal | City, Owner, No. | Pitch | No. Pcs. | Length | Body, Mounts Flaps | SAT | Holes Dbld. | Tuning Holes | Additional Data | Ill. Source |
|---|---|---|---|---|---|---|---|---|---|---|---|
| **PICCOLOS** | | | | | | | | | | | |
| 1. | | Washington: DCM 53 | C | | 30.0 | grena, silver | | | | Open g♯. | |
| 2. | | Washington: DCM 344 | C | | 31.4 | grena, silver | | | | Open g♮. | |
| 3. | | Munich Stadtmuseum 42-352 | C | | 31.5 | grena, silver | | | | Closed g♯. | |

BOEHM & GREVE

BOEHM & MENDLER

## BOEHM & MENDLER (cont.)                                                        BOEHM & MENDLER (cont.)
BOEHM & MENDLER (cont.)

### FLUTES

| Young No. | No. Keys and Metal | City, Owner, No. | Pitch | No. Pcs. | Length | Body, Mounts Flaps | SAT | Holes Dbld. | Tuning Holes | Additional Data | Ill. Source |
|---|---|---|---|---|---|---|---|---|---|---|---|
| 1. | | Bonn BH (Zimmermann 83) | C | 3 pcs | 69.0 | cocus, silver | | | | Open g♯. | |
| 2. | | New York: MMA 23.273 | C | 3 pcs | 71.1 | silver, gold lip pl | | | | Open g♯. Schlief key | Ill. MMA flute checklist |
| 3. | silver | Nürnberg MIR 328 | C | 3 pcs | 68.3 | boxw, brass | | | | | |
| 4. | | Nürnberg MIR 329 | C | | 68.5 | ebony, silver | | | | | Probably the one Ill. Karl Ventzke *Die Boehmflöte* abb. 1-p |
| 5. | | Oklahoma City: R.W. Payne | C | | 60.3 | silver | | | | Closed g♯. Stamped "Boehm & Mendler No. 550 Model." Modern mechanism. | |
| 6. | 15 silver | Zurich: Walter Thut | C | 3 pcs | 60.2 | silver, gold lip pl | | | | Perhaps made by Mendler, not B&M | |
| 7. | | Washington: DCM 24 | G | | 87.0 | boxw, brass | | | | 13 raised-edge holes in 2-pc tube (only) | Ill. DCM's *The Flute & Flute Playing* |
| 8. | | Washington: DCM 49 | G | | 86.5 | cocus head, silver body | | | | Open g♯. | Ill. DCM's *The Flute & Flute Playing* |
| 9. | | Washington: DCM 52 | C | | 68.7 | grena, silver | | | | Open g♯. | Ill. DCM's *The Flute & Flute Playing* |
| 10. | | Washington: DCM 57 | C | | 68.5 | grena, silver | | | | Open g♯. | Ill. DCM's *The Flute & Flute Playing* |
| 11. | | Washington: DCM 59 | C | | 67.5 | wood head, silver body | | | | Open g♯. Lowest tone b. | Ill. DCM's *The Flute & Flute Playing* |
| 12. | | Washington: DCM 61 | D♭ | | 56.3 | grena, silver | | | | Open g♯. Lowest tone eb' | Ill. DCM's *The Flute & Flute Playing* |
| 13. | | Washington: DCM 92 | C | | 67.1 | silver, gold | | | | Open g♯. Octave key. Lowest tone b. | Ill. DCM's *The Flute & Flute Playing* |
| 14. | | Washington: DCM 134 | C | | 65.0 | silver, gold | | | | Open g♯. | Ill. DCM's *The Flute & Flute Playing* |
| 15. | | Washington: DCM 147 | C | | 66.5 | cocus, silver | | | | Closed g♯, orig open. | Ill. DCM's *The Flute & Flute Playing* |
| 16. | | Washington: DCM 155 | | | 16.9 | grena, silver | | | | Foot joint only. Lowest tone b. | Ill. DCM's *The Flute & Flute Playing* |
| 17. | | Washington: DCM 156 | | | 16.9 | cocus, silver | | | | Foot joint only. Lowest tone b. | Ill. DCM's *The Flute & Flute Playing* |
| 18. | | Washington: DCM 157 | C | | 66.5 | cocus, silver | | | | Open g♯. | Ill. DCM's *The Flute & Flute Playing* |
| 19. | | Washington: DCM 161 | C | | 67.5 | silver, gold | | | | Special closed g♯, Schlief key. Lowest tone b. | Ill. DCM's *The Flute & Flute Playing* |
| 20. | | Washington: DCM 201 | G | | 83.5 | silver, ebonite | | | | Open g♯. | Ill. DCM's *The Flute & Flute Playing* |

## BOEHM & MENDLER *(cont.)* BOEHM & MENDLER *(cont.)*

### FLUTES *(cont.)*

| Young No. | No. Keys and Metal | City, Owner, No. | Pitch | No. Pcs. | Length | Body, Mounts Flaps | SAT | Holes Dbld. | Tuning Holes | Additional Data | Ill. Source |
|---|---|---|---|---|---|---|---|---|---|---|---|
| 21. | | Washington: DCM 233 | C | | 69.8 | silver, gold | | | | Open g♯, Schlief key. Lowest tone b. | Ill. DCM's *The Flute & Flute Playing* |
| 22. | | Washington: DCM 263 | C | | 68.2 | silver, gold | | | | Open g♯, Schlief key. Lowest tone b. | Ill. Girard's *The Flute* |
| 23. | | Washington: DCM 306 | C | | 66.5 | grena, silver | | | | Open g, Schlief key, wood thinned w raised edges at tone holes & embouch. | |
| 24. | | Washington: DCM 415 | C | | 64.0 | cocus head, phosphor bronze | | | | Open g♯. 1 of 3 made in this metal, but B found it too hard to work it. | |
| 25. | | Washington: DCM 416 | G | | 88.3 | wood lip plate, phosphor bronze | | | | Open g♯, Schlief key. 1 of the 3 cited directly above. | |
| 26. | | Washington: DCM 609 | G | | 87.6 | silver, gold, hard rubber lip plate | | | | Closed g♯, orig open; Schlief key | |
| 27. | | D. Shorey, Cranberry Island, Me. | | | | | | | | Mr. Shorey, a dealer, listed this in March, 1980. | |
| 28. | | Düren: Karl Ventzke, No. 1 | | | | | | | | | |
| 29. | | Ann Arbor: H. deKornfeld | | | | wood | | | | | |
| 30. | | Ann Arbor: G. Stout | | | | silver | | | | | |
| 31. | | Anfhausen: R. von Fröhlich | | | | silver | | | | | |
| 32. | | Madison: R. Cole | | | | silver | | | | | |
| 33. | | Munich: Stadtmuseum 79-13 | | | | cocus | | | | | |
| 34. | | Stuttgart: H. Böhm | | | | silver | | | | | |
| 35. | | Stuttgart: H. Böhm | | | | ebony | | | | | |
| 36. | | Weiblingen: P. Thalheimer | | | | cocus | | | | | |

# BOEHM, but which firm undetermined BOEHM, but which firm undetermined

| | | | | | | | | | | | |
|---|---|---|---|---|---|---|---|---|---|---|---|
| 1. | | Markneukirchen: F. Berndt | | | | | | | | | |
| 2. | | Munich: H. Prager | | | | | | | | | |
| 3. | | Munich: H. Prager | | | | | | | | | |
| 4. | | New Orleans: J. Swain | | | | | | | | | |
| 5. | | Oxford: Pitt Rivers Museum | | | | | | | | | |
| 6. | | Oxford: Pitt Rivers Museum | | | | | | | | | |
| 7. | | Seattle: Jack Peters | | | | | | | | | |
| 8. | | Seattle: Jack Peters | | | | | | | | | |
| 9. | | Bremen | | | | | | | | | |
| 10. | | Bremen | | | | | | | | | |
| 11. | | Tattnang: H. Steinkrauss | | | | | | | | | |

| Young No. | No. Keys and Metal | City, Owner, No. | Pitch | No. Pcs. | Length | Body, Mounts | Flaps | SAT | Holes Dbld. | Tuning Holes | Additional Data | Ill. Source |
|---|---|---|---|---|---|---|---|---|---|---|---|---|
| **BOEKHOUT** | | | | | | | | | | | | |
| **SOPRANO RECORDER** | | | | | | | | | | | | |
| 1. | | New York MMA 89.4.912 | B♮ | 2 pc | 34.3 | ebony, ivory | | | | | | |
| **ALTO RECORDERS** | | | | | | | | | | | | |
| 1. | | Hague Ea 27-X-52 | | 3 pc | 51.0 | ebony, ivory | | | | | | |
| 2. | | xBerlin 2790 | | 3 pc | 49.5 | boxw | | | | | | |
| 3. | | Zurich Bellerive 128 | | 3 pc | 51.8 | boxw, unmtd | | | | | | |
| **BASS RECORDERS** | | | | | | | | | | | | |
| 1. | 1 brass | Berlin 2824 | F | 3 pc | 105.2 | box, unmtd | tr | SATW | | | Floor peg. Crook into top. | Ill Sachs, Taf. 25 |
| 2. | 1 brass | Munich DM 10226 | F | 3 pc | 101.5 | boxw, brass | ro | | | | | |
| 3. | 2 brass | Brussels 1039 | E | 3 pc | 103.0 | maple, unmtd | tr | SATW | | | 2nd key is Hole 3. | |
| 4. | 2 brass | Brussels 1040 | E | 3 pc | 104.8 | dark wood, unmtd | sq-cors | SATW | | | 2nd key is Hole 3, Hole 7 cp missing. Floor peg. Crook into top. | |
| 5. | 2 brass | Leningrad 408 | | 3 pc | 142.0[1] | box, unmtd | tr | SATW | | | 2nd key is Hole 3. Floor peg. Crook into top. | Ill Hunt, Pl XV. LOM 67. |
| **RECORDER OF UNDETERMINED PITCH** | | | | | | | | | | | | |
| 1. | | London Guy Oldham | | | | | | | | | | |
| **FLUTE** | | | | | | | | | | | | |
| 1. | 1 silver | xBerlin 2678 | C | | 64.5 | boxw, ivory | sq | | | | Lowest tone d' | |
| **OBOES** | | | | | | | | | | | | |
| 1. | 3 silver | Hague Ea 24-1937 | | 3 | 58.3 | ebony, silver | C below,[3] E♭s same but smaller | SATW | 3&4 dbl | | Carved child's head at top. Lowest tone c' | Ill Hague '74 exhib., p 52. |
| 2. | 3 silver | Hague Ea 16-X-1952 | | 3 | 58.0 | boxw, unmtd | sq E♭, ro C | SATW | 3&4 dbl | | Lowest tone c' | Ill. Hague '74 exhib. catalogue, p 52. LOM 76 |
| **CLARINETS** | | | | | | | | | | | | |
| 1. | 2 brass | Brussels 2561 | C | | 48.0[2] | boxw, ivory | sq [4] | SATW | | | Lowest tone f. Bore 1.4 cm. | Ill. this book, Pl. XI |

---

[1] Including its crutch (floor peg)

[2] Without mouthpiece or barrel, missing only very recently.

[3] The touch on the C key is also very ornate. This is an unusually beautiful key.

[4] a' key CP is notched (D).

| Young No. | No. Keys and Metal | City, Owner, No. | Pitch | No. Pcs. | Length | Body, Mounts | Flaps | SAT | Holes Dbld. | Tuning Holes | Additional Data | Ill. Source |
|---|---|---|---|---|---|---|---|---|---|---|---|---|

**BOEKHOUT** *(cont.)*                                                   **BOEKHOUT** *(cont.)*

BASSOON

| 1. | | Selhof Inventory, per Langwill 5th ed. | | | | | | | | | | |

# BOIE                                                                   **BOIE**

FLUTES

| 1. | 1 | London: Horniman 308 | D | | 62.8 | boxw, horn | | | | | | |
| 2. | 2 silver | Washington: DCM 467 | C | | 62.4 | ebony, ivory | | | 3 upper joints | | Keys e♭ & g♯, 1 upper joint with an added key. | |
| 3. | x2 silver | xBerlin 2683 | C | | 61.0 | | sq | | | | Keys e♭ & g♯. | |
| 4. | 2 silver | Göttingen, Univ. of, 612 | | | 52.3 | boxw, ivory | | | | | | |
| 5. | 4 silver | Washington: DCM 401 | C | | 62.7 | ebony, ivory | | | | | | |
| 6. | 4 silver | Washington: DCM 1355 | C | | 64.2 | ebony, ivory | | | 3 upper joints | | | |
| 7. | x4 | xBerlin 104 | C | | 61.5 | ebony, ivory | sq | | | | Has bell. Keys e♭, f, g♯ & b. Ft. jt marked "Schneider." | Ill Sachs, pl 25 |
| 8. | 4 brass | Göttingen, Univ. of, 314 | C | | 61.3 | ebony, ivory | | | | | | |
| 9. | 6 silver | Eisenach I-121 | C | | 61.85 | ebony, ivory | sq[2] | | | | More details, Heyde Eisenach, p 208. | |
| 10. | 7 brass | Leipzig 3351[1] | C | | 65.75 | boxw, horn | ov (Y) | | | | By F. Boie II?[1] Flaps curved to the body. | Ill. Heyde Leipzig, taf 10 |
| 11. | 9 brass | Leipzig 3490[1] | C | | 69.4 | boxw, ivory | ov (Y) | | | | By F. Boie II[1]. Flaps curved to the body. Badly warped. | Ill. Heyde Leipzig, taf 13 |
| 12. | 9 brass | Berlin 3994 | C | | 68.2+ | boxw, horn | ov (Y) | | | | Flaps curved to the body. | |
| 13. | head jt only | Bremen: Focke Museum | | | — — — | | — — — | — — — | | | | |

CLARINETS

| 1. | 6 brass | Hamburg MHG 1924.242 | Bb | | 66.5 | boxw, horn | sq | | | | 1-pc bell & lower joint. Bore 1.4 | |
| 2. | 12 brass | Hamburg MHG 1912.1558 | A | 5 pc | (57.0) | boxw, horn | sq | | | | Mouthpiece & bbl missing. Bore 1.4 | Ill. Schröder catalogue, pl 19c |

[1] Dr. Heyde thinks Leipzig 3351 may be by F. Boie II and states that Leipzig 3490 *is*. Until a distinction can be made between the respective stamps of I & II, they will be listed together, as above.

[2] decorated as in type (E) but with a notch on either side next to the point where the shank joins the flap.

| Young No. | No. Keys and Metal | City, Owner, No. | Pitch | No. Pcs. | Length | Body, Mounts Flaps | SAT | Holes Dbld. | Tuning Holes | Additional Data | Ill. Source |
|---|---|---|---|---|---|---|---|---|---|---|---|

# BRESSAN

**BRESSAN**

| | | | | | | | | | | *GSJ No.* | |
|---|---|---|---|---|---|---|---|---|---|---|---|
| **SOPRANO RECORDER** | | | | | | | | | | | |
| 1. | | Chesham Bois: Edgar Hunt | B | 3 pc | 36.7 | boxw, unmtd | | | | 1. Headjoint marked "4". | Ill. Hunt, Pl 9 |

| | | | | | | | | | | | |
|---|---|---|---|---|---|---|---|---|---|---|---|
| **ALTO RECORDERS** | | | | | | | | | | | |
| 1. | | Washington: DCM 127 | F | 3 | 50.3 | boxw, ivory | | | | 2. | LOM 63 |
| 2. | | Washington: DCM 1181 | F | 3 | 50.8 | boxw, ivory | | | | 3. | |
| 3. | | Chester: Grosvenor Mus I | E | 3 | | fruitw, ivory | | | | 4. | 1 of these 2 ill. Montagu, *BC*, Pl 26 |
| 4. | | Chester: Grosvenor Mus II | E | 3 | | fruitw, ivory | | | | 5. | 1 of these 2 ill. Montagu, *BC*, Pl 26 |
| 5. | | Chesham Bois: Edgar Hunt | E | 3 | 50.4 | boxw, ivory | | | | 6. | Ill. Hunt. Pl 9 |
| 6. | | Vienna C. 166 | | 3 | 47.0 | boxw, unmtd | | Holes 3, 6 & 7 double! | | 7. | |
| 7. | | Leamington Spa: M. Byrne | | 3 | 50.4 | fruitw, ivory | | No holes doubled | | 8. | |
| 8. | | Haslemere: Carl Dolmetsch | F | | | boxw, ivory | | | | 9. | |
| 9. | | Prague 1369E | | 3 | | boxw, ivory | | | | 10. | Ill. Buchner, *MITA*, Pl 152 |
| 10. | | London: Reuben Greene | | | | | | | | 11. | |
| 11. | | Paris C. 394, E. 283[1] | | 3 | 52.0 | tortoise[2], ivory | | | | 12. | |
| 12. | | Ilford: late E. Halfpenny[3] | | 3 | | pear, unmtd | | | | 13. | Ill. GSJ IX, Pl VIIIb |
| 13. | | Oxford: Baines, loan to Bate[4] | | 3 | 50.4 | boxw, unmtd | | | | 43. | |
| 14. | | Amsterdam: Frans Brüggen | F | 3 | 50.5 | boxw, ivory | | | | 45. | |
| 15. | | London? Michael Oridge | | | | | | | | 46. | |
| 16. | | Stockholm F. 173 | | 3 | 50.8 | ebony, ivory | | | | 47. | |
| 17. | | Berlin 2801 | E | 3 | 50.0 | boxw, ivory | | | | 30. | |
| 18. | | Amsterdam: F. Brüggen[5] | F | 3 | 50.5 | boxw, ivory | | | | | |
| 19. | | xLeipzig 1130 | | 3 | 51.5 | boxw, ivory | | | | | |

[1] Attributed to Bressan, not stamped.
[2] Tortoise-finish on wood.
[3] Headjoint by Bressan, rest by Stanesby.
[4] Middle joint by Bressan, rest by Harris.
[5] A second Bressan alto now owned by Mr. Brüggen, ex Spiegel.

| Young No. | No. Keys and Metal | City, Owner, No. | Pitch | No. Pcs. | Length | Body, Mounts Flaps | SAT | Holes Dbld. | Tuning Holes | Additional Data | Ill. Source |
|---|---|---|---|---|---|---|---|---|---|---|---|
| **BRESSAN** *(cont.)* | | | | | | | | | | | |
| ALTO RECORDERS *(cont.)* | | | | | | | | | | GSJ No. | |
| 20. | | Reported *Early Music* 10/79 | | | | ivory mts | | | | | |
| 21. | | Reported *Early Music* 10/79 | | | | ivory mts | | | | | |
| **"VOICE FLUTES"** | | | | | | | | | | | |
| 1. | | Chester: Grosvenor Mus[1] | D | 3 | | | | | | 14. | Ill. Montagu, *BC*, Pl 26? |
| 2. | | Washington: DCM 834[2] | D | 3 | 57.5 | wood,[3] ivory | | | | 15. | |
| 3. | | Washington: DCM 989 | D | 3 | 60.7 | wood, ivory | | | | 16. | |
| 4. | | Bury St. Edmunds: Moyse's Hall | D | | | | | | | 17. | |
| 5. | | Chester: Grosvenor Mus | D | 3 | | | | | | 18. | Ill. Montagu, BC, Pl 26? |
| 6. | | Oxford: Pitt Rivers Museum | D | 3 | 60.8 | boxw, ivory | | | | 19. | Ill. GS Exhib. '68, Pl II-2 |
| 7. | | Bath: Mrs Robin Eden | D | | | | | | | 20. | |
| 8. | | Salisbury, N.C.: Dale Higbee | D | 3 | 60.95 | boxw, unmtd | | | | 21. | |
| 9. | | Amsterdam: F. Brüggen[4] | D | 3 | 60.5 | boxw, ivory | | | | 39. | Ill. Montagu, *BC*, Pl 25 |
| 10. | | Amsterdam: F. Brüggen[4] | D | 3 | 60.5 | maple, ivory | | | | 40. | Ill. Montagu, *BC*, Pl 25 |
| **TENOR RECORDERS** | | | | | | | | | | | |
| 1. | 1 | Chester: Grosvenor Mus | C | 3 pcs | | ivory | | | | 22. | Ill. Montagu, *BC*, Pl 26 |
| 2. | 1 silver | xBerlin 96 | C | 3 | 67.5 | boxw, ivory | cp ro | | | x23 | |
| 3. | 1 | Brunswick 80 | B | | 68.0 | boxw, ivory | | | | 29. | |
| 4. | 1 | Hague 52 | C | | | | | | | 31. | |
| 5. | | London: Guy Oldham | | | | | | | | 32. | |
| 6. | | Bologna 1825 | C | | | boxw, unmtd | | | | 36. Note 5 | |
| 7. | | Bologna 1834 | C | | | boxw, ivory | | | | 37. Note 5 | |
| 8. | | London: W. Avery | | | | | | | | 42. | |
| 9. | 1 | Milan: Cast. Sforzesco 316[6] | C | 3 | 67.5 | ivory | | | | 44. | |

[1]This instrument has been said to be in eb' and designated "alto" to distinguish it from "treble" and "voice flute" recorders in other keys, but another report has this one in d' and therefore easily confused with GSJ No. 18, a "voice flute" in d'.
[2]Headjoint by Bressan, the rest of different wood and unmarked.

[3]Two types of wood.
[4]Both of these previously in the collection of W. Oler.
[5]These are tenors in C, not altos ("trebles") as previously reported.
[6]Another frustrating instance of Milan's complete renumbering of every instrument in successive editions of their catalogue.

This Bressan recorder is No. 316 in the 1963 edition, No. 188 in 1953 edition, and No. 107 in an earlier-still edition. How wonderful to have updated revisions with such frequency, but how shortsighted to renumber every item included! Numbers—ALL numbers—once assigned, should be left unchanged thereafter, FOREVER.

**BRESSAN** *(cont.)*

**TENOR RECORDERS** *(cont.)*

GSJ No.

**BRESSAN** *(cont.)*

| Young No. | No. Keys and Metal | City, Owner, No. | Pitch | No. Pcs. | Length | Body, Mounts | Flaps | SAT | Holes Dbld. | Tuning Holes | Additional Data | Ill. Source |
|---|---|---|---|---|---|---|---|---|---|---|---|---|
| 10. | 1 brass | Hague Ea 28-X-1952 | | 3 | 68.0 | d brn. wood ivory | | | | | | |
| 11. | 1 copper | Copenhagen E. 129 | | 3 | 69.8 | | ——— ——— | | | | Key a replacement | |

**BASS RECORDERS**

| Young No. | No. Keys and Metal | City, Owner, No. | Pitch | No. Pcs. | Length | Body, Mounts | Flaps | SAT | Holes Dbld. | Tuning Holes | Additional Data | Ill. Source |
|---|---|---|---|---|---|---|---|---|---|---|---|---|
| 1. | 1 | Chester: Grosvenor Mus | F | 3+peg | 107.5 | wood, ivory | (U) | | | | 24. Note 1 | Ill. Montagu, *BC*, Pl 26 |
| 2. | 1 brass | London: V&A 293-1882 | F | 3+peg | 108.0 | fruitw, ivory | sq | | | | 25. Key a replacement? peg missing. Note 1. | Ill. Baines cat., Fig. 116 |
| 3. | 1 silver | Norwich: St Peter Hungate Mus | F | 3+peg | 109.2 | boxw, ivory | sq | | | | 26. peg missing? Note 1. | Ill. GS Exhib' 68, Pl II-3 |
| 4. | 1 | Prague 370E | F | 3+peg | | wood, ivory | (U) | | | | 27. | Ill. Buchner, *MITA*, No.153 |
| 5. | 1 silver | near Dublin: anon. | F | 3+peg | 107.9 | pearw, ivory | (U) | | | | 28. Peg missing. Note 2. | Ill. GSJ XXXII, Pl XXXI |
| 6. | 1 silver | Antwerp: Vleeshuis Mus | F | 3+peg | 109.0 | wood, unmtd | ro | | | | 41. Peg missing. | Ill. Vleeshuis cat., Pl III |

**TRANSVERSE FLUTES**

| Young No. | No. Keys and Metal | City, Owner, No. | Pitch | No. Pcs. | Length | Body, Mounts | Flaps | SAT | Holes Dbld. | Tuning Holes | Additional Data | Ill. Source |
|---|---|---|---|---|---|---|---|---|---|---|---|---|
| 1. | 1 silver | Washington: DCM 1207 | C | 3 | 62.7 | boxw, ivory | tr | SATW | | | 33. | Ill. Bate *Flute*, Pl II-d; Ill. AMIS III, p. 25; Ill. GSJ XV, Pl V. LOM 70 |
| 2. | 1 silver | London: Guy Oldham | C | 3 | | boxw, ivory | tr? | | | | 34. | Ill. Bate *Flute*, Pl II-b |
| 3. | 1 silver | London: V&A 452-1898 | C | 4 | 61.5 | ebony, silv [3] | tr | | | | 35. | Ill. Baines cat., Fig. 122; Ill. GSJ XIII, Pl VIII |

# BROD

**BROD**

**OBOES**

| Young No. | No. Keys and Metal | City, Owner, No. | Pitch | No. Pcs. | Length | Body, Mounts | Flaps | SAT | Holes Dbld. | Tuning Holes | Additional Data | Ill. Source |
|---|---|---|---|---|---|---|---|---|---|---|---|---|
| 1. | 8 silver | Paris C. 483, E. 379 | | | 57.9 | grena, silver | dome w lip | | 3&4 dbl | 1 th. | Keys mtd on posts & axles | |
| 2. | 11 silver | Oxford: Bate 207 | | | 59.2 | violet, silver [4] | dome w lip | SATK | 3&4 dbl | 0 th | Keys mtd on posts & axles | Ill. Bate *Oboe*, Pl V. LOM 230 |
| 3. | silver | Biebrich | | | | | | | | | | Ill. Heckel, *Der Fagott*, p 10 |
| 4. | | Paris C. 1512 | | | | | | | | | | |
| 5. | | Edinburgh: Rendall | | | | | | | | | | |
| 6. | | New York: late J Marx | | | | | | | | | | |
| 7. | | New York: late J Marx | | | | | | | | | | |
| 8. | | Nürnberg MI 457 (loan Ventzke) | | | | | | | | | c. 1839 | |

[1] Detailed measurements of these first three are given in GSJ VIII, p 30-31.

[2] Full account of this instrument (bought in Newfoundland!) is in GSJ XXXII, p 131.

[3] Silver inlay on body.

[4] With ivory bell ring.

| Young No. | No. Keys and Metal | City, Owner, No. | Pitch | No. Pcs. | Length | Body, Mounts | Flaps | SAT | Holes Dbld. | Tuning Holes | Additional Data | Ill. Source |
|---|---|---|---|---|---|---|---|---|---|---|---|---|
| **BROD** (cont.) | | | | | | | | | | | | |
| **ENGLISH HORNS** | | | | | | | | | | | | |
| 1. | 9 nick silv | Oxford: Bate 249 | | | 70.5 | maple, silver | cupped | | 3 dbl | | Keys mtd on posts & axles. Straight form. | EAMI 583. Ill. Bate *Oboe*, Pl VI |
| 2. | 9 | London: Horniman 178 | | | 70.0 | wood, silver | cupped | | | | Keys mtd on posts & axles. Straight form. | Ill. Horniman, *WIEAM*, Pl 12 |
| 3. | 12 | Edgware: Boosey & Hawkes 234 | | | | maple, silver | | | | | Straight form | |
| 4. | | Royal Military Exhibition No. 212, per Langwill | | | | | | | | | | |
| 5. | | Loup Sale, Paris, 1888, No. 203, per Langwill | | | | | | | | | | |
| **BASS OBOE** | | | | | | | | | | | | |
| 1. | 10 brass | Scarsdale: Rosenbaum 96 | | | 96.7 | rosew, brass | dome w lip | | 0 dbl. | 0 th. | Keys mtd on posts & axles. Unusual! Straight form. | LOM 233 |

# GEORGE CATLIN, HARTFORD

GEORGE CATLIN, HARTFORD

| Young No. | No. Keys and Metal | City, Owner, No. | Pitch | No. Pcs. | Length | Body, Mounts | Flaps | SAT | Holes Dbld. | Tuning Holes | Additional Data | Ill. Source |
|---|---|---|---|---|---|---|---|---|---|---|---|---|
| **BASS CLARINET** | | | | | | | | | | | | |
| 1. | 6 brass | Dearborn: H. Ford Mus. 77.68.1 | | | 80.4 | maple, ivory | spade[1] | SATK | | | Guard-medallion over R thumb keys but now missing. Brass bands. | Ill. this book, Pl. VII |
| **BASSOONS** | | | | | | | | | | | | |
| 1. | 4 brass | Dearborn: H. Ford Mus. 76.27 | | | 121.3 | maple, brass | spade[1] | SATK | | | Keys mtd in saddles | Ill. GSJ XXX, Pl III Ill. this book, Pl. VII |
| 2. | 6 brass | Delmar, N.Y.: Clifford Allanson | | | 122.3 | maple, brass | (U) | SATK | | | Keys mtd in saddles | Ill. GSJ XXX, Pl IV |

# CATLIN BACON

CATLIN BACON

| Young No. | No. Keys and Metal | City, Owner, No. | Pitch | No. Pcs. | Length | Body, Mounts | Flaps | SAT | Holes Dbld. | Tuning Holes | Additional Data | Ill. Source |
|---|---|---|---|---|---|---|---|---|---|---|---|---|
| **BASS CLARINET** | | | | | | | | | | | | |
| 1. | 9 brass | Letchworth State Park, N.Y. | | | 84.0 | maple, ivory | spade[1] | SATK | | | brass bell | Ill. GSJ XXX, Pl V |
| **BASSOON** | | | | | | | | | | | | |
| 1. | 6 brass | N.J. (town unknown) [2] | | | 122.5 | maple, brass | | SATK | | | | |

[1] This unique coverplate design has been found thus far only on instruments made in Hartford 1799-1820 by Catlin, Uzal Miner and perhaps other associates. Robert Eliason gives a full account in GSJ XXX and has christened this flap shape 'the Hartford spade.'

one flap on H. Ford 77.68.1    H. Ford 76.27    Letchworth bass clarinet

[2] Robert Eliason examined this instrument while a member of the Smithsonian staff. The owner eventually "lost" the bassoon, even as the Smithsonian believed they were acquiring it. It has not resurfaced.

## CATLIN BLISS

### BASSOON

| | | | | | | | | | | | | |
|---|---|---|---|---|---|---|---|---|---|---|---|---|
| 1. | 6 brass | Dearborn: H. Ford Mus. 77.68.2 | | | 121.8 | maple, brass | (U) | SATW | | | Keys mtd in saddles . Flat table | |

## CATLIN, PHILADELPHIA

### FLUTES

| | | | | | | | | | | | | |
|---|---|---|---|---|---|---|---|---|---|---|---|---|
| 1. | 4 silver | Washington: DCM 1182 | C | 5 pc | 62.3 | rosew, ivory | salt-spoon | SATK | | | Metal lined headjoint. | |
| 2. | 6 silver | Mt. Vernon Estates, Va. | C | 5 pc | | boxw, ivory | All plugs | SATK | | | Plugs fit into silver bushings. Barrel stamped G. ASTOR/LONDON | |
| 3. | 8 silver | Hayward, Cal.: D.L. Parker | C | 5 pc | 68.0 | rosew, silver | salt-spoon | SATK | | | Metal-lined head jt. Foot to C. | |

## COLLIER

### FLUTES

GSJ No.

| | | | | | | | | | | | | |
|---|---|---|---|---|---|---|---|---|---|---|---|---|
| 1. | 1 silver | Essen: J.F. Hanchet[1] | | | 53.2+[2] | boxw, ivory | Sq | – – – | | 1. | Key a replacement. 2 keys added later, embouchure enlarged. | |
| 2. | 1 silver | Munich: Stadt-museum 43/170 | | 4 pc | 59.45 | boxw, ivory | Sq(F) | SATK | | | 3 keys added later in blocks. | |
| 3. | 1 | Peebles: F.E. Dodman | | | | boxw, ivory | | | 2 upper jts | 18. | Ft jt missing. 2 keys added later. | |
| 4. | 3 | Cambridge University | | 4 pc | | boxw, ivory | Sq | | | | | |
| 5. | 5 silver | Oxford: Bate 113 | | | 57.3+[2] | boxw, ivory | Sq | | 3 upper jts | 4. | To c♯. | |

### CLARINETS

| | | | | | | | | | | | | |
|---|---|---|---|---|---|---|---|---|---|---|---|---|
| 1. | 5 brass | Keighley: Cliffe Castle Mus. | B♭ | | | boxw, unmtd | | | | 11. | Mthpc+bbl=1. | Ill. GSJ XVIII, Pl Vc |
| 2. | 5 brass | Edinburgh: Rendall | B♭ | 4 | 60.4 | boxw, unmtd | Sq | | | 12. | Bore 1.38. Mthpc+bbl=1;2 pc body; 3 pc+bell=4 total | |
| 3. | 5 brass | Glasgow Univ. Music Dept. | C | – – – | – – – | wood, ivory | | | | 13. | Only lower jt by T. Collier | |
| 4. | 5 | Ilford: late E. Half-penny | B♭ | 4 | | boxw, ivory | Sq | | | 14. | 3 pc+bell=4 total | Ill. GSJ XVIII, Pl Ve |
| 5. | 5 brass | Berwick on Tweed: C. Brackenbury | B♭ | 4 | | boxw, unmtd | Sq | | | 17. | 3 pc+bell=4 total. | Ill. GSJ XVIII, Pl VIa |

[1] Formerly Oxford: Bate 13
[2] Anthony Baines' catalogue of the Bate Collection, Oxford, gives only the length from the center of the embouchure, rather than from the extreme end of the head joint. Such lengths will be given here with the sign+ to indicate that the overall length is actually slightly longer.

| Young No. | No. Keys and Metal | City, Owner, No. | Pitch | No. Pcs. | Length | Body, Mounts | Flaps | SAT | Holes Dbld. | Tuning Holes | | Additional Data | Ill. Source |
|---|---|---|---|---|---|---|---|---|---|---|---|---|---|
| **COLLIER** *(cont.)* | | | | | | | | | | | | | **COLLIER** *(cont.)* |
| OBOES | | | | | | | | | | | | | |
| 1. | 2 brass | Cuxton: Marshall Coll. | | | | boxw, unmtd | | | | | 2. | type C[3] | |
| 2. | 2 brass | West Tapping Church | | | | boxw, ivory | | | | | 3. | type C | |
| 3. | 2 silver | Swindon Museum | | | | wood, ivory | | | | | 6. | type D[3] | |
| 4. | 2 silver | New Haven: Yale | | | 56.85 | boxw, unmtd | Oct(R) | SATK | 3&4dbl | 2th | 7. | type D | Ill. Bate *Oboe*, Pl III-6 |
| 5. | 2 silver | Berwick/Tweed: C. Brackenbury | | | | unmtd | | | | | 8. | type D | |
| 6. | 3 silver | Cambridge: C.R.F. Maunder | | | | boxw, unmtd | Oct | SATK | 3&4dbl | 2th | 5. | type D. Exhaustive analysis, GSJ XXXI, p 36-43 | |
| TENOR OBOES IN F | | | | | | | | | | | | | |
| 1. | 2 brass | Glasgow: Glen Coll | | | 76.8 | boxw, ivory | Sq | | | | 9. | Swallowtail | Ill. GSJ V, Pl I-B |
| 2. | 2 brass | London: Guy Oldham | | | 71.7 | maple, unmtd | Sq | | | | 10. | No swallowtail | |
| BASSOONS | | | | | | | | | | | | | |
| 1. | 5 | St. Albans City Mus. | | | | maple | | | | | 16. | | |
| 2. | 9 | Keighley | | | | | | | | | 15. | | |
| **CRONE** | | | | | | | | | | | | | **CRONE** |
| FLUTES | | | | | | | | | | | | | |
| 1. | 1 silver | Washington: Smithsonian 381288 | | 4 pcs | 60.9[2] | boxw, ivory[3] | Sq | SATW | | | | Key missing, as is cap. In poor condition. | |
| 2. | 1 brass | Amsterdam: Jaap Frank | | | | wood, ivory | | | | | | | |
| 3. | 1 brass | Copenhagen E. 139 | | | 31.1 | boxw, unmtd | | SATW | | | | No initials. | |
| 4. | 1 | Berlin (ex Hart) | | | | | | | | | | | |
| 5. | 10 silver | Washington DCM 744 | | | 65.6 | ivory, silver | | | | | | "I.A. CRONE/AMSTERDAM" | |
| 6. | | Lucerne: Tribschen 120 | | | | | | | | | | "I.A. CRONE" | |
| OBOES | | | | | | | | | | | | | |
| 1. | 2 | Prague 1335E | | | | | | | | | | "I.A. CRONE/LEIPZIG" | |
| 2. | 2 brass | Copenhagen C. 457 | | | 56.9 | boxw, unmtd | Sq-cors | | 3 dbl. | 2 th. | | | |
| 3. | 2 | Poznan 170 | | | 58.0 | | | | | | | | |
| 4. | 3 | Amsterdam: deVries | | | | | | | | | | | |
| 5. | 3 | Amsterdam: deVries | | | | | | | | | | | |

[1] In GSJ II, p 12-17, the late Eric Halfpenny summarized external appearance-types of early oboes under the designations 'Type A, Type B,' etc. 'Type C' is the so-called 'English straight model' with a very plain, unornamented profile without decorative turnings, while 'Type D' is the more common profile created by various combinations of 'bulbs,' 'onions,' 'spools,' 'knobs,' etc. See GSJ II, Pl III, for many examples.

[2] Length without its cap, which is missing.

[3] The ivory mounts have been covered with a thin metal band for added strength, perhaps in repair of cracked ivory.

CRONE (cont.)

| Young No. | No. Keys and Metal | City, Owner, No. | Pitch | No. Pcs. | Length | Body, Mounts | Flaps | SAT | Holes Dbld. | Tuning Holes | Additional Data | Ill. Source |
|---|---|---|---|---|---|---|---|---|---|---|---|---|
| **CRONE** (cont.) | | | | | | | | | | | | |
| OBOES (cont.) | | | | | | | | | | | | |
| 6. | 2 brass | Zurich: W. Burger | | | 55.0 | boxw, unmtd | Sq C, oct E♭ | | | | | |
| 7. | 3 brass | Markneukirchen 1116 | | | 58.65 | boxw, ivory | | SATW | 3 dbl. | 2th. | Long gentle upper bulb. Very small upper holes. No initial. | |
| CLARINETS | | | | | | | | | | | | |
| 1. | 5 | xBerlin 2869 | E♭ | | 47.5 | unmtd | | | | | | |
| 2. | 2 brass | Hague Ea 58-X-1952 | D | | 54.2 | boxw | | | | | "G. Crone" (Gottlieb) | Ill. Hague '74 Exhib catalogue, p 30 |
| BASSOONS | | | | | | | | | | | | |
| 1. | 8 | Leipzig 1387 | | | | | | | | | | |
| 2. | | Nieuw Loosdrecht: W. Jansen | | | | | | | | | | Ill. Jansen, fig. 203,128,93 |
| 3. | 8 | Leipzig 1383 | | | | | | | | | | Ill. Jansen, fig. 208 |
| 4. | 8 | Lilienfeld Heimatmus. 6 | | | | | | | | | bell joint replacement | Ill. Jansen, fig. 584 |

# C. DELUSSE

C. DELUSSE

| Young No. | No. Keys and Metal | City, Owner, No. | Pitch | No. Pcs. | Length | Body, Mounts | Flaps | SAT | Holes Dbld. | Tuning Holes | Additional Data | Ill. Source |
|---|---|---|---|---|---|---|---|---|---|---|---|---|
| FLUTES | | | | | | | | | | | | |
| 1. | 1 silver | Paris E. 2147 | C | 4 pc | 64.5 | boxw, ivory | Sq | | | | Crowned C. | |
| 2. | 1 | Paris | C | 4 pc | 62.0 | boxw, unmtd | Sq | | | | Crowned C. | Ill. JJ, GT&BR, no. 91. |
| 3. | 1 silver | London: J. Montagu II 2 | C | 4 pc | 62.7 | rosew, ivory | Ro | SATW | | | Crowned C. Almost hemispherical ivory cap, with silver collar. | |
| 4. | | Broadway: Snowhill Manor | | | | | | | | | | |
| BASS FLUTES | | | | | | | | | | | | |
| 1. | 5 brass | Paris C. 1108, E. 1079 | | | 102.1 | boxw, ivory | E♭ Sq[1] | SATW | | | Crowned C. Headjt is wood w brass U. | |
| 2. | 5 | Paris. Private. | C | | 100.0 | boxw, ivory | E♭ Sq[1] | | | | No initial. Head jt is wood w brass U. | Ill. JJ, GT&BR, no. 94. |
| FLAGEOLET D'OISEAU A POMPE | | | | | | | | | | | | |
| 1. | | Paris C. 373, E. 591. | | | ca.22.0 | dark wood | | | | | Typical French flageolet shape. | |
| GALOUBET | | | | | | | | | | | | |
| 1. | | Paris C. 364 | | | | | | | | | | |
| PITCH PIPES | | | | | | | | | | | | |
| 1. | | Paris C. 741, E. 342 | | | 18.56 | rosew, ivory | | | | | | |
| 2. | | Paris C. 742 | in case | | 17.5 | boxw, unmtd | | | | | Crowned C. | |
| 3. | | Paris C. 743 | | | 17.15 | boxw | | | | | Crowned C. | Ill. JJ, GT&BR, no. 84. |

[1] Remaining flaps are in middle of four keys (on holes 1, 3, 4, & 6).

**C. DELUSSE** *(cont.)*              **C. DELUSSE** *(cont.)*

**OBOES**

| Young No. | No. Keys and Metal | City, Owner, No. | Pitch | No. Pcs. | Length | Body, Mounts | Flaps | SAT | Holes Dbld. | Tuning Holes | Additional Data | Ill. Source |
|---|---|---|---|---|---|---|---|---|---|---|---|---|
| 1. | 2 brass | London Horniman 202 | | (59.0) | | boxw, ivory | Sq Eb, ro C | | 3&4 dbl. | | Crowned C. Bell by T. Lot. | |
| 2. | 2 silver | Paris C. 2182 | | | 57.1 | boxw, unmtd | long oct | SATW | 3 dbl. | 2 th | Crowned C. Swallowtail. | |
| 3. | 2 silver | Paris E. 1807 | | ( ) | | boxw, unmtd | long sq-cors | SATW | 3&4 dbl. | 2 th | Crowned C. Top jt by Dobner & Consort. Swallowtail. | |
| 4. | 2 silver | Paris C. 180, E. 2180 | | | 57.15 | ebony, ivory | long oct | SATW | 3&4 dbl. | 2 th | Crowned C. ½ swallowtail. | |
| 5. | 2 silver | Leningrad 505 | | | 58.7 | boxw, unmtd | long oct | SATW | 3&4 dbl. | | No initial, acc to Blagodatov. | |
| 6. | 2 silver | Vienna: G. Stradner | | | 55.95 | boxw, ivory | long oct | SATW | 3&4 dbl. | | Crowned C. | |
| 7. | 2 | Vienna: R. Clemencic | | | | | | | | | Now 9 keys | |
| 8. | 2 silver | Oxford: Bate 202 | | | 56.1 | violet?, ivory | ro | SATW c,SATK eb | 3&4 dbl. | | Crowned C. Now 5 keys. | |
| 9. | 3 brass | Paris C. 480, E. 387 | | | 56.5 | boxw, ivory | long oct | SATK | 3&4 dbl. | 2 th[1] | Crowned C. 3 upper joints. | LOM 175 |
| 10. | 3 silver | Oxford: Bate 20 | | | 57.2 | cedar? silver | ro | SATK | 3&4 dbl. | 2 th[1] | Crowned C. F# key is original. | EAMI 565. |
| 11. | 7 silver | Paris C. 481, E. 263 | | | 56.5 | boxw, ivory | b, c', eb' all oct[2] | SATK | 3&4 dbl. | 2 th[1] | Crowned C. Swallowtail. | |
| 12. | 9 silver | Paris C. 1114 | | | 55.8 | boxw, ivory | All keys replacements | | 3&4 dbl. | 2 th[2] | Crowned C. | |
| 13. | 12 silver | Paris C. 479, E. 367 | | | 56.1 | cedar, silver | all shallow dome | | | 3&4 dbl. | 2 th[1] | Crowned C. | |
| 14. | | Basel: Michel Piguet | | | | | | | | | | |
| 15. | | Basel: Michel Piguet | | | | | | | | | | |
| 16. | | Samary sale no. 104 per Langwill | | | | | | | | | | |
| 17. | | Loup sale no. 208 per Langwill | | | | | | | | | | |
| 18. | | Loup sale no. 209 per Langwill | | | | | | | | | | |
| 19. | | Milan 118[3] | | | | | | | | | | |

**COR ANGLAIS**

| | | | | | | | | | | | | |
|---|---|---|---|---|---|---|---|---|---|---|---|---|
| 1. | 7 brass | Paris C. 499 | | | | | | | | | | |

**OCTAVE (?) BASSOON**

| | | | | | | | | | | | | |
|---|---|---|---|---|---|---|---|---|---|---|---|---|
| 1. | 7 brass | Paris[4] | | | | | | | | | bBelonged to and gift from Eugene Jancourt | |

**CONTREBASSE OBOE**

| | | | | | | | | | | | | |
|---|---|---|---|---|---|---|---|---|---|---|---|---|
| 1. | 8 brass | Paris C. 459, E. 150 | | | 204.0[5] | wood[6] | Cps (N) & (V) | SATW | | | Crowned C. Keys on holes 1,3, 4, &6, also for C & Eb, plus 2 for left thumb. Bass crook. | Ill. this book, Pl. XIII |

[1] One tuning hole now used for low B.
[2] Low c#', bb', c all round; f#' square.
[3] In 1953 edition? etc.
[4] See Jansen, p. 354. This may be the "English Horn".
[5] Without crook. With crook 211.0 cm.
[6] Wood stained black.

# JOHANN CHRISTOPH DENNER JOHANN CHRISTOPH DENNER

| Young No. | No. Keys and Metal | City, Owner, No. | Pitch | No. Pcs. | Length | Body, Mounts | Flaps | SAT | Holes Dbld. | Tuning Holes | GSJ XX | Nickel (Additional Data) | Ill. Source |
|---|---|---|---|---|---|---|---|---|---|---|---|---|---|
| **SOPRANINO RECORDER** | | | | | | | | | | | | | |
| 1. | | Basel 1956.630 | | 2 pc | 26.95 | ivory, unmtd | | | | | A-1 | S a | Ill. Hunt, Pl XIV |
| **SOPRANO RECORDER** | | | | | | | | | | | | | |
| 1. | | Eisenach 115[1] | | 1 pc | 32.15 | plum, unmtd | | | | | A-2 | S b. Supplementary stamp [1] | EAMI 419. Color ill. Heyde catalogue, also B & W photo of stamp. |
| **ALTO RECORDERS** | | | | | | | | | | | | | |
| 1. | | Munich DM 63053 | G | 3 pc | 45.1 | ebony, ivory | | | | | A-3 | AB dd. Only head jt ICD; rest HOTTETERRE | |
| 2. | | Basel 1878.19 | F | 3 pc | 51.5 | boxw, unmtd | | | | | A-3 | AB dd. | |
| 3. | | Neuwied a R: Giesbert | | 3 pc | 44.8 | ivory | | | | | A-4 | AB aa. | |
| 4. | | Vienna H.U. Staeps | D | 3 pc | 49.5 | boxw, ivory | | | | | A-5 | AB bb. | Ill. Hunt, Pl XIV. |
| 5. | | Scarsdale Rosenbaum 1 | F | 3 pc | 47.52 | plum, unmtd | | | | | A-6 | AB cc. | LOM 42 |
| 6. | | Stockholm 163 | | 3 pc | 50.1 | boxw, unmtd | | | | | A-48 | Only head jt is ICD; mid jt ID & fir tree; ft unmarked. | |
| 7. | | Bavaria anonymous | F | 3 pc | 50.5 | ivory, unmtd | | | 6th and 7th holes dbl! | | | | Ill. GSJ XXXV |
| 8. | | Bavaria anonymous | | 3 pc | 45.3 | boxw, horn[2] | | | | | | | Ill. GSJ XXXV |
| 9. | | xNürnberg MI 139 | | 3 pc | 50.0 | boxw | | | | | | | |
| 10. | | USA: anon | | | | | | | | | | | Ill. GSJ XXXV |
| **TENOR RECORDERS** | | | | | | | | | | | | | |
| 1. | | xSalzburg 239 | D | | 65.0 | | | | | | A-8 | TB cc. | |
| 2. | | Nürnberg MIR 208 | C♯ | 3 pc | 58.5 | plum, unmtd | | | | | A-47 | TB bb. | |
| 3. | | Stockholm 1005 | | 3 pc | 65.0 | plum, ivory | | | | | | | LOM 43 |
| 4. | | Amsterdam: F. Bruggen | | | | pear | | | | | | ex-E.Buser | |
| **BASSET RECORDER [3]** | | | | | | | | | | | | | |
| 1. | 1 brass | Nürnberg MIR 213 | A | 2 pc | 83.0 | maple, brass | Ro | SATK | | | A-9 | BB aa. Edge-blown | Ill. GSJ XX, Pl III. |
| **BASS RECORDERS [3]** | | | | | | | | | | | | | |
| 1. | 1 brass | Leipzig 1141 | F | 3 pc[4] | 94.3 | cherry, brass | sq-cors | SATW | | | A-10 | BB dd. Crook into top. | Ill Heyde catalogue, Pl 4. |
| 2. | 1 | xLeipzig 1142 | | 3 pc | 102.5 | pear | | | | | | | |

[1] On the bottom surface of the foot joint is stamped "I.D. Felbinger . 1682" the significance of which is not established.

[2] A repair.

[3] Satisfactory definitions do not seem to exist for the terms 'basset' and 'bass,' at least as applied to members of the recorder family. I have elected to apply the term 'basset' only to one recorder that is both higher pitched and slightly smaller than the others I have called 'bass.'

[4] Bass recorders are commonly described as 'three piece' (in analogy to three-piece sopranos, altos, and tenors that are comprised of head joint, main joint, and foot) even though many basses require a detachable crook, sometimes a separate mouthpiece on the end of it, and almost always have a detachable cap to form the wind chamber within the head joint.

**JOHANN CHRISTOPH DENNER** *(cont.)*  **JOHANN CHRISTOPH DENNER** *(cont.)*

## BASS RECORDERS *(cont.)*

| Young No. | No. Keys and Metal | City, Owner, No. | Pitch | No. Pcs. | Length | Body, Mounts Flaps | SAT | Additional Data | Ill. Source |
|---|---|---|---|---|---|---|---|---|---|
| | | | | | | | | *GSJ XX* Nickel | |
| 3. | 1 brass | Leipzig 1143 | E♭ | 3 pc | 106.7 | cherry, brass sq-cors | SATW | A-11 BB dd. Crook into top. | Ill. Hevde catalogue, Pl 4. |
| 4. | 1 brass | Bavaria anonymous | F | 3 pc | 102.85 | cherry, brass sq-cors | SATW | Crook into top. | Ill. GSJ XXXV |
| 5. | 1 brass | Bavaria anonymous | F | 3 pc | 101.9 | cherry, brass sq-cors | SATW | Crook into top. | Ill. GSJ XXXV |
| 6. | 1 brass | Nürnberg MI 88 | F♯ | 3 pc | 95.3 | plum, brass sq | SATW | A-12 BB dd. Crook into top. | Ill. GSJ XX, Pl IIIc. |
| 7. | 1 brass | Nürnberg MIR 214 | G | 3 pc | 89.2 | maple, unmtd ro | SATK | A-13 BB ee. Crook into top. Key a replacement? Crook missing. | |
| 8. | 1 brass | Munich BNM Mu 173 | F | 3 pc | 87.0 | ivory, brass sq | SATI | A-14 BB cc. Crook into side. Ivory mouthpiece. | Ill. Hunt, Pl VIII. |
| 9. | 1 brass | Munich BNM Mu 175 | | 3 pc | 90.12 | plum, brass ro | SATW | A-15 BB bb. Edge-blown. | |
| 10. | 1 brass | Munich BNM Mu 179 | E | 3 pc | 103.3 | maple, brass sq | SATW | A-16 BB ff. Crook into top. Crook replacement. | LOM 45. |
| 11. | 1 brass | Berlin 92 | E | 3 pc | 103.0 | boxw, brass sq | SATW | A-17 BB dd. Crook into top. Crook missing. | |
| 12. | 1 brass | Brunswick 84 | | 3 pc | 102.0 | boxw | | A-18 BB ff. Crook missing. | |
| 13. | 1 brass | Linz 156 | F♯ | 3 pc | 89.0 | plum, brass ro | SATW | A-19 BB ff. Crook into side. | |
| 14. | 1 brass | Linz 157 | F | 3 pc | 98.5 | maple, brass ro | SATW | A-20 BB ff. Crook into side. | |
| 15. | 1 brass | Linz 158 | F | 3 pc | 104.0 | maple, brass sq | SATW | A-21 BB ff. Crook into top. Crook a replacement. | |
| 16. | 1 | Salzburg 3/13 | | 3 pc | 89.0 | maple | | A-22 BB ff. Edge-blown. Cp missing. | |
| 17. | 1 brass | Hague Ea 703-1933 | | 3 pc | 100.0 | maple, brass | | A-23 BB ff. Crook into side. | |
| 18. | 1 brass | Paris C. 1388. E. 1516. | F♯ | 3 pc | 90.5 | wood, brass tr | SATW | A-24 BB ff. Crook into top. | |
| 19. | 1 brass | Paris C. 1511 | | 3 pc | 98.0? | wood, brass sq | SATW | A-25 BB ff. Crook into top. Foot joint missing. As is, 72.5 cm high. | |
| 20. | 1 brass | Leningrad 407 | | 3 pc | 90.0 | maple, brass sq | SATW | A-46 Crook into top.[1] | Ill. Blagodatov cat. LOM 44 |
| 21. | 1 brass | Gottweig Abbey | | 3 pc | 93.1 | wood, brass sq | | BB ff. Crook into top. Crook missing. | Ill. GSJ XXI, Pl VIa |
| 22. | 1 brass | Gottweig Abbey | | 3 pc | 93.1 | wood, brass sq | | BB ff. Crook into top. Crook missing. | Ill. GSJ XXI, Pl VIa |
| 23. | 1 brass | Vienna: G. Stradner | | 3 pc | 97.0 | maple, brass sq | | BB ff. Crook into top. Ivory mouthpiece. Bought in Cremona! | |
| 24. | 1 brass | Hague Ea 30-X-1952 | | 3 pc | 88.3 | boxw, brass | | BB ff. Crook into side. Crook missing. | |
| 25. | 1 (missing) | Eisenach L-1 | | 3 pc | 101.7 | boxw, brass | | | |
| 26. | 1 brass | Frankfurt am Oder | | | 94.0 | boxw, brass | | | |
| 27. | | Venice, per P Hailperin | | | | ivory | | | |
| 28. | | Venice, cons.B.Marcello[2] | | | | boxw, brass | | | |

[1] The headjoint cap is decorated with concentric rings cut into the surface ca. 4 mm. apart.     [2] per Alfredo Bernardini, Rome.

| Young No. | No. Keys and Metal | City, Owner, No. | Pitch | No. Pcs. | Length | Body, Mounts | Flaps | SAT | Holes Dbld. | Tuning Holes | Additional Data | | | Ill. Source |
|---|---|---|---|---|---|---|---|---|---|---|---|---|---|---|
| **JOHANN CHRISTOPH DENNER** *(cont.)* | | | | | | | | | | | | | **JOHANN CHRISTOPH DENNER** *(cont.)* | |

## JOHANN CHRISTOPH DENNER *(cont.)*

### RECORDERS OF UNDETERMINED PITCH

| | | | | | | | | | | | *GSJ XX* | *Nickel* | | |
|---|---|---|---|---|---|---|---|---|---|---|---|---|---|---|
| 1. | | Versailles: Bricqueville Collection, according to Langwill | | | | | | | | | A-26 | | | |
| 2. | | London: Royal Military Exhibition 1890, No. 3, according to Langwill | | | | | | | | | A-27 | | | |

### ALTO POMMER

| | | | | | | | | | | | | | | |
|---|---|---|---|---|---|---|---|---|---|---|---|---|---|---|
| 1. | 1 brass | Frankfurt a M X436 | | 1 pc | 77.0 | boxw, brass | | | | | A-28 | P | Bell is a replacement | Ill. this book, Pl. X |

### OBOES

| | | | | | | | | | | | | | | |
|---|---|---|---|---|---|---|---|---|---|---|---|---|---|---|
| 1. | 3 brass | Nürnberg MI 155 | D | 3 pc | 49.65 | plum, unmtd | sq Eb, ro C | SATW | 3&4 dbl | 2th | A-29 | O ee | | Ill. Ott, Pl 56. LOM 51 |
| 2. | 3 | xNürnberg MI 153 | D | 3 pc | 50.0 | boxw, unmtd | | | | | | O cc | | |
| 3. | 3 brass | xNürnberg MI 154 | D | 3 pc | (37.5) | boxw, unmtd | sq Eb, ro C | | 3&4 dbl | | | O dd | | |
| 4. | 3 | xBerlin 2942 | D | 3 pc | 49.5 | boxw, unmtd | | | | | A-31 | O bb | | Ill. Sachs 1922, Pl 26 |
| 5. | 3 | xBerlin 291 | C | 3 pc | 57.0 | boxw | | | | | | O aa | Bell is missing, even in Sachs 1922 | |
| 6. | 3 brass | Leningrad 508 | C | 3 pc | 56.8 | plum, unmtd | trap (L) eb, ro C | SATW | 3&4 dbl | 2th | A-49 | | | LOM 50 |
| 7. | 3 brass | Sigmaringen 281 | C | 3 pc | 56.5 | boxw, unmtd | trap (L) eb, ro C | SATW | 3&4 dbl | 2th | | | | |
| 8. | 3 brass | Venice 34[1] | | | | boxw | | | | | A-30 | O ff | | |

### TENOR OBOES

| | | | | | | | | | | | | | | |
|---|---|---|---|---|---|---|---|---|---|---|---|---|---|---|
| 1. | 2 brass | Leipzig 1547 | F♯ | 3 pc | 80.4 | boxw, unmtd | sq | SATW | 3&4 dbl | 2th | A-32 | AO bb. | Bell flares but bulb inside | |
| 2. | 2 brass | Berlin 1071 | E | 3 pc | 85.0 | boxw, unmtd | sq-cors | SATW | 3&4 dbl | 2th | A-33 | AO aa. | Bell flared | |
| 3. | 2 brass | Linz W. 120, Mu 24 | F♯ | 3 pc | 70.0 | boxw, unmtd | sq Eb, ro C | SATW | 3&4 dbl | 2th | A-35 | OdC. | Bell flared | |
| 4. | 2 brass | Sigmaringen 293 | F♯ | 3 pc | 79.8 | boxw, unmtd | sq(D) | SATW | 3&4 dbl | | | | Bell flared. Both cps D design. | |

### BARITONE OBOE

| | | | | | | | | | | | | | | |
|---|---|---|---|---|---|---|---|---|---|---|---|---|---|---|
| 1. | 2 brass | Nürnberg MI 94 | C♯ | 3 pc[2] | 96.3 | plum,[3] unmtd | sq Eb, sq-corsC | SATW | 0 dbl | 2th | A-34 | TO. | 2 upper jts. | Ill. Ott, Pl 56 |

---

[1] Langwill had listed this oboe as in Verona, as reported in GSJ XX, but there is no such instrument there. Alfredo Bernardini, Rome, confirms that this oboe is in Venice and supplies the details given here.

[2] Plus brass crook. Paul Hailperin believes that the bell may be of maple.

| Young No. | No. Keys and Metal | City, Owner, No. | Pitch | No. Pcs. | Length | Body, Mounts | Flaps | SAT | Holes Dbld. | Tuning Holes | Additional Data | Ill. Source |
|---|---|---|---|---|---|---|---|---|---|---|---|---|

**JOHANN CHRISTOPH DENNER** *(cont.)*

### RACKETT

| Young No. | No. Keys and Metal | City, Owner, No. | Pitch | No. Pcs. | Length | Body, Mounts | Flaps | SAT | Holes Dbld. | Tuning Holes | Additional Data | Ill. Source |
|---|---|---|---|---|---|---|---|---|---|---|---|---|
| | | | | | | | | *GSJ XX* | *Nickel* | | | |
| 1. | | Vienna GdM 173 | | | 24.7[1] | maple, brass [2] | | | | | d. 1709[3] Ivory bell. | |

### CHALUMEAUX [4]

| Young No. | No. Keys and Metal | City, Owner, No. | Pitch | No. Pcs. | Length | Body, Mounts | Flaps | SAT | Holes Dbld. | Tuning Holes | Additional Data | Ill. Source |
|---|---|---|---|---|---|---|---|---|---|---|---|---|
| 1. | 2 brass | Munich BNM Mu 136 | D | 3 pc | 50.0 | boxw, unmtd | sq | SATW | 0 dbl | 0th    A-37    C. | Bore 1.42-1.43 cm. | EAMI 618. LOM 52 |
| 2. | 2 brass | xNürnberg MI 196 | D | 3 pc | 51.0 | boxw, unmtd | sq | | | | Bore 1.5 cm. | |
| 3. | 2 brass | xNürnberg MI 197 | D | 3 pc | | boxw, unmtd | sq | | | | Bore 1.5-1.7 cm. | |
| 4. | 2 brass | xNürnberg MI 149 | C | 3 pc | 55.0 | boxw, unmtd | sq | | | | Bore 1.5 cm. | |

### CLARINETS[5]

| Young No. | No. Keys and Metal | City, Owner, No. | Pitch | No. Pcs. | Length | Body, Mounts | Flaps | SAT | Holes Dbld. | Tuning Holes | Additional Data | Ill. Source |
|---|---|---|---|---|---|---|---|---|---|---|---|---|
| 1. | 3 brass | Berkeley:U.Cal.19 | D | 3pc | 52.9 | boxw,unmtd[6] | sq a'& 8ve;ro e | | 3,4,6, (2X)7 | 0 | Main jt + bell=2pcs. Mthpc & bbl missing Given length is main jt + bell. | Ill. & details, Hoeprich, GSJ XXXIV |
| 2. | | Reported Hoeprich:*GSJ XXXIV* | | | | | | | | | | |

### FAGOTTINO

| Young No. | No. Keys and Metal | City, Owner, No. | Pitch | No. Pcs. | Length | Body, Mounts | Flaps | SAT | Holes Dbld. | Tuning Holes | Additional Data | Ill. Source |
|---|---|---|---|---|---|---|---|---|---|---|---|---|
| 1. | 3 brass | Boston MFA 17.1922 | C | | 63.5 | maple, brass | sq.[7] | SATK | | A38    F dd. | Keys: B♭, D, F. Keys may be repacements. | Ill. Bessaraboff. LOM 49. |

### BASSOONS

| Young No. | No. Keys and Metal | City, Owner, No. | Pitch | No. Pcs. | Length | Body, Mounts | Flaps | SAT | Holes Dbld. | Tuning Holes | Additional Data | Ill. Source |
|---|---|---|---|---|---|---|---|---|---|---|---|---|
| 1. | 3 brass | Berlin 2969 | C | | 120.0 | maple, brass | sq-cors | SATW | | A-39    F aa | Keys: B♭, D, F. | LOM 47 |
| 2. | 3 brass | Berlin 2970 | C | | 126.0 | maple, brass | sq-cors | | | A-40    F bb | Keys: B♭, D, F. | EAMI 591 |
| 3. | 3 brass | Brussels 427[8] | C | | 123.0 | maple, brass | ro | SATK | | A-41    F cc | Keys: B♭, D, F. | Color Ill. Bragard-deHen, IV-15 |
| 4. | x3 brass | xNürnberg MI 126 | C | | 120.0 | beech! brass | | | | F ee | Keys: B♭, D, F | Drawing: Sachs *Handbuch*, fig. 141 |
| 5. | 4 brass[6] | Leningrad 528 | C | | 119.5 | maple, brass | sq-cors but G♯ trap | SATW | | A-50 | Keys: B♭, D, F, G♯[9] | LOM 48 |
| 6. | 6 brass[7] | Salzburg 15/2 | C | | - - - | maple, brass | | | | | Keys: B♭, D, F, F♯,2XG♯[10] | Ill. Birsak, Pl IX & p 40 |

[1] Diameter of body 8.7 cm.

[2] Ivory bell.

[3] But for the soprano recorder in Eisenach, the date on which may or may not be that of manufacture, this rackett is the only known *dated* instrument by Johann Christoph Denner(d.1707!)

[4] (added in press) Dr. J.H. van der Meer believes on the basis of John's description that these 3 lost Nürnberg instruments were true "clarinets" with flared bell, not "chalumeaux" with recorder-like footjoints.

[5] Added in press. Included here for completeness' sake. I remain unconvinced that the Berkeley instrument is by JCD. See pg. 25, fn.2.

[6] Horn ring at top of bell is probable repair.

[7] Hardly "square", very uneven, in fact.

[8] Jansen, p.355, says that Brussels 998 is also by J.C.Denner, but both Mahillon and J. Tilman's checklist of 1975 find No. 998 to be *without* stamp.

[9] Possibly only three keys originally, without G♯.

[10] The F♯ was certainly added later. The double G♯ keys are less certain. (A bassoon and a fagottino both by Scherer, in Zurich's Museum Bellerive, also have double G♯ keys.) Is this an ICD innovation, an experiment not used thereafter by him, or is it a later addition by someone else? I have not examined the instrument personally. It would be interesting to know if the block in which the duplicate G♯ is mounted is an integral piece with the boot joint itself.

| Young No. | No. Keys and Metal | City, Owner, No. | Pitch | No. Pcs. | Length | Body, Mounts Flaps | SAT | Holes Dbld. | Tuning Holes | GSJ XX | Nickel | Additional Data | Ill. Source |
|---|---|---|---|---|---|---|---|---|---|---|---|---|---|

## JOHANN CHRISTOPH DENNER *(cont.)*

### CHORIST FAGOTTE/DULCIANS

| Young No. | No. Keys and Metal | City, Owner, No. | Pitch | No. Pcs. | Length | Body, Mounts Flaps | SAT | Holes Dbld. | Tuning Holes | GSJ XX | Nickel | Additional Data | Ill. Source |
|---|---|---|---|---|---|---|---|---|---|---|---|---|---|
| 1. | 2 silver | Nürnberg MI 125 | C | | 96.1 | maple, silver [1] | | | | A-42 | D bb | Keys: E, F. Gedakt. | Ill. GSJ XX, Pl IIId. LOM 46. |
| 2. | 2 | Nürnberg MI 106 | C | | --- | maple, brass --- --- | | | | A-43 | D dd; | Keys: E, F. Keys, bell, & crook all missing | Ill. GSJ XX, Pl IIIe |
| 3. | 2 brass | Nürnberg MIR 403 | C | | 94.2 | maple, brass | | | | A-44 | D cc | Keys: E, F. Gedakt. | Ill. GSJ XX, Pl IIIf; Jansen fig. 4 |
| 4. | 2 brass | Leipzig 1360 | C | | 93.8 | maple, brass | | | | A-45 | D aa | Keys: E, F. Gedakt. | |
| 5. | 2 brass | Meron, Tirol 6844 | C | | 94.0 | maple, brass | | | | | | Keys: E, F. Gedakt. Crook, E key cover, and F touch all missing. | Ill. GSJ XXXII |

*JOHANN CHRISTOPH DENNER (cont.)*

# JACOB DENNER

### ALTO RECORDERS

| Young No. | No. Keys and Metal | City, Owner, No. | Pitch | No. Pcs. | Length | Body, Mounts Flaps | SAT | Holes Dbld. | Tuning Holes | GSJ XX | Additional Data | Ill. Source |
|---|---|---|---|---|---|---|---|---|---|---|---|---|
| 1. | | Nürnberg MI 139 | E | | 49.4 | boxw, unmtd | | | | B-1 | AO dd. | Ill. Ott, Pl 56. Ill. GSJ XX, Pl IVa. |
| 2. | | Nürnberg MI 140 | E | | 50.0 | boxw, ivory | | | | B-2 | AO ee. Ivory beak. | Ill. Ott, Pl 56. Ill. GSJ XX, Pl IVb. |
| 3. | | Copenhagen 34 | F | | 50.0 | boxw, unmtd | | | | B-3 | AO bb. | Ill. Hammerich, p 20. Ill. GSJ XXI, Pl VIIIb |
| 4. | | Paris C. 399, E. 195 | F | | 49.5 | boxw, unmtd | | | | B-4 | AO gg. Upper jt "C. Rykel." Rest ID. | |
| 5. | | London RCM 63 | F | | 49.7 | ivory [2] | | | | B-5 | AO cc. | Ill. GSJ XXI, Pl VIIIc |
| 6. | | Neuwied a R | | | | | | | | B-6 | | |
| 7. | | Ann Arbor 506 | F | | 50.2 | boxw | | | | B-26 | AO aa. Head jt replacement | GSJ XXI, ill. Pl VIIIa & details p 88. |
| 8. | | Bavaria anonymous | F | | 49.7 | boxw, unmtd | | | | | | Ill. GSJ XXVIII, Pl II & p 10. Also ill. GSJ XXXV |
| 9. | | Bavaria anonymous | F | | 47.2 | boxw, unmtd | | | | | | Ill. GSJ XXVIII, Pl II & p 10. Also ill. GSJ XXXV |
| 10. | | Oettingen | | | 50.1 | | | | | | AO ff. | |
| 11. | | Sigmaringen 304 | | | | boxw | | | | | Head jt ID, rest Rykel [3] | |

### TENOR RECORDERS

| Young No. | No. Keys and Metal | City, Owner, No. | Pitch | No. Pcs. | Length | Body, Mounts Flaps | SAT | Holes Dbld. | Tuning Holes | GSJ XX | Additional Data | Ill. Source |
|---|---|---|---|---|---|---|---|---|---|---|---|---|
| 1. | | Brussels 1026 | B | | 64.0 | boxw, unmtd | | | | A-7 | T bb. Incorrectly listed as ICD by both Mahillon & GSJ XX | |
| 2. | 1 brass | xBerlin 224 | B | | 66.5 | boxw | | | | | T aa. | |
| 3. | 1 brass | Scarsdale: Rosenbaum | | | 68.0 | boxw, unmtd ro | SATW | | | | | |

*JACOB DENNER*

---

[1] all richly engraved.

[2] Highly carved. Interesting how rarely either Denner makes an instrument body of ivory vs. their contemporaries.

[3] The main jt is stamped 'Rijkel' and the foot jt 'Rijkel & Haka,' this last the only stamp I've seen with both names.

| Young No. | No. Keys and Metal | City, Owner, No. | Pitch | No. Pcs. | Length | Body, Mounts | Flaps | SAT | Holes Dbld. | Tuning Holes | Additional Data | Ill. Source |
|---|---|---|---|---|---|---|---|---|---|---|---|---|

## JACOB DENNER (cont.)

GSJ XX   Nickel

### BASS RECORDER

| Young No. | No. Keys and Metal | City, Owner, No. | Pitch | No. Pcs. | Length | Body, Mounts | Flaps | SAT | Holes Dbld. | Tuning Holes | Additional Data | Ill. Source |
|---|---|---|---|---|---|---|---|---|---|---|---|---|
| 1. | 1 brass | Nürnberg MI 95 | E | | 98.5 | maple, unmtd | sq | SATW | | | Stamped "H. SCHELL" and "I. DENNER CORRIGIERT" | |

### FLUTES

| Young No. | No. Keys and Metal | City, Owner, No. | Pitch | No. Pcs. | Length | Body, Mounts | Flaps | SAT | Holes Dbld. | Tuning Holes | Additional Data | Ill. Source |
|---|---|---|---|---|---|---|---|---|---|---|---|---|
| 1. | 1 brass | Brussels 1056 | C | 4 pc | 63.5 | boxw, ivory | sq | SATK | 1 upper jt | B-7 | Q b. | | |
| 2. | 1 silver | Nürnberg MI 257 | C | 4 pc | 65.0 | boxw, ivory | tr | SATW | 2 upper jts | B-8 | Q c. | | |
| 3. | 1 gold pl | xBerlin L.G. | C | 3 pc | 66.5 | ivory | sq | | 2 ft jts, one to C | B-9 | Q a. | | Ill. Sachs, pl 25. Ill. Bowers, AMIS 3, pl 24. |

### CLARINETS

| Young No. | No. Keys and Metal | City, Owner, No. | Pitch | No. Pcs. | Length | Body, Mounts | Flaps | SAT | Holes Dbld. | Tuning Holes | Additional Data | Ill. Source |
|---|---|---|---|---|---|---|---|---|---|---|---|---|
| 1. | 2 brass | Nürnberg MI 149 | D | 3 pc | 54.4 | boxw, unmtd | tr(L)a' | SATW | 0 dbl | B-21 | K d. | | EAMI 621. Ill. Ott, Pl 56. |
| 2. | 2 brass | xNürnberg MI 196 | D | 4 pc[1] | 51.0 | boxw, unmtd | | | | K e. | | | |
| 3. | 2 brass | xNürnberg MI 197 | D | 3 pc | 51.0 | boxw, unmtd | | | | K f. | | | |
| 4. | 2 brass | Berlin 223 | C | 4 pc[1] | 58.0 | boxw, unmtd | tr(L)a' sq oct key | SATW | 0 dbl | B-22 | K a. | | Ill. Otto, p 139 |
| 5. | 2 brass | Brussels 912 | C | 4 pc[1] | 60.0 | boxw, unmtd | tr a', long sq oct key | SATW | 0 dbl | B-23 | K c. | | Ill. Kroll, Pl. 4; LOM 79. |
| 6. | 3 brass[2] | xBrussels 414[2] | A | | 71.0 | | | | | | K b | | |

### DISCANT POMMER

| Young No. | No. Keys and Metal | City, Owner, No. | Pitch | No. Pcs. | Length | Body, Mounts | Flaps | SAT | Holes Dbld. | Tuning Holes | Additional Data | Ill. Source |
|---|---|---|---|---|---|---|---|---|---|---|---|---|
| 1. | 1 brass | Frankfurt a M X437 | | 2 pc | 56.3 | plum, brass | ro | | 0 dbl | 2 th | B-10 | DP | EAMI 538. Ill. Epstein, Pl 3 <br> Ill. this book, Pl. X |

### OBOES

| Young No. | No. Keys and Metal | City, Owner, No. | Pitch | No. Pcs. | Length | Body, Mounts | Flaps | SAT | Holes Dbld. | Tuning Holes | Additional Data | Ill. Source |
|---|---|---|---|---|---|---|---|---|---|---|---|---|
| 1. | 3 brass | Nürnberg MI 90 | | | 53.5 | boxw, unmtd | sq Eb, ro C | SATW | 0 dbl | | B-11 | O dd. | Ill. GSJ XX, Pl IVc |
| 2. | 3 brass | Nürnberg MIR 370 | | | 57.7 | boxw, unmtd | sq E♭, ro C | SATW | 3 dbl | | B-12 | O ee. | Ill. GSJ XX, Pl IVd |
| 3. | 3 brass | Nürnberg MIR 371 | | | 57.6 | boxw, unmtd | sq E♭, ro C | SATW | 3 dbl | | B-13 | O ff. | Ill. GSJ XX, Pl IVe |
| 4. | 3 brass | Nürnberg MIR 372 | | | 57.5 | boxw, unmtd | tr Eb, ro C | SATW | 3&4 dbl | | B-14 | O gg. Upper jt only by ID; rest by I.S.W. | Ill. GSJ XX, Pl IVf |
| 5. | 3 gold pl | Vienna 332 | | | 57.3 | ivory, silver | all ro | SATI | 3&4 dbl | 2 th | B-15 | O hh. | |
| 6. | 3 brass | New Haven, ex Bate | | | 56.0 | boxw, unmtd | tr E♭, sq C | SATW | 3 dbl | 2 th | B-16 | O bb. | Ill. Bate *Oboe*, Pl II-5 |

[1] The fourth piece is created by a divided main section. Mouthpiece and barrel remain a single unit.

[2] Mahillon reported an A clarinet with three keys 'by Denner' (Brussels 414), which seems to have been lost since. Nickel questions its authenticity, especially the bell joint which carried the third key. The University of California, Berkeley, Music Department owns a three-keyed early clarinet which Prof. David Boyden has long hoped might be a Denner instrument. Its maker's stamp is indeed in a scroll like the Denner stamps, but the name itself is illegible. Holes 3, 4, 6, and two 'saucers' for the 7th finger are all *double*. Its turnings are not like any other Denner clarinet, but its keys are very much like one or the other Denner. Added in press: see more recent opinion under J.C. Denner's chalumeaux and clarinets, page 23.

25

**JACOB DENNER** *(cont.)* | | | | | | | | | | | | | **JACOB DENNER** *(cont.)*

| | | | | | | | | | | | | | |
|---|---|---|---|---|---|---|---|---|---|---|---|---|---|
| OBOES *(cont.)* | | | | | | | | | | | *GSJ XX* | *Nickel* | |
| 7. | 3 silver | New York MMA 89.4.1566 | | | 57.1 | boxw, ivory | tr(L)e♭, ro C | SATW | 3 dbl | 2 th | B-17 | O cc. | |
| 8. | 3 brass | New York MMA 89.4.893 | | | 57.5 | boxw, unmtd | tr(L)e♭, ro C | SATW | 3 dbl | 2 th | B-18 | OdA bb. | |
| 9. | 3 brass | Leningrad 1135 | | | (61.3) [1] | boxw, unmtd | all tr | SATW | 3&4 dbl | 2 th | B-26 | O aa. | LOM 78 |
| 10. | 3 brass | Zurich: W. Burger | | | 57.2 | boxw, unmtd | tr(L)e♭, ro C | SATW | 3 dbl | 2 th | B-27 | O ii.  Bell also stamped "H.I.1754" | |
| 11. | 2 brass | London, Sotheby's, 5/3/79. | | | ——— | boxw, ivory | ro | ——— | 3&4 dbl | | | Lower jt is by another maker. late 18C. | |

| | | | | | | | | | | | | | |
|---|---|---|---|---|---|---|---|---|---|---|---|---|---|
| OBOES D'AMORE | | | | | | | | | | | | | |
| 1. | 3 brass | Cincinnati 25 | | | 61.8 | boxw, unmtd | all sq | | 3 dbl | | B-19 | OdA aa.  Straight form, bulb bell | Ill. GSJ XXVIII |
| 2. | 3 brass | Bavaria anonymous | | | 62.5 | boxw, unmtd | tr E♭, sq C | SATW | 3 dbl | | | Straight form, bulb bell. | Ill. GSJ XXXV |
| 3. | 3 brass | Bavaria anonymous | | | 61.7 | boxw, unmtd | tr E♭, ro C | SATW | 3 dbl | | | Straight form, bulb bell. | Ill. GSJ XXXV |

| | | | | | | | | | | | | | |
|---|---|---|---|---|---|---|---|---|---|---|---|---|---|
| TENOR OBOE | | | | | | | | | | | | | |
| 1. | 3 brass | Berlin 516 | | | 81.0 | plum, unmtd | all rec | SATW | 3 dbl | | B-20 | OdC aa.  Straight form, bulb bell | |

| | | | |
|---|---|---|---|
| OBOE DA CACCIA | | | |
| 1. | 3 brass | xLeipzig 1340 | |

| | | | | | | | | | | | | | |
|---|---|---|---|---|---|---|---|---|---|---|---|---|---|
| BASSOONS | | | | | | | | | | | | | |
| 1. | 5 brass | Rheinfelden 1.1 | | | | maple, brass | sq | | | | 1 th | Wing & crook replacement | Ill. Roth, p 6 |
| 2. | 4 brass | Linz W. 129, Mu 33 | | | ——— | maple, brass | sq-cors, but G♯ sq | SATW | | | ——— | Bell damaged, reduced to socket only | |

# J. H. EICHENTOPF | | | | | | | | | | | | | # J. H. EICHENTOPF

| | | | | | | | |
|---|---|---|---|---|---|---|---|
| ALTO RECORDER | | | | | | | |
| 1. | | Nürnberg MIR 200 | F | 3 | 48.34 | boxw, unmtd | |

| | | | | | | | |
|---|---|---|---|---|---|---|---|
| TENOR RECORDER | | | | | | | |
| 1. | 1 brass | Stockholm 165 | C | 3 | 66.5 | boxw, unmtd | |

| | | | | | | | | |
|---|---|---|---|---|---|---|---|---|
| FLUTE | | | | | | | | |
| 1. | 1 silver | Leipzig 1244 | C | 4 pc | | ivory, unmtd | sq(C) | SATK |

| | | | | | | | | |
|---|---|---|---|---|---|---|---|---|
| | | | | | | | | Ill. Heyde Leipzig, Taf. 9 |

[1] The upper joint is stampled "Eichentopf" and is clearly from an oboe d'amore! This was discovered by Paul L Hailperin, Grant Moore, and Felix Raudonikas, to whom I am grateful for the news of this fact.

## J. H. EICHENTOPF (cont.)

| Young No. | No. Keys and Metal | City, Owner, No. | Pitch | No. Pcs. | Length | Body, Mounts | Flaps | SAT | Holes Dbld. | Tuning Holes | Additional Data | Ill. Source |
|---|---|---|---|---|---|---|---|---|---|---|---|---|
| **OBOES** | | | | | | | | | | | | |
| 1. | 3 brass | Halle MS 420 | | | 57.1 | boxw, unmtd | tr E♭s, ro C | SATW | 3&4 dbl | 2th | Very bad warp | Ill. Eppelsheim Bach. |
| 2. | 2 brass | Lisbon MI-76 SK | | | 57.5 | boxw, unmtd | | | 3&4 dbl | 2th | | |
| 3. | | xLeipzig 1325 | | | | | | | | | | |
| **OBOES D'AMORE** | | | | | | | | | | | | |
| 1. | 3 brass | Berlin 73 | A | | 62.0 | boxw, unmtd | ro | SATW | 3&4 dbl | 0 th | | Ill. Eppelsheim Bach |
| 2. | 2 brass | Brussels 971 | A | | 61.1 | boxw, unmtd | tr e♭s, ro C | SATW | 3&4 dbl | 0 th | | Ill. GSJ XXVIII Pl. VIb + details. LOM 80 |
| 3. | 2 brass | Leipzig 1335 | A | | 60.95 | boxw, unmtd | | | | | | |
| 4. | 2 brass | Leipzig 1336 | A | | 61.0 | boxw, unmtd | ro | SATW | | | | |
| 5. | 2 brass | Stockholm Nordiska 77.223 | A | | 61.0 | boxw, unmtd | e♭(Y), ro C | SATW | 3&4 dbl | 0 th | | |
| 6. | 2 brass | Paris C.473, E.205 | A | | 62.0 | boxw, unmtd | all tr, C-cors | SATW | 3&4 dbl | 0 th | Horn around lower jt socket, undoubted repair | LOM 81 |
| 7. | 2 brass | Paris C. 178 | A | | 60.72 | boxw, unmtd | tr | SATW | 3&4 dbl | | 9 more keys & 2 rings added later. | |
| 8. | 2 brass | Leipzig 1337[1] | A | | 61.1 | boxw, unmtd | all ro, C oval | SATW | 3&4 dbl | | | |
| 9. | 2 brass | Leipzig 1337a[1] | A | | | boxw, unmtd | | | | | | |
| 10. | 2 brass | Venice, con. B.Marcello | A | | | bxwd, unmtd. | | | | | These details from A. Bernardini, Rome. | |
| **OBOES DA CACCIA** | | | | | | | | | | | | |
| 1. | 3 brass | Stockholm 170 | | | 83.9 | boxw[2] | tr | SATW | 3&4 dbl | 2 th | d. 1724 | ill. GSJ XXV & XXVI |
| 2. | 3 brass | Copenhagen E-70 | | | 84.2 | boxw[2] | tr | SATW | 3&4 dbl | 2 th | d. 1724. LH e♭ key missing. | ill. GSJ XXV & XXVI LOM 83 |
| **OCTAVE BASSOON** | | | | | | | | | | | | |
| 1. | 3 brass | Halle MS 522 | | | 64.5 | maple, brass | ro | SATW | | | F in saddle, B♭ & D in blocks. Wing not original. Dec. bell ring. | |
| **BASSOONS** | | | | | | | | | | | | |
| 1. | 4 brass | Nürnberg MI 127 | | | 126.9 | maple, brass | ro(V) | SATW | | | B♭ & D in blocks, F & G♯ in saddles. Dec. bell ring. | Ill. Eppelsheim Bach. LOM 86. |
| 2. | 4 brass | Linz W. 136, Mu 35 | | | 126.5 | boxw, brass | ro(V) | SATW | | | All 4 keys in blocks. *Very* heavy because of boxwood. Dec. bell ring. | |
| **QUART BASSOON** | | | | | | | | | | | | |
| 1. | 4 brass | Lübeck 1893/63 | | | 160.0 | maple, brass | ro(V) | | | | B♭ & D in blocks, F & G♯ in saddles. Dec. bell ring. | Ill. Lübeck booklet |

[1] Reported by P. Hailperin in GSJ XXV both stamped "Hirschstein" but made by Eichentopf. I found only one of these, No. 1337, in 1979

[2] leather covered, with brass bell.

| Young No. | No. Keys and Metal | City, Owner, No. | Pitch | No. Pcs. | Length | Body, Mounts Flaps | SAT | Holes Dbld. | Tuning Holes | Additional Data | Ill. Source |
|---|---|---|---|---|---|---|---|---|---|---|---|
| **J. H. EICHENTOPF** *(cont.)* | | | | | | | | | | | **J.H. EICHENTOPF** *(cont.)* |
| HORNS | | | | | | | | | | | |
| 1. | | Salzburg: Museum Caro-lino Augusteum 24/3 | F | | | | | | | dated 1738 | Ill. Birsak Brass, taf VIII |
| 2. | | Greifensee: Bernoulli Collection 134 | | | | | | | | dated 1735 | |
| 3. | | Prague 85E | | | | | | | | dated 1735 | |
| 4. | | Prague 86E | | | | | | | | | |
| 5. | | Munich: Deutsches Museum 1976/856 | | | | | | | | dated 1722. "IOHANN HEINRICH EICHGENTOBF IN LEIPZIG ANNO 1722." | Ill. Langwill |
| TRUMPET | | | | | | | | | | | |
| 1. | | Brunswick Stadt-museum 76 | C | | | | | | | dated 1726 | |
| TROMBONES | | | | | | | | | | | |
| 1. | | Bremen Focke Museum | | | | all brass | | | | dated 1723. Air column length: 360.5 Bell diameter 15.5 | |
| 2. | | ex-Breslau 69, now Poznan? | | | | | | | | dated 1733 | |

# A. EICHENTOPF

**A. EICHENTOPF**

| Young No. | No. Keys and Metal | City, Owner, No. | Pitch | No. Pcs. | Length | Body, Mounts Flaps | SAT | Holes Dbld. | Tuning Holes | Additional Data | Ill. Source |
|---|---|---|---|---|---|---|---|---|---|---|---|
| CONTRABASSOON | | | | | | | | | | | |
| 1. | 3 brass | Leipzig 3394 | | 5 pcs | ca. 267.0 | maple, brass | Cps(U) | SATW | | dated 1714. 5 pcs. exactly like ordinary bassoon. Keys B♭, D, F (no G♯) | Ill. MGG |

# M. EISENMENGER

**M. EISENMENGER**

| Young No. | No. Keys and Metal | City, Owner, No. | Pitch | No. Pcs. | Length | Body, Mounts Flaps | SAT | Holes Dbld. | Tuning Holes | Additional Data | Ill. Source |
|---|---|---|---|---|---|---|---|---|---|---|---|
| ALTO RECORDERS | | | | | | | | | | | |
| 1. | | Munich DM 818 | F | 3 pcs | 49.2 | boxw, unmtd | | | | No finger holes! Apparently never completed to that step. | |
| 2. | | Munich DM 819 | F | 3 pcs | 49.1 | lead! unmtd | | | | No finger holes. | |
| FLUTES | | | | | | | | | | | |
| 1. | 1 brass | Eisenach I-114 | | 4 pcs | 59.9 | boxw, ivory | CP sq | SATW | | | Ill. colour Heyde Eisenach, opp. p 204 |
| 2. | | Innsbruck: Dr. Senn | | | | | | | | | |

## J. G. EISENMENGER

J. G. EISENMENGER

### FLUTE

| | | | | | | | | | | | | |
|---|---|---|---|---|---|---|---|---|---|---|---|---|
| 1. | 1 brass | Niederalteich: Ruhland | | | | boxw, ivory | | | | | | |

### FLUTE D'AMOUR

| | | | | | | | | | | | | |
|---|---|---|---|---|---|---|---|---|---|---|---|---|
| 1. | 1 brass | Nürnberg MIR 345 | | | 71.0 | boxw, unmtd | sq | SATK | | | Key quite crude, unlike other Eisem Eisenmenger specimens. | |

### ENGLISH HORN IN F

| | | | | | | | | | | | | |
|---|---|---|---|---|---|---|---|---|---|---|---|---|
| 1. | 3 brass | Brussels 425 | | | 85.7 | cherry? ivory | tr E♭, | SATW | 3&4 dbl. | | Bulb bell. Straight form. | Ill. Mahillon |

### BASSET HORN

| | | | | | | | | | | | | |
|---|---|---|---|---|---|---|---|---|---|---|---|---|
| 1. | 9 brass | Munich BNM Mu 128[1] | | | | maple, brass | long sq: 8ve, a' c' g♯,f; ro f♯, e, d, c. | SATK | | | Rectangular form! Mthpc. & bbl missing. Bell new? Air column (existing pcs) ca. 105.0 cm. long. Some keys show silver plating, others traces of copper. Bore ca. 1.3-1.4 cm. | Ill. this book, Pl. IV |

### BASSOON

| | | | | | | | | | | | | |
|---|---|---|---|---|---|---|---|---|---|---|---|---|
| 1. | 5 boxw | Biebrich: Heckel F-1 | | | 120.0 | reddish maple, brass | Flaps varied[1] | SATW | | | All joints stamped. 5th key is L thumb E♭. I believe all 5 keys are original. All keys in saddles. Flat table on bass joint for key accuracy. Keys have decorative carving, bell has decorative brass ring around top. | |

[1] Eisenmenger (1698-1742) worked principally in Mannheim, slightly before the emergence of the celebrated Mannheim orchestra. That same orchestra was eventually transferred to Munich. This basset horn is recorded as the gift of the Munich royal theatre (orchestra) to the Bayerisches Nationalmuseum at some point in the 19th century. Not often can ownership be traced as clearly. At the same time, I remain uneasy about certain details of this instrument.

BASSET HORN:

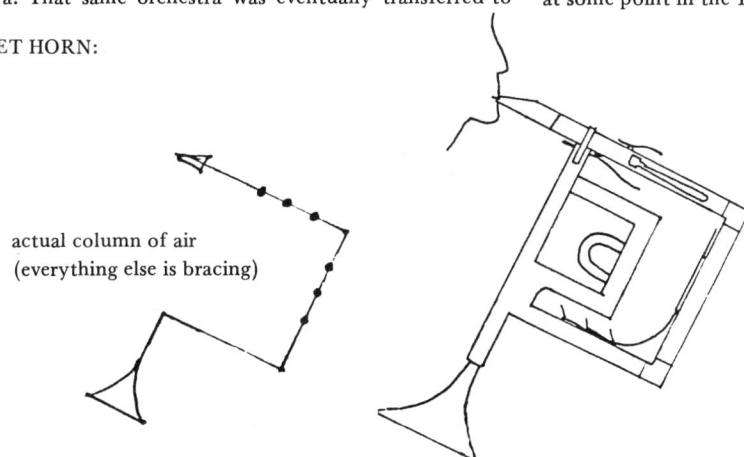

actual column of air (everything else is bracing)

BASSOON: Bb flap

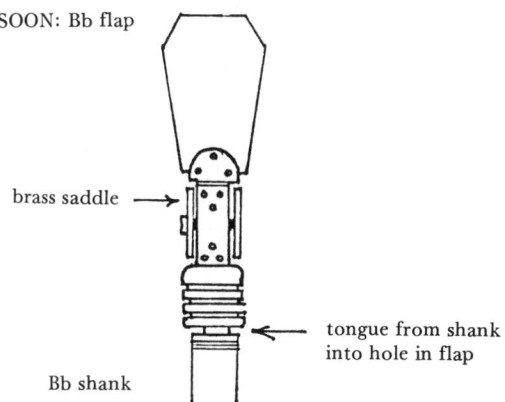

brass saddle →

tongue from shank into hole in flap

Bb shank

D flap

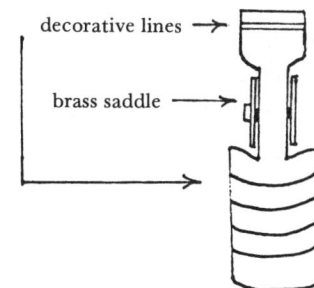

decorative lines →

brass saddle →

# FINKE

## FLUTES

| | | | | | | | | | | | | |
|---|---|---|---|---|---|---|---|---|---|---|---|---|
| 1. | 4 brass | Munich DM 5477 | C | 4 pcs | 63.0 | boxw, ivory | sq | | 3 up jts | | Keys mounted in blocks. | |
| 2. | | Bochum Grumbt | | | | | | | | | | |

## OBOES

| | | | | | | | | | | | | |
|---|---|---|---|---|---|---|---|---|---|---|---|---|
| 1. | 8 brass | Eisenach I-153 | | | 56.45 | boxw, unmtd | oct | | 3 dbl | 2 th | Keys mounted in blocks and knobs. | Ill. Heyde Eisenach, Foto 232 |
| 2. | | Paris E. 2177 | | | | | | | | | | |

## CLARINETS

| | | | | | | | | | | | | |
|---|---|---|---|---|---|---|---|---|---|---|---|---|
| 1. | 5 | Milan Sci & Tech | | | | boxw | | | | | | |
| 2. | 6 brass | Hague Ea 113-1950 | | | 53.3 | boxw, horn | | | | | | |
| 3. | | Oxford: Bate 476a | | | | | | | | | Keys mounted in blocks. Divided lower jts and bell, only. | |

## BASSOONS

| | | | | | | | | | | | | |
|---|---|---|---|---|---|---|---|---|---|---|---|---|
| 1. | 8 | xBerlin 63 | | | 127.5 | maple, brass | | | | | F-G♯ rollers. | |
| 2. | 8 | Stockholm 345 | | | | | | | | | | |
| 3. | 8 | ex Morley-Pegge | | | | | | | | | | |
| 4. | 8 brass | Copenhagen E. 175 | | | 128.0 | maple, brass | sq-cors | SATK | 1 th[1] | | Keys in saddles. | |
| 5. | 8 brass | Copenhagen E. 248 | | | 125.5 | maple, brass | sq-cors | SATK | 0 th. | | Keys in saddles. | |
| 6. | 8 | Oslo: Norsk Folkmuseum | | | | | | | | | | |
| 7. | 9 brass | Bonn BH (Zimmermann 117) | | | 126.5 | maple, brass | sq-cors | | | | Keys in saddles. | |
| 8. | 10 brass | Copenhagen E. 249 | | | 126.0 | maple, brass | | SATK | | | B♭ & D in blocks, rest in saddles. Flat table on bass jt. | |
| 9. | 12 brass | Copenhagen E. 250 | | | 126.4 | maple, brass | ro | SATK | 1 th | | Keys mainly in saddles. Ivory bushed low C hole. | |
| 10. | 12 brass | Leipzig 3560 | | | | maple, brass | ro | | | | | |
| 11. | 13 brass | Biebrich: Heckel F-14a | | | 126.9 | | | | | | Only stamp is on brass top-boot band. | |

## CONTRABASSOON

| | | | | | | | | | | | | |
|---|---|---|---|---|---|---|---|---|---|---|---|---|
| 1. | 7 brass | Huddersfield, Tolson Mem. Mus. | | | 202.0 | maple, brass | | | | | Experimental finger holes plugged. Water key. Floor spike. | |

## BASS HORNS

| | | | | | | | | | | | | |
|---|---|---|---|---|---|---|---|---|---|---|---|---|
| 1. | 3 | Leipzig 1890 | | | | | | | | | | |
| 2. | 11 brass | Leipzig 3933 | | 8 pcs | | maple, brass | | | | | dated 1848 | |
| 3. | 4 | xBerlin 501 | | | | maple | | | | | | |

[1] tuning hole ivory bushed

| Young No. | No. Keys and Metal | City, Owner, No. | Pitch | No. Pcs. | Length | Body, Mounts | Flaps | SAT | Holes Dbld. | Tuning Holes | Additional Data | Ill. Source |
|---|---|---|---|---|---|---|---|---|---|---|---|---|

# FLOTH

### FLUTE

| | | | | | | | | | | | | |
|---|---|---|---|---|---|---|---|---|---|---|---|---|
| 1. | 1 brass | Leipzig 3440 | in F? | | 51.75 | boxw, horn | | | | | | |

### OBOES

| | | | | | | | | | | | | |
|---|---|---|---|---|---|---|---|---|---|---|---|---|
| 1. | 2 silver | Cincinnati Art Museum 26 | C | | 57.1 | ebony, ivory | ro | | | | ½ swallowtail C. Turnings very unusual, modern. "Contemporary" look. | |
| 2. | 2 | Leningrad 1119 | C | | 55.5 | boxw, ivory | | | 3 dbl. | | | |
| 3. | 2 brass | Prague 201E | C | | (55.25) | boxw, unmtd | sq-cors | SATK | 3 dbl. | | undated. Keys mounted in knobs. Bell stamped 'GRUNDMANN ET FLOTH' | |
| 4. | 8 brass | Copenhagen E. 237 | C | | 57.4 | boxw, ivory | sq-cors | SATK | 3 dbl. | | d. 1805. 4 keys originally? (c', c♯', e♭', g♯') f', low b, b♭', & oct added? | |
| 5. | 9 silver | New Haven: Yale 196 | C | | 56.9 | boxw, unmtd | sq-cors | SATK | 3 dbl. | | undated. 5 keys originally? (c', e♭', f', g♯', b♭'); f', low b, oct added? | LOM 177 |
| 6. | 10 silver | Stockholm F. 284 | C | | 55.9 | boxw, ivory | sq-cors | SATK | 3 dbl. | 2 th[1] | d. 1805. Horn mt on lower jt. | |

### CLARINET

| | | | | | | | | | | | | |
|---|---|---|---|---|---|---|---|---|---|---|---|---|
| 1. | | Sweden: Gävle Museum 11795 | | | | | | | | | | |

### BASSOONS

| | | | | | | | | | | | | |
|---|---|---|---|---|---|---|---|---|---|---|---|---|
| 1. | 6 brass | Stockholm Nordiska Mus. 71108 | | | | | | | | | | |
| 2. | 7 brass | Hague Ea 127-1950 | | | 125.0 | | | | | | Correction GSJ XXXI: F is swallowtail, not C. 2 wing keys. No F♯. | |

# FORNARI

### FLUTES

| | | | | | | | | | | | | |
|---|---|---|---|---|---|---|---|---|---|---|---|---|
| 1. | 1 | Munich: BNM Mu 162 | | | 31.0 | boxw, horn | | | | | d. 1819 | |
| 2. | | Venice | | | | | | | | | reported flute, 1 pc by Fornari, rest by Schlegel | |

### OBOES

| | | | | | | | | | | | | |
|---|---|---|---|---|---|---|---|---|---|---|---|---|
| 1. | 2 ivory | Leipzig 1327 | | | 55.9 | ebony, ivory | long sq[2] C, sq Eb | SATK | 3 dbl. | 2th. | undated 3 upper jts. Long C key is offset and for L4![3] | Ill. this book, Pl. 00 |
| 2. | 2 brass[4] | Leipzig 1328 | | | 55.9 | ivory, wood | long sq C, sq Eb | SATI | 3 dbl. | 2th. | d. 1792 | Ill this book, Pl. 00 |

---

[1] tuning hole is now low b, one of several keys added later.
[2] Fornari used the design illustrated to the right for a great many if not a majority of his CPs. It is both distinctive and quite handsome. Even when *not* indicated above (by '2'), it is almost sure that many other instruments by him have CPs in this design.
[3] This is the only instance of this which I know.
[4] gold plate over brass

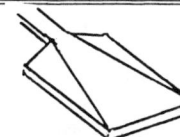

FORNARI (cont.)                                                                                                    FORNARI (cont.)

## OBOES (cont.)

| Young No. | No. Keys and Metal | City, Owner, No. | Pitch | No. Pcs. | Length | Body, Mounts Flaps | SAT | Holes Dbld. | Tuning Holes | Additional Data | Ill. Source |
|---|---|---|---|---|---|---|---|---|---|---|---|
| 3. | 2 ivory | Boston MFA 17.1906 | | | 56.5 | ebony, ivory  long sq[1] | SATW | 3 dbl. | 2 th. | d. 1815  2 upper jts. | |
| 4. | 2 silver | Copenhagen C. 458 | | | 55.9 | boxw, ivory  sq[1] | SATW | 3 dbl. | 2 th. | | |
| 5. | 2 | Lisbon 145 | | | | | | | | d. 1807 | |
| 6. | | Bern 36776 | | | | | | | | d. 1814 | |
| 7. | | Venice | | | | | | | | | |
| 8. | | Venice | | | | | | | | | |
| 9. | | Venice | | | | | | | | | |
| 10. | | Venice | | | | | | | | | |
| 11. | | Rome | | | | | | | | | |

## ENGLISH HORNS

| Young No. | No. Keys and Metal | City, Owner, No. | Pitch | No. Pcs. | Length | Body, Mounts Flaps | SAT | Holes Dbld. | Tuning Holes | Additional Data | Ill. Source |
|---|---|---|---|---|---|---|---|---|---|---|---|
| 1. | 2 brass | Scarsdale: Rosenbaum 92 | | | 77.7 | maple,[2] horn  sq[1] | SATW | 3 dbl. | 2 th. | d. 1795  curved  C ½ swallowtail. | LOM 236 |
| 2. | 2 brass | Copenhagen C. 462 | | | 76.5 | maple,[2] horn | | | | d. 1809  curved | |
| 3. | 2 | Modena 47 | | | | | | | | curved | |
| 4. | 2 | Verona 54 | | | | | | | | d. 1792 | |
| 5. | 2 | Kilmarnock: H. deWalden | | | | | | | | | |
| 6. | 2 ivory | Oxford Bate 251 | | | 75.1 | maple,[2] ivory  sq[1] | | 3 dbl. | | curved  Finger holes ivory bushed. | Ill. Bate Oboe, Pl VII |
| 7. | 2 | Basel: M. Piguet | | | | | | | | curved | |
| 8. | 2 | Milan 390 | | | 76.0 | ebony | SATW | 3 dbl. | | d. 1815  curved  3rd key (g♯) added later. | |
| 9. | | Richmond: E.C. Murray | | | | | | | | d. 1809 | |
| 10. | 2 brass | Boston MFA 17.1920[3] | | | ca 75.0 | pear[4], horn & ivory | | 3 dbl. | | undated  curved  RME No. 210, apparently | Ill. Bessaraboff, Pl IV |
| 11. | 8 | Royal Military Exhib. | | | | | | | | curved | |
| 12. | 10 G. silver | Munich DM 34503 | | | 76.0 | wood,[5]ivory | | 3 dbl. | | d. 1820  curved  Keys mtd in blocks & saddles. | |
| 13. | | Venice: Cons B. Marcello | | | | | | | | | |
| 14. | | Venice: Cons. B.Marcello | | | | | | | | | |
| 15. | 12 G. silver | New York MMA 89.4.889 | | | 77.4 | maple[2], ivory dome | SATK | 3 dbl. | | d. 1832  curved  Keys mounted on posts and axles. | |
| 16. | | Rome: Museo St. Cecilia | | | | leath[4] | | | | d. 1822  curved | |

[1] Fornari used the design illustrated to the right for a great many if not a majority of his CPs. It is both distinctive and quite handsome. Even when *not* indicated above (by '1'), it is almost sure that many other instruments by him have CPs in this design.

[2] black leather covered

[3] Full description by Bessaraboff, p 124. I believe however that he is mistaken in his guess that Fornari (whose stamp is the only one on the instrument) simply repaired it, and that it was made 30-40 years earlier by an anonymous maker. The instrument *looks* like a Fornari English horn to which additional keys have been added in at least two stages.

[4] Leather covered

[5] Light leather covered

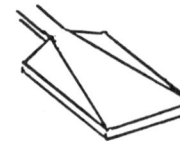

| Young No. | No. Keys and Metal | City, Owner, No. | Pitch | No. Pcs. | Length | Body, Mounts Flaps | SAT | Holes Dbld. | Tuning Holes | Additional Data | Ill. Source |
|---|---|---|---|---|---|---|---|---|---|---|---|
| **BASS CLARINET** | | | | | | | | | | | |
| 1. | 26 brass | New York MMA 1636[1] | | | 166.5 | wood, brass | | | | undated   bassoon form | Ill. Crosby Brown cat, p 134 |
| **BASSOON** | | | | | | | | | | | |
| 1. | 10 | Milan: Conservatorio | | | | | | | | per W. Jansen | |

# J.G. FREYER

| Young No. | No. Keys and Metal | City, Owner, No. | Pitch | No. Pcs. | Length | Body, Mounts Flaps | SAT | Holes Dbld. | Tuning Holes | Additional Data | Ill. Source |
|---|---|---|---|---|---|---|---|---|---|---|---|
| **FLUTES** | | | | | | | | | | | |
| 1. | 1 | Stockholm 539 | C | | | | | | | | |
| 2. | 2 silver | Nürnberg MI 329 | C | 4 pc | 63.8 | boxw, ivory | sq(F) | SATK | | | |
| 3. | 4 silver | Nürnberg MI 343 | C | 4 pc | 63.8 | ebony, ivory | sq(F) | SATK | 3 | | Keys mtd in blocks. Upper jts' lengths: no. 1 16.4; no. 2 15.7; no. 3 15.0[2] | |
| 4. | 5 silver | Washington DCM 979 | C | | 62.8 | boxw, ivory | | | | | | |
| 5. | 5 silver | Lübeck | C | | | ebony | | | | | | |
| 6. | 6 silver | Hamburg MHG 1912.1568a | C | 5 pc | 65.0 | boxw, ivory | | | | | | |
| 7. | 6 silver | Hamburg MHG 1912.1568b | C | 5 pc | 65.0 | boxw, ivory | | | | | | |
| 8. | 8 silver | Brussels 620 | C | 4 pc | 63.9 | ebony, ivory | sq(F) | SATK | 4 | | 2 ft jts. 1 has only d♯ key, other c, c♯, d♯.[3] | |
| 9. | | Lübeck | C | | | ebony | | | | | | |
| 10. | | Bremen | | | | | | | | | | |
| **BASSET HORNS** | | | | | | | | | | | |
| 1. | 9 brass | New York MMA 53.56.12 | | 7 pc | 101.7 | boxw, ivory | sq | SATK | | | Keys in blocks & knobs. | Ill. Winternitz MIWW, p 237 |
| 2. | 9 brass | Berlin 4769 | | 7 pc | 98.0 | boxw, ivory | sq | SATK | | | Keys in blocks & knobs except g♯ in saddle (added?) Bell angled up. | |
| 3. | 14 brass | Paris C. 548 | | | | boxw | | | | | | |
| **BASSOONS** | | | | | | | | | | | |
| 1. | 8 | Stockholm: Nordiska Mus | | | | | | | | | | |

[1] From 1904 Crosby Brown Collection catalogue, p 135: ". . . constructed . . . similar to a bassoon, with tenor and bass joints inserted into a wooden butt and the mouthpiece placed on a curved brass crook. The instrument is mounted with 26 brass keys, some on saddles, others on pins. The finger holes are covered by a patent lever mechanism. . . . The mechanism appears to have been much altered. . . . This instrument is said to have been constructed by Fornari of Venice in the 18th century. In its present state, a large number of keys and other mechanism have been added."

[2] Keys are e♭', f' with 2 touches, g♯', and a♮'. In case very much like Kirst's, with end plugs to suspend joints within case.

[3] Other keys are 2xf', g♯', a♮', and c".

## FREYER & MARTIN

### FLUTES

| | | | | | | | | | | | |
|---|---|---|---|---|---|---|---|---|---|---|---|
| 1. | 1 | Peine: G. Hart | | | | | | | | Accompanying case marked 1816. | |
| 2. | 1 | Stockholm 539 | | | | | | | | | |
| 3. | 6 silver | Washington DCM 873 | | | 63.3[1] | pear, ivory | | | | 3 upper jts. With no. 2 62.5, with no. 3 61.6 | |

### OBOE

| | | | | | | | | | | | |
|---|---|---|---|---|---|---|---|---|---|---|---|
| 1. | 2 brass | Markneukirchen 36 | | | 56.3 | boxw, ivory | SATK | 3 dbl. | 2 th. | | |

### BASSET HORN

| | | | | | | | | | | | |
|---|---|---|---|---|---|---|---|---|---|---|---|
| 1. | | Hague | | | | | | | | | |

### BASSOON

| | | | | | | | | | | | |
|---|---|---|---|---|---|---|---|---|---|---|---|
| 1. | 7 brass | Biebrich: Heckel | | | | | | | | | |

### BASS HORN

| | | | | | | | | | | | |
|---|---|---|---|---|---|---|---|---|---|---|---|
| 1. | | Stockholm | | | | | | | | | |

## J. B. GAHN

### SOPRANO RECORDERS

| | | | | | | | | | | | |
|---|---|---|---|---|---|---|---|---|---|---|---|
| 1. | | Zurich: W. Burger | | 3 pc | 30.7 | ivory | | | | | |
| 2. | | London: J.A. MacGillivray | | | | ivory | | | | | |
| 3. | | Aachen: Dr. W. Willms | | | | | | | | | |

### ALTO RECORDERS

| | | | | | | | | | | | |
|---|---|---|---|---|---|---|---|---|---|---|---|
| 1. | | Leipzig 1126 | | 6 pc [2] | 50.2 | ivory, unmtd | | | | Plain. | See Heyde Leipzig p 137, drawing, Photo too, Tafel 7. |
| 2. | | Copenhagen E. 95 (ex 36) | | 3 pc | 50.1 | ivory, unmtd | | | | Highly carved ivory. | |
| 3. | | London: Guy Oldham | | | | ivory | | | | | |
| 4. | | Amsterdam: Frans Brüggen | f' | 6 pc [2] | 43.8 | ivory, unmtd | | | | | |

[1] With upper joint No. 1.

[2] Since three recorders listed here have been found to consist of 6 pieces rather than the usual 3, it may well turn out that many other Gahn recorders are also of six-piece construction though appearing to be in three pieces.

FREYER & MARTIN

J. B. GAHN

**J.B. GAHN** (cont.)

ALTO RECORDERS (cont.)

| Young No. | No. Keys and Metal | City, Owner, No. | Pitch | No. Pcs. | Length | Body, Mounts Flaps | SAT | Holes Dbld. | Tuning Holes | Additional Data | Ill. Source |
|---|---|---|---|---|---|---|---|---|---|---|---|
| 5. | | Zurich: W. Burger | g' | | 43.5 | ivory, unmtd | | | | | |
| 6. | | Leipzig 3243 | | | 44.4 | ivory, unmtd | | | | Plain. | Ill. Heyde Leipzig, Tafel 7 |
| 7. | | Leipzig 3022 | | 3 pc | | boxw | | | | Highly carved wood. "attributed to" Gahn | Ill. Heyde Leipzig, Tafel 6 |
| 8. | | Munich BNM Mu 34 | | 3 pc | 50.4 | boxw, unmtd | | | | | |
| 9. | | Neuwied a R: Giesbert | f#' | | 44.6 | ivory | | | | | |
| 10. | | Neuwied a R: Giesbert | e' | | 50.8 | boxw | | | | Middle jt by R. Haka. | |
| 11. | | Nürnberg MIR 204 | | 3 pc | 50.0 | ivory, unmtd | | | | In very nice case. | |
| 12. | | New York MMA 89.4.909 | f' | 6 pc[1] | 48.6 | ivory, unmtd | | | | Highly carved ivory. "Foot sections not original." | Ill. MMA Recorder checklist, 1976. |
| 13. | | Aachen: Dr. W. Willms | | | | | | | | | |

TENOR RECORDER

| Young No. | No. Keys and Metal | City, Owner, No. | Pitch | No. Pcs. | Length | Body, Mounts Flaps | SAT | Holes Dbld. | Tuning Holes | Additional Data | Ill. Source |
|---|---|---|---|---|---|---|---|---|---|---|---|
| 1. | | Aachen: Dr. W. Willms | | | | | | | | | |

BASS RECORDER

| Young No. | No. Keys and Metal | City, Owner, No. | Pitch | No. Pcs. | Length | Body, Mounts Flaps | SAT | Holes Dbld. | Tuning Holes | Additional Data | Ill. Source |
|---|---|---|---|---|---|---|---|---|---|---|---|
| 1. | | Aachen: Dr. W. Willms | | | | | | | | | |

OBOES

| Young No. | No. Keys and Metal | City, Owner, No. | Pitch | No. Pcs. | Length | Body, Mounts Flaps | SAT | Holes Dbld. | Tuning Holes | Additional Data | Ill. Source |
|---|---|---|---|---|---|---|---|---|---|---|---|
| 1. | 3 brass | Brunswick 93 | | | 57.0 | ivory | | 3&4 dbl. | | | |
| 2. | 3 brass | Stockholm Nordiska Mus 77333 | in D? | | 50.0 | boxw | | | | C key missing. Listed as "piccolo oboe by I.B. Gann" | |
| 3. | | Hammer Auction 1487[2] | | | | | | | | | |

# GEDNEY

FLUTES

| Young No. | No. Keys and Metal | City, Owner, No. | Pitch | No. Pcs. | Length | Body, Mounts Flaps | SAT | Holes Dbld. | Tuning Holes | Additional Data | Ill. Source |
|---|---|---|---|---|---|---|---|---|---|---|---|
| 1. | 1 | Keighley Museum | | | | | | | | GSJ No. 2. | |
| 2. | 6 | Sevenoaks: C.M. Champion | | 4 | | boxw | | | 3 | GSJ No. 1. Dated 1769. | Ill. Baines WITH, pl XXVI |

BASS FLUTE

| Young No. | No. Keys and Metal | City, Owner, No. | Pitch | No. Pcs. | Length | Body, Mounts Flaps | SAT | Holes Dbld. | Tuning Holes | Additional Data | Ill. Source |
|---|---|---|---|---|---|---|---|---|---|---|---|
| 1. | 1 silver | Edinburgh: Galpin Soc. Collection | G | 4 | 91.6 | boxw, ivory sq | | | | GSJ No. 3. | |

[1] Since three recorders listed here have been found to consist of 6 pieces rather than the usual 3, it may well turn out that many other Gahn recorders are also of six-piece construction though appearing to be in three pieces.

[2] This may be the same instrument as that listed here as in Stockholm's Nordiska Museum, currently on loan to the Musik Museet.

| Young No. | No. Keys and Metal | City, Owner, No. | Pitch | No. Pcs. | Length | Body, Mounts Flaps | SAT | Holes Dbld. | Tuning Holes | Additional Data | Ill. Source |
|---|---|---|---|---|---|---|---|---|---|---|---|

**GEDNEY** *(cont.)*

**OBOE**

| | | | | | | | | | | | |
|---|---|---|---|---|---|---|---|---|---|---|---|
| 1. | 2 silver | Colchester: Colchester & Essex Mus. | | | | boxw, ivory | | | | GSJ No. 4. Engraved keys. | |

**TENOR OBOE**

| | | | | | | | | | | | |
|---|---|---|---|---|---|---|---|---|---|---|---|
| 1. | 2 brass | Boston MFA 17.1912 | F | 3[1] | 84.8 | boxw, unmtd sq | SATW C; SATK Eb. | 0 dbl. | 2 th. | GSJ No. 5. | Ill; Bessaraboff, pl IV |

**BASSOONS**

| | | | | | | | | | | | |
|---|---|---|---|---|---|---|---|---|---|---|---|
| 1. | 4 brass | London: Horniman Mus. 205 | | | 122.3 | maple, brass | | | | GSJ No. 6. Dated 1765. Bell not original. | Ill. JJ, GT & BR, no. 101 |
| 2. | 6 brass | London: RAM office | | | | | | | | | |

# GOLDE

**OBOES**

| | | | | | | | | | | | |
|---|---|---|---|---|---|---|---|---|---|---|---|
| 1. | 10 brass | Halle MS 422 | | | 56.0 | boxw, ivory | | | | | |
| 2. | 11 brass | London: Horniman 42 | | | 55.7 | boxw, ivory | | | | Lowest tone b♮. 2 upper jts. Carse says is Sellner system. In case. | |
| 3. | 11 G.silver | Leningrad 2219 | | | 55.0 | boxw, ivory | | 3 dbl. | | | |
| 4. | 12 | Lübeck | | | | boxw, ivory | | 3 dbl. | | Lowest tone b♮. | |
| 5. | 12 G.silver | London: Horniman 153 | | | 56.4 | boxw, ivory | 2 rings | | | Lowest tone b♮. 2 upper jts. 3 levers for for b♭'. In original case. | Ill.[2] |
| 6. | 12 brass | Zurich: Museum Bellerive 114 | | | 56.0 | boxw, ivory | slight dome | | 3 dbl. | 2 th. | |
| 7. | 13 brass | Nürnberg MIR 384 | | | 55.8 | boxw, ivory | slight dome | SATK | 3 dbl. | | Lowest tone b♭. | |
| 8. | 13 silver | Hague 1116 | | | 56.1 | grena, ivory | ro, flat but lip | SATK | | | Rollers on c, c♯, & e♭. | |
| 9. | 13 | Philadelphia: S. Schoenbach | | | | | | | | | | |
| 10. | 13 silver | Stockholm 1941.43 | | | 54.9 | boxw, ivory | ro, flat but lip | SATK | 3 dbl. | 0 th. | | |
| 11. | 13 brass | Paris E.2179 | | | 54.9 | boxw, ivory | slight dome | | 3 dbl. | 1 th. | | |
| 12. | 13 silver | Düren: Karl Ventzke, ex Heckel | | | 55.9 | boxw, ivory | | | 3 dbl. | | 3 keys on posts and axles. | |

[1] Plus (missing) crook.　　　[2] Ill. Horniman WIEAM, pl 5 (no. 30).

| Young No. | No. Keys and Metal | City, Owner, No. | PITCH | No. Pcs. | Length | Body, Mounts | Flaps | SAT | Holes Dbld. | Tuning Holes | Additional Data | Ill. Source |
|---|---|---|---|---|---|---|---|---|---|---|---|---|
| **GOLDE** *(cont.)* | | | | | | | | | | | | **GOLDE** *(cont.)* |
| **OBOES** *(cont.)* | | | | | | | | | | | | |
| 13. | 13 silver | New York City: the late Josef Marx | | | 54.15 | boxw, ivory | | SATK | 3 dbl. | 0 th. | All keys in blocks except f' & one bb'. | |
| 14. | 15 G.silver | Vienna NB 608 | | | 55.25 | boxw, ivory | ro, flat but lip | SATK | 3 dbl. | 0 th. | Lowest tone bb. Most keys in saddles, 2 posts & axles. | |
| **ENGLISH HORNS** | | | | | | | | | | | | |
| 1. | 11 brass | London: RCM 82 | | | 76.8 | maple,[1] ivory | ro, flat | | | | | Lowest tone c. Curved. Keys in brass saddles. | EAMI 578 |
| 2. | 11 G.silver | Leningrad 1115 | | | | ivory | | | 3 dbl. | | | |
| 3. | 12 silver pl. | Hague Ea 132-1950 | | | 70.5 | wood,[2] ivory | | | | | Curved. | |
| 4. | 12 G.silver | Stockholm F. 292 | | | ca 79.0 | wood,[1] ivory | slight dome | SATK | 0 dbl. | 1 th. | Curved. Grenadilla bell. | LOM 238 |
| 5. | 13 brass | Leningrad 525 | | | 78.0 | wood, ivory | | | 3 dbl. | | | |
| 6. | | Zurich: Allgemein 2689 | | | | wood,[3] ivory | slight dome | | | | Lowest tone bb. Curved. | Ill. Jakob Allgemein, p 33 |
| 7. | | Leipzig 1348 | | | | | | | | | | |
| 8. | | Mengelberg Auction 936[4] | | | | | | | | | | |
| **CLARINETS** | | | | | | | | | | | | |
| 1. | 11 brass | Leipzig 3252 | A | 5 pcs[5] | 61.0+ | boxw, ivory | sq w chamfer (C) | | | | Keys mtd in knobs and saddles. | |
| 2. | 11 silver | Leipzig 3248 | Bb | 6 pcs | 64.9 | ebony, ivory | sq w chamfer (C) | | | | Keys mtd in knobs and saddles. | |
| 3. | 12 brass | Leipzig 3251 | C | 5 pcs[5] | 51.7+ | boxw, ivory | sq w chamfer (C) | | | | Keys mtd in knobs and saddles. | |
| 4. | 12 | Halle MS 384 | A | | | | | | | | | |
| 5. | 13 Germ. silver | Cambridge: N.J. Shackleton | Bb | | 58.5 | ebony, ivory | slight dome | | | | | |
| 6. | | Graz 1395 | | | | | | | | | | |
| 7. | | Graz 1392 | | | | | | | | | | |

[1] Black leather covered.
[2] Brown leather covered.
[3] Leather covered.
[4] Per Langwill.
[5] Plus (missing) mouthpiece.

| Young No. | No. Keys and Metal | City, Owner, No. | Pitch | No. Pcs. | Length | Body, Mounts | Flaps | SAT | Holes Dbld. | Tuning Holes | Additional Data | Ill. Source |
|---|---|---|---|---|---|---|---|---|---|---|---|---|
| **GOLDE** *(cont.)* | | | | | | | | | | | | **GOLDE** *(cont.)* |
| **BASS CLARINETS** | | | | | | | | | | | | |
| 1. | 17/18? brass | Hamburg MHG 1928.323 | | | 108.0 | wood,[1] | | | | | Angular. Some rollers. | |
| 2. | 18 brass | Hamburg MHG 1928.324 | | | 108.0 | wood, ivory | | | | | Angular. Some rollers. | |
| 3. | 18 G.silver | Hamburg MHG 1928.322 | | | 108.0 | ebony, silver[2] | | | | | Angular. No rollers. | |
| **BASSOON** | | | | | | | | | | | | |
| 1. | | Hanover, private collection[3] | | | | | | | | | French system! | |

# GRASSI

**GRASSI**

| Young No. | No. Keys and Metal | City, Owner, No. | Pitch | No. Pcs. | Length | Body, Mounts | Flaps | SAT | Holes Dbld. | Tuning Holes | Additional Data | Ill. Source |
|---|---|---|---|---|---|---|---|---|---|---|---|---|
| **SOPRANINO RECORDER** | | | | | | | | | | | | |
| 1. | | Leipzig 1113 | f" | 3 pcs | 25.3 | boxw, horn | | | | | Block made of cypress. | Ill. Heyde Leipzig, Tafel 5 |
| **FLUTES** | | | | | | | | | | | | |
| 1. | 1 silver | London: RCM 326/FL 3 (Ridley) Geneva: Ernst per Langwill | C | 4 pcs. | 61.0 | ebony, ivory | | | 1 up jt. | | | |
| **OBOES** | | | | | | | | | | | | |
| 1. | 2 brass | Washington Smithsonian 95.298 | | | 57.1 | boxw, ivory | ——— | ——— | 3&4 dbl. | 2 th. | Keys are replacements. 3 upper joints. | |
| 2. | 2 brass | Quito, Ecuador 3450 | | | 55.7 | boxw, ivory | | | | | "Keys mounted in wood saddles." | Ill. Rephann |
| 3. | 2 | Leningrad 1107 | | | 55.6 | boxw, unmtd | | | 3 dbl. | | | |
| 4. | 2 | Stockholm 1954.55/24 | | | ——— | boxw | | | | | Lower jt & bell by Grassi; upper jt by Engelhard. | |
| 5. | 2 | Modena 21 | | | | | | | | | | |
| 6. | 2 brass | Vermillion, U. of S.D. 1314 | | | 54.7 | boxw | | oct. | SATW | 3 dbl. | | |
| **ENGLISH HORNS** | | | | | | | | | | | | |
| 1. | 2 brass | Leipzig 1344 | | | 78.3 | wood,[4] horn | | | 3 dbl. | 2 th. | Curved. Bulb bell. | |
| 2. | 2 brass | New York MMA 89.4.888 | F | 3 pcs | 74.9 | boxw,[5] horn | | | 3 dbl. | | Curved. Bulb bell. | |
| 3. | 2 brass | Paris C.487 | | | | | | | | | Gift of Charles Triebert. | |

[1] Ivory knee is only mount.
[2] Ivory knee.
[3] Per Will Jansen.
[4] Brown leather-covered.
[5] Leather covered.

| Young No. | No. Keys and Metal | City, Owner, No. | Pitch | No. Pcs. | Length | Body, Mounts | Flaps | SAT | Holes Dbld. | Tuning Holes | Additional Data | Ill. Source |
|---|---|---|---|---|---|---|---|---|---|---|---|---|

## GRAVES & Co., WINCHESTER, N.H. Woodwinds

GRAVES & Co., WINCHESTER, N.H. Woodwinds

### FIFES

| Young No. | No. Keys and Metal | City, Owner, No. | Pitch | No. Pcs. | Length | Body, Mounts | Flaps | SAT | Additional Data | Ill. Source |
|---|---|---|---|---|---|---|---|---|---|---|
| 1. | 0 keys | Dearborn: H. Ford Museum 77.68.4 | C | 1 pc | 39.5 | boxw, brass | | | | |
| 2. | 0 keys | Winchester: Wheeler | B? | 1 pc | 44.5 | boxw, brass | | | | |

### PICCOLOS

| Young No. | No. Keys and Metal | City, Owner, No. | Pitch | No. Pcs. | Length | Body, Mounts | Flaps | SAT | Additional Data | Ill. Source |
|---|---|---|---|---|---|---|---|---|---|---|
| 1. | 1 brass | New Paltz, NY: M. Zadro | | 3 pc | 31.8 | apple, ivory | ro | | Key mounted in block. | Ill. Eliason Graves, p 7. |
| 2. | 1 brass | Dearborn: H. Ford Museum 78.2 | D | 3 pc | 32.0 | boxw, brass | ro | | Key mounted in block. | |

### FLUTES

| Young No. | No. Keys and Metal | City, Owner, No. | Pitch | No. Pcs. | Length | Body, Mounts | Flaps | SAT | Additional Data | Ill. Source |
|---|---|---|---|---|---|---|---|---|---|---|
| 1. | 1 brass | Washington: DCM 1274 | C | 4 pc | 61.4 | pear, ivory | flat ro | | | |
| 2. | 4 | Springfield: K.C. Parker | C | | 60.0+ | pear | saltsp | | | |
| 3. | 5 silver | New Haven: Yale 441 | C | 5 pc | 59.95 | rosew, ivory | saltsp | SATK | | |
| 4. | 6 silver | Washington: Smithsonian 59.58 | C | 5 pc | 60.4 | rosew, ivory | saltsp | | | |
| 5. | 8 silver | New Haven: Yale 416 | C | 5 pc | 66.7 | boxw, ivory | saltsp | | Especially beautiful boxwood. | Ill. Eliason Graves, p 7. |

### CLARINETS

| Young No. | No. Keys and Metal | City, Owner, No. | Pitch | No. Pcs. | Length | Body, Mounts | Flaps | SAT | Additional Data | Ill. Source |
|---|---|---|---|---|---|---|---|---|---|---|
| 1. | 5 brass | Washington DCM 274 | C | 5 pc | 59.8 | boxw, ivory | flat ro | | Mouthpiece missing. | |
| 2. | 5 brass | New Haven: Yale 419 | Bb | 6 pc | 60.4+ | boxw, ivory | flat ro | SATK | Mouthpiece missing. | |
| 3. | 5 brass | Dearborn: H. Ford Mus. 73.40 | Eb | 6 pc | 43.7 as is | boxw, ivory | flat ro | | Mouthpiece missing. (43.7 cm is without mthpc.) | |
| 4. | 5 brass | Massapequa, NY: W. Maynard | Bb | 6 pc | | boxw, ivory | flat ro | | | |
| 5. | 5 brass | New York: MMA 89.4.899 | Bb | 6 pc | 66.1 | boxw, ivory | flat ro | SATK | | |
| 6. | 5 brass | Wolfeboro, NH, E. Thomas | C | 6 pc | 58.5 | boxw, ivory | flat ro | | | |
| 7. | 5 brass | Northampton, Mass. Hist. Society | Eb | 5 pc | | rosew, ivory | flat ro | | Bell missing. | |
| 8. | 5 brass | Williamstown, Mass., Williams Coll. | Eb | 6 pc | | boxw, ivory | | | | |
| 9. | 5 brass | Dearborn: Robert E. Eliason | Eb | 5 pc | 49.0 | pear | flat ro | | | |
| 10. | 5 brass | Vermillion: Univ. of S.D. 2653 | Eb | 5 pc | 53.0+ | boxw, ivory | flat ro | | Mouthpiece not orig; given height is without mouthpiece. | |
| 11. | 6 brass | Claremont, California: Janssen | Bb | 5 pc | 66.0 | boxw, ivory | flat ro | | Metal mouthpiece. | |

| Young No. | No. Keys and Metal | City, Owner, No. | Pitch | No. Pcs. | Length | Body, Mounts | Flaps | SAT | Holes Dbld. | Tuning Holes | Additional Data | Ill. Source |
|---|---|---|---|---|---|---|---|---|---|---|---|---|

## GRAVES & CO., WINCHESTER, N.H. Woodwinds *(cont.)*

GRAVES & CO., WINCHESTER, N.H. Woodwinds *(cont.)*

### CLARINETS *(cont.)*

| Young No. | No. Keys and Metal | City, Owner, No. | Pitch | No. Pcs. | Length | Body, Mounts | Flaps | SAT | Additional Data | Ill. Source |
|---|---|---|---|---|---|---|---|---|---|---|
| 12. | 6 brass | Dearborn: Henry Ford Mus. 73.39[1] | C | 6 pc | 53.4+ | boxw, ivory | flat ro | | Mouthpiece missing. Given height is without mouthpiece. | |
| 13. | 8 brass | Springfield: K.C. Parker[1] | C | 6 pc | 53.0+ | boxw, ivory | flat ro | | Bell and barrel by Hopkins. | |
| 14. | 8 brass | Carmel, Cal. Rosario Mazzeo | A | | | boxw, ivory | | | | |
| 15. | 11 G.silver | Hanover, N.H.: Dartmouth Coll. 157-30-18134 | | | | | | | | |
| 16. | 12 brass | Springfield: K.C. Parker | B♭ | 5 pc | 65.2 | boxw, ivory | flat ro | | Eliason says is stamped B but is actually in C. | Ill. Eliason, Graves, p 7 |
| 17. | 13 brass | New Haven: Yale 425 | C | 5 pc | 57.9 | rosew, ivory | flat ro | SATK | All keys in integral blocks. F-F♯ rollers. | |
| 18. | 13 brass | Dearborn: Robert Eliason | C | | 58.6 | boxw, ivory | flat ro | | Metal mouthpiece. "Kendall Model," "top of the line." [2] | |
| 19. | 13 brass | Dearborn: Henry Ford Mus. 78.51 | B♭ | 5 pc | 59.4+ | boxw, ivory | flat ro | | Mouthpiece missing. (59.4 high without it) | |

# GRAVES & Co., WINCHESTER, N.H. Brasses

GRAVES & Co., WINCHESTER, N.H. Brasses

### KEYED BUGLES

| Young No. | No. Keys and Metal | City, Owner, No. | Pitch | No. Pcs. | Length | Body, Mounts | Additional Data | Ill. Source |
|---|---|---|---|---|---|---|---|---|
| 1. | 7 | Deerfield, Mass.: Historic Deerfield | B♭ | | | copper, brass | Labeled "J. Keat for Graves & Co." | |
| 2. | 7 | Dearborn: H. Ford Mus. 73.60.1 | B♭ | | | copper, brass | Labeled "J. Keat for Graves & Co." | |
| 3. | 9 | Milwaukee: Fred Benkovic | B♭ | | | copper, brass | Labeled "J. Keat for Graves & Co." | |
| 4. | 9 | Dearborn: H. Ford Mus. 28.18.17 | B♭ | | | copper, brass | | Ill. Eliason Graves, p 13 |
| 5. | 9 | Washington: Smithsonian 237,754 | B♭ | | 48.7 | copper, brass | Actually in C with B♭ crook. 7 basic keys + Eliason's type 9 & 11. Bell diameter 14.0. | LOM 277 |
| 6. | 9 | Interlochen: Natl. Music Camp | B♭ | | | copper, brass | | |
| 7. | 10 | Ohio: David Karstadt | B♭ | | | copper, G.silver | | |
| 8. | 10 | Dearborn: H. Ford Museum 28.18.166 | e♭ | | | copper, G.silver | | |
| 9. | 9 | Dearborn: H. Ford Museum 28.18.144 | e♭ | | | copper, brass | | |

[1] Stamped GRAVES & ALEXANDER        [2] Has brass bushings in each covered hole.

| Young No. | No. Keys and Metal | City, Owner, No. | Pitch | No. Pcs. | Length | Body, Mounts Flaps | SAT | Holes Dbld. | Tuning Holes | Additional Data | Ill. Source |
|---|---|---|---|---|---|---|---|---|---|---|---|

**GRAVES & CO., WINCHESTER, N.H. Brasses** *(cont.)*      **GRAVES & CO., WINCHESTER, N.H. Brasses** *(cont.)*

**KEYED BUGLES** *(cont.)*

| Young No. | No. Keys and Metal | City, Owner, No. | Pitch | No. Pcs. | Length | Body, Mounts Flaps | SAT | Holes Dbld. | Tuning Holes | Additional Data | Ill. Source |
|---|---|---|---|---|---|---|---|---|---|---|---|
| 10. | 9 | Dearborn: H. Ford Museum 74.142.2 | e♭ | | | copper, brass | | | | Key 6 missing. | |
| 11. | 9 | Dearborn: H. Ford Museum 28.18.182 | e♭ | | | copper, brass | | | | | Ill. Eliason Graves, p 13 |
| 12. | 9 | New York MMA | e♭ | | | copper, G.silv | | | | | |
| 13. | 9 | Urbana: University of Illinois | e♭ | | | copper, brass | | | | | |
| 14. | 9 | New Haven: Yale 180 | e♭ | | 48.2 | copper, brass | | | | | LOM 276 |
| 15. | 9 | Rochester: Martin Lessen | e♭ | | | copper, brass | | | | | |
| 16. | 9 | Milwaukee: Judy Plant | e♭ | | | copper, brass | | | | Straight brass crook. Bell diameter 10.7 | |
| 17. | 9 | Washington: Smithsonian 95,580 | e♭ | | | copper, brass | | | | | |
| 18. | 9 | Milwaukee: Fred Benkovic | e♭ | | | copper, brass | | | | | |
| 19. | 9 | Springfield: Kenneth C. Parker | e♭ | | | copper, brass | | | | Tuning shank and mouthpiece missing. Bell diameter 11.0 | |
| 20. | 10 | Washington: Robert Sheldon | e♭ | | 33.5 as is | copper, nickel silver | | | | Tuning shank. Reportedly used in the inaugural parade of U.S. President W.H. Harrison | |
| 21. | 9 | Vermillion: USD 1339 | e♭ | | 33.65 | copper, brass | | | | | |

**ALTO OPHICLEIDE**

| Young No. | No. Keys and Metal | City, Owner, No. | Pitch | No. Pcs. | Length | Body, Mounts Flaps | SAT | Holes Dbld. | Tuning Holes | Additional Data | Ill. Source |
|---|---|---|---|---|---|---|---|---|---|---|---|
| 1. | 10 | Dearborn: H. Ford Museum 28.18.13 | | | | brass | | | | Also called "quinticlave" | |

**BASS OPHICLEIDE IN B♭**

| Young No. | No. Keys and Metal | City, Owner, No. | Pitch | No. Pcs. | Length | Body, Mounts Flaps | SAT | Holes Dbld. | Tuning Holes | Additional Data | Ill. Source |
|---|---|---|---|---|---|---|---|---|---|---|---|
| 1. | 9 | Milwaukee: Fred Benkovic | | | | brass | | | | | |

**TRUMPETS**

| Young No. | No. Keys and Metal | City, Owner, No. | Pitch | No. Pcs. | Length | Body, Mounts Flaps | SAT | Holes Dbld. | Tuning Holes | Additional Data | Ill. Source |
|---|---|---|---|---|---|---|---|---|---|---|---|
| 1. | | Scarsdale: Dorothy & Robert Rosenbaum | e♭ | | | brass | | | | 3 Vienna valves | Ill. Eliason Graves, p 10 |
| 2. | | Milwaukee: Fred Benkovic | F | | | brass | | | | 2 Stölzel valves. Labeled "J. Keat for Graves & Co." | Ill. Eliason Graves, p 13 |
| 3. | | Claremont, Cal.: Janssen | B♭ | | | brass | | | | 3 Vienna valves | |
| 4. | | New Jersey: Robert Helmacy | B♭ | | | brass | | | | 3 Vienna valves | |

| Young No. | No. Keys and Metal | City, Owner, No. | Pitch | No. Pcs. | Length | Body, Mounts Flaps | SAT | Holes Dbld. | Tuning Holes | Additional Data | Ill. Source |
|---|---|---|---|---|---|---|---|---|---|---|---|

## GRAVES & CO., WINCHESTER, N.H. Brasses (cont.)

### LOW BRASS

| | | | | | | | | | | | |
|---|---|---|---|---|---|---|---|---|---|---|---|
| 1. | | Dearborn: H. Ford Mus. 28.18.60 | E♭ | | | brass | | | | Alto horn. 3 Vienna valves. Also called a "trombcello" | Ill. Eliason Graves, p 10 |
| 2. | | Dearborn: H. Ford Mus. 28.18.29 | F | | | brass | | | | Bass trombone. Slide extension handle. | Ill. Eliason Graves, p 11 |
| 3. | | New York City: Frederick Selch | F | | | | | | | Bass trombone. | |
| 4. | | Windsor, Vermont: Constitution House | F | | | copper w brass | | | | Tuba. 5 Berlin valves. | Ill. Eliason Graves, p 11 |

# GRAVES & Co., BOSTON

GRAVES & Co. BOSTON

### KEYED BUGLES

| | | | | | | | | | | | |
|---|---|---|---|---|---|---|---|---|---|---|---|
| 1. | 9 keys | Springfield: Kenneth C. Parker | e♭ | | | copper, brass | | | | | |
| 2. | 9 | Warrensburg, Mo.: CMSU | e♭ | | | copper, brass | | | | Bell diameter 11.3 32.4 overall length. | |
| 3. | 10 | Milwaukee: Fred Benkovic | e♭ | | | copper, silver | | | | | |
| 4. | 11 | Claremont, Cal.: Janssen Coll. | e♭ | | | copper, brass | | | | | |
| 5. | 12 | Washington: Smith-sonian 68/610 | e♭ | | | engraved silver | | | | 34.0 without lead pipe. | Ill. Eliason Graves, p 20, fig 24 |

### CORNETS

| | | | | | | | | | | | |
|---|---|---|---|---|---|---|---|---|---|---|---|
| 1. | | Milwaukee: Fred Benkovic | e♭ | | | German silver | | | | 3 rotary valves. Over-the-shoulder. | |
| 2. | | Ann Arbor: U. of Mich. | e♭ | | | German silver | | | | 3 rotary valves. Removable bell. | Ill Eliason Graves, p 14, fig 22 |
| 3. | | New Haven: Yale 397 | B♭ | | | brass | | | | 3 rotary valves. 12.65 bell diameter. 25.5 overall length. 36.25 overall height. Circular. | Ill. Eliason Graves, p 14, fig. 23. LOM 273. |
| 4. | | St. Johnsbury, Vt.: Arthur Graves | e♭ | | | silver | | | | 3 rotary valves. "GILMORE, GRAVES" | |

### TUBAS

| | | | | | | | | | | | |
|---|---|---|---|---|---|---|---|---|---|---|---|
| 1. | | Pittsfield, Mass: Berkshire Museum | E♭ | | | German silver | | | | 4 Paine valves. Over-the-shoulder. | |
| 2. | | Washington: Robert Sheldon | | | | | | | | | |

# A. GRENSER

# A. GRENSER

## FLUTES

| Young No. | No. Keys and Metal | City, Owner, No. | Pitch | No. Pcs. | Length | Body, Mounts | Flaps | SAT | Holes Dbld. | Tuning Holes | Additional Data | Ill. Source |
|---|---|---|---|---|---|---|---|---|---|---|---|---|
| 1. | 1 brass | Washington: DCM 140 | C | 4 pc | 63.0 | boxw, ivory | sq | SATK | 2 upper jts[1] | | Undated. Register. | |
| 2. | 1 brass | Paris E. 1632 | C | 4 pc | 61.4 as is | boxw, ivory | sq | ——— | | | Undated. Ft. jt. missing. Present one by L. Lot. | |
| 3. | 1 silver | Washington: DCM 619 | C | 4 pc | 46.3 as is | boxw, ivory | sq | SATW | ——— | | Undated. Upper jt. missing. Present one G.A. Rottenburgh. | |
| 4. | 1 silver | Bonn (Zimmermann 51) | C | 4 pc | 63.5 | ebony, ivory | sq | | 3 upper jts | | Undated. | |
| 5. | 1 silver | Aachen: W. Willms | C | 4 pc | 61.35 as is | boxw, ivory | sq | SATW | | | d. 1789. Ivory cap missing. | |
| 6. | 1 silver | Stockholm 203 | C | 4 pc | 65.43 | boxw, ivory | sq | SATK | 3 upper jts[2] | | Undated. Cap is black horn. | |
| 7. | 1 silver | Vienna GdM 370 | C | 4 pc | 62.5 | ebony, ivory | sq | SATK | 3 upper jts | | Undated. | |
| 8. | 1 silver | Nürnberg MIR 297 | C | 4 pc | 63.85 | boxw, ivory | sq(F) | SATW | 7 upper jts | | Undated. Register. In nice case. | Ill. van der Meer Wegweiser, p 1 . LOM 163 |
| 9. | 1 silver | Nürnberg MIR 292 | C | 4 pc | 63.1 | boxw, horn | sq | SATK | 3 upper jts | | Undated. | |
| 10. | 1 silver | Vienna: Nikolas Harnoncourt | C | | 65.45 | | | | | 7 upper jts | | Ex Frederick the Great. | |
| 11. | 1 silver | Leipzig 3145 | C | 4 pc | 62.7 | boxw, ivory | sq(C) | | | | d. 1796. | |
| 12. | 1 silver | Hague Ea 14-1935 | C | 4 pc | 65.9 | boxw, ivory | sq | | 5 upper jts | | Undated. Register. | |
| 13. | 1 silver | Hague Ea 96-1950 | C | 4 pc | 62.3 | boxw, ivory | sq | | | | d. 1796. | |
| 14. | 1 brass | Copenhagen E. 142 | C | 4 pc | 67.0 | ivory, unmtd | sq | | | | Undated. Ornately engraved key. | |
| 15. | 1 silver | Paris: P. Suzanne | C | 4 pc | | boxw, ivory | sq | | | | | |
| 16. | 1 silver | Meopham, Kent: N. Benn | C | 4 pc | 63.75 | boxw, ivory | sq | | 6 upper jts | | Undated. Register. | |
| 17. | 1 key missing | Hague Ea 8-1944 | C | 4 pc | 62.6 | boxw, ivory | | | 3 upper jts | | Undated. | |
| 18. | 1 silver | Sotheby auction 1977 | C | 4 pc | 55.3[3] | boxw, ivory | sq | | | | Undated. "Key of unusual sprung construction." | |
| 19. | 2 silver | Washington: DCM 949 | C | 4 pc | 60.1 | ebony, ivory | sq(F) | SATW | | | d. 1789. Register. | |
| 20. | 2 | ex Offenbach am Main[4] | C | | | | | | | | | |
| 21. | head jt only | Washington: DCM 997 | | ——— | ——— | boxw, ivory | ——— | ——— | | | Undated. Rest of flute by Schlegel. | |
| 22. | 1 brass | Rome: Museo d.S.M. | | | | boxw, ivory | | | | | Undated | |

## OBOES

| Young No. | No. Keys and Metal | City, Owner, No. | Pitch | No. Pcs. | Length | Body, Mounts | Flaps | SAT | Holes Dbld. | Tuning Holes | Additional Data | Ill. Source |
|---|---|---|---|---|---|---|---|---|---|---|---|---|
| 1. | 3 brass[5] | Peine: G. Hart | C | 3 pc | 56.0 | boxw, unmtd | sq eb, sq-corsC | SATW | 3 dbl. | 2 th. | Undated. Variant stamp no. 1 "GRENTZER" Only instance! | |
| 2. | 2 brass | Leipzig 1315 | C | 3 pc | 58.3 | boxw, unmtd | sq-cors | SATW[6] | 3 dbl. | | Undated. Variant stamp no. 11. | |

[1] Marked 5 & 7 respectively.

[2] Correction, GSJ XXXI. Now 3 upper jts, at least 2 of which appear to belong to the rest of the instrument.

[3] Sounding length.

[4] This collection was sold "some time ago" and no records were kept, either of the instruments themselves or to whom they were sold. The University of Göttingen has at least some of them, but I did not see this flute there at the time of a visit in 1978.

[5] This oboe has duplicate e♭ keys.

[6] The eb key is a later replacement, spring attached to the key.

| Young No. | No. Keys and Metal | City, Owner, No. | Pitch | No. Pcs. | Length | Body, Mounts | Flaps | SAT | Holes Dbld. | Tuning Holes | Additional Data | Ill. Source |
|---|---|---|---|---|---|---|---|---|---|---|---|---|

**A. GRENSER** *(cont.)*

OBOES *(cont.)*

| 3. | 2 brass | Leipzig 1316 | C | 3 pc | 56.7 | boxw, horn | long oct | SATK | 3 dbl. | 2 th. | Undated. Wide middle socket is only horn. Repair? | |
| 4. | 2 silver[1] | Leipzig 3524 | C | 3 pc | 56.9 | boxw, ivory | long oct | SATW | 3&4 dbl. | 2 th. | d. 1790. 3rd key (g♯') added. | |
| 5. | 2 brass | Washington: DCM 1118 | C | 3 pc | 58.0 | boxw, ivory | ro | | 3 dbl. | 2 th. | Undated. Variant stamp no. 6. Keys & top bulb replacement[2] | |
| 6. | 2 brass | Vienna: G. Stradner | C | 3 pc | 56.8 | boxw, unmtd | long oct | SATK | 3&4 dbl. | 2 th. | Undated. 2 upper joints. | |
| 7. | 2 brass | Vienna: G. Stradner | C | 3 pc | 42.7 as is | boxw, horn | long oct | SATW | 3 dbl. | | Undated. Bell missing. Unmounted but for top ring. | |
| 8. | 2 brass | Markneukirchen 3825 | C | 3 pc | 58.8 | boxw, ivory | sq-cors | SATK | 3 dbl. | 2 th. | Undated. | |
| 9. | 2 silver | Binningen: E. Buser | C | 3 pc | 58.2 | boxw, ivory | sq-cors | SATW[3] | 3 dbl. | | Undated. 3 added keys. | |
| 10. | 2 brass | Poznan 166 | C | 3 pc | 58.0 | boxw, unmtd | | | 3 dbl. | | Undated. | |
| 11. | 2 silver | Basel: Michel Piguet | C | 3 pc | 57.7 | boxw, ivory | sq-cors | | 3 dbl. | | d. 1778. MP "plays exceptionally well." | |

OBOE D'AMORE

| 1. | 6 | Grenoble[4] | | | 79.0 | | | | | | | |

OBOE DA CACCIA

| 1. | | Florence, per Langwill[5] | | | | | | | | | | |

ENGLISH HORNS

| 1. | 2 | Florence Conservatory 136 | | | 81.5 | | sq? | | 3 dbl. | | Straight form. | Drawing, Gai catalogue, p 209 |
| 2. | 3 brass | Salzburg 13/5 (G. 191) | | | 78.0 | cherry, leather | sq | | | | Bell glued to lower jt. Curved form. | Ill. Birsak catalogue, pl VIII |

CLARINETS

| 1. | 4 brass | Leipzig 1472 | C | 4 pc | 57.1 | boxw, ivory | sq | SATW | 3&7 dbl. | | d. 1777. No f♯ key. Mthpc, bbl, main jt, long bell. Mthpc not orig. | LOM 101 |
| 2. | 5 brass | Leipzig 1473 | B♭ | 6 pc | 53.5 as is | boxw, ivory | sq | SATW | 3 dbl. | | Undated. Has f♯. 4 pcs+ missing bbl and mthpc=6 originally. | |
| 3. | | Halsingborg P. 666[6] | | | | | | | | | | |
| 4. | 5 brass | Stuttgart: G. Hase | B♭[7] | | | boxw, horn | | | | | | |

[1] Correction, GSJ XXXI. This oboe has 2 silver keys, not brass.
[2] Dayton C. Miller himself made the replacement keys and spliced on a topmost piece to the broken upper joint, but the turnings he made are inappropriate. They resemble Fornari.
[3] The C spring is attached to the wood; the e♭ key spring obviously was similarly attached originally, but a replacement spring is attached to the key.
[4] The name of the museum is not known. No reply to several inquiries. This is suspiciously long for an oboe d'amore, to say the least.
[5] Probably the same instrument listed here as an English horn.

Gai's catalogue lists no oboe da caccia. But see stamp, Langwill 5th ed., p 219.
[6] This instrument is *not* among those transferred to Stockholm recently.
[7] According to T.E. Hoeprich. The Hase list says it is in A.

**A. GRENSER** *(cont.)*              A. GRENSER *(cont.)*

### BASSET HORNS

| Young No. | No. Keys and Metal | City, Owner, No. | Pitch | No. Pcs. | Length | Body, Mounts | Flaps | SAT | Additional Data | Ill. Source |
|---|---|---|---|---|---|---|---|---|---|---|
| 1. | 8 brass | Stockholm 553 | | 8 pc | — — — | boxw, horn | sq | | d. 1784. Angular. Bore 1.45. 7 pc + oval brass bell. [2] | Ill. Saam & EAMI 642 [1] |
| 2. | 9 brass | Munich DM 10224 | | 7 pc | 95.5 [3] | boxw, horn | sq(C) | SATK | undated. Angular. Bore 1.32. 6 pc + oval brass bell. Keys mtd in knobs & blocks. | |
| 3. | 9 brass | Hague Ea 601-1933 | | 7 pc | 93.7 | boxw, horn | sq or sq-cors | SATK | d. 1795. Angular. Bore 1.45-1.47. 6 pc + round brass bell. Mthpc & bbl not orig. | |
| 4. | 10 brass | Hague Ea 600-1933 | | 7 pc | 98.5 | boxw, horn | sq or sq-cors | SATK | d. 1795. Angular. Bore 1.45-1.47. 6 pc + round brass bell. | |
| 5. | 13 brass | Darmstadt Kg 67: 132 | | 7 pc | 98.5 | boxw, horn | sq(C) + 1 U-shape | SATK | undated. Angular. Bore 1.38. 6 pc + round brass bell | |

### BASS CLARINET

| | | | | | | | | | |
|---|---|---|---|---|---|---|---|---|---|
| 1. | 9 brass | Darmstadt Kg 67: 133 | | | 73.8 | boxw, brass | sq exc. a'&g♯' oct. | SATK | d. 1795. Bore 1.43. 6 pc orig but mthpc and neck missing. Repro. made 1981 by R. Weber, copied from Stockholm. |

### BASSOONS [4]

| Young No. | No. Keys and Metal | City, Owner, No. | Length | Body, Mounts | Flaps | SAT | Additional Data | Ill. Source |
|---|---|---|---|---|---|---|---|---|
| 1. | 4 brass | Prague 1336E | 120.0 | maple, brass | (X) | SATW | d. 1775 B♭, D, F, G♯. Keys in blocks. Broad shanks. [5] Brass bell ring. Flat table. | Ill. GSJ XXIV, pl XVI |
| 2. | 4 brass | Nürnberg: Friedemann Hellwig | 123.2 | maple, brass | see note 6 | SATW | d. 1776 B♭, D, F, G♯. Keys in blocks. Broad shanks. Bell replacement? Flat table. | |
| 3. | 4 brass | Copenhagen E. 140 DISCANT | 67.0 | maple, brass | sq-cors | SATW | undated B♭, D, F, G♯. Keys in blocks, notched. | |
| 4. | 4 brass | Prague 1775E | 123.2 | maple, brass | (X) | SATW | undated B♭, D, F, G♯. Keys in blocks, notched. Brass bell ring. Flat table. [7] | |
| 5. | 5 brass | Frankfurt am Oder [8] | 119.6 | maple, brass | | | d. 1772 | |

---

[1] Variant stamp no. 8 is ill. by Dr. Saam and pg. 46 this book.

[2] Knee is not original. All keys mounted in knobs or blocks.

[3] I measure curved or angular woodwinds from mouthpiece tip to bell rim, going over the outside of the curve/angle. This is not wholly satisfactory but is of more interest than simple overall height perpendicular to the bell rim.

[4] The bassoons are listed chronologically by date with the undated specimens inserted according to my guess as to their original number of keys. This of course is strictly speculative, however interesting.

[5] August Grenser's keys frequently have notches, singly or in groups of three along each edge of their broad shanks. Often, too, there are projecting points or barbs along the key edges as a purely decorative embellishment. This fondness for decoration is also seen in grooves around the edges of flat tables on many of his bass joints, with additional decorative carving there as well, e.g. Paris C. 505, E. 188, in some instances. This characteristic is not at all common, and it is interesting that August Grenser's pupil, F.G.A. Kirst of Potsdam, does the same thing and only on bassoons.

[6] A unique coverplate shape is found on this bassoon:

[7] Two wing keys and Eb for L4 added.

[8] The Museum Viadrina lists this instrument as made by Heinrich Grenser, but in 1772 he would have been eight years old. The initials 'A' and 'H' are very easily misread in the Grenser stamp, so in GSJ XXXI I attributed this instrument to August. The Museum has not confirmed my suspicion or corrected it.

**A. GRENSER** *(cont.)* A. GRENSER *(cont.)*

BASSOONS *(cont.)*

| | | | | | | | | | | | | |
|---|---|---|---|---|---|---|---|---|---|---|---|---|
| 6. | 5 ivory | Paris C. 505, E. 188 | | | 124.5 | maple, brass | oval-top(x) | SATW | | | d. 1779  B♭, D, F, G♯, E♭ L Th. Keys in blocks. 2 brass wing keys added. Carved design on flat table. | LOM 190 |
| 7. | 5 brass | Leipzig 1376 | | | 125.7 | maple, brass | oval-top(x) | SATW | | | d. 1782  B♭, D, F, G♯, E♭ L Th. Keys in blocks. Flat table grooved. | |
| 8. | 5 ivory | Leipzig 1377 | | | 126.4 | maple, brass | sq-cors | SATW | | | d. 1786  B♭, D, F, G♯, E♭ L Th. Keys in blocks. Ivory F♯ and 2 brass wing keys added. | Ill. Jansen, fig.214(left) |
| 9. | 5 brass | Leipzig 1378 | | | 127.4 | maple, brass | sq-cors | SATW | | | d. 1788  B♭, D, F, G♯, E♭ L4. Keys in blocks. | Ill. Jansen, fig. 214 (right) |
| 10. | 5 brass | Biebrich: Heckel KG, F-6 | | | 125.7 | maple, brass | long sq-cors | SATW | | | undated  B♭, D, F, G♯, E♭ L Th. Original 5 keys in blocks, others saddles. Grooved flat table. | |
| 11. | 6 brass | Poznan 177 | | | 125.0 | maple, brass | sq-cors | | | | d. 1796  B♭, D, F, G♯, E♭ L Th, F♯. Keys in blocks. Flat table. | |
| 12. | 8 boxwd | Stockholm 1966-67/ 61 | | | 126.5 | maple, brass | sq-cors | | | | d. 1797  B♭, D, F, G♯, E♭ L4, F♯, C♯L4. Wing by H. Grenser, 2 wing keys. Bell unmarked. | |
| 13. | 10 brass | Nieuw Loosdrecht: W. Jansen | | | 126.3 | maple, brass | | | | | undated  No maker's stamp but Mr. Jansen sure by comparison it is by AG. | Ill. Jansen, fig. 203 |
| 14. | 10 brass | Copenhagen 1976-10  Leipzig: H. Heyde | | | 125.5 | maple, brass | oct,[1] | SATK | | 1 tuning hole | undated  B♭, D, F, G♯, E♭ L4, F♯, C♯L4, Low B♮. 2 wing jts. No notches. | |

SERPENTS

| | | | | | | | | | | | | |
|---|---|---|---|---|---|---|---|---|---|---|---|---|
| 1. | no keys | Lübeck 3587f | | | | leather-covered wood, brass ferrules | | | | | dated 1783 | |
| 2. | no keys | Stockholm,[2] | | | | | | | | | undated | |

# A. GRENSER II A. GRENSER II

FLUTE

| | | | | | | | | | | | | |
|---|---|---|---|---|---|---|---|---|---|---|---|---|
| 1. | 6 brass | Eisenach BH I-125 | C | | 68.45 | boxw, ivory | Cps sq (E) | | | | c' & c♯' mtd in blocks, rest in saddles. | Ill. color Heyde Eisenach, p 205[3] |

[1] All flaps replacements?  Odd looking.

[2] Was transferred to Stockholm from Vastmanlands Länsmuseum, where it had been No. 6285.

[3] The stamp is illustrated B&W p. 212.

GRENTZER ← 1. Oboe | 3 brass keys Boxwood 56.0 cm | Pastor Gunter Hart Peine

2. Flute | 4 silver keys Ebony 62.9 cm | Markneukirchen 56 → GRENSER DRESDEN

A. GRENSER DRESDEN ← 3. Flute | 1 key missing Boxwood, ivory, 62.6 cm | Hague Ea 8-1944

4. Oboe | 2 brass keys Boxwood, ivory 58.0 cm | Washington DCM 1118 | * * * → A. GRENSER

A. GRENSER DRESDEN ← 5. Flute | 1 brass key Boxwood, ivory 63.0 cm | Washington DCM 140

6. Flute | 7 brass keys Boxwood, ivory 68.45 (Dr. Heyde says is by A. Grenser II) | Eisenach I-125 Foot to c' → GRENSER DRESDEN

A. GRENSER ← upper jt

7. Oboe | 2 brass keys Boxwood, unmtd, 58.4 cm | Leipzig 1315

G ← lower jt & bell

8. Flute | 1 brass key Boxwood, ivory Unique touch: | Hague Ea 9-1942 → GRENSER DRESDEN

← 9. Basset horn | 8 brass keys as reported in Saam (drawing) | Stockholm 553

10. Flute | 4 silver keys Ebony, ivory, 62.2 cm | Bonn BH (Zimmermann 46) → GRENSER DRESDEN

A. GRENSER IN DRESDEN 1784 2

11. Piccolo | 1 brass key Boxwood, ivory, 30.5 cm | Bonn BH (Zimmermann 30) → GRENSER DRESDEN

All stamps with 'H. GRENSER' but without his usual crossed swords   or Saxon crown trademark, are collected on the page "H. GRENSER II?"

# H. GRENSER

H. GRENSER

| Young No. | No. Keys and Metal | City, Owner, No. | Pitch | No. Pcs. | Length | Body, Mounts | Flaps | SAT | Keys mtd. in | Trade-mark | Additional Data | Ill. Source |
|---|---|---|---|---|---|---|---|---|---|---|---|---|
| **ALTO RECORDER** | | | | | | | | | | | | |
| 1. | | xBerlin 2810 | E | 3 | | boxw, ivory | | | | crown | Keys d', e', & f♯'. "clarinet-like bell" | |
| **FLUTES** | | | | | | | | | | | | |
| 1. | Headjt | Berlin 2725 | C | --- | --- | ebony, ivory | --- | --- | --- | crown | Rest lost in 19th century. | |
| 2. | 1 silver | Niederalteich: K. Ruhland | C | 4 | 61.9 | boxw, ivory | sq (C) | | block | crown | Upper joint "Stengel, Baireuth" | |
| 3. | 1 silver | Nürnberg MIR 294 | C | 4 | 61.3 | boxw, ivory | sq (C) | SATK | block | crown | 3 upper joints. | |
| 4. | 1 silver | Leipzig 1241 | C | 4 | 63.9 | boxw, ivory | trap(C) | SATK | knob | swords | Register. | Ill. Heyde Leipzig, pl 10 |
| 5. | 1 silver | Berlin 102 | C | 4 | 63.0 | ebony, ivory | trap | SATK | knob | swords | 2 keys added in saddles. | |
| 6. | 1 silver | Cologne Stadtmus I/14 | D | 4 | 60.0 | ebony, ivory | sq | SATK | knob | swords | | |
| 7. | 1 silver | Washington Smithson 95.297 | C | 4 | 63.9 | boxw, ivory | sq(G) | SATK | knob | swords | 7 upper joints. Register. | LOM 164 |
| 8. | 1 brass | Washington DCM 1378 | C | 4 | 61.4 | boxw, horn | sq | | | crown | 5 upper joints. | |
| 9. | 1 brass | Helsinki 31064: 3 | C | 4 | 62.5 | boxw | | | | crown | 2 upper joints. | |
| 10. | 1 brass | Munich: Albert Müller | E♭? | 4 | 58.0 | boxw, horn | sq | | | crown | | |
| 11. | 2 silver | Munich: Stadtmuseum 40/173 | C | 4 | 62.6 | ebony, ivory | sq | SATK | knob | swords | 2nd key (g♯') is original. 3rd key (f') added. | |
| 12. | 2 silver | Göttingen, Univ. of, 338 | C | 4 | 61.0 | boxw, ivory | sq (C) | SATK | block | crown | (Second key is f', mtd in added block.) | |
| 13. | 2 silver | Zurich: Allgemein 2692 | C | 4 | 66.3 | ebony | | | | crown | 5 upper joints. Cased with another HG flute, Y. 32 | |
| 14. | 3 silver | Leipzig 3497 | C | 4 | 62.93 | ebony, ivory | sq (C) | | block | swords | Other 2 keys in saddles. 1 silv-pl brass (4th) key added. | Ill. Heyde Leipzig [1] |
| 15. | 3 | Leipzig: Herbert Heyde | C | | | | | | | | Reported by William Waterhouse. | |
| 16. | 3 brass | Leipzig 3146 [2] | C | 4 | 62.8 | ebony, ivory | | | blocks | swords | Keys all later replacements, but originals all in blocks. | |
| 17. | 4 silver | Washington DCM 644 | C | 4 | 65.5 | ebony, ivory | oval(Y) | SATK | | crown | 3 upper joints. | |
| 18. | 4 silver | Washington DCM 767 | C | 4 | 62.6 | ebony, ivory | sq | SATK | | crown | Headjoint stamped "Tuerlinckx," upper jt unmarked. | |
| 19. | 4 silver | Ingolstadt Stadtmus. 2699 | C | 4 | 61.5 | ebony, ivory | sq (C) | SATK | block | crown | But for eb', other keys mtd in saddles. These probably added. | |
| 20. | 4 silver | Hamburg 1912.1565 | C | 4 | 61.9 | ebony, ivory | sq | SATK | blocks | crown | f' cp missing. | |
| 21. | 4 silver | Cologne: van Hünerbein | C | 4 | | ebony, ivory | | | | | | |
| 22. | 4 silver | Vernon, B.C.: Karen | C | 4 | 62.7 | ebony, ivory | sq | | blocks | swords | keys e♭', f', g ', bb. Screw in cap. | |
| 23. | 4 | xBerlin 2685 | C | 4 | 64.5 | ebony, ivory | ro | | | swords | | Ill. Sachs, pl 25 |

[1] Pl 12. Excellent details on page 92. Heyde says this is a "luxurious, extremely well-made" instrument.

[2] Correction of error in GSJ XXXI. Not a terzflöte and not dated.

| Young No. | No. Keys and Metal | City, Owner, No. | Pitch | No. Pcs. | Length | Body, Mounts | Flaps | SAT | Holes Dbld. | Tuning Holes | Additional Data | Ill. Source |
|---|---|---|---|---|---|---|---|---|---|---|---|---|

**H. GRENSER** *(cont.)*

**FLUTES** *(cont.)*

| | | | | | | | | | Keys mtd. in | Trade-mark | | |
|---|---|---|---|---|---|---|---|---|---|---|---|---|
| 24. | 4 brass | Leipzig 3214 "Terz" | F | 4 | 51.1 | boxw, ivory | oval(Y) | | blocks | swords | | Ill. Heyde Leipzig, Pl. II |
| 25. | 4 brass | Celle: Dr. H. Moeck | C | 4 | 62.7 | boxw, horn | | | | crown | 3 upper joints. | |
| 26. | 4 | Leipzig: Herbert Heyde | C | | | | | | | | Reported by William Waterhouse. | |
| 27. | 5 silver | Washington DCM 996 | C | 4 | 61.5 | ebony, ivory | sq | | | swords | "Germany" stamped on upper joint, although Miller acquired it in Germany! | |
| 28. | 5 brass | Poznan 153[1] | C | 4 | 62.5 | boxw, unmtd | sq | SATK | | swords | Knob for e♭, f in block, rest in saddles. | |
| 29. | 5 silver | Stockholm 22649 | C | 4 | 65.1 | boxw, ivory | sq | SATK | | swords | Knob for e♭, rest in blocks. No register. Thumb holes in all 3 upper jts. | LOM 165. |
| 30. | 6 silver | Stockholm 366 | C | 4 | 65.0 | ebony, ivory | sq | SATK | | swords | | |
| 31. | 6 silver | Stockholm 237 | C | 4 | 66.0 | ebony, horn | oval (Y) | SATK | | swords[2] | Dot design around edge of flaps. Unique. | |
| 32. | 6 silver | Bochum Grumbt | C | 4 | 69.5 | ebony, ivory | | | | crown | 2 upper joints. Foot to B? or C? | |
| 33. | 7 brass | Stockholm F. 218 | C | 4 | | boxw, ivory | | | | crown | 3 upper joints. Cased. | |
| 34. | 8 silver | Zurich Allgemein 2692 | C | 4 | 69.8 | ebony | | | | crown | Cased with similar 2-keyed HG flute, Y. 13. | |
| 35. | 8 silver | Kassel: Littmann-Gutbier | C | 4 | 69.5 | ebony, ivory | sq | | | swords | Knob for e♭, rest in blocks but for g♯ in saddle. | |

**OBOES**

| | | | | | | | | | | | | |
|---|---|---|---|---|---|---|---|---|---|---|---|---|
| 1. | 2 silver | Hamburg 1927.102 | C | 3 | 55.5 | boxw, unmtd | oct | SATW | 3 | 2 swords | Keys mtd in knobs. | |
| 2. | 2 silver | Haslemere Dolmetsch 58 | C | 3 | 55.9 | boxw, ivory | | | 3 | 2 crown | Keys mtd in knobs. | |
| 3. | 2 brass | Leipzig 1317[3] | C | 3 | 56.75 | boxw, unmtd | sq-cor | c'W, e♭'K | 3 | 2 swords | Keys mtd in knobs. | |
| 4. | 2 brass | Scarsdale Rosenbaum | C | 3 | 56.2 | boxw, unmtd | oct | c'W, e♭'K | 3 | 2 swords | Keys mtd in knobs. | |
| 5. | 2 brass | Kassel: Littmann-Gutbier | C | 3 | 56.0 | boxw, unmtd | oct | | 3 | 2 crown | Keys mtd in knobs. | |
| 6. | 2 brass | Sigmaringen 300 | C | 3 | 55.5 | boxw, unmtd | sq-cor (C) | SATK | 3 | swords | Keys mtd in knobs. | |
| 7. | 3 brass | Prague 202E | C | 3 | 54.9 | boxw, unmtd | sq-cor (N) | SATK | 3 | 2 swords | Keys mtd in knobs. 3rd key is octave key, mtd in saddle. | |
| 8. | 3 | Milan: Cast. Sforz 381 | C | 3 | 57.0 | boxw | | SATW | 2 | swords | 2 up jts. 3rd key is g♯'. | |
| 9. | 4 silver | Bologna 1793 | C | | 55.8 | boxw, ivory | oct | | | crown | 3rd & 4th keys (f' and 8ve) added.[4] | |
| 10. | 5 brass | Leningrad 514 | C | 3 | 57.8 | boxw, ivory | oct | SATK | | crown | Keys mtd in blocks. Keys c', c♯', e♭', g♯', b♭'. | |
| 11. | 7 silver | Arnsburg: R. Menger | | | | | | | | | 2 up jts. In handsome case. | ill Stauder Alte Instrumente |
| 12. | 7 silver | Berlin 5200 | C | 3 | 56.5 | boxw, ivory | sq-cor (0)[5] | SATK | 3 | 2 crown | 2 up jts. Keys mtd in kn & bl. In nice case. | |

---

[1] Probably two keys originally, e♭' and f', in knob and block, respectively. Other keys added later in saddles.

[2] Correction of error in GSJ XXXI. Crown is on foot joint only.

Other pieces stamped with crossed swords.

[3] Another H. Grenser oboe listed in GSJ XXXI as in Leipzig is in fact by another maker.

[4] originally had 2 e♭' keys? per Alfredo Bernardini, Rome.

[5] Octave key flap is round.

| Young No. | No. Keys and Metal | City, Owner, No. | Pitch | No. Pcs. | Length | Body, Mounts | Flaps | SAT | Holes Dbld. | Tuning Holes | Trade-mark | Additional Data | Ill. Source |
|---|---|---|---|---|---|---|---|---|---|---|---|---|---|

**H. GRENSER** *(cont.)* **H. GRENSER** *(cont.)*

**OBOES** *(cont.)*

| Young No. | No. Keys and Metal | City, Owner, No. | Pitch | No. Pcs. | Length | Body, Mounts | Flaps | SAT | Holes Dbld. | Tuning Holes | Trade-mark | Additional Data | Ill. Source |
|---|---|---|---|---|---|---|---|---|---|---|---|---|---|
| 13. | 7 silver | Stockholm 451 | C | 3 | 55.5 | boxw, ivory | sq-cor[1] | SATK | 3 | 2 | crown | c♯' key a replacement? | |
| 14. | 7 silver | Lisbon MI-76 No. 129 | C | 3 | 55.5 | boxw, ivory | oct[2] | SATK | 3 | | crown | | |
| 15. | 8 brass | Nürnberg MIR 381 | C | 3 | 56.7 | boxw, unmtd | sq-cor[2] | SATK | 3 | 2[3] | crown | | |
| 16. | 8 brass | New York MMA X307 | C | 3 | 55.6 | boxw, unmtd | sq-cor (N)[2] | SATK | 3 | 2[3] | crown | Keys mtd in kn, bl & sad. | LOM 176 |
| 17. | 8 silver | Lisbon MI-76LC | C | 3 | 56.5 | boxw, ivory | sq[2] | | | | crown | | |
| 18. | 9 brass | Geneva M d'A&H 556 | C | 3 | 56.8 | boxw, ivory | oct[2] | | | | crown | 3 up jts | |
| 19. | 9 brass | Stockholm F. | C | 3 | 56.3 | boxw, ivory | sq-cor | SATK | 3 | 2 | crown | | |
| 20. | 10 brass | Berlin 2954 | C | 3 | 56.5 | boxw, ivory | sq-cor | SATK? | | | crown | Keys mtd in kn, bl, & sad. | |
| 21. | 10 silver | Lisbon 4-25 | C | 3 | 56.2 | boxw, ivory | oct | | | | crown | | |
| 22. | 10 silver | Bonn BH (Zimmermann 97) | C | 3 | 57.5 | boxw, ivory | sq-cors | SATK | 3 | 2[3] | swords | The keys 2Xf♯', g♯', b♭', & 8ve have square flaps *with* corners. | |
| 23. | ---- | Quito 3449 | C | 3 | (20.5) | boxw, ivory | | | | | | Upper joint only. | |
| 24. | | Amsterdam: H. deVries[4] | | | | | | | | | | | |
| 25. | | Amsterdam: H. deVries[4] | | | | | | | | | | | |

**OBOES D'AMORE (?)**

| Young No. | No. Keys and Metal | City, Owner, No. | Pitch | No. Pcs. | Length | Body, Mounts | Flaps | SAT | Holes Dbld. | Tuning Holes | Trade-mark | Additional Data | Ill. Source |
|---|---|---|---|---|---|---|---|---|---|---|---|---|---|
| 1. | 2 | Naples Museo st-mu[5] | | | 60.4 | | | | | | | | ill E. Santagata cat. (1930) |
| 2. | | Naples Museo st-mu[5] | | | | | | | | | | | |

**ENGLISH HORNS**

| Young No. | No. Keys and Metal | City, Owner, No. | Pitch | No. Pcs. | Length | Body, Mounts | Flaps | SAT | Holes Dbld. | Tuning Holes | Trade-mark | Additional Data | Ill. Source |
|---|---|---|---|---|---|---|---|---|---|---|---|---|---|
| 1. | 2 brass | Lisbon 4.46 | | | | wood[6] | | | | | | Angular form. | |
| 2. | 2 brass | New York MMA 1980.111 | | | 75.00 | boxw, ivory | sq | SATK | 3 | | swords | 2 up jts. Keys mtd in knobs. Angular form. | |

**CLARINETS**

| Young No. | No. Keys and Metal | City, Owner, No. | Pitch | No. Pcs. | Length | Body, Mounts | Flaps | SAT | Holes Dbld. | Tuning Holes | Trade-mark | Additional Data | Ill. Source |
|---|---|---|---|---|---|---|---|---|---|---|---|---|---|
| 1. | 5 brass | Ingolstadt Stadtmus 2703 | Bb | 6[7] | 56.5 | boxw, horn | sq | SATK | 0 | | crown | Missing: middle jt. Bell ring integral. | |
| 2. | 5 brass | Lancaster, Pa. Hist. Soc. | C | 6[7] | 60.95 | boxw, ivory | sq | | | | crown | Missing: mouthpiece. | |
| 3. | 5 brass | Berlin 522 | C | ?[8] | 60.5 | boxw, ivory | sq | | 3&7 | | swords[9] | Missing: all but upper jt. Bore 1.5. | |
| 4. | 5 brass | Haarlem: Piet Honingh | Bb | 6[7] | 60.0 | boxw, horn | sq | SATK | 0 | | swords[9] | Missing: mouthpiece. Long keys extendable. | |
| 5. | 6 brass | Göttingen, Univ. of, 943 | A | 6[7] | 61.8 | boxw, ivory | sq(C) | SATK | 0 | | crown | Missing: mouthpiece. Bore 1.4. | |

---

[1] The c' and eb' keys are sq-cor, but the others are round.

[2] Octave key flap is round.

[3] One tuning hole now converted to b and other one plugged.

[4] Mr. deVries, at one time a member of the Concertgebouw Orchestra, has declined to provide information about his collection, but on one occasion said he owned at least two oboes by H. Grenser.

[5] I am indebted to Mr. N.J. Shackleton for calling these two instruments to my attention just as this book is going to press. He also reports the sad news that the concert hall in which this entire collection was stored, burned in 1973 resulting in the loss of the entire collection. One of the two instruments is listed, however, in a 1930 catalogue, hence at least these few details. Mr. Shackleton points out that since the overall height of 60.0 cm is said to include a staple, the instrument may well be an oboe rather than oboe d'amore.

[6] *Not* leather-covered.

[7] One section missing of original 6. See "additional details" at left.

[8] Only the upper joint survived WW2. Other details from Sachs' catalogue (1922).

[9] This is the only known instance when the crossed swords are *below* "H. GRENSER". On the lower joint only, there is also a crown *above* "H. GRENSER".

| Young No. | No. Keys and Metal | City, Owner, No. | Pitch | No. Pcs. | Length | Body, Mounts | Flaps | SAT | Holes Dbld. | Tuning Holes | Additional Data | Ill. Source |
|---|---|---|---|---|---|---|---|---|---|---|---|---|
| **H. GRENSER** *(cont.)* **CLARINETS** *(cont.)* | | | | | | | | | | Trade-mark | | |
| 6. | 6 brass | Ann Arbor: U. Mich. 615 | Bb | 6 | 65.0 | boxw, ivory | sq | | | crown | | |
| 7. | 6 brass | xBerlin 523 | Bb | | 68.0 | boxw, ivory | | | 3 | crown | Lost in WW2. Bore 1.5. | |
| 8. | 8 brass | Berlin 83 | Bb | 6 | 64.0 | boxw, ivory [2] | sq | SATK | 0 | crown [3] | Bore 1.5 | EAMI 630 |
| 9. | 8 brass | Stockholm 43554 | Bb/A | 6 [1] | 62.8 [4] | boxw, ivory | sq | SATK | | crown | Missing: mouthpiece. Belonged to Finnish virtuoso, B.H. Crusell. | |
| 10. | 9 brass | Oxford: Bate 432 | Bb | 6 [1] | 59.3 | boxw, ivory | sq | SATK | 3 | crown | Missing: mouthpiece. Bell ring integral. Bore 1.44 | LOM 182 |
| 11. | 10 brass | Biebrich: Heckel K-6 | C | 6 [1] | 53.1 | boxw, ivory | sq | SATK | 0 | crown | Missing: mouthpiece. | |
| 12. | 11 brass | Biebrich: Heckel K-7 | Bb/A | 6 [1] | 63.1 | boxw, ivory | sq | SATK | 0 | crown | Mouthpiece is a replacement. Long keys extendable. | LOM 181 |
| 13. | 11 brass | Markneukirchen 123 | Bb | 6 | 67.0 | boxw, horn | sq | SATK | 0 | | | |
| 14. | 11 brass | Markneukirchen 124 | A | 6 | 70.8 | boxw, horn | sq | SATK | 0 | | | |
| **BASSET HORNS** | | | | | | | | | | | | |
| 1. | 8 brass [5] | Oxford: Bate 489 | F | 7 | 105.95 [6] | boxw, horn | sq | SATK | | swords | Bore 1.42. Angular form with oval brass bell. Ivory mthpc & knee. All keys mtd in blocks. | ill. Baines WITH, pl XXVIII; LOM 187. |
| 2. | 14 brass | Ann Arbor: U. Mich, 633 | F | | | boxw, ivory | sq | | | crown | Angular form with oval brass bell. | |
| 3. | 14 brass | Burgdorf, Schloss 13-1124 | F | | 98.0 | boxw, ivory | sq | | | | Angular form with oval brass bell. | |
| 4. | 15 brass | Zurich Allgemein 2685 | F | 7 | | boxw, ivory | sq | | | crown | Angular form with oval brass bell. Keys mtd in blocks & saddles. 3 alternate barrels. Cased. | ill Jakobs, opp p 33. |
| 5. | 16 brass | Stockholm 1225 | F | 7 | 108.0 [7] | boxw, brass | sq(C) | SATK | | crown | Bore 1.5. Angular form with oval brass bell. Keys mtd in blocks & saddles. | |
| **BASS CLARINET** | | | | | | | | | | | | |
| 1. | 8 brass | Stockholm 1957-58/28 | | | 80.4 | boxw, brass | sq [8] | SATK | 0 | swords | Bore 1.4-1.48. Dated 1793, HG's only dated instrument. All keys in blocks. | EAMI 647. LOM 245. |
| **FAGOTTINI** | | | | | | | | | | Keys other than Bb, D, and F | | |
| 1. | 5 ivory | Hague Ea 402-1933 | C | crown [9] | 66.5 | maple, brass | oval | | | G♯ | Keys mtd in saddles. | |
| 2. | 5 brass | Frankfurt a M X26.469 | C | crown | 68.0 | maple, brass | oval | | | G♯, F♯ . | Keys mtd in saddles. | |
| 3. | 6 ivory | Berlin 2973 | C | crown | 65.0 | maple, brass | sq-cors | SATK | | G♯, F♯, E♭ L4 | Keys mtd in saddles. | EAMI 598. |

[1] One section missing of original 6. See "additional details" at left.
[2] But horn ring (replacement?) at top of the lower joint.
[3] Correction of GSJ XXXI. There is a crown on the lower joint, bell and barrel are unmarked, and the upper joint stamp is illegible. It all looks like the same instrument, but not sure.

[4] This height is without the mouthpiece and with the A upper joint.
[5] Basset keys for c & d are extendable.
[6] Estimated air column length, as given in 1968 Galpin Society Exhibition catalogue.

[7] Measured from mouthpiece tip to bell rim over outside of angle.
[8] Except g♯ for R4 is round, and a' for L1 is sq-cors.
[9] One star under maker's name.

| Young No. | No. Keys and Metal | City, Owner, No. | Pitch | No. Pcs. | Length | Body, Mounts | Flaps | SAT | Holes Dbld.<br>*Keys other than Bb, D, and F* | Tuning Holes | Additional Data | Ill. Source |
|---|---|---|---|---|---|---|---|---|---|---|---|---|

**H. GRENSER** *(cont.)*

**BASSOONS**

| | | | | | | | | | *Keys other than*<br>*Bb, D, and F* | | | |
|---|---|---|---|---|---|---|---|---|---|---|---|---|
| 1. | 5 brass | Markneukirchen 125 | C | crown | 126.0 | maple, brass | sq-cors | | | | Keys mtd in blocks. Flat table. Strange. Looks early for HG. | |
| 2. | 7 ivory | London: Horniman 197 | C | swords | 125.2[1] | maple, brass | sq-cors | | G♯, E♭L4, WW. | | Keys mtd in saddles. Bell is modern. | ill Carse MWI, pl XI-E & XII-E. |
| 3. | 7 brass | Copenhagen E. 165 | C | swords | 125.0 | maple, brass | sq-cors | SATK | G♯, E♭L4, WW. | | Keys mtd in saddles. Flat table. | |
| 4. | 7 brass | Prague 369E | C | swords | 124.0 | maple, brass | sq-cors | | G♯, E♭L4, WW. | | Keys mtd in blocks. Decorative bell ring and notches on F key. Wing keys in saddles and added. | |
| 5. | 7 brass | Zurich: W. Burger | C | crown | 130.0 [1] | maple, brass | oval | | G♯. F♯, E♭L4, W (C♯, W) [2] | | Keys mtd in saddles. Bell replacement. Only wing & boot stamped. | |
| 6. | 7 brass | Harburg uber Donau-wörth | C | swords | 125.5 | maple, brass | sq-cors | SATK | G♯, E♭L4, WW. | | Keys mtd in saddles. Groove around flat table. | |
| 7. | 8 bxwd | Brussels 4353 | C | swords | 129.9 | maple, brass | sq-cors | SATK | G♯, F♯, E♭L4, WW | | Keys mtd in saddles. Bell not original? | |
| 8. | 8 brass | Zurich: Allgemein 2686 | C | crown | 130.0 | maple, brass | ro | | G♯, F♯, E♭L4, WW | | 2 wing jts. | |
| 9. | 8 brass | Vienna: N. Harnoncourt | C | crown | 126.0 | maple, brass | ro | SATK | G♯, F♯, E♭L4, WW | 1 | Keys mtd in saddles. Oval flaps on wing keys. | |
| 10. | 8 brass | Hague Ea 418-1933 | C | crown | 128.8 | maple, brass | oval | SATK | G♯, F♯, E♭L4, WW | | Keys mtd in saddles. 2 wing jts. | ill Hague '74 exhib cat., p 32. Ill. this book, Pl. V |
| 11. | 8 bxwd | Hague Ea 570-1933 | C | swords | 126.1 | maple, brass | sq-cors | SATK | G♯, F♯, E♭L4. WW (C♯) [2] | 1 | Keys mtd in saddles. Flat table. Box-wood-veneered metal. C♯ key added. | LOM 191. Ill. this book, Pl. V |
| 12. | 8 brass | Hague Ea 148-1950 | C | crown | 125.7 | maple, brass | oval | SATK | G♯. F♯, E♭L4, WW (C♯, B♭) [2] | 0 | Keys mtd in saddles. The 2 later keys are on axles. | Ill. this book, Pl. V |
| 13. | 8 ivory | Hague 61-X-1952 | C | swords | 126.2 | maple, brass | ro | SATK | G♯, F♯, E♭L4, WW (B♭) [2] | 1 | Keys mtd in saddles. Keys added later now removed. | Ill. this book, Pl. V |
| 14. | 8 brass | Göttingen, Univ. of, 95 | C | crown | 125.47 | maple, brass | oval | SATK | G♯, F♯, E♭L4, WW | 0 | Keys mtd in saddles. | |
| 15. | 8 brass | Frankfurt a M 26.573 | C | crown | 125.7 | maple, brass | ro | | G♯, F♯, E♭L4, WW | | Keys mtd in saddles. G♯ key missing so now 7 keys. Flat table. | |
| 16. | 8 brass | Hamburg 1928.390 | C | crown | 124.0 | maple, brass | sq-cors | | G♯. | | Keys mtd in saddles. | |
| 17. | 8 brass | Munich Stadtmuseum 40/191 | C | crown | 125.2 | maple, brass | sq-cors | SATK | G♯, F♯, E♭L4, WW | | Keys mtd in saddles. Flat table. Wing by Finke. | |

[1] Height has been altered. See details.    [2] In parentheses are *sure* added keys, not included in number given in column at left.

| Young No. | No. Keys and Metal | City, Owner, No. | Pitch | No. Pcs. (Trade-mark) | Length | Body, Mounts | Flaps | SAT | Holes Dbld. (Keys other than Bb, D, and F) | Tuning Holes | Additional Data | Ill. Source |
|---|---|---|---|---|---|---|---|---|---|---|---|---|
| **H. GRENSER** *(cont.)* | | | | | | | | | | | | |
| **BASSOONS** *(cont.)* | | | | | | | | | | | | |
| 18. | 8 brass | Nürnberg: F. Hellwig | C | swords | 126.6 | maple, brass | sq-cors | SATK | G#, F#, Eb L4, WW | 0 | Keys mtd in saddles. Flat table. | |
| 19. | 8 brass | Bonn BH (Zimmermann 115) | C | swords | 126.0 | maple, brass | sq-cors | | G#, F#, Eb L4. WW | | | |
| 20. | 8 ivory | Brussels 183 | C | crown | 126.25 | maple, brass | sq-cors | SATK | G#, F#, Eb L4, WW | 1 | Keys mtd in saddles. Tuning hole now plugged. Ivory bushed C-hole. Brass saddles recessed into body. | |
| 21. | 8 brass | Leipzig 1385 | C | swords | 126.4 | maple, brass | sq-cors | SATK | G#, F#, Eb L4, WW | | Keys mtd in saddles. | |
| 22. | 8 ivory | Leipzig 1386 | C | crown | 129.7 | maple, brass | oval | SATK | G#, F#, Eb L4, WW | 0 | Keys mtd in saddles. Brass saddles recessed into body. | Ill. Jansen, fig. 595 (left) |
| 23. | 8 brass | Leipzig 1387 | C | swords | | | | | | | | Ill. Jansen, fig. 595 (mdl) |
| 24. | 8 brass | Darmstadt Kg 67: 129 | C | crown | 128.0 | maple, brass | | | G#. | | 2 wing jts. Belonged to Carl Mangold, 1st bsn, Darmstadt court orch. [1] | |
| 25. | 8 brass | Washington: US Marine Band | C | swords | 124.5 | maple, brass | | | | | Keys mtd in blocks. Key mts converted to saddles later. | |
| 26. | 8 brass | Lisbon MIC 197, Fag.1 | C | crown | 126.5 | maple, brass | sq-cors | | | | | |
| 27. | 8 brass | xBerlin 511 | C | swords | 126.5 | maple, brass | | | G#, F#, Eb L4, WW | | Keys mtd in blocks. Some keys also in saddles. | |
| 28. | 8 boxw | xBerlin 2971 | C | crown | 129.5 | maple, brass | | | G#, F#, Eb L4, WW | | | |
| 29. | 9 brass | Leipzig 1388 | C | swords | 126.5 | maple, brass | sq-cors | SATK | G#, F#, Eb L4, WW, Bb R Th. | | Keys mtd in saddles. Brass saddles recessed into body. | Ill. Jansen, fig. 547, 595 (right) |
| 30. | 9 brass | Antwerp Vleeshuis 67.1.158. | C | swords | 126.5 | | | | G#, Eb L4 | | | |
| 31. | 9 brass | Hamburg 1912.1548 | C | swords | 126.2 | maple, brass | sq-cors | SATK | G#, F#, Eb L4, WW, C R1 | 1 | Keys mtd in saddles. 2 wing jts. | |
| 32. | 9 brass | London: Horniman 211 | C | crown | 128.3 | maple, brass | oval | | G#, F#, Eb L4, WW, C#L4 | | Keys mtd in saddles. 2 wing jts. | ill Carse MWI, pl XIII-H & XIV-H |
| 33. | 9 brass | Stockholm 2154 | C | crown | 131.5 | maple, brass | oval | | G#, F#, Eb L4, WW, C#L4 | 1 | Keys mtd in saddles. 2 wing jts. 9th key is on only one. | |
| 34. | 9 brass | Bonn BH (Zimmermann 116) | C | crown | 128.0 | maple, brass | ro | | G#, F , Eb L4, WW, C#. | | Keys mtd in saddles. | |
| 35. | 9 brass | Kassel: Littmann-Gutbier | C | crown | 125.0 | | | | | | | |

[1] 1808–?

## H. GRENSER (cont.)
### BASSOONS (cont.)

Trade-mark column / Keys other than Bb, D, and F

| Young No. | No. Keys and Metal | City, Owner, No. | Pitch | Trademark | Length | Body, Mounts | Flaps | SAT | Keys other than Bb, D, and F | Tuning Holes | Additional Data | Ill. Source |
|---|---|---|---|---|---|---|---|---|---|---|---|---|
| 36. | 9 brass | Stockholm 1973-74/21 | C | crown | 126.0 | maple, brass | oval | SATK | | | | |
| 37. | 9 brass | Poznan 180 | C | crown | 134.0 | maple, brass | oval(Y) | | G♯ F♯, E♭L4, WWW | | Keys mtd in saddles. Wide key shanks, at least in photo. Wood? Ivory-bushed C-hole. | |
| 38. | 9 brass | Amsterdam: H. de Wit Jr. | C | crown | 126.1 | maple, brass | oval | | | | | |
| 39. | 10 brass | Stockholm 120 | C | crown | 126.0 | maple, brass | oval | SATK | G♯ F♯, E♭L4, WWW, C R Th. | 1 | Keys mtd in saddles. Flat table. | |
| 40. | 10 brass | Vienna: Klose (ex-Heckel F7) | C | swords | 124.5 | maple, brass | sq-cors | | G♯, F♯, E♭L4, WW B♭ R3[1] | 0 | Keys mtd in saddles. | |
| 41. | 10 brass | Linkopings Museum[2] | C | crown | 127.0 | maple, brass | | | G♯ F♯, E♭L4, WW | | | |
| 42. | 11 boxw | Vienna NE 348 | C | swords | 125.5 | maple, brass | sq-cors | SATK | G♯, F♯, E♭L4, WW C♯RTh. | | Keys mtd in saddles. | ill Schlosser, pl LIV. |
| 43. | 13 brass | Basel 1904.312 | C | swords | 124.6 | maple, brass | ro | | G♯, F♯, E♭L4, WWW, etc | | Keys mtd in saddles.[3] | |
| 44. | 14 brass | Stockholm 1954-55/26 | C | swords | | maple, brass | sq-cors | | G♯, F♯, E♭L4, WWW etc | 1 | Keys mtd in saddles. Whichever keys added, beautifully done! | |
| 45. | | Cologne: Prof. E. Schamberger | | | | | | | | | | |
| 46. | brass | Edgware: Boosey & Hawkes. | | | | | | | | | Boot joint only. Carries 4 keys. | |

## HUNTING HORN

| | | | | | | | | | | | | |
|---|---|---|---|---|---|---|---|---|---|---|---|---|
| 1. | | Ann Arbor: U. of Mich. | | | | | | | | | Reported lost or misplaced, 1977. Reconfirmed November 1979. | EAMI 694. |

## BASS HORN

| | | | | | | | | | | | | |
|---|---|---|---|---|---|---|---|---|---|---|---|---|
| 1. | 3 brass | Zurich: Museum Bellerive | | | | | | | | | Maple. Bassoon shape. | |

[1] Plus others.
[2] Full name of museum: Ostergotlands & Linkopings Museum.

[3] Bell looks like a replacement, or perhaps just a very wide ring was added at the end? Doubtful that the ring was original.

| Young No. | No. Keys and Metal | City, Owner, No. | Pitch | No. Pcs. | Length | Body, Mounts | Flaps | SAT | Holes Dbld. | Tuning Holes | Additional Data | Ill. Source |
|---|---|---|---|---|---|---|---|---|---|---|---|---|

## HEINRICH OTTO GRENSER

HEINRICH OTTO GRENSER

Stamp Variants

### FLUTES

| | | | | | | | | | | | | |
|---|---|---|---|---|---|---|---|---|---|---|---|---|
| 1. | 1 brass | Washington: loan to Smithsonian | | | 62.7 | boxw, unmtd | sq(F) | | H. GRENSER DRESDEN ✳ | | Unusual touch shape. | |
| 2. | 8 silver | Berlin 4019 | | 5 pc | 66.7 | ebony, ivory | sq | | ✳ H. GRENSER DRESDEN ✳ | | Only 5 pc flute known with Grenser stamp. Has tuning barrel. Unlike usual Grenser practice, only the barrel has maker's stamp. Rest is unmarked. Foot to C. | |

### BASSOON

| | | | | | | | | | | | | |
|---|---|---|---|---|---|---|---|---|---|---|---|---|
| 1. | 9 brass | Nieuw Loosdrecht: Will Jansen | | | | maple, brass | | | ✳ H. GRENSER DRESDEN ✳ | | | |

### CONTRABASSOON IN F

| | | | | | | | | | | | | |
|---|---|---|---|---|---|---|---|---|---|---|---|---|
| 1. | 5 brass | Brussels 1000 | | | 186.6 | maple, brass | ro | SATK | ✳ H. GRENSER DRESDEN ✳ | | Keys mtd in saddles. 1 th, now plugged. B♭, D, F, G♯, E♭ L4. Usual bassoon shape. | LOM 195 |

## H. GRENSER & WIESNER

H. GRENSER & WIESNER

### FLUTES

| | | | | | | | | | | | | |
|---|---|---|---|---|---|---|---|---|---|---|---|---|
| 1. | 6 brass | Hamburg MHG 1928.297 | | | 60.0 | boxw, ivory | | | | | Keys: e♭', long & short f', g♯', b', c trill | |
| 2. | 6 brass | Markneukirchen 618 | C | 4 pc | 60.7 | boxw, ivory | sq | | | | No register. | |

### OBOES

| | | | | | | | | | | | | |
|---|---|---|---|---|---|---|---|---|---|---|---|---|
| 1. | 2 brass | Stockholm 706 | | | --- | | --- | --- | | | Upper jt only. | |
| 2. | 2 silver | Stockholm 2456 | | | --- | | --- | --- | | | Upper jt only. | |
| 3. | 4 silver | Linkopings Stads Museum 11.222 | | | 56.0 | | | | | | | |
| 4. | 7 brass | Stockholm 1964-65/9 | | | 55.7 | boxw, horn | sq-cors | SATK | | | 3 dbl. | |
| 5. | 8 | Lund Kulturhistoriska Mus | | | | boxw, ivory | | | | | | |

**H. GRENSER & WIESNER** *(cont.)*

CLARINETS

| | | | | | | | | | | | |
|---|---|---|---|---|---|---|---|---|---|---|---|
| 1. | 5 | Kalmar Slott Och Mus 14.281 | | | 64.0 | | | | | | |
| 2. | 8 brass | Hamburg MHG 1912.1555 | | | 67.5 | boxw, horn | | | | | |
| 3. | 10 brass | Hamburg MHG 1912.1556 | | | 63.0 | boxw, horn | | | | | |
| 4. | 11 silver | Stockholm 2151 | A | | | | | | | | |
| 5. | 11 silver | Stockholm 2152 | C | | | | | | | | |
| 6. | 11 | Hamburg 1912.1557 | A | | | boxw | | | | | |
| 7. | 11 silver | Stockholm 239 | B♭ | | | ebony, ivory | | | | | |
| 8. | 11 brass | Stockholm Nordiska 43,5536 | | | 50.4 as is | | | | | | |

ALTO CLARINETS

| | | | | | | | | | | | |
|---|---|---|---|---|---|---|---|---|---|---|---|
| 1. | 11 brass | Stockholm 330 | F | | | boxw | | | | | |
| 2. | 11 brass | Stockholm 313 | F | | | | | | | Dated 1850. Stamped "WIESNER" | |

BASSET HORNS

| | | | | | | | | | | | |
|---|---|---|---|---|---|---|---|---|---|---|---|
| 1. | 15 brass | Basel 1906.3158 | F | | 103.0 | boxw, ivory, brass bell | | | | | |
| 2. | 15 brass | Boston MFA 17.1883 | E♭! | 7 | 98.0 | boxw, ivory, ebony | | | | Oval bell. Bore 1.5 cm. Was Royal Mil. Exhib., London, No. 273. Chromatic extension to C. See GSJ XXV, p 13. | Ill. Bessaraboff, pl III |

BASSOONS

| | | | | | | | | | | | |
|---|---|---|---|---|---|---|---|---|---|---|---|
| 1. | 6 silver | Stockholm 1972-73/20 | | | 67.5 | maple, silver | | | | DISCANT. | |
| 2. | 9 | Florence Conservatory 138 | | | | | | | | 2 wing jts. | |
| 3. | 10 brass | Stockholm 914 | | | | | | | | | |
| 4. | 10 brass | Leipzig 3204 | | | | maple, brass | ro | SATK | | Saddles. B♭, D, F, G♯, F♯, E♭L4, B♭ R Th, WW, C♯L4. | |
| 5. | | Halsingborg, maybe now Stockholm? | | | | | | | | | |

BASS HORN

| | | | | | | | | | | | |
|---|---|---|---|---|---|---|---|---|---|---|---|
| 1. | 5 brass | Hague Ea 483-1933 | | | 252.0 [1] | | | | | Brass bell and neck-crook. | |

[1] Overall air column length.

## GRIESSLING & SCHLOTT

GRIESSLING & SCHLOTT

### FLUTES

| | | | | | | | | | | | | |
|---|---|---|---|---|---|---|---|---|---|---|---|---|
| 1. | 2 silver | Munich Stadtmuseum 47/28 | C | 4 pc | 61.2 | ebony, ivory | sq(A) | SATK | | | Keys eb' & g#'. No register. Cap missing. | |
| 2. | 5 silver | Bonn BH (Zimmermann 59) | C | | | | sq | | | | | |
| 3. | x5 brass | xLeipzig 1234 | C | | 52.8 | | | | | | Lost in WW2. TERZFLOTE | |
| 4. | 6 brass | Leipzig 3024 | C | 4 pc | 69.85 | boxw, ivory | sq(D) | SATK | | | 3 upper jts, 2 ft jts. 1 ft to D, 1 to C. | Ill. Heyde Leipzig, Taf 10 |
| 5. | 7 silver | Lübeck | C | | | | | | | | | |
| 6. | 8 brass | Washington DCM 146 | C | 5 pc | 66.5 | boxw, ivory | dome | SATK | | | 1 upper jt. No register. | |
| 7. | 8 | Cologne: Hammer Sale No. 1452 | C | | | | | | | | | |
| 8. | | Halsingborg 101 | C | | | | | | | | | |

### OBOES

| | | | | | | | | | | | | |
|---|---|---|---|---|---|---|---|---|---|---|---|---|
| 1. | 7 | Cologne: Hammer Auction No. 1481. | | | | | | | | | | |
| 2. | brass | Leningrad 517 | | | 55.7 | | | | | | | |

### CLARINETS

| | | | | | | | | | | | | |
|---|---|---|---|---|---|---|---|---|---|---|---|---|
| 1. | 5 brass | Oxford: Bate 4004 | Eb | 6 pc | 43.6 | boxw, ivory | sq | SATK | | | Ebony mthpc. Keys in blocks & knobs. | LOM 183 |
| 2. | 5 | Leipzig 1485 | | | | | | | | | | |
| 3. | 5 | Leipzig 1486 | | | | | | | | | | |
| 4. | 11 | Berlin 3569 | A | | | | | | | | | |
| 5. | 11 brass | Berlin 3570 | C | 6 pc | | | sq(C) | | | | Keys in blocks & knobs. Especially beautiful keys. | |
| 6. | 11 | Hamburg MHG 1912.1557 | | | | boxw | sq | | | | Also marked "Grenser & Wiesner"! | |
| 7. | 12 | Lübeck | | | | boxw | | | | | | |
| 8. | x13 silver | xBerlin 1060 | C | | 59.0 | boxw, ivory | | | | | | |

### BASSET HORNS

| | | | | | | | | | | | | |
|---|---|---|---|---|---|---|---|---|---|---|---|---|
| 1. | 9 | Copenhagen C. 495 | | | | | | | | | | |
| 2. | 12 brass | Washington: Smithsonian 384.091 | F | 7 pc | 108.0 | boxw, ivory | sq | SATK | | | 3 bbl jts. Length given is with shortest. Bore 1.46. | LOM 188. |
| 3. | 12 brass | London: Horniman 167 | | | 102.0 | boxw, brass, ivory knee | | | | | Bore 1.5 | |
| 4. | 12 brass | Oxford: Bate 486 | | | | boxw, ivory | | | | | Sharply angled at knee. Bell and bbl are replacements. | |
| 5. | 15 brass | Hamburg MHG 1924.216 | | | 103.0 | boxw, ivory | | | | | Sharply angled at knee. | Ill. Kroll Clarinet, pl 15 |
| 6. | 15 | Berlin 1207 | | | 75.0 | | | | | | Bore 1.5. | |
| 7. | 16 | Leipzig 1550 | | | | | | | | | | |

| Young No. | No. Keys and Metal | City, Owner, No. | Pitch | No. Pcs. | Length | Body, Mounts | Flaps | SAT | Holes Dbld. | Tuning Holes | Additional Data | Ill. Source |
|---|---|---|---|---|---|---|---|---|---|---|---|---|

**GRIESSLING & SCHLOTT** (*cont.*)                                                                 **GRIESSLING & SCHLOTT** (*cont.*)

BASSOONS

| | | | | | | | | | | | | |
|---|---|---|---|---|---|---|---|---|---|---|---|---|
| 1. | 7 brass | London: W. Waterhouse | | | 124.4 | maple, brass | ro | | | | Saddles. | |
| 2. | 8 brass | Stockholm 360 | | | | maple, brass | ro | | | | Saddles. B♭, D, F, G♯, F♯, E♭L4, WW | |
| 3. | 10 brass | Eisenach I-161 | | | | maple, brass | ro | | | | Saddles. B♭, D, F, G♯, F♯, E♭L4, WW C♯L4 | |
| 4. | | Leipzig | | | | | | | | | | |
| 5. | | Glasgow | | | | | | | | | | |
| 6. | 9 | Nürnberg MI 258 | | | | maple | ro[1] | | | | | |

CORNET A PISTONS

| | | | | | | | | | | | | |
|---|---|---|---|---|---|---|---|---|---|---|---|---|
| 1. | | Paris 1404 | | | | | | | | | | |

BUGLES

| | | | | | | | | | | | | |
|---|---|---|---|---|---|---|---|---|---|---|---|---|
| 1. | | Boston: MFA 17.19691 | | | 52.5 | brass | | | | | | |
| 2. | | Lübeck | | | | | | | | | Half-moon form | |
| 3. | | Lübeck | | | | | | | | | Half-moon form | |

HIFTHORN (WATCHMAN'S HORN)

| | | | | | | | | | | | | |
|---|---|---|---|---|---|---|---|---|---|---|---|---|
| 1. | | Copenhagen 172 | | | | | | | | | | |

BASS HORNS

| | | | | | | | | | | | | |
|---|---|---|---|---|---|---|---|---|---|---|---|---|
| 1. | 4 | Stockholm 52 | | | | | | | | | | |
| 2. | 5 | Lübeck | | | | wood, ivory | | | | | | |

SERPENT

| | | | | | | | | | | | | |
|---|---|---|---|---|---|---|---|---|---|---|---|---|
| 1. | | Stockholm 88 | | | | | | | | | | |

# GRUNDMANN                                            *Dated*                                            # GRUNDMANN

FLUTE

| | | | | | | | | | | | | |
|---|---|---|---|---|---|---|---|---|---|---|---|---|
| 1. | 1 brass | Seattle: Jerome Kohl[2] | C | 4 | 61.6 | boxw, ivory | trap | SATK | | undated | No register. No screw in cap. Cylindrical ft. | |

OBOE D'AMORE

| | | | | | | | | | | | | |
|---|---|---|---|---|---|---|---|---|---|---|---|---|
| 1. | 2 brass | xBerlin 2957[3] | | 3 | 61.5 | boxw, unmtd | | | | 1774[4] | Bulb bell. | original ill Sachs cat., pl 26 |

[1] Jansen says 7 flaps are round and 2 are square.

[2] Not only is this the only known Grundmann flute, the Ns in GRUNDMANN are reversed on all four joints as on oboes 4 & 5, making likely a date near 1768, a period when I have conjectured that Grundmann briefly used a flawed stamp. In addition, there is neither date nor DRESDEN on any of the clearly-original joints. Most unusual of all, there are no crossed swords (as found on every other Grundmann instrument) but instead a bouquet or spray of 3 or 4 flowers(?), resembling but not a fleur de lys. I think it must be earlier than oboes 4 & 5, before the crossed swords were adopted. Could it have been made in Leipzig before Grundmann went to Dresden (in the 1740's?)?

[3] Fortunately, copies of these two instruments were made by Wilhelm Heckel before their loss in WW2. The copies are illustrated in *Der Fagott* and are now in the collection of Karl Ventzke, Düren.

[4] Sachs says the oboe d'amore is dated 1774, but gives no date for the tenor. For the latter, Heckel specifies "1750" but may be estimating. If correct, this would be the earliest(?) or earliest dated(?) known Grundmann instrument.

| | | | | | | | | | | | | |
|---|---|---|---|---|---|---|---|---|---|---|---|---|
| **GRUNDMANN** *(cont.)* | | | | | | | | | | *Date* | | **GRUNDMANN** *(cont.)* |
| TENOR OBOES (Straight form) | | | | | | | | | | | | |
| 1. | 2 brass | xBerlin 249[1] | F | 3 | 85.0 | boxw, unmtd | | | | 1750 [2] | Bulb bell. | copy ill Heckel Der Fagott, p 10 |
| 2. | 2 brass | Geneva: Musée Instrs.163 | F | 3 | | | | | | 1776 | Bulb bell. | |
| ENGLISH HORNS (Angular form) | | | | | | | | | | | | |
| 1. | 2 silver[3] | Kremsmunster Abbey | F | 3 | 81.73 | boxw, horn | oct(Q) | c'W, eb'K | 3 | 1791 | Flared bell but bulb inside. | |
| 2. | 2 silver[3] | Kremsmunster Abbey | F | 3 | 82.1 | boxw, horn | long sq | SATK | 3 | 1793 | Flared bell but bulb inside. | |
| 3. | 2 brass | Liverpool: City Museum | F | 3 | | | sq | | | 1791 | Flared bell but "considerable inner lip" | EAMI 577 |
| CLARINETS | | | | | | | | | | | | |
| 1. | 4 brass | Paris, seen 1964 [4] | | 6 | | boxw, unmtd | | | | 1775 | Mthpc & middle jt missing. Large, heavy instr. Massive, well-made keys. | |
| 2. | 5 brass | Poznan 184 (ex Breslau) | | | 65.5 | | | | 3 | 1759 | Mthpc & bbl missing. | |
| BASSET HORNS | | | | | | | | | | | | |
| 1. | 7 brass | Boston MFA 17.1881 | F | | 91.8 | boxw, horn | sq | a'W, rest K | | 1791 | Angular form. Brass bell angled toward audience. | ill Bessaraboff, pl III |
| 2. | 8 brass | Lübeck 4424 | F | | | boxw, horn | sq(C) | W & K mixed | | 1792 | Angular form. Oval brass bell. Keys mtd in knobs & blocks. | |
| 3. | 8 brass | Lübeck 4423 | F | | | boxw, horn | sq(C) | W & K mixed | | 1792 | Angular form. Oval brass bell. Keys mtd in knobs & blocks. | |
| 4. | 8 brass | Hamburg 1912.1560 | F | | 103.0 | boxw, ivory | long sq | SATK | | 1787 | Angular form. Ro brass bell. Keys mtd in knobs & blocks. Bore 1.4-1.42. | ill[5]. LOM 186. |
| 5. | 8 brass | Hamburg 1922.70 | F | | 99.0 | boxw, horn | sq | | | 1799 | Angular form. Ro brass bell. Keys mtd in knobs & blocks. | ill[5]. |
| BASSOONS | | | | | | | | | | | | |
| 1. | 4 brass | Breslau 109 [6] | | | | maple | | | | | | |
| 2. | | Biebrich Heckel [7] | | | | | | | | | | |
| 3. | 10 brass | Nieuw Loosdrecht: Jansen | | | 128.0 | maple, brass | sq-cors | | | 1780 | | Ill. Jansen, fig. 203 |
| 4. | | Austria [8] | | | | | | | | | | |

[1] Fortunately, copies of these two instruments were made by Wilhelm Heckel before their loss in WW2. The copies are illustrated in *Der Fagott* and are now in the collection of Karl Ventzke, Düren.

[2] Sachs says the oboe d'amore is dated 1774, but gives no date for the tenor. For the latter, Heckel specifies "1750" but may be estimating. If correct, this would be the earliest(?) or earliest dated(?) known Grundmann instrument.

[3] Silver plating on brass.

[4] Seen by the author in 1964 at Vian Antiquities.

[5] In the well known photo of seven basset horns from Hamburg, in both Kroll and Rendall.

[6] Not listed in the 1949 Poznan catalogue, so apparently not transferred there.

[7] Reported by Will Jansen.

[8] Reported by David Skulski.

| Young No. | No. Keys and Metal | City, Owner, No. | Pitch Date | No. Pcs. | Length | Body, Mounts | Flaps | SAT | Holes Dbld. | Tuning Holes | Additional Data | Ill. Source |
|---|---|---|---|---|---|---|---|---|---|---|---|---|

**GRUNDMANN** *(cont.)*

**OBOES**

| | | | | | | | | | | | | |
|---|---|---|---|---|---|---|---|---|---|---|---|---|
| 1. | 2 brass | Prague 643E | undated | | 58.4 | boxw, unmtd | c' sq-cor[2] | SATW[1] | 3 | 2 | | |
| 2. | 2 brass | Prague 1702E | undated | | 58.35 | boxw, unmtd | c' sq-cor[2] | SATW[1] | 3 | 2 | | |
| 3. | 2 brass | Niederalteich: Ruhland | undated | | 58.5 | boxw, unmtd | c' sq-cor[2] | SATW[1] | 3 | 2 | | |
| 4. | 2 silver | Hamburg 1912.1549 | 1768 | | 59.3 | boxw, unmtd | oct(Q) | SATW | 3 | 2 | Ns in GRUNDMANN reversed, all 3 pcs[3] 1 added key. | |
| 5. | 2 brass | Brussels 2331 | undated | | 56.6 | boxw, unmtd | oct(Q) | SATW | 3&4 | 2 | Ns in GRUNDMANN reversed, mid jt only. 2 added keys. | |
| 6. | 2 brass | Cologne Stadtmus I/29 | undated | | 57.0 | boxw, unmtd | c' sq-cor[2] | SATW | 3 | 2 | Mid jt earlier than rest? | |
| 7. | 2 brass | Leningrad 518 | 17?? | | 56.8 | boxw, unmtd | oct(Q) | SATW[1] | 3 | 2 | 7 added keys. | LOM 173 |
| 8. | modern | Berlin 1005 | 1774 | | 57.1 | boxw, unmtd | all keys replaced | | 3 | 2 | Modern cupped keys, on posts and axles. All added keys. | |
| 9. | 2 silver | Great Yarmouth: J. Norris / J. Norris | 1774 | | 57.15 | boxw, ivory | | | 3&4 | 2 | N's in Grundmann revised, all 3 pcs. | |
| 10. | 2 silver | xBerlin 586 | 1777 | | 56.5 | boxw, unmtd | | | | | | |
| 11. | 2 silver | Harburg über Donau-wörth. | 1779 | | 57.2 | boxw, unmtd | oct(Q) | SATW | 3 | 2 | Added keys have ro flaps. 2 added keys. | |
| 12. | 2 silver | Hamburg 1912.1550 [4] | 1779 | | 57.5 | boxw, unmtd | oct(Q) | SATW | 3 | 2 | | ill Schroder Hamburg, pl 19e |
| 13. | 2 brass | Poznan 167 (ex Breslau) | 1780 | | 56.5 | boxw, unmtd | oct(Q) | | 3 | 2 | Upper jt by Peukert & Sohn. 5 added keys. | |
| 14. | 4 brass | xBerlin 635 | 1781 | | 57.0 | boxw, unmtd | | | | | 4 original keys: c', c#', eb', 8ve. | |
| 15. | 2 brass | Nürnberg MIR 377 | 1782 | | 55.8 | boxw, unmtd | oct(Q) | SATK | 3 | 2 | | ill MGG "oboe" |
| 16. | 2 | Bern: Karl Burri | 1783? | | | boxw | | | | | | |
| 17. | 10 brass | Poznan 168 (ex Breslau) | 1788 | | 57.0 | boxw, unmtd | | | | | | |
| 18. | 2 silver | London: RCM 75 | 1791 | | 55.0 | boxw, unmtd | oct(Q) | SATW | 3 | 2 | 6 added keys. | |
| 19. | 2 brass | Nürnberg MIR 378 | 1792 | | 56.6 | boxw, ivory | oct(Q) | SATW | 3 | 2 | | |
| 20. | 2 silver | Vienna GdM 146 | 1793 | | 57.3 | boxw, unmtd | oct(Q) | SATW | 3 | 2 | 1 added key. The added key is 8ve on detachable clamp. | |
| 21. | 3 brass | Leipzig 3499 | 1793 | | 57.3 | boxw, unmtd | oct(Q) | SATW | 3 | 2 | 5 added keys, but now removed. g#' is (original) 3rd key. | |
| 22. | 7 silver | xBerlin 587 | 1793 | | 56.0 | boxw | | | 3 | 2 | | |

[1] The c' key spring is attached to the body (SATW), but the eb' spring is attached to the underside of the key (SATK) (on five different oboes above).

[2] The eb' flap is square, with its corners intact (on four different oboes above).

[3] But the N in DRESDEN is not reversed. Also, see Grundmann flute 1.

[4] Having reported this instrument in GSJ XXXI "Lost in 1939-45," as I'd been informed by the Museum, I then "found" it far back on a low shelf during a more recent visit to the Museum in 1978.

| Young No. | No. Keys and Metal | City, Owner, No. | Pitch | No. Pcs. | Length | Body, Mounts | Flaps | SAT | Holes Dbld. | Tuning Holes | Additional Data | Ill. Source |
|---|---|---|---|---|---|---|---|---|---|---|---|---|

## GRUNDMANN (cont.)

### OBOES (cont.)

| Young No. | No. Keys and Metal | City, Owner, No. | Pitch | No. Pcs. | Length | Body, Mounts | Flaps | SAT | Holes Dbld. | Tuning Holes | Additional Data | Ill. Source |
|---|---|---|---|---|---|---|---|---|---|---|---|---|
| 23. | 2 brass | Leipzig 1330 | 1794 | | 57.0 | boxw, ivory | oct(Q) | SATW [1] | 3 | 2 | 6 added keys. Perhaps all 8 keys are replacements? | |
| 24. | 10 brass | Hamburg 1912.1551 | 1797 | | 56.8 | boxw, ivory | oct(Q) | SATK | 3 | 2 | 0? added keys. Seem likely original. | LOM 172. |
| 25. | 2 brass | Basel: R. Hildebrand | 1799 | | 57.2 | boxw, horn | oct(Q) | SATK | 3 | 2 | Many added keys, but now removed. | |
| 26. | 2 brass | Hamburg 1924.213 | 1799 | | 57.23 | boxw, ivory | oct(Q) | SATK | 3 | 2 | 3 added keys. G♯', b♭', 8ve are added. | ill Schroder Hamburg, pl XVf |
| 27. | 2 brass | Hamburg 1912.1552 | 1799 | | 56.5 | boxw, unmtd | oct(Q) | SATK | 3 | 2 | 9 added keys. Swallowtail amputated. | LOM 174 |
| 28. | 3 silver | Leningrad 1143 | 1800 | | 56.0 | boxw, unmtd | oct(Q) | SATW | 3 | 2 | 6 added keys. Original keys c', c♯', e♭', maybe g♯'. | |
| 29. | 3 | Grenoble | | | 57.0 | | | | | | | |
| 30. | 3 silver | Paris C.476, E.605 | | | (60.0) | boxw, unmtd | oct(Q) | SATK | 3 | 2 | Replacement bell by Panormo. Only known Grundmann oboe with 2X e♭'. | |
| 31. | 10 modern | Basel 1956.338 | | | 56.9 | boxw, horn | oct(Q) | SATK | 3 | 2 | All added keys? Short added section to extend length for b & b♭. | |
| 32. | | Geneva: Mme. Teyssere-Vuilleumier [1] | | | | | | | | | | |
| 33. | 2 brass | Munich: BNM Mu 133 | undated | | 56.5 | boxw, ivory | oct(Q) | SATW | 3 | 2 | 1 added key. Added key is f'. Only top jt stamped. | |
| 34. | 2 brass | Brussels 962 | undated | | 55.8 | boxw, horn | oct(Q) | SATW | 3 | 2 | Tuning slide in top jt. [2] | Color ill Bragard-de Hen, pl IV-14 |

## GRUNDMANN ET FLOTH

### OBOES [3]

| Young No. | No. Keys and Metal | City, Owner, No. | Dated Pitch | No. Pcs. | Length | Body, Mounts | Flaps | SAT | Holes Dbld. | Tuning Holes | Additional Data | Ill. Source |
|---|---|---|---|---|---|---|---|---|---|---|---|---|
| 1. | 2 brass | Lübeck 1937: 20 | 1800 | | 56.7 | boxw, unmtd | sq-cor | SATK | 3 | 2 | 1 tuning hole now b♮. 7 added keys have round flaps. | |
| 2. | 2 brass | Assen, Neth., Mus H-1911-2 | no | | 56.7 | pear, unmtd | sq-cor | SATW? | 3 | 2 | | |

### ENGLISH HORN

| Young No. | No. Keys and Metal | City, Owner, No. | Dated Pitch | No. Pcs. | Length | Body, Mounts | Flaps | SAT | Holes Dbld. | Tuning Holes | Additional Data | Ill. Source |
|---|---|---|---|---|---|---|---|---|---|---|---|---|
| 1. | 2 brass | Lisbon 4.17 [4] | no | | 73.3 | boxw, ivory | | | 3 | | Angular form. Angle very slight. | |

[1] Michel Piguet reported originally that Mme. H. Teyssere-Vuilleumier owned *two* Grundmann oboes, as was listed in GSJ XXXI, but now believes there is only one. The owner has ignored repeated pleas for even brief details.

[2] As pointed out in GSJ XXXI, the bell of this instrument is the only known instance of the GRUNDMANN/GRENSER stamp. Its mid jt is stamped GRUNDMANN (only) and its upper jt is unstamped. The bell has neither DRESDEN nor date. In design and style, it is a late Grundmann oboe. There is nothing to suggest a partnership with any Grenser at any time. I also believe that *all* Grundmann instruments were dated (on their bells in most instances), at least beginning in 1768. The only *undated* oboes but for the 1st 3 above have, I suspect, replacement bells. However illogical, perhaps a Grenser made a replacement bell for this Grundmann oboe and used individual-letter dies to stamp GRUNDMANN above GRENSER. It will be seen throughout this book how often oboe bells are replacements, much like clarinet mouthpieces. Why were clarinet *bells* not as fragile as oboe bells?

[3] An oboe is listed under FLOTH which carries that stamp on its upper and lower jts, but the bell is stamped GRUNDMANN ET FLOTH. This is Prague 201E.

[4] Stamped FLOTH ET GRUNDMANN.

| Young No. | No. Keys and Metal | City, Owner, No. | Pitch | No. Pcs. | Length | Body, Mounts Flaps | SAT | Holes Dbld. | Tuning Holes | Additional Data | Ill. Source |
|---|---|---|---|---|---|---|---|---|---|---|---|

**GRUNDMANN ET FLOTH** (cont.)    **GRUNDMANN ET FLOTH** (cont.)

**BASSET HORN**

| Young No. | No. Keys and Metal | City, Owner, No. | Pitch | No. Pcs. | Length | Body, Mounts Flaps | SAT | Holes Dbld. | Tuning Holes | Additional Data | Ill. Source |
|---|---|---|---|---|---|---|---|---|---|---|---|
| 1. | 8 brass | Stockholm[1] | 1802 | 6 pc | | boxw, horn | sq | SATK | | | Bore 1.45-1.5 cm. Ro brass bell. 6 pcs including (missing) mthpc. Angular form. | |

# HAKA    # HAKA

**SOPRANINO RECORDER**

| Young No. | No. Keys and Metal | City, Owner, No. | Pitch | No. Pcs. | Length | Body, Mounts Flaps | SAT | Holes Dbld. | Tuning Holes | Additional Data | Ill. Source |
|---|---|---|---|---|---|---|---|---|---|---|---|
| 1. | | xNurnberg MI 142 | | 1 pc | 25.0 | ivory | | | | | |

**SOPRANO RECORDERS**

| Young No. | No. Keys and Metal | City, Owner, No. | Pitch | No. Pcs. | Length | Body, Mounts Flaps | SAT | Holes Dbld. | Tuning Holes | Additional Data | Ill. Source |
|---|---|---|---|---|---|---|---|---|---|---|---|
| 1. | | xBerlin 2784 | e♭" | 2 pc | 31.5 | boxw, brass | | | | | |
| 2. | | Berwick on Tweed: Brackenbury | | 1 pc | 33.65 | ivory | | | | GS Exhib' 68, No. 23 (not ill.) | |
| 3. | | Leipzig 1115 | | 2 pc | 34.3 | boxw, ivory | | | | | Ill. Heyde Leipzig, taf. 5 |
| 4. | | Amsterdam: Frans Bruggen | c" | 2 pc | 35.0 | grena, ivory | | | | | |
| 5. | | xBerlin 2786 | b' | 1 pc | 36.0 | boxw, unmtd | | | | "quartflöte". Onion-shaped beak. | |

**ALTO RECORDERS**

| Young No. | No. Keys and Metal | City, Owner, No. | Pitch | No. Pcs. | Length | Body, Mounts Flaps | SAT | Holes Dbld. | Tuning Holes | Additional Data | Ill. Source |
|---|---|---|---|---|---|---|---|---|---|---|---|
| 1. | | Paris: late Comtesse de Chambure | e' | | | ebony, ivory | | | | | |
| 2. | | xBerlin 2798 | e' | | 49.5 | boxw, ivory | | | | | |
| 3. | | Sigmaringen 304 | | 3 pc | | boxw | | | | FOOT only. Foot jt marked "RIJKEL & HAKA", only instance known. Head jt by J. Denner, md jt by Rijkel. | |

**BASS RECORDER**

| Young No. | No. Keys and Metal | City, Owner, No. | Pitch | No. Pcs. | Length | Body, Mounts Flaps | SAT | Holes Dbld. | Tuning Holes | Additional Data | Ill. Source |
|---|---|---|---|---|---|---|---|---|---|---|---|
| 1. | | Goteborg 12 | F | | | | | | | | |

**FLAGEOLET**

| Young No. | No. Keys and Metal | City, Owner, No. | Pitch | No. Pcs. | Length | Body, Mounts Flaps | SAT | Holes Dbld. | Tuning Holes | Additional Data | Ill. Source |
|---|---|---|---|---|---|---|---|---|---|---|---|
| 1. | | xBerlin 2738 | g'" | 1 pc | 11.66 | palisander, silver | | | | | |

**CANNE FLUTE**

| Young No. | No. Keys and Metal | City, Owner, No. | Pitch | No. Pcs. | Length | Body, Mounts Flaps | SAT | Holes Dbld. | Tuning Holes | Additional Data | Ill. Source |
|---|---|---|---|---|---|---|---|---|---|---|---|
| 1. | | Hague Ea 532-1933 [2] | | | 95.7 | brown wood, ivory head | | | | 7 fingerholes on front, 1 on back. | |

[1] Cary Karp has reported that this instrument's parts are stamped FLOTH but for the "curiously built lower piece" which is stamped GRUNDMANN ET FLOTH.

[2] The style of this instrument is such that Dr. C.C. von Gleich, Director of the Music Department of the Gemeente Museum, believes there must have been a second Richard Haka at an appreciably later date.

| Young No. | No. Keys and Metal | City, Owner, No. | Pitch | No. Pcs. | Length | Body, Mounts Flaps | | SAT | Holes Dbld. | Tuning Holes | Additional Data | Ill. Source |
|---|---|---|---|---|---|---|---|---|---|---|---|---|

**SHAWMS AND DEUTSCHE SCHALMEI**

| | | | | | | | | | | | | |
|---|---|---|---|---|---|---|---|---|---|---|---|---|
| 1. | 0 | Hague Ea 21-X-1952 | | 2 | 62.0 | boxw, brass | | | 0 | 3 | Fontanelle w 2 brass bands. Brass bell rim. | ill. Langwill p 80[1]; EAMI 535 |
| 2. | 0 | Hague Ea 18-X-1952 | | 2 | 61.6 | boxw, brass | | | 0 | 3 | Fontanelle w 2 brass bands. Brass bell rim. | ill. Langwill p 80[2] |
| 3. | 0 | Stockholm 145 | | 2 | 62.2 | boxw, brass | | | 0 | 4+peg | Fontanelle w 2 brass bands. Brass bell rim. | |
| 4. | 1 brass | New Haven: Yale 438 | | 2 | 65.4 | boxw, brass | sq-cor | SATW | 0 | 4 | Key added. Fontanelle w 2 brass bands. Brass bell rim & top rim[3] | LOM 73 |
| 5. | | xBerlin 2930 | | 2 | 61.5 | boxw, brass | | | | | | |
| 6. | | Copenhagen E. 27 | | 2 | 61.8 | boxw, brass | | | 0 | 4+peg | Fontanelle w 2 brass bands. Brass bell rim & top rim. | |
| 7. | 1 brass | Hague Ea 19-X-1952 | | 2 | 83.6 | boxw, brass | ro | SATW | 0 | | Alto shawm. | ill Hague '74 Exhib cat., p 57, no. 28. |
| 8. | | Berlicum: E. van Tright | | | | | | | | | | |
| 9. | | Mengelberg auction 963 | | | | | | | | | This or the next may have become Canon Galpin's, then Yale's (no. 4 above). | |
| 10. | | Royal Mil. Exhib. 146 | | | | | | | | | | |

**OBOES**

| | | | | | | | | | | | | |
|---|---|---|---|---|---|---|---|---|---|---|---|---|
| 1. | 1 silver | Hague 20-X-1952[4] | | 3 | 52.0 | ebony, silver | | | 0 | | Metal box over key flap and mechanism. | EAMI 540[5] |
| 2. | 3 brass | Hague 6-1952 | | 3 | 57.8 | wood, unmtd | c'ro[6] | SATW | 3&4 | 2 | | ill Hague '74 Exhib cat., p 57, no. 30. |
| 3. | 3 brass | Stockholm 155 | | 3 | 54.95 | boxw, brass | c' oval (Y)[8] | SATW | 3&4 | 2 | | |
| 4. | 2 silver | Bremen: R. Müller | | | | | | | | | | |
| 5. | | xBerlin 2936 | | | | | | | | | | |
| 6. | | Bruges: B. Kuijken | | | | | | | | | | |

**TENOR OBOES**

| | | | | | | | | | | | | |
|---|---|---|---|---|---|---|---|---|---|---|---|---|
| 1. | 3 brass | Vienna GdM 151 | | 3 | 83.8 | boxw? unmtd | c'oval (Y)[7] | SATW | 3&4 | 2 | Brass crook. | |
| 2. | 3 brass | Vienna GdM 152 | | 3 | 84.1 | boxw? unmtd | c'oval (Y)[7] | SATW[8] | 3&4 | 2 | Brass crook. | |

---

[1] Second from left.

[2] At extreme left.

[3] Also has detachable pirouette.

[4] This has also been designated a Deutsche schalmei, but in my opinion it is not. It is the earliest oboe of which I know.

[5] Also ill (1) Langwill 5 ed., p 80, 3rd from left; (2) Hague '74 Exhib cat, p 57, no. 29.

[6] The eb' key's flap is trap(L).

[7] The eb' key's flaps are sq(D).

[8] The eb' key spring is attached to the key, undoubtedly a replacement spring.

HALE

| Young No. | No. Keys and Metal | City, Owner, No. | Pitch | No. Pcs. | Length | Body, Mounts | Flaps | SAT | Holes Dbld. | Tuning Holes | Additional Data | Ill. Source |
|---|---|---|---|---|---|---|---|---|---|---|---|---|

## FLUTES

| Young No. | No. Keys and Metal | City, Owner, No. | Pitch | No. Pcs. | Length | Body, Mounts | Flaps | SAT | Holes Dbld. | Tuning Holes | Additional Data | Ill. Source |
|---|---|---|---|---|---|---|---|---|---|---|---|---|
| 1. | 1 silver | Washington DCM 1194 | A | | 72.2 | boxw, ivory | | | | | GSJ no. 5. | |
| 2. | 6 silver | Washington DCM 385 | C | | 68.8 | satinw, ivory | | | | | GSJ no. 1. 3 upper jts. Foot to c'. | |
| 3. | 6 | London: Horniman 170 | D | | 68.1 | boxw, ivory | | | | | GSJ no. 2. | |
| 4. | 6 | London: Guy Oldham | | | | | | | | | GSJ no. 4. | |
| 5. | 6 | Bristol: R. Mickleburgh | | | | | | | | | GSJ no. 11. | |
| 6. | 6 silver | Cambridge: N. Shackleton | | | 66.8 | rosew, ivory | sq | SATK | | | Foot to c'. | |
| 7. | 8 | Edinburgh: Rendall Coll. | | | | | | | | | GSJ no. 3. | |
| 8. | | Gloucester | | | | | | | | | | |

## OBOES

| Young No. | No. Keys and Metal | City, Owner, No. | Pitch | No. Pcs. | Length | Body, Mounts | Flaps | SAT | Holes Dbld. | Tuning Holes | Additional Data | Ill. Source |
|---|---|---|---|---|---|---|---|---|---|---|---|---|
| 1. | 2 silver | London: Kneller Hall 59 | C | | | | | | | | Keys and mounts missing. | |

## CLARINETS

| Young No. | No. Keys and Metal | City, Owner, No. | Pitch | No. Pcs. | Length | Body, Mounts | Flaps | SAT | Holes Dbld. | Tuning Holes | Additional Data | Ill. Source |
|---|---|---|---|---|---|---|---|---|---|---|---|---|
| 1. | 5 | London: Guy Oldham | C | | | | | | | | GSJ no. 13. Mouthpiece is a replacement. | |
| 2. | 5 | London: R. Muffet | | | | | | | | | GSJ no. 8. | |
| 3. | 5 brass | Qualicum, B.C. Canada [1] | | | | boxw, ivory | | | | | Mthpc + bbl = 1 pc; lower jt + bell = 1 pc. | |
| 4. | 5 brass | New York MMA 1976.7.7 | C | | 58.5 | boxw, ivory | sq | SATK | | | 4 pcs. Very slim body. Mthpc + bbl = 1 pc. | |
| 5. | 5 brass | Cambridge: N. Shackleton | C | | 60.7 | boxw, ivory | sq | SATK | | | Mthpc + bbl = 1 pc; alternate mthpc & bbl separate; lower jt + bell = 1 pc. | |
| 6. | 5 | anonymous (GSJ XXV) | C | | | | | | | | GSJ no. 14. "I.HALE/LONDON/LATE/ COLLIER/O" | |
| 7. | 6 | Hereford City Museum 2997 | C | | | boxw, ivory | | | | | GSJ no. 12. Stock and bell by Cramer & & Son, 20 Pall Mall. | |
| 8. | 6 brass | Cambridge: N. Shackleton | Bb | | 67.2 | boxw, ivory | sq | SATK | | | Mthpc + bbl = 1 pc; alternate mthpc & bbl separate; lower jt + bell = 1 pc. | |
| 9. | 8 | Manchester: Watson | | | | | | | | | GSJ no. 7. | |

## BASSOONS

| Young No. | No. Keys and Metal | City, Owner, No. | Pitch | No. Pcs. | Length | Body, Mounts | Flaps | SAT | Holes Dbld. | Tuning Holes | Additional Data | Ill. Source |
|---|---|---|---|---|---|---|---|---|---|---|---|---|
| 1. | 6 brass | Cambridge: C.R.F. Maunder | C | | | | (U) | | | | GSJ no. 9. | Ill. & X-ray photo, GSJ X, p 30 |
| 2. | 8 | London: Reuben Greene | C | | | | | | | | GSJ no. 10. Crook marked 4C. | |
| 3. | 8 brass | Vermillion: USD 574 | C | | 123.8 | maple, brass | | SATW | | | Wing joint by W. Milhouse, London, SATK | |

[1] In the collection of the late Edward Eames.

# A. HOPKINS

## A. HOPKINS

## FLUTES

| Young No. | No. Keys and Metal | City, Owner, No. | Pitch | No. Pcs. | Length | Body, Mounts | Flaps | SAT | Holes Dbld. | Tuning Holes | Additional Data | Ill. Source |
|---|---|---|---|---|---|---|---|---|---|---|---|---|
| 1. | 1 brass | Sturbridge Village 10-17-29 | C | 4 pc | 61.0 | boxw, ivory | flat sq | | | | | |
| 2. | 1 brass | New York City: Robert A. Lehman | C | 4 pc | 60.1 | boxw, ivory | flat sq | | | | | |
| 3. | 1 brass | Rockport, Maine: John Shortridge | C | 4 pc | 61.25 | boxw, ivory | flat sq | | | | | |
| 4. | 4 brass | Rockport, Maine: John Shortridge | C | 5 pc | 61.0 | boxw, ivory | flat ro | | | | | |
| 5. | 4 brass | Scarsdale: D & R Rosenbaum | C | 4 pc | 61.0 | boxw, ivory | flat ro | SATK | | | | LOM 168 |
| 6. | 4 brass | New Haven: Yale 218 | C | 4 pc | 61.0 | boxw, ivory | flat ro | SATK | | | 1 ivory ring replaced with (old) crude, pewter one. | |
| 7. | 4 brass | Baltimore: S. Forrest | | | | | | | | | | |
| 8. | 4 brass | Northampton His. Soc. | C | 5 pc | 60.6 | boxw, ivory | flat ro | SATK | | | 5th pc is tuning bbl on head jt. | |
| 9. | 4 silver | Washington: DCM 131 | C | 5 pc | 59.6 | boxw, ivory | | | | | 5th pc is tuning bbl on head jt. | |
| 10. | 4 silver | Washington: DCM 1225 | C | 5 pc | 60.9 | boxw, ivory | | | | | 5th pc is tuning bbl on head jt. | |
| 11. | 4 silver | Torrington Hist. Soc. | C | 5 pc | 61.0 | boxw, ivory | saltsp | SATK | | | Long C key added to original 4. 5th pc is tuning bbl. | |
| 12. | 8 silver | New York City: Frederick Selch | D | 5 pc | 68.0 | rosew, silver | saltsp | SATK | | | c', c#', & d#' plug type. Foot to c'. | |
| 13. | 9 silver | Washington: DCM 901 | C | 5 pc | 66.2 | rosew, silver | saltsp | | | | Foot to c'. 5th pc is tuning bbl. Head jt lined with brass. | |

## FLAGEOLET

| Young No. | No. Keys and Metal | City, Owner, No. | Pitch | No. Pcs. | Length | Body, Mounts | Flaps | SAT | Holes Dbld. | Tuning Holes | Additional Data | Ill. Source |
|---|---|---|---|---|---|---|---|---|---|---|---|---|
| 1. | | Litchfield Hist. Soc. | | | | | | | | | | |

## CLARINETS

| Young No. | No. Keys and Metal | City, Owner, No. | Pitch | No. Pcs. | Length | Body, Mounts | Flaps | SAT | Holes Dbld. | Tuning Holes | Additional Data | Ill. Source |
|---|---|---|---|---|---|---|---|---|---|---|---|---|
| 1. | 5 brass | Washington: Smithsonian 373.850 | C | 6 pc | 60.0 | boxw, ivory | flat sq | SATK | | | | EAMI 629 |
| 2. | 5 brass | Dearborn: H. Ford Museum 77.68.7 | C | 6 pc | 59.4 | boxw, ivory | flat sq | SATK | | | | |
| 3. | 5 brass | Victoria, Univ. of, | C | 6 pc | 59.2 | boxw, ivory | flat sq | SATK | | | | LOM 179 |
| 4. | 5 brass | New York City: F. Selch | C | 6 pc | 58.6 | boxw, ivory | flat sq | SATK | | | | |
| 5. | 5 brass | New York City: F. Selch (2nd one) | C | 6 pc | 59.1 | boxw, ivory | flat sq | SATK | | | | |
| 6. | 5 brass | New Haven: Yale 417 | C | 6 pc | 58.3 | boxw, ivory | flat sq | | | | | |
| 7. | 5 brass | New Haven: Yale 468 | C | 6 pc | 59.2 | boxw, ivory | flat sq | | | | | |
| 8. | 5 brass | San Diego: Miss C. Hale | C | 6 pc | 58.4 | boxw, ivory | flat sq | SATK | | | | |
| 9. | 5 brass | Middlebury, Conn.: G. Somers | | 6 pc | | boxw, ivory | flat sq | SATK | | | | |
| 10. | 5 brass | New Haven: Goldie's Music | C | 6 pc | 59.4 | boxw, ivory | flat sq | | | | | |

**A. HOPKINS** *(cont.)*

CLARINETS *(cont.)*

| | | | | | | | | | | | | |
|---|---|---|---|---|---|---|---|---|---|---|---|---|
| 11. | 5 brass | Vermillion: Univ. of SD | C | 6 pc | (53.0)[1] | boxw, ivory | flat sq | SATK | | | mid and lower jts stamped "J.M. Camp," Hopkins' successor. | |
| 12. | 5 brass | Washington: Smithsonian 54.253 | B♭ | 6 pc | 59.4[1] | boxw, ivory | flat sq | | | | 6th key is a'-b' trill. | |
| 13. | 5 brass | Litchfield Hist. Soc. | E♭ | 6 pc | 50.0[1] | boxw, ivory | flat sq | | | | Bell by J.M. Camp. | |
| 14. | 5 | Nazareth Moravian Hist. Soc. | B♭ | | | | | | | | | |
| 15. | 6 brass | Washington: R. Sheldon | C | 6 pc | 53.1[1] | boxw, ivory | flat sq | SATK | | | 6th key is a' - b' trill. | |
| 16. | 7 brass | Dearborn: H. Ford Mus. 72.79 | C | 6 pc | 59.8 | boxw, ivory | flat sq | SATK | | | | |
| 17. | 5 brass | W. A. Bartlett | C | 6 pc | | boxw, ivory | flat sq | SATK | | | | |
| 18. | 5 brass | Vermillion, Univ. of S.D. 2721 | A | 6 pc | 59.1[1] | boxw, ivory | flat sq | SATK | | | | |
| 19. | 5 brass | De Witt, N.Y.: D'Mello | C | | | boxw, ivory | flat sq | | | | | |
| 20. | 6 brass | Silver Spring, Md: Dale | B♭ | 6 pc | 59.1[1] | boxw, ivory | flat sq | | | | Mthpc. missing | |

# HOTTETERRE (No Initial)

*Actual Stamp*

ALTO RECORDERS

| | | | | | | | | | | | | |
|---|---|---|---|---|---|---|---|---|---|---|---|---|
| 1. | | Paris E. 979.2.8 [2] | | 3 | 48.0 | ivory, unmtd | | | | | HOTTETERRE/ anchor | Ill. (1) Harrison-Rimmer 127; (2) JJ-GT-BR 73 |
| 2. | | Paris: late Chambure [3] (2nd one) | | | | maple, ivory | | | | | HOTTETERRE | |
| 3.[4] | | Nordenham: H. Ritz | | | | boxw | | | | | HOTTETERRE | |

TENOR RECORDERS

| | | | | | | | | | | | | |
|---|---|---|---|---|---|---|---|---|---|---|---|---|
| 1. | 1 brass | Leningrad 405 | | 3 | 68.0 | boxw, unmtd | Flap ro | SATW | | | (both) HAUTERRE & HOTTETERRE / fleur de lys | LOM 55 |
| 2. | 1 brass | Paris E.590, C. 402 | | 3 | 68.35 | maple, ivory | Flap ro | SATK | | | HOTTETERRE / anchor | Ill. JJ-GT-BR 75; EAMI 430; LOM 56 |
| 3. | 1 brass | Paris E.979.2.9 [2] | | 3 | 71.0 | maple? ivory | Flap ro | SATK | | | HOTTETERRE / anchor  Only ft jt is stamped | |
| 4. | 1 silver | Amsterdam: F. Brüggen | | 3 | | grena, ivory | Flap ro | SATK | | | HOTTETERRE / anchor  Only head jt is stamped | Ill. this book, Pl. VIII |

BASS RECORDERS

| | | | | | | | | | | | | |
|---|---|---|---|---|---|---|---|---|---|---|---|---|
| 1. | 1 brass | Paris C.413, E. 589 | | 3 [5] | 116.2 | maple, ivory | Flap ro | SATW | | | HOTTETERRE / anchor  Crook goes into side. | EAMI 430; LOM 57 |
| 2. | 1 brass | Paris E.979.2.10 [2] | | 3 [5] | 107.1 | maple, ivory | Flap ro | SATW | | | 6 pt star / HOTTETERRE Crook goes into top. | Ill. JJ-GT-BR 77 |

[1] Given height is without (missing) mouthpiece.

[2] Ex Comtesse de Chambure

[3] According to Bob Marvin, GSJ XXV (1972), p 40

[4] Added in press, thanks to Paul Hailperin.

[5] Three sections plus brass crook

| Young No. | No. Keys and Metal | City, Owner, No. | Pitch | No. Pcs. | Length | Body, Mounts | Flaps | SAT | Holes Dbld. | Tuning Holes | Additional Data | Ill. Source |
|---|---|---|---|---|---|---|---|---|---|---|---|---|

## HOTTETERRE (No Initial) *(cont.)*

HOTTETERRE (No Initial) *(cont.)*

### TRANSVERSE FLUTES

| Young No. | No. Keys and Metal | City, Owner, No. | Pitch | No. Pcs. | Length | Body, Mounts | Flaps | SAT | Holes Dbld. / Actual stamp | Tuning Holes | Additional Data | Ill. Source |
|---|---|---|---|---|---|---|---|---|---|---|---|---|
| 1. | 1 silver | Berlin 2670 | | 3 | 70.5 | boxw, ivory | Flap ro | SATI | HOTTETERRE / anchor | | | Ill. Winternitz 171; EAMI 466; LOM 58 [1] |
| | 1 | La Couture-Boussey Museum 11 [2] | | 3 | 70.5 | boxw, ivory | Flap ro | SATI | HOTTETERRE / anchor | | COPY. See footnote 2. | Ill. JJ-GT-BR 87 |
| 2. | 1 silver | Leningrad 471 | | 3 | 70.5 | boxw, ivory | Flap ro | SATI | HOTTETERRE / anchor | | | Ill. Blagodatov; LOM 59 |
| 3. | 1 | Graz: Landesmus. Johanneum | | 3 | | ebony, ivory | Flap sq | | HOTTETERRE / anchor | | | Ill. AMIS 3, p 23 |

# L. HOTTETERRE

L. HOTTETERRE

### ALTO RECORDERS

| Young No. | No. Keys and Metal | City, Owner, No. | Pitch | No. Pcs. | Length | Body, Mounts | Flaps | SAT | Holes Dbld. | Tuning Holes | Additional Data | Ill. Source |
|---|---|---|---|---|---|---|---|---|---|---|---|---|
| 1. | | Munich DM 63053 | | 3 | --- | ebony, ivory | | | fleur de lys / L / HOTTETERRE [3] | | Lower 2 jts. only. Upper jt "I.C. DENNER" | |
| 2. | | Washington DCM 326 | | 3 | 52.5 | boxw, ivory | | | fleur de lys / L / HOTTETERRE | | | LOM 54 |

### OBOE

| Young No. | No. Keys and Metal | City, Owner, No. | Pitch | No. Pcs. | Length | Body, Mounts | Flaps | SAT | Holes Dbld. | Tuning Holes | Additional Data | Ill. Source |
|---|---|---|---|---|---|---|---|---|---|---|---|---|
| 1. | 2 silver | Amsterdam: F. Brüggen | | 3 | 57.5 | boxw, ivory | Flaps ro | SATW | L. / HOTTETERRE | | 3 & 4 dbl. 2 tuning holes. Bell unstamped. | Ill. this book, Pl. VIII |

# N. HOTTETERRE

N. HOTTETERRE

### ALTO RECORDER

| Young No. | No. Keys and Metal | City, Owner, No. | Pitch | No. Pcs. | Length | Body, Mounts | Flaps | SAT | Holes Dbld. | Tuning Holes | Additional Data | Ill. Source |
|---|---|---|---|---|---|---|---|---|---|---|---|---|
| 1. | | Scarsdale: D & R Rosenbaum | | 3 | 51.0 | boxw, unmtd | | | 6 pt star / N / HOTTETERRE | | tortoise finish | LOM 53 |

### TENOR RECORDER

| Young No. | No. Keys and Metal | City, Owner, No. | Pitch | No. Pcs. | Length | Body, Mounts | Flaps | SAT | Holes Dbld. | Tuning Holes | Additional Data | Ill. Source |
|---|---|---|---|---|---|---|---|---|---|---|---|---|
| 1. | | Blois: ex Petit [4] | | | | | | | 5 pt star / N / HOTTETERRE | | | |

### OBOE

| Young No. | No. Keys and Metal | City, Owner, No. | Pitch | No. Pcs. | Length | Body, Mounts | Flaps | SAT | Holes Dbld. | Tuning Holes | Additional Data | Ill. Source |
|---|---|---|---|---|---|---|---|---|---|---|---|---|
| 1. | 3 brass | Brussels 2320 | | 3 | (59.0) | boxw, ivory | Flaps ro | SATW | 5 pt star / N / HOTTETERRE | | 3 & 4 dbl. 2 tuning holes. Bell "DEBEY" | EAMI 550; LOM 60 |

---

[1] Also illustrated in AMIS 3.

[2] This instrument is reported to be a reproduction, copied after the original now in Berlin. I am indebted to Mme. Florence Abondance of the Musée Instrumental, Paris, for this information, which has come only as the present book has gone to press.

[3] Upper joint stamped "I.C. DENNER"

[4] Again with thanks to Mme. Abondance for calling this instrument to my attention. The instrument may now be in the possession of the Bousquet-Leroux family.

| Young No. | No. Keys and Metal | City, Owner, No. | Pitch | No. Pcs. | Length | Body, Mounts Flaps | SAT | Holes Dbld. | Tuning Holes | Additional Data | Ill. Source |
|---|---|---|---|---|---|---|---|---|---|---|---|

## KELMER

KELMER

CLARINETS

| | | | | | | | | | | | |
|---|---|---|---|---|---|---|---|---|---|---|---|
| 1. | 2 brass | Leipzig 1469 | C | 3 pc | 55.2 | boxw, horn   trap | SATW | 0 dbl. | | 8ve key hole higher than a' hole. | |
| 2. | 3 brass | xBerlin 79 | D | 3 pc | | maple, unmtd?sq? | | 0 dbl. | | Keys e, a', speaker. | Ill. Kroll Clarinet, pl 6 |

## A. KINIGSPERGER

A. KINIGSPERGER

OBOE

| | | | | | | | | | | | |
|---|---|---|---|---|---|---|---|---|---|---|---|
| 1. | 3 brass | Munich: Deutsches Museum 25968 | | 3 pc | 56.0 | boxw, unmtd  trap(K) | SATW | 3&4 | 2 th | | |

TENOR OBOES

| | | | | | | | | | | | |
|---|---|---|---|---|---|---|---|---|---|---|---|
| 1. | 3 brass | Hague Ea 8-1942 | | 3 pc | 71.0 | boxw         sq | | | | | |
| 2. | 3 brass | Nürnberg MIR 393 | | 3 pc + crook | 71.4 | plumw?, horn  trap(K) | | 3&4 | 2 th | Straight form, bulb bell | |

BARITONE OBOE

| | | | | | | | | | | | |
|---|---|---|---|---|---|---|---|---|---|---|---|
| 1. | 3 brass | Brussels 977 | | 3 pc + crook | 92.0[1] | cherry, unmtd  trap(K) | SATW | 3&4 | 2 th | Straight form, bulb bell. | Ill. Mahillon II, p 25. |

## J. W. KENIGSPERGER

J. W. KENIGSPERGER

TENOR RECORDERS

| | | | | | | | | | | | |
|---|---|---|---|---|---|---|---|---|---|---|---|
| 1. | 1 brass | Salzburg 3/7 (G.238) | | 3 pc | 67.5 | maple, unmtd  ro | | | | | Stamp (but not instr.) ill. Birsak catalogue, taf IV |
| 2. | 1 brass | Munich: Deutsches Museum 17233 | | 3 pc | 69.6 | maple, unmtd  sq | | 0 | | | |

OBOE

| | | | | | | | | | | | |
|---|---|---|---|---|---|---|---|---|---|---|---|
| 1. | 3 brass | Boston: MFA 17.1908 | | 3 | 57.0 | pear, horn     trap(K) | SATW | 3&4 | 2 th | | Ill. Bessaraboff, pl I |

OBOES D'AMORE

| | | | | | | | | | | | |
|---|---|---|---|---|---|---|---|---|---|---|---|
| 1. | | Weishaupt & Co., per Langwill | | | | | | | | | |
| 2. | | Savoy Sale 78d, per Langwill | | | | | | | | | |

TENOR OBOES

| | | | | | | | | | | | |
|---|---|---|---|---|---|---|---|---|---|---|---|
| 1. | 3 brass | Stockholm 1007 | | 3 pc | 70.35 | plumw?,unmtd trap(K) | SATW | 3&4 | | Straight form, bulb bell | LOM 93 |
| 2. | 3 brass | Stockholm F.289 | | 3 pc | 70.85 | plumw?,unmtd trap(K) | SATW | 3&4 | | Straight form, bulb bell | Ill. Halsingborg cat. Pl X |

[1] With crook and reed.

## J. W. KENIGSPERGER *(cont.)* J. W. KENIGSPERGER *(cont.)*

### CLARINET

| Young No. | No. Keys and Metal | City, Owner, No. | Pitch | No. Pcs. | Length | Body, Mounts | Flaps | SAT | Holes Dbld. | Tuning Holes | Additional Data | Ill. Source |
|---|---|---|---|---|---|---|---|---|---|---|---|---|
| 1. | 3 brass | Munich BNM Mu 110 | G | 3 pc | 51.8 | plumw?, bone | trap(K) | SATW | 0 | | Mthpc+bbl=1 pc; main joint; long bell = 3 pc. | LOM 100 |

### BASSOONS

| Young No. | No. Keys and Metal | City, Owner, No. | Pitch | No. Pcs. | Length | Body, Mounts | Flaps | SAT | Holes Dbld. | Tuning Holes | Additional Data | Ill. Source |
|---|---|---|---|---|---|---|---|---|---|---|---|---|
| 1. | 3 brass | Nürnberg MIR 404 | | 4 | 119.0 | maple, brass | trap[1] | SATW | | | Fat, heavy turnings | |
| 2. | 3 brass | Halle MS 435 | | | 114.5 | maple, brass | | | | | | |
| 3. | 3 brass | Munich Stadtmuseum 52-49 | | 4 | 113.9 | maple, brass | trap[2] | SATW | | | 4th key added (G♯). Fat, heavy turnings. | LOM 103 |

## F. KONIGSPERGER F. KONIGSPERGER

### CLARINET D'AMOUR

| Young No. | No. Keys and Metal | City, Owner, No. | Pitch | No. Pcs. | Length | Body, Mounts | Flaps | SAT | Holes Dbld. | Tuning Holes | Additional Data | Ill. Source |
|---|---|---|---|---|---|---|---|---|---|---|---|---|
| 1. | 4 brass | Munich: Deutsches Museum 18869 | G | 3 pc | 79.0 | maple, horn | sq | | 0 dbl. | | | |

### BASSET HORN

| Young No. | No. Keys and Metal | City, Owner, No. | Pitch | No. Pcs. | Length | Body, Mounts | Flaps | SAT | Holes Dbld. | Tuning Holes | Additional Data | Ill. Source |
|---|---|---|---|---|---|---|---|---|---|---|---|---|
| 1. | 7 brass | Berlin 578 | F | 7 pc | 95.0[3] | boxw, horn | U-shape | SATW | 4 dbl. | | Only horn mt is around kasten top socket. Bore 1.4. Right angle form. | Ill. Sachs catalogue, taf 29 |

### BASSOON

| Young No. | No. Keys and Metal | City, Owner, No. | Pitch | No. Pcs. | Length | Body, Mounts | Flaps | SAT | Holes Dbld. | Tuning Holes | Additional Data | Ill. Source |
|---|---|---|---|---|---|---|---|---|---|---|---|---|
| 1. | | reported by Dr. J.H. van der Meer, 1975 | | | | | | | | | | |

## KIRST KIRST

### PICCOLO

| Young No. | No. Keys and Metal | City, Owner, No. | Pitch | No. Pcs. | Length | Body, Mounts | Flaps | SAT | Holes Dbld. | Tuning Holes | Additional Data | Ill. Source |
|---|---|---|---|---|---|---|---|---|---|---|---|---|
| 1. | 1 | Florence 111 | | | | | | | | | | |

### FLUTES

| Young No. | No. Keys and Metal | City, Owner, No. | Pitch | No. Pcs. | Length | Body, Mounts | Flaps | SAT | Holes Dbld. (upper jts) | Tuning Holes | Additional Data | Ill. Source |
|---|---|---|---|---|---|---|---|---|---|---|---|---|
| 1. | 1 silver | Berlin 4895 | C | 4 pc w 1) | 63.64 | ebony, ivory | sq(E) | SATK | 4 | | 1) 16.4; 2) 15.7; 3) 15.0; 4) 14.26. No register. | LOM 166 |
| 2. | 1 silver | Salzburg 6/9 | C | 4 pc | 63.0 | ebony, ivory | | | 4 | | 1) 16.5; 2) 15.8; 3) 15.0; 4) 14.5. Register. | |
| 3. | 1 silver | **Bonn BH** (Zimmermann 52) | C | 4 pc | 63.2 | boxw, ivory | sq | SATK | 3 | | | |
| 4. | 1 silver | Stockholm F-183 | C | 4 pc w 1) | 63.3 | boxw, ivory | sq(F) | | 3 | | 1) 16.4; 2) 15.73; 3) 14.75. In mahogany veneered case. | |
| 5. | 1 silver | Stockholm F-192 | C | 5 pc w 2) | 63.4 | ebony, ivory | sq | | 3 | | 5th pc is tuning bbl. Added g♯. | |

[1] B♭ and D flaps are notched (K).
[2] B♭ and D flaps are notched (K), F and G are octagonal.
[3] Measured from mouthpiece tip over outside of right angle to bell rim. Actual height perpendicular to bell rim is 46.0.

| Young No. | No. Keys and Metal | City, Owner, No. | Pitch | No. Pcs. | Length | Body, Mounts | Flaps | SAT | Holes Dbld. | Tuning Holes | Additional Data | Ill. Source |
|---|---|---|---|---|---|---|---|---|---|---|---|---|

**KIRST** *(cont.)*

**FLUTES** *(cont.)* — *upper jts.*

| Young No. | No. Keys and Metal | City, Owner, No. | Pitch | No. Pcs. | Length | Body, Mounts | Flaps | SAT | Holes Dbld. | Tuning Holes | Additional Data | Ill. Source |
|---|---|---|---|---|---|---|---|---|---|---|---|---|
| 6. | 1 silver | Munich: Albert Müller | C | 4 pc | | ebony, ivory | sq | | | | | |
| 7. | 1 brass | Düren: Karl Ventzke, ex Hart | C | | | boxw, ivory | sq | | | | | |
| 8. | 1 brass | Hague: Rob van Acht | C | 4 pc | | boxw, ivory | sq(F) | | 3 | | | Ill. Hutchings: *Mozart* |
| 9. | 1 brass | Bonn BH (Zimmermann 53) | C | | 63.0 | boxw, ivory | sq | | 3 | | | |
| 10. | 1 brass | Berlin 473, by loan | C | 4 pc | 63.7 | boxw, ivory | sq | SATK | 3 | | Only ft is stamped. No register. | |
| 11. | 1 | Dorking: Lady Jeans | C | | | | | | | | | |
| 12. | 1 | Stockholm 1957-58/32 | | 4 pc | | | | | | | | |
| 13. | ? | Leipzig 3265 | C | 4 pc | — | boxw, ivory | | | 3 | | Lower jt and ft jt lost. | |
| 14. | 2 silver | Berlin 4986 | C | 4 pc | 62.62 | ebony, ivory | sq(E) | SATK | 4 | | | |
| 15. | 4 silver | Leningrad 1136 | C | 4 pc | 60.7 | boxw, ivory | sq(E) | SATK | 1 (no. 2) | | 5th touch (to make cross f') added in ivory saddle. [1] | LOM 167 |
| 16. | 4 brass | Halle MIS 340 | C | 4 pc | 62.2 | boxw, ivory | | | 1 (no. 2) | | | |
| 17. | 4 silver | xLeipzig 1255 | C | 4 pc | 64.0 | boxw, ivory | | | 3 | | | |
| 18. | 5-7 silver | Nürnberg MI 409, by loan [2] | C | 5 pc | 73.0 | ebony, ivory | sq | SATK | 3 | | | |
| 19. | 5 8 silver | Berlin 4214 | C | 4 pc | 70.5 w 1) | ebony, ivory | sq | SATK | 4 | | 2 ft jts. With 1) upper jt, 70.5 & 63.5 | |
| 20. | 5 silver | Peine: Günter Hart | C | | | | | | | | | |
| 21. | 5 silver | Washington: DCM 934 | C | 4 pc | 61.3 | ebony, ivory | sq | SATK | 1 | | Register. | |
| 22. | 6 silver | Aachen: Dr. W. Willms | C | | 61.7 | ebony, ivory | sq | SATK | | | | |
| 23. | 6-8 silver | Washington: DCM 995 | C | 4 pc | 68.7 w 1)+C ft | ebony, ivory | sq | SATK | 4 | | Register in d' foot. 2nd ft jt. to c'. | |
| 24. | 7 silver | Oxford: Bate 118 | C | 4 pc | 54.0 [3] | ebony, ivory | sq | | | | Has both d♯' & e♭'. Upper jt marked "I" | |
| 25. | | Stuttgart: G. Hase | | | | | | | | | | |

**FLUTE D'AMOUR**

| Young No. | No. Keys and Metal | City, Owner, No. | Pitch | No. Pcs. | Length | Body, Mounts | Flaps | SAT | Holes Dbld. | Tuning Holes | Additional Data | Ill. Source |
|---|---|---|---|---|---|---|---|---|---|---|---|---|
| 1. | 1 silver | Bonn BH (Zimmermann 41) | A | 4 pc | 78.2 | boxw, ivory | sq | | 3 | | | |

**OBOES** — *Holes double*

| Young No. | No. Keys and Metal | City, Owner, No. | Pitch | No. Pcs. | Length | Body, Mounts | Flaps | SAT | Holes Dbld. | Tuning Holes | Additional Data | Ill. Source |
|---|---|---|---|---|---|---|---|---|---|---|---|---|
| 1. | 3 brass | Munich Stadtmuseum [4] | C | | 57.9 w 1) | boxw, ivory | oct(Q) | SATK | 3 | 2 th | 3rd key is c♯'. 4 upper jts. [5] | |
| 2. | 4 | Florence Conservatory 128 | C | | 55.7 | | | | | | | No. 111 in Lete Bargagna catalogue, n.d. |

---

[1] To engage f' key in integral wooden block for LH4. Register.
[2] From Karl Ventzke, Düren.
[3] Sounding length, embouchure to ft. end.
[4] Not as yet assigned a collection number.
[5] The fourth doesn't match the others and must be a later acquisition.

## KIRST *(cont.)*         KIRST *(cont.)*

### ENGLISH HORN

| Young No. | No. Keys and Metal | City, Owner, No. | Pitch | No. Pcs. | Length | Body, Mounts | Flaps | SAT | Holes Dbld. | Tuning Holes | Additional Data | Ill. Source |
|---|---|---|---|---|---|---|---|---|---|---|---|---|
| 1. | 2 silver | Kremsmünster Abbey | F | | 74.8 | black leath-covered wood, silver | sq(G) | SATK | 3 | 2 th | Bulb bell, sickle form. | |

### CLARINET

| Young No. | No. Keys and Metal | City, Owner, No. |
|---|---|---|
| 1. | 5 | Breslau 117[1] |

### BASSET HORNS

| Young No. | No. Keys and Metal | City, Owner, No. | No. Pcs. | Length | Body, Mounts | Flaps | SAT | Additional Data | Ill. Source |
|---|---|---|---|---|---|---|---|---|---|
| 1. | 8 brass | Leipzig 1528 | | (86.0) | boxw?, ivory | sq | SATK | Angular form. 5 pcs + missing mthpc & bbl. | |
| 2. | 9 | xBerlin 2914 | | (75.0) | | | | Angular form. Bore 1.5. Keys d, e♭, e, f, f♯, g♯, c♯', a', b'. | |
| 3. | 9 | Leipzig 1529 | | | | | | | |
| 4. | 9 brass | Hamburg 1912.1561 | | 89.0 | black leath cov wood [2] | sq | SATK | Sickle form. Bore 1.44. Bell an amusing replacement. | Ill. Schroder catalogue, pl 20b [3] |
| 5. | 12 brass | Eisenach I-149 | 7 pc | 105.3 | boxw, ivory | sq | | Angular form. | Color ill. Heyde Eisenach, p 228 |
| 6. | | Halsingborg 137 | | | boxw, ivory | sq | | Angular form. Not known if now in Stockholm or not. | Ill. Halsingborg catalogue, pl XI |

### BASSOONS

| Young No. | No. Keys and Metal | City, Owner, No. | Length | Body, Mounts | Flaps | SAT | Additional Data | Ill. Source |
|---|---|---|---|---|---|---|---|---|
| 1. | 5 brass | Poznan 178 | 125.0 | maple, brass | mixed | | Brass decorative bell ring. | Ill. Szulc Poznan |
| 2. | 5 brass | Cologne Stadtmus I/65 | 123.0 | maple, brass | oct(Q) | SATW [4] | 2 bells! One wood, one brass, widely flared & longer [5] | |
| 3. | 6 brass | Hamburg 1928.387 | 123.0 | maple, brass | oct(Q) | SATW [6] | Nicely decorated keys[5]. Bell ring. | Ill. Schroder catalogue. LOM 191 |
| 4. | 7 brass | London: W. Waterhouse | 123.3 | maple, brass | oct(Q) | SATK | Nicely decorated keys [5] No bell ring | Ill. this book, Pl. VI |
| 5. | 7 brass | Biebrich: Heckel F-7a | 124.15 | black lacq maple, brass | oct(Q) | SATW [7] | d. 1801 [8]. c♯ flap sq. A replacement? Nicely decorated keys,[5] but no bell ring. | |
| 6. | 10 ivory | Brighton R5773/73 | | maple, brass | oct(Q) | | Brass decorative bell ring. | Ill. GS'68 Exhib, pl 12 |
| 7. | 7 brass | Frankfurt a M: 15.032 [9] | | maple, brass | ro [10] | | Ivory-bushed c-hole. Ornate ½ swallowtail. | |

---

[1] But not listed in 1949 Poznan catalogue with other instruments transferred to Poznan from Breslau.

[2] One ivory band plus 2 brass bands. Body tube clearly made in curved halves, (cornett-fashion) then joined.

[3] Also ill. Rendall Clarinet, pl 6b

[4] But E♭L4 and wing key springs attached to keys.

[5] Kirst uses both notches and small barbs to decorate the shanks of his keys very attractively. This is one of the more conspicuous influences he exhibits of his teacher, August Grenser. In addition, he uses a flat table on the bass joints, a projecting (protective, integral) knob below the F flaps, and (often but not consistently) a decorative brass ring around the tops of his bell joints. Both celebrated makers' bassoons tend to have an 'old fashioned' look, while their respective flutes are models of elegant sophistication.

[6] E♭L4 and D springs are attached to the wood, suggesting that the others probably were originally; now however the others are attached to the keys.

[7] B♭, D, and G♯ springs are attached to the wood; the others to the keys.

[8] The only dated Kirst instrument.

[9] In GSJ XXXI, I identified this instrument as by H. Grenser. I am grateful to William Waterhouse for correcting this error.

[10] F and G♯ are octagonal.

| Young No. | No. Keys and Metal | City, Owner, No. | Pitch | No. Pcs. | Length | Body, Mounts Flaps | SAT | Holes Dbld. | Tuning Holes | Additional Data | Ill. Source |
|---|---|---|---|---|---|---|---|---|---|---|---|

# KLENIG

## ALTO RECORDER

| | | | | | | | | | | | |
|---|---|---|---|---|---|---|---|---|---|---|---|
| 1. | | Amsterdam: Mrs. Misset-Oudheusden | | | | ivory | | | | | |

## OBOE

| | | | | | | | | | | | |
|---|---|---|---|---|---|---|---|---|---|---|---|
| 1. | 2 brass | Hamburg MHG 1928.359 | | | 57.3 | boxw, ivory   ro | | 3&4 dbl | | | Ill. Schröder catalogue, pl 19d |

## CHALUMEAUX

| | | | | | | | | | | | |
|---|---|---|---|---|---|---|---|---|---|---|---|
| 1. | 2 brass | Stockholm 141 | F | | 49.0 | boxw, unmtd   trap | SATK | | | Bore 1.3 (top) & 1.2 (lower). Speaker key hole opposite a' hole. | Ill. Rendall Clarinet, pl I: ill. Grove 6 vol. 4, p 111 |
| 2. | 2 brass | Stockholm 142 | F | | 49.0 | boxw, unmtd   trap | SATW | | | Bore 1.32 (top) & 1.22 (lower). Speaker key hole opposite a' hole. Mthpc not original. | LOM 98 |

# S. KOCH

## DOUBLE RECORDER ("Akkord-Querschnabelflöte)

| | | | | | | | | | | | |
|---|---|---|---|---|---|---|---|---|---|---|---|
| 1. | G. silver | xBerlin 823 | | | | | | | | | |

## CZAKAN

| | | | | | | | | | *Keys mtd. in* | | |
|---|---|---|---|---|---|---|---|---|---|---|---|
| 1. | 1 silver | xLeipzig 1172 | | | | | | | | | |
| 2. | 7 brass | Berlin 2829 | | | | | | | | blocks | | |
| 3. | 7 brass | Leipzig 3246 | | | | dome | | | | blocks | | |

## WALKING STICK FLUTE (recorder)

| | | | | | | | | | | | |
|---|---|---|---|---|---|---|---|---|---|---|---|
| 1. | 1 brass | Munich Stadtmuseum 41-397 | | | | | | | | 2 round holes at top to blow into. 7 fingerholes on front+[1] | LOM 227 |

## PICCOLO

| | | | | | | | | | | | |
|---|---|---|---|---|---|---|---|---|---|---|---|
| 1. | 1 silver | Hague Ea 12-1937 | | | | | | | | | Ill. Hague '74 Exhib. cat., p 17 |

## FLUTES

| | | | *Foot to* | | | | | | | | |
|---|---|---|---|---|---|---|---|---|---|---|---|
| 1. | 7 silver | Zurich: W. Burger | C | 5 pc | 68.0 | ebony, ivory   plug | | | blocks | | |
| 2. | 7 silver | Leningrad 1741 | G | 4 pc | 72.2 | ebony, bone | | | | U-bend. | |
| 3. | 8 silver | Hague Ea 17-1951 | B | 5 pc | 67.3 | ebony, ivory   plug | | | | 5th pc is tuning bbl. | |
| 4. | 9 silver | Markneukirchen 2027 | B | 5 pc | (70.4) | ebony, ivory | | | blocks | Head jt and bbl not original. | |
| 5. | 9 silver | Washington: DCM 595 | B | 5 pc | 71.6 | ebony, ivory, silver   flat ro [2] | | | | | |

[1] +closed key and 2 more holes further down that emit the bell note.     [2] Except for 3 plug keys for lowest pitches.

| Young No. | No. Keys and Metal | City, Owner, No. | Pitch | No. Pcs. | Length | Body, Mounts | Flaps | SAT | Holes Dbld. | Tuning Holes | Additional Data | Ill. Source |
|---|---|---|---|---|---|---|---|---|---|---|---|---|

**S. KOCH** *(cont.)*

**FLUTES** *(cont.)*

*Foot to* (under Pitch); *Keys mtd in* (under Tuning Holes)

| Young No. | No. Keys and Metal | City, Owner, No. | Pitch | No. Pcs. | Length | Body, Mounts | Flaps | SAT | Holes Dbld. | Keys mtd in | Additional Data | Ill. Source |
|---|---|---|---|---|---|---|---|---|---|---|---|---|
| 6. | 9 silver | Aachen: Dr. W. Willms | B♭ | | 70.15 | ebony | flat ro [1] | | | knobs & blocks | 8 flaps vs. 9 touches. Brass liners in knobs and blocks. | |
| 7. | 9 silver | Göttingen, Univ. of, 335 | B | 4 pc | 70.0 | ebony, ivory | | | | blocks | Head jt, bbl, main jt, long lower jt. | |
| 8. | 9 silver | Munich Stadtmuseum 78-30 | B | 4 pc | 70.1 | ebony, ivory | flat ro [1] | | | blocks | | |
| 9. | 10 silver | Washington: DCM 1039 | B | 4 pc | 70.1 | cocus, silver | dome | | | | Head, bbl, main jt, long lower jt. | |
| 10. | 10 silver | Edinburgh: Melville-Mason | | 4 pc | | cocus, silver | clam [2] | | | | Metal lined head jt. | |
| 11. | 10 silver | Berlin 4982 | B | 5 pc | 71.1 | cocus, ivory | plug | | | | | |
| 12. | 10 silver | Berlin 2693 | A | 4 pc | 87.0 | ebony, ivory | ——— | ——— | | | All keys missing. Were a, b♭, b♮, c', c♯'-d♯', 2Xf', g♯', b♭', c". | |
| 13. | 11 silver | Amsterdam: Henk de Wit, Jr. | B | | | ebony, silver | | | | | 3 plug keys on ft jt. Koch name on oval silver plate. Long B♮ key L4. | |
| 14. | 11 silver | Oxford: Bate 119 | A | 4 pc | 78.6 | rosew, silver | clam [2] | | | blocks, lined | Head jt, bbl, main jt, long lower jt. | Ill. Bate Flute. LOM 219 |
| 15. | 12 silver | Washington: DCM 15 | A | 4 pc | 79.5 | ebony, silver | ro, lip | | | blocks | Head jt, bbl, main jt, long lower jt. | |
| 16. | 13 ——— | Berlin 2694 | A♭ | 4 pc | 87.0 | boxw, ivory | ——— | ——— | | | U-bend. Keys missing, but were a♭, a, b♭, b♮, c', c♯'-d♯'. 2Xf', 2Xg♯', b♭', c", 8ᵛᵉ. | |
| 17. | 14 silver | Washington: DCM 256 | G | 5 pc | 70.5 | ebony, silver | plug | | | | Head jt, bbl, main jt, lower jt, ft jt with U-bend. | Ill. Bate Flute, pl 7j |
| 18. | 15 silver | Washington: DCM 231 | G | 4 pc | 88.0 | ebony, silver | plug | | | | Long lower jt, no ft jt. | |
| 19. | 15 silver | Berlin 3981 | G | 4 pc | 71.5 | cocus, ivory | plug | | | | Lower jt doubles back on itself for 19 cm. | |

## ALTO FLUTE

| Young No. | No. Keys and Metal | City, Owner, No. | Pitch | No. Pcs. | Length | Body, Mounts | Flaps | SAT | Holes Dbld. | Tuning Holes | Additional Data | Ill. Source |
|---|---|---|---|---|---|---|---|---|---|---|---|---|
| 1. | 13 silver | Edinburgh: Melville-Mason | G | | 90.6 | ebony, ivory, | clam [2] | | | | Lower keys pewter plugs. Metal lined head jt. Ivory embouchure. | |

## OBOES

| Young No. | No. Keys and Metal | City, Owner, No. | Pitch | No. Pcs. | Length | Body, Mounts | Flaps | SAT | Holes dbl | Tuning Holes | Additional Data | Ill. Source |
|---|---|---|---|---|---|---|---|---|---|---|---|---|
| 1. | 10 brass | Basel 1913.301 | | | 56.15 | boxw, ivory | ro | | 3 | 0 | All keys in integral blocks. | |
| 2. | 10 silver | Basel 1956.625 | | | 56.0 | boxw, ivory | ro | | 3 | 0 | All keys in saddles except those in lower knobs. | |
| 3. | 11 brass | Hamburg MHG 1912.1553 | | | 55.5 | boxw, horn | ro | SATK | 3 | | Only upper lip of top spool is horn, rest unmtd. 13 touches. | |
| 4. | 11 silver | Leningrad 1145 | | | 56.4 | boxw, ivory | | | | | | |
| 5. | 11 brass | Ann Arbor: U. of Michigan 669 | | | 56.0 | boxw, ivory | ro | | 3 | | 12 touches. | |

---

[1] Except for 3 plug keys for lowest pitches.    [2] Koch used this "clam" or "scallop"-shell design for flaps occasionally. Very handsome.

**S. KOCH** *(cont.)*

**OBOES** *(cont.)*

| Young No. | No. Keys and Metal | City, Owner, No. | PITCH | No. Pcs. | Length | Body, Mounts | Flaps | SAT | Holes Dbld. | Tuning Holes | Additional Data | Ill. Source |
|---|---|---|---|---|---|---|---|---|---|---|---|---|
| 6. | 11 G. Silver | Vienna 443 | | | 56.8 | ebony, ivory | dome | SATK | 0 | | b L Th, c', c♯', e♮', f♯'R3, eb'L4, f'R3, f'L4, g♯'L4, B♭R1, c"R1, 8 ve. 13 touches. | |
| 7. | 12 silver | Bonn BH (Zimmermann 98) | | | 55.4 | ebony, ivory | | | 3&4 | | All keys in knobs & blocks. | Ill. Zimmermann, p 27 |
| 8. | 12 brass | Berlin 4166 | | | 56.62 | boxw, ivory | | | 3 | | | |
| 9. | 12 silver | Munich Stadtmuseum 41-2 | | | 54.3 | boxw, ivory | ro | SATK | 3 | 0 | Everything in saddles except long b. Sellner system. | LOM 228 |
| 10. | 13 silver | Oxford: Bate 210 | | | 55.3 | ebony, ivory | dome | | | | keys on posts & axles. GS Exhib '68, 92. | Ill. Harrison-Rimmer, pl 195; ill. Montagu, RM, Pl. 36 |

**ENGLISH HORNS**

| Young No. | No. Keys and Metal | City, Owner, No. | PITCH | No. Pcs. | Length | Body, Mounts | Flaps | SAT | Holes Dbld. | Tuning Holes | Additional Data | Ill. Source |
|---|---|---|---|---|---|---|---|---|---|---|---|---|
| 1. | 8 brass | Nürnberg MIR 397 | | | 77.3 | boxw, ivory | | | 3 | | Angular form. | |
| 2. | 10 brass | Ann Arbor: U. of Michigan 672 | | | 78.0 | dark wood | | | | | Angular form. Bulb bell. 11 touches. | |
| 3. | 11 brass | Leipzig 1349 | | | 78.7 | boxw, ivory | ro | | | | keys in blocks. Angular form. | EAMI 579 |
| 4. | 11 brass | Düren: Karl Ventzke, ex Heckel EH4 | | | c77.0 | boxw, ivory | | | | | | |
| 5. | 14 silver | Nürnberg MIR 399 | | | c80.3 | boxw, ivory | | | | | Angular form. Ivory bushed Hole 1. | |

**CLARINETS**

| Young No. | No. Keys and Metal | City, Owner, No. | PITCH | No. Pcs. | Length | Body, Mounts | Flaps | SAT | Holes Dbld. | Tuning Holes | Additional Data | Ill. Source |
|---|---|---|---|---|---|---|---|---|---|---|---|---|
| 1. | 5 brass | Zell-Riedichen: Paul Hailperin | C | | 51.5[1] | boxw, ivory | | | | | Mthpc missing. | |
| 2. | 5 | Salzburg 18/16 | D | | 50.5[2] | boxw | ro | | | | keys in blocks & knobs. 6 pcs, but mthpc missing & replaced. | |
| 3. | 7 brass | Hague Ea 116-1950 | Eb | | 43.3[3] | boxw, ivory | sq | | | | 6 pcs, but mthpc missing. | Ill. Hague '74 Exhib, p 30 |
| 4. | 8 brass | Basel 1912.296 | | | 58.5 | boxw, ivory | sq | | | | keys in blocks & knobs. | |
| 5. | 8 | Stuttgart: G. Hase | G | | | | | | | | | |
| 6. | 10 G.silver | Nürnberg MIR 447 | | | 36.4 | rosew, silver | | | | | keys on posts & axles. | |
| 7. | 10 G.silver | Nürnberg MIR 450 | Bb/A | | 50.0 | grena, ivory | | | | | 5 pcs. 2 upper jts & 2 lower jts. 50.0 w longer, 48.0 w shorter. | |
| 8. | 14 silver | Edinburgh: Melville-Mason | C | | 52.1 | boxw, ivory, silver | flat ro | | | | Metal tuning slide. Speaker hole on front, key behind as usual. 5 pcs. | |
| 9. | 16 brass | London: Horniman 198B | Bb | | 67.7 | dark w, horn | | | | | 5 pcs. | |
| 10. | 17 G.silver | Vienna GdM 123 | C | | 59.0 | boxw, silver | dome | | | | 5 pcs. 2 upper joints. Bore 1.46 | |
| 11. | 17 G.silver | Vienna GdM 124 | Bb/A | | 64.2/ 65.8 | boxw, silver | dome | | | | 5 pcs. Bore 1.4 | |

---

[1]This length without its mouthpiece, which is missing.    [2] This length with a modern, replacement mouthpiece.    [3] Without mouthpiece.

## S. KOCH (cont.)

### BASSET HORNS

| | | | | | | | | | | | | |
|---|---|---|---|---|---|---|---|---|---|---|---|---|
| 1. | 15 | Stockholm 2360 | | | | boxw, ivory, brass | | | | | Keys mtd in blocks & knobs. 6 pcs. | |
| 2. | 12 brass | Stockholm F.327 | | | 107.3 | boxw, brass | | | | | Long lower jt, short upper jt. Oval bell. 8 pcs. | Ill. Halsingborg catalogue, pl XI |
| 3. | 17 brass | Vienna Techn Museum 15380/26 | | | 98.5 | maple? silver, brass | | | | | Keys mtd in knobs & blocks. | |

### BASSOON

| | | | | | | | | | | | | |
|---|---|---|---|---|---|---|---|---|---|---|---|---|
| 1. | 7 brass | Amsterdam: Henk de Wit, Jr. | | | 123.5 | maple, brass | flat, shield(U) | | | | 2 wing keys. Brass bell ring. | |

### CONTRABASSOON

| | | | | | | | | | | | | |
|---|---|---|---|---|---|---|---|---|---|---|---|---|
| 1. | 5 | xBerlin 2975 | | | 167.75 | maple, brass | | | | | | |

# KRAUS

### CLARINETS D'AMOUR

| | | | | | | | | | | | | |
|---|---|---|---|---|---|---|---|---|---|---|---|---|
| 1. | 3 brass | Brunswick 105 | F | | 72.5 | dark wood, horn | | | | | "KRAUS" | |
| 2. | 3 brass | Munich: BNM Mu 107 | F | | 66.3 | cherry? plum? trap | | SATW | | | "I.KRAVS". No mthpc, no bbl, brass neck, upper jt, lower jt, bell | |
| 3. | 3 | xBerlin 293 | | | 74.0 | pear, horn | | | | | "I.KRAVS" | |
| 4. | 3 brass | Scarsdale: Dorothy & Robert Rosenbaum | | | 74.0 | boxw, horn | sq | SATW | | | "I.KRAVS". Brass crook. | |

### FAGOTTINI

| | | | | | | | | | | | | |
|---|---|---|---|---|---|---|---|---|---|---|---|---|
| 1. | 3 brass | Munich: BNM Mu 120 | G | | 80.0 | maple, brass | (U) | SATW | | | "I.KRAVS". Crook + 4 pc. Slight hollow in bell. | |
| 2. | 3 brass | Scarsdale: Dorothy & Robert Rosenbaum | G | | 79.5 | boxw, brass | (U) | SATW | | | "I.KRAVS". Crook + 4 pc, bell & bass jt separate. | LOM 104 |
| 3. | 4 brass | Paris 501 | G | | 76.9 | maple, brass | | SATK | | | "I.KRAVS". 4 pc, bell & bass jt separate. g key missing. | |
| 4. | 4 brass | Salzburg 15/7 | | | 71.0 | maple | sq | | | | "I.KRAVS" 3 pc, bell & bass jt not separate.[1] | |
| 5. | 4 brass | Eisenach I-158 | F | | | cherry, brass | sq | | | | "C.KRAVSS"[2] 4 pc, bell and bass jt separate. | |

### BASSOON

| | | | | | | | | | | | | |
|---|---|---|---|---|---|---|---|---|---|---|---|---|
| 1. | 4 brass | Nürnberg MI 373 | | | 125.5 | maple, brass | (V) | SATW | | | "I.KRAVS". Crook + 4 pc. Bb&D in blocks, F&G in saddles. Hollow in bell. | |

[1] Stamp but not instrument illustrated in Birsak catalogue, Taf. XIV.

[2] Or "C.KRAVSE," says Dr. Heyde in his catalogue. I believe, however, that what he is reading as a sixth letter in the last name is instead a design that occurs as well before the initial at the left. I'd bet there is in fact only one 18th century woodwind maker named Kraus, whose initial is "I".

# KRESS

# KRESS

## BASSET RECORDER

| 1. | 1 brass | Brunswick 82 | F | | 96.0 | red wood | | | | Edge blown. Richly turned. Said in catalogue to be 16th century. [1] | |

## OBOES

| 1. | 3 brass | Munich: BNM Mu 145 | | | 57.0 | boxw, unmtd trap(I) | SATW | 3&4 dbl. | 2 th. | | One of these ill. Harrison-R, No. 129. |
| 2. | 3 brass | Munich: BNM Mu 146 | | | 57.0 | boxw, unmtd trap(I) | SATW | 3&4 dbl. | 2 th. | | One of these ill. Harrison-R, No. 129. |

## TENOR OBOES

| 1. | 3 brass | Copenhagen 103, E.81 | F | | 74.0 | boxw, unmtd | SATW | 3&4 dbl. | 0 th. | Bulb bell. Straight form. | Ill. Hammerich [2] |
| 2. | 3 brass | Linz W. 121. | | | 75.0 | | | 3&4 dbl. | 0 th. | Bulb bell. Curved form. | |

## DULCIAN OR SORDUN

| 1. | 5 brass | Salzburg 8/1 | C | | 73.0 | maple? brass sq(C) or trap(I) | | | | | Stamp & instr. ill. Birsak catalogue, pl [3] |

# KÜSS

# KÜSS

## OBOES

| 1. | 3 brass | New York City: late J. Marx | | | | boxw, ivory | | | | | |
| 2. | 8 brass | Vienna: G. Stradner | | | | boxw, ivory | | | | | |
| 3. | 11 brass | Stockholm 312 | | | 54.9 | boxw, unmtd [4] sq-cors (N) | SATK | 3 dbl. | | Keys mtd. in knobs & blocks, all integral. | |
| 4. | 11 brass | Washington: Smithsonian 95.299 | | | 55.0 | boxw, ivory oct(Q) | SATK | 3 dbl. | 2 th. | Keys mtd. in knobs & blocks. | |
| 5. | 12 | Prague 9024 (seen 1964) | | | | | | | | | |
| 6. | 12 | Prague 12046 (seen 1964) | | | | | | | | | |
| 7. | 13 brass | Zell-Riedichen: P. Hailperin | | | | boxw, ivory | | | | | |
| 8. | 13 | Prague 12052 (seen 1964) | | | | | | | | No inner bell rim. | |
| 9. | 13 G.silver | Munich: D M 34508 | | | 54.7 | boxw, ivory dome | | 3 dbl. | | | |
| 10. | 13 brass | Munich Stadtmuseum 42-209 | | | 55.0 | boxw, ivory dome | SATK | 3 dbl. | 0 th. | Keys mtd. in blocks. Key names. [5] | |

---

[1] But unlikely for the maker of these other instruments with the same (?) stamp.

[2] Page 27 in Hammerich catalogue.

[3] Plates XIV and IV, respectively.

[4] But for one silver ring that is clearly a repair.

[5] b, c' c♯', 2Xeb', 2Xf', f♯', g♯', b♭' w 2 touches, b'-c" trill, c"-d" trill, 8ve key.

| | | | | | | | | | | | | |
|---|---|---|---|---|---|---|---|---|---|---|---|---|

## KÜSS (cont.)
### OBOES (cont.)

| Young No. | No. Keys and Metal | City, Owner, No. | Pitch | No. Pcs. | Length | Body, Mounts | Flaps | SAT | Holes Dbld. | Tuning Holes | Additional Data | Ill. Source |
|---|---|---|---|---|---|---|---|---|---|---|---|---|
| 11. | 14 brass | New York City: late J. Marx | | | 54.15 | boxw, ivory | flat ro | SATK | 3 dbl. | | Keys mtd. in blocks. Tuning jt in upper jt. | |
| 12. | 14 brass | New York City: late J. Marx | | | 55.0 | boxw, ivory | dome | SATK | 3 dbl. | | Keys mtd. in knobs & blocks. | |
| 13. | 14 nickel silv | Scarsdale: D & R Rosenbaum | | | 54.2 | boxw, ivory | dome | SATK | 3 dbl. | 2 th | Keys mtd. in blocks. | |
| 14. | 15 silver | Munich Stadtmuseum 41-316 | | | 55.3 | ebony, ivory | dome | SATK | 3 dbl.[3] | | Keys mtd. in blocks.[1] | LOM 229 |

### ENGLISH HORNS

| Young No. | No. Keys and Metal | City, Owner, No. | Pitch | No. Pcs. | Length | Body, Mounts | Flaps | SAT | Holes Dbld. | Tuning Holes | Additional Data | Ill. Source |
|---|---|---|---|---|---|---|---|---|---|---|---|---|
| 1. | 10 brass | Boston: MFA 17.1919, B. 144 | | | 78.8 | boxw, ivory | dome | SATK | 3 dbl. | | Keys mtd. in blocks. Angular form. | Ill. Bessaraboff, pl IV |
| 2. | 10 brass | Leningrad 1118 | | | 77.0 | | | | 3 dbl. | | | |
| 3. | 12 | Prague 472 | | | | | | | | | | |
| 4. | 12 brass | Halle MS 432 | | | 77.5 | boxw, ivory | | | | | Angular form. | |

### CLARINETS

| Young No. | No. Keys and Metal | City, Owner, No. | Pitch | No. Pcs. | Length | Body, Mounts | Flaps | SAT | Holes Dbld. | Tuning Holes | Additional Data | Ill. Source |
|---|---|---|---|---|---|---|---|---|---|---|---|---|
| 1. | 5 brass | Cambridge: N. Shackleton | E♭ | | 48.25 | boxw, horn | CPs ro | | | | Brass tuning slide connecting barrel and body. | |
| 2. | 13 brass | Leningrad 1360 | | | 51.4 | boxw, ivory | CPs dome | | | | Keys mtd. in blocks.[2] Mthpc missing. | |

### BASSET HORN

| Young No. | No. Keys and Metal | City, Owner, No. | Pitch | No. Pcs. | Length | Body, Mounts | Flaps | SAT | Holes Dbld. | Tuning Holes | Additional Data | Ill. Source |
|---|---|---|---|---|---|---|---|---|---|---|---|---|
| 1. | | Loup Sale no. 188, per Langwill. | | | | | | | | | | |

### BASSOONS

| Young No. | No. Keys and Metal | City, Owner, No. | Pitch | No. Pcs. | Length | Body, Mounts | Flaps | SAT | Holes Dbld. | Tuning Holes | Additional Data | Ill. Source |
|---|---|---|---|---|---|---|---|---|---|---|---|---|
| 1. | 5 | Prague, per W Jansen | | | | | | | | | | |
| 2. | 9 | Prague (seen 1964) | | | | | | | | | | |
| 3. | 9 | Biebrich: Heckel Museum | | | | | | | | | | |
| 4. | 9 | Biebrich: Heckel Museum | | | | | | | | | | |
| 5. | 9 | Nazareth, Pa. | | | | | | | | | | |
| 6. | 9 brass | Binningen, Schweiz.: E.W. Buser | | | 128.0 | maple, brass | | | | | Keys recessed into wood body. | |
| 7. | 9 brass | Leningrad 219 | | | 128.7 | maple, brass | | | | | | |
| 8. | 9 brass | Stuttgart: G. Hase | | | | | | | | | | |
| 9. | 10 brass | Zurich: W Burger | | | 126.0 | maple, brass | | | | | Keys recessed into wood body with metal channel. | |
| 10. | 10 | Milan: Prof. E Muccetti | | | | | | | | | | |
| 11. | 10 | Celle: H Moeck | | | | | | | | | | |
| 12. | 11 brass | Zurich: W Burger | | | 125.6 | maple, brass | | | | | Keys mounted in saddles. | |
| 13. | 11 | xBerlin 1218 | | | | | ro | | | | Keys recessed into wood. | |
| 14. | 11 brass | Edinburgh: L.G. Langwill | | | | | | | | | | |
| 15. | 11 brass | Salzburg 15/13 | | | 127.5 | maple, brass | ro | | | | Keys recessed into wood. | |

[1] b, c', c♯', 2Xe♭', 2Xf', f♯', g♯', b♭' w 2 touches, b'-c" trill, c"-d" trill, 8ve key.

[2] Or recessed into body.

| Young No. | No. Keys and Metal | City, Owner, No. | Pitch | No. Pcs. | Length | Body, Mounts | Flaps | SAT | Holes Dbld. | Tuning Holes | Additional Data | Ill. Source |
|---|---|---|---|---|---|---|---|---|---|---|---|---|
| 16. | 15 brass | Nieuw Loosdrecht: W Jansen | | | | | dome | | | | Keys recessed into wood. Wing keys telescope. Flared wooden bell. | |

**CONTRABASSOON**

| | | | | | | | | | | | | |
|---|---|---|---|---|---|---|---|---|---|---|---|---|
| 1. | 5 | Prague 376E | | | 166.6 | | | | | | | |
| 2. | 5 brass | Copenhagen E.105 | | | 167.0 | maple, brass | ro | SATK | | | Keys in saddles. Top hairpin & crook of brass. Upright bell. | LOM 259 |
| 3. | 6 brass | Vienna: G Stradner | | | 167.5 | | ro | | | | Crook missing. | |
| 4. | 6 brass | Nürnberg MI 129 | | | 168.6 | dk maple, brass | ro | | | | Crook missing. | |

# LEMPP                                                              **LEMPP**

## OBOES

| | | | | | | | | | | | | |
|---|---|---|---|---|---|---|---|---|---|---|---|---|
| 1. | 2 | Prague 21E (seen in 1964) | | | | | | | | | | |
| 2. | 2 brass | Brussels 963 | | | 57.4 | boxw, unmtd | | SATK | 3 dbl. | | 2 upper jts (no. 1 22.5; no. 2 22.0) | |
| 3. | 2 brass | Linz 116 | | | 54.5 | boxw, unmtd | | | 3 dbl. | | | |
| 4. | 2 brass | Munich: Dr. M Schmid | | | 55.7 | boxw, ivory | sq-cors | | 3 dbl. | | The eb key is on the *left* side! Only instance known to the author. | |

## TENOR OBOE

| | | | | | | | | | | | | |
|---|---|---|---|---|---|---|---|---|---|---|---|---|
| 1. | 2 brass | Vienna 153 | | | 82.3 | boxw, unmtd | trap eb, sq-cors C | SATW | | | Straight form, bulb bell. Keys in *round* knobs. | |

## ENGLISH HORN

| | | | | | | | | | | | | |
|---|---|---|---|---|---|---|---|---|---|---|---|---|
| 1. | 2 brass | Zell-Riedichen: P Hailperin | | | 77.2 | black leath on box? horn | | SATW C, 3 dbl. SATK Eb | | | Curved form, bulb bell. | |

## BASS CLARINET

| | | | | | | | | | | | | |
|---|---|---|---|---|---|---|---|---|---|---|---|---|
| 1. | 7 brass | Linz 147 | | | 57.0 | box/maple? horn | flat sq | | | | Keys mounted in blocks & saddles. Curved-outward brass bell. Bore 2.0 Bassoon shape. | |

## BASSOONS

| | | | | | | | | | | | | |
|---|---|---|---|---|---|---|---|---|---|---|---|---|
| 1. | 8 brass | New Haven: Yale 442 | | | 122.24 | maple, brass | U-shape | | | | Bb key missing. D, Eb, F, G♯, F♯, 2 wing. | |
| 2. | | Vienna Techn Museum (seen 1964) | | | | | | | | | | |

| Young No. | No. Keys and Metal | City, Owner, No. | Pitch | No. Pcs. | Length | Body, Mounts Flaps | SAT | Holes Dbld. | Tuning Holes | Additional Data | Ill. Source |
|---|---|---|---|---|---|---|---|---|---|---|---|
| **LEMPP** *(cont.)* | | | | | | | | | | | **LEMPP** *(cont.)* |
| CONTRABASSOONS | | | | | | | | | | | |
| 1. | 5 brass | Brussels 1002 | | | 156.7 | maple, brass | | | | Originally 11 pcs, but missing uppermost 3 = 8 pcs now.[1] | |
| 2. | 5 brass | Linz 140 | | | 159.0 | maple, brass, horn | | | | Originally 10 pcs, but missing crook = 9 now. | |
| **LIEBAV** | | | | | | | | | | | **LIEBAV** |
| FLUTE | | | | | | | | | | | |
| 1. | 1 silver | Bonn BH (Zimmermann 39) | | | 65.0 | boxw, ivory | | | | 3 upper joints. | |
| CHALUMEAUX | | | | | | | | | | | |
| 1. | 2 brass | Stockholm 139 | C | | 33.0 | boxw | | 7 dbl. | | Bore 1.18 (at bottom 1.19) | Ill. Grove 6, vol. 4, p 111 |
| 2. | 2 brass | Stockholm 143 (now missing) | | | | | | | | | |
| **LINDNER**[2] | | | | | | | | | | | **LINDNER** |
| FLUTES | | | | | | | | | | | |
| 1. | 6 brass | Leipzig 3144 | C | 4 pc | 64.1 | boxw, ivory flat ro | | | | Stamp: "L. LINDNER / AUGSBURG". All keys mounted in integral blocks. | |
| 2. | 6 | Nürnberg MIR | | | | | | | | | |
| 3. | 7 silver | Zurich: Willi Burger | C | 4 pc | 69.5 | ebony, unmtd flat ro | | | | Stamp: L. LINTNER star & crown. All keys mounted in integral blocks. | |
| 4. | 7 | exOffenbach am Main | | | | | | | | | |
| 5. | 9 silver | Washington: DCM 972 | C | | 69.1 | ebony, silver | | | | Stamp: "L. LINTNER / AUGSBURG". | |
| 6. | | Kaiserlautern | | | | | | | | | |
| 7. | | Kaiserlautern | | | | | | | | | |
| 8. | | Bern 25088 | | | | | | | | | |
| TENOR OBOES | | | | | | | | | | | |
| 1. | 3 brass | Munich: BNM Mu 143 | F | | 77.8 | plum? unmtd trap eb', ro c' | | 3&4 | | Stamp: "LINDNER / o". Flared bell. | |
| 2. | 3 brass | Munich: BNM Mu 148 | F | | 75.0 | plum? unmtd trap eb', ro c' | | 3&4 | | Stamp: "LINDNER / L". Bulb bell. | |
| 3. | 3 brass | Paris C. 486 | | | | | | | | | |

[1] Missing are the small inverse boot, its extension, and crook.

[2] Although Langwill lists only L. Lindner (sic) of Augsburg (1766-1840) and his presumed father, Johann Georg Lintner, who made only brasses, it would appear certain that there was an early (early 18C) Lindner, who made the tenor oboes and the well-known early clarinet on the following page. I have been unable to learn details of Mr. Clemencic's Lindner bassoon, which surely is also by this earlier Lindner.

**LINDNER** *(cont.)*     **LINDNER** *(cont.)*

**TENOR OBOES** *(cont.)*

| Young No. | No. Keys and Metal | City, Owner, No. | Pitch | No. Pcs. | Length | Body, Mounts | Flaps | SAT | Holes Dbld. | Tuning Holes | Additional Data | Ill. Source |
|---|---|---|---|---|---|---|---|---|---|---|---|---|
| 4. | 3 | Berlin 2961 | | | 83.5 | maple, horn | | | 3&4 | | Stamp: "LINDNER" | |
| 5. | 3 | xBerlin 292 "ALTOBOE" | g | | 78.0 | boxw | trap eb', ro c' | | 3&4 | | Stamp: "LINDNER". Flared bell.[1] | Ill. Sachs, taf 26 |
| 6. | | Royal Military Exhib. No. 207 | | | | | | | | | | |

**BASSOON**

| | | | | | | | | | | | | |
|---|---|---|---|---|---|---|---|---|---|---|---|---|
| 1. | 4 | Vienna: R. Clemencic | | | | | | | | | | |

**WATCHMAN'S HORN**

| | | | | | | | | | | | | |
|---|---|---|---|---|---|---|---|---|---|---|---|---|
| 1. | | Leipzig 1553 | | | | | | | | | | |

**CLARINET**

| | | | | | | | | | | | | |
|---|---|---|---|---|---|---|---|---|---|---|---|---|
| 1. | 3 brass | Brussels 913 | A | 3 pc | 72.0 | red-brown wood, unmtd | sq[2] | SATW | | | Stamp: "LINDNER". Bore 1.35-1.4. 3 pc: mthpc-bbl, main, bell. | Ill. Mahillon, II |

# D. LOT     **D. LOT**

**FLUTES**

| Young No. | No. Keys and Metal | City, Owner, No. | Pitch | No. Pcs. | Length | Body, Mounts | Flaps | SAT | Holes Dbld. | Tuning Holes | Additional Data | Ill. Source |
|---|---|---|---|---|---|---|---|---|---|---|---|---|
| 1. | 1 brass | Leipzig 3266 | | 4 pcs | --- | boxw, horn | | | | | Incomplete. Head jt and upper jt lost in WW2 | |
| 2. | 1 brass | Leningrad 462 | | 4 pcs | 61.0 | boxw, horn | | | | | | |
| 3. | | Prague 1362E | | | | | | | | | Keller says "D. LOTT" | |

**OBOES**

| | | | | | | | | | | | | |
|---|---|---|---|---|---|---|---|---|---|---|---|---|
| 1. | 3 | xBerlin 2943 | | | 58.5 | boxw, ivory | | | | | Sachs says "D. LOTT". More keys added later. | |
| 2. | 3 | xBerlin 2946 | | | 58.0 | boxw | | | | | Sachs says "D. LOT" | |
| 3. | | Hague 81 | | | | | | | | | | |
| 4. | | Leipzig 1319 | | | | | | | | | | |

**BASSOONS**

| | | | | | | | | | | | | |
|---|---|---|---|---|---|---|---|---|---|---|---|---|
| 1. | 4 brass | Brussels 2322 | | | | maple, brass | (X) | SATW | | | Bb&D in blocks, F & G# in saddles. F touch replacement. Touches wide, flat | |

---

[1] Sachs calls Berlin 292 an 'altoboe in g,' making the curious remark that such instruments differ from the English horn because of its bulb bell. Bierdimpfl in 1883 called the two Munich specimens by the same term, 'altoboe,' even though one of them now has (did it then?) a bulb bell and both are in f. Sachs called Berlin 2961 an oboe da caccia.

[2] But 3rd key (D) shape.

## G. LOT[1]

**FLUTES**

| | | | | | | | | | | | |
|---|---|---|---|---|---|---|---|---|---|---|---|
| 1. | | Munich: BNM 29[2] | | | 60.5 | | | | | | |
| 2. | | Munich: BNM 33.[2] | | | 60.5 | | | | | | |
| 3. | 1 | xBerlin 2680 | B | | 64.0 | boxw, ivory | | | | | |

**GALOUBET**

| | | | | | | | | | | | |
|---|---|---|---|---|---|---|---|---|---|---|---|
| 1. | | Paris C. 363 | | | | palisander, ivory | | | | | |

**FLAGEOLET**

| | | | | | | | | | | | |
|---|---|---|---|---|---|---|---|---|---|---|---|
| 1. | | Sax sale, no. 11, per Langwill | | | | | | | | | |

## M. LOT

**FLUTES**

| | | | | | | | | | | | |
|---|---|---|---|---|---|---|---|---|---|---|---|
| 1. | 1 brass | Washington: DCM 804 | C | 4 pc | 61.8 | boxw, horn | sq | SATW | | | 1 upper jt. |
| 2. | 1 brass | Brussels 3767 | D? | 4 pc | 52.7 | boxw, unmtd | | SATW | | | |
| 3. | 2 | Leningrad 469 | | 4 pc | 67.0 | rosew, horn | | | | | Wooden end cap on head joint. |
| 4. | | Paris 1104 | | | 61.8 | boxw, horn | | | | | |
| 5. | | Hague 1429 | | | | | | | | | |

**OBOES**

| | | | | | | | | | | | |
|---|---|---|---|---|---|---|---|---|---|---|---|
| 1. | 2 brass | Brussels 1980 | | | 56.7 | | sq-cors | SATW | 3&4 dbl. | 2 th. | Concave bell. | |
| 2. | 2 | xBerlin 2947 | | | 60.75 | boxw | | | | | | Ill. Sachs catalogue, taf 26 |

**TENOR OBOES**

| | | | | | | | | | | | |
|---|---|---|---|---|---|---|---|---|---|---|---|
| 1. | 3 brass | London: RCM 76 | | | 81.0 | boxw, ivory | ro C, sq e♭. | | 3&4 dbl. | | Straight form. Bulb bell. | |
| 2. | 3 brass | xBerlin 2960 | | | 77.5 | boxw, brass | | | 3&4 dbl. | | Straight form. Keys in blocks & knobs. | |
| 3. | 6 or more? | Halsingborg 120 | | | | | ro C | | 3&4 dbl. | | Straight form. Bulb bell. | Ill. Halsingborg catalogue, pl X |

**CLARINET**

| | | | | | | | | | | | |
|---|---|---|---|---|---|---|---|---|---|---|---|
| 1. | 4 brass | xBerlin 2878 | B♭ | | 61.5 | | | | | | |

**FAGOTTINI**

| | | | | | | | | | | | |
|---|---|---|---|---|---|---|---|---|---|---|---|
| 1. | 3 brass | London: RCM | C | | | | | | | | |
| 2. | 5 brass | Oxford: Bate 334 | C | | 63.6 | maple, brass | (V) | | | | Keys in saddles. Crook not original. | EAMI 596-597 |

---

[1] The ubiquitous Gilles Lot is best known perhaps because his 'basse tube' was mentioned in the Paris newspaper *L'Avant-Coureur* of May 11, 1972, with the exasperating but fascinating result that all subsequent accounts of the history of the early bass clarinet have had to refer to (or defer to) the otherwise negligible G. Lot and his presumed "first."

[2] Jane Bowers has reported in her excellent study of the early 18th century flute published in AMIS *Journal* 3, that Dr. Georg Himmelheber, Director of the Bayerisches Nationalmuseum, has said that these two flutes are not by *Gilles* Lot but by *Thomas* Lot, and are presumably therefore Nos. Mu 172 and Mu 176 reported under that maker (Young nos. 12 and 13).

| | | | | | | | | | | | |
|---|---|---|---|---|---|---|---|---|---|---|---|
| **M. LOT** *(cont.)* | | | | | | | | | | | **M. LOT** *(cont.)* |

## BASSOON

| | | | | | | | | | | | |
|---|---|---|---|---|---|---|---|---|---|---|---|
| 1. | 4 | Rothenburg ob Tauber | | | | | | | | | |

# T. LOT

T. LOT

## RECORDERS

| | | | | | | | | | | | |
|---|---|---|---|---|---|---|---|---|---|---|---|
| 1. | 0 keys | Leningrad 401 | (alto) | | 50.0 | boxw, unmtd | | | | 3 fingerholes, only! | |

## PICCOLO IN C

| | | | | | | | | | | | |
|---|---|---|---|---|---|---|---|---|---|---|---|
| 1. | 1 brass | Washington: DCM 667 | | | 33.0 | | sq | | | | |

## FLUTES

| Young No. | No. Keys and Metal | City, Owner, No. | Pitch | No. Pcs. | Length | Body, Mounts Flaps | SAT | Additional Data | Ill. Source |
|---|---|---|---|---|---|---|---|---|---|
| 1. | 1 silver | Washington: DCM 615 | D | 4 pc | 63.6 | boxw, ivory sq(F) | | | Ill. AMIS 3, fig 38 |
| 2. | 1 silver | Washington: DCM 984 | E♭ | 4 pc | 52.7 | boxw, ivory sq(F) | | | |
| 3. | 1 silver | Dorking: Lady Jeans | | 4 pc | 64.0 | boxw, ivory sq | | 3 upper joints. | Ill. GS exhib' 68, ill. 46 |
| 4. | 1 silver | Boston: MFA 41 | C | 4 pc | 64.5 | boxw, ivory sq | SATW | Elliptical embouchure. *Square* touch! | |
| 5. | 1 | Regensburg: Museum der Stadt | | | | | | | |
| 6. | 1 silver | Brussels 2379 | C | 4 pc | 61.9 | ivory, black horn sq | | 2 upper joints. | Ill. Bragard-deHen |
| 7. | | York: York Castle Museum | | | | | | | |
| 8. | 1 | Hague | | 4 pc | | wood, ivory | | | Ill. AMIS 3, fig 36 |
| 9. | 1 silver | Paris C.1389, E.1517 | | 4 pc | 64.3 | boxw, unmtd sq | SATW | Cap missing. 1 upper joint. No register. | |
| 10. | 1 gold | London: Horniman | C | 4 pc | | olive, ivory sq | | 5 upper joints. | Ill. JJ-GT-BR, pl 37 |
| 11. | 1 silver | London: Horniman Museum 263 | C | 4 pc | | tulip, ivory sq [1] | | 5 upper joints. | Ill. AMIS 3, fig 34 |
| 12. | 1 silver | Munich: BNM Mu 172& Mu 293 | C | 4 pc | 67.5 | tulip? ivory sq | SATK | Head cap missing. 5 upper joints. | Ill. AMIS 3, fig 35. LOM 68 |
| 13. | 1 silver | Munich: BNM Mu 176& Mu 293 | C | 4 pc | ? | tulip? ivory | SATK | Head cap missing. 5 upper joints. Ft. joint missing. | LOM 68 |
| 14. | 1 silver | Copenhagen E. 102 | C | | 63.3 | ivory, unmtd | SATK | | |
| 15. | 1 | Paris: Conserv. Natl. Arts & Met. | G | 4 pc | | wood, ivory | | | Ill. AMIS 3, fig 37 |
| 16. | 4 | Bologna 1836 | | | | rosew, ivory | | | |
| 17. | | Bricqueville Collection | | | | | | | |
| 18. | | Halsingborg 105, now Stockholm | | | | | | | |

[1] Well known instance of much more ornate key on more elegant flute, presumably intended for aristocratic student, while companion flute has rather utilitarian key on unpretentious flute, intended for teacher.

|---|---|---|---|---|---|---|---|---|---|---|---|

## T. LOT *(cont.)*

### BASS FLUTES

| | | | | | | | | | | | |
|---|---|---|---|---|---|---|---|---|---|---|---|
| 1. | 5 brass | Leningrad 473 | C | 6 pc | 102.5 | maple? ivory sq e♭[1] | SATW | | | U-bend head jt. | Lom 72 |
| 2. | 5 brass | Brussels 449 | C | 6 pc | 126.0 | cherry? plum? sq e b.[1] ivory | SATW | | | U-bend head jt. | Ill. Mahillon, Vol. ! |
| 3. | | Paris: Musee des Arts & Metiers[2] | | | | | | | | | |

### OBOES

| | | | | | | | | | | | |
|---|---|---|---|---|---|---|---|---|---|---|---|
| 1. | 2 silver | xBerlin 2948 | | | 59.5 | boxw | | | | | |
| 2. | 2 silver | Oxford: Bate 24 | | | 60.0 | boxw, ivory | sq | 2 th. | | | Ill. Bate Oboe, pl 3 |
| 3. | 2 | Leningrad 512 | | | 60.1 | boxw, horn | | 3&4 dbl. | | | |
| 4. | | Basel: Michel Piguet | | | | | | | | | |
| 5. | bell only | London: Horniman | | | | | | bell only | | | |
| 6. | 1 jt only | Bochum: Grumbt Collection 5 | | | | | | 1 joint only. | | | |

### TENOR OBOE

| | | | | | | | | | | | |
|---|---|---|---|---|---|---|---|---|---|---|---|
| 1. | 3 brass | Leningrad 524 | | | 80.0 | boxw, ivory | sq | SATW | 3 dbl. | | Straight form, flared bell. | LOM 94 |
| 2. | 3 brass | Leningrad ?[3] | | | 80.0 | boxw, ivory | sq | SATW | 3 dbl. | | Straight form, flared bell. | |

# MAYRHOFER

| BASSET HORNS | | | BODY DETAILS | | SAT | | | Est. length air column | main joint only | av.[4] bore | KEY DETAILS |
|---|---|---|---|---|---|---|---|---|---|---|---|
| 1. 6 brass | Nürnberg MI 133[5] | | brown leath cov. boxw sickle form | 5 pc: (mthpc)[6], bbl, main jt, kasten, (bell) | SATW | 4 dbl | leath. patched[7] Oct. X-section | 113.0 | 51.0 | 1.28 | F has swallowtail touch. C, E, F, G♯, A', speaker. CPs trap C, rectangle E, rest sq-cors. |
| 2. 6 brass[8] | Bonn BH (Zimmermann 154) | | brown leath cov. boxw sickle form | 5 pc: (mthpc)[6], (bbl), main jt kasten, (bell) | | 4 dbl | leath. patched[7] Oct. X-section | ? | 52.4 | 1.31 | F has swallowtail touch. C, E, F, G♯, A', speaker[8]. CPs trap-cors F, sq-cors A' & speaker[9] |
| 3. 7 brass | Passau Oberhausmuseum[10] | | brown leath cov. boxw sickle form | 5 pc: (mthpc)[6], (bbl), main jt, kasten, bell | SATW (F SATK) | 4 dbl | Oct. X-section | 114.0 | 54.4 | 1.21 | F has swallowtail touch. C, E, F, F♯, G♯, A', speaker. CPs all sq-cors. |

### BASS CLARINET

| | | | | | | | | | | | |
|---|---|---|---|---|---|---|---|---|---|---|---|
| 1. 7 brass | Munich Stadtmuseum 52-50[11] | | brown leath cov boxw sickle form | 6 pc: (mthpc), (bbl), upper jt, lower jt, loop, (bell) | SATW | 0 dbl | Oct. X-section | 177.1 | (two) 96.2 | 1.63 | F has swallowtail touch. C, E, F, F♯, G♯, A', speaker. CPs trap-cors C, rest all sq-cors. See AMIS J, VII, p 36. |

---

[1] Other keys hinged from end.

[2] According to J. Bowers' dissertation, *The French Flute School from 1700 to 1760,* University of California at Berkeley, 1977.

[3] I examined an *identical* pair in June 1978. This second one is not listed by Blagodatov.

[4] An average of opposing measurements if the bore has become elliptical.

[5] LOM 185.

[6] Pieces in parentheses are missing, although in most cases are replaced.

[7] In such a way to indicate that keys were mounted there at one time, perhaps only experimentally before the instrument left the makers' workshop.

[8] The Oberhausmuseum instrument has its G♯ and F♯ on the *left* side of the instrument, playable only with the left hand lowermost.

[9] C and E flaps are square, look as though they might be replacements.

[10] Formerly Hamburg MHG 1927.159.

[11] LOM 244.

**MAYRHOFER** *(cont.)*

Nürnberg basset horn swallowtail

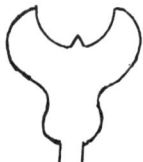

Nürnberg basset horn closed key touches

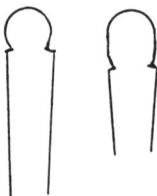

Tracing of bass clarinet swallowtail (reduced size)

**MAYRHOFER** *(cont.)*

bass clarinet's basset key touch

# MEACHAM (ALL)

## J. MEACHAM, JR., HARTFORD

| | | | | | | | | | | | | |
|---|---|---|---|---|---|---|---|---|---|---|---|---|
| 1. Oboe | 2 brass | Letchworth N.Y. Park Museum | C | | 57.7 | boxw, ivory | ro | | | | | Ill. GSJ XXX, Pl. V; AMIS V-VI, fig. 1. |
| 1. Bassoon | 4 brass | Madison, Wisc.: R. Lottridge | | | 121.0 | maple, brass | spade[1] | | | | | Ill. AMIS V-VI, Fig. 2. ill. this book, Pl. 00 |

## J. MEACHAM, ALBANY

| | | | | | | | | | | | | |
|---|---|---|---|---|---|---|---|---|---|---|---|---|
| 1. Flute | 1 brass | New Haven: Yale 432 | | 4 | 50.4 | boxw, ivory | sq | SATK | | | | Ill. AMIS V-VI, fig. 3. |
| 1. Clarinet | 5 brass | Delmar, N.Y.: C. Allanson | C | | | | | | | | | Ill. AMIS V-VI, fig. 4. |

## MEACHAM, ALBANY

| | | | | | | | | | | | | |
|---|---|---|---|---|---|---|---|---|---|---|---|---|
| 1. Bassoon | 4 brass | New York: MMA 89.4.884 | | | 121.4 | maple, brass | | SATW | | | | |
| 1. Flute | 1 silver | Washington: loan to Smithsonion | C | | 59.7 | boxw | ro | | | | Pewter plug-type flap, Register in foot jt. | |
| 1. Clarinet | | Iowa City: H. Voxman | | 6 | | boxw, ivory | sq | | | | | |

## J. & H. MEACHAM, ALBANY

| | | | | | | | | | | | | |
|---|---|---|---|---|---|---|---|---|---|---|---|---|
| 1. Flute | 4 brass | Concord Antiquarian Society | C | | 59.1 | boxw, ivory | | | | | | |
| 2. Flute | 1 silver | Washington: DCM 1154 | C | 4 | 60.5 | boxw, ivory | | | | | Unicorn head below stamp! | Ill. AMIS V-VI, fig. 5. |
| 3. Flute | 1 silver | Milwaukee: F. Benkovic | | | | boxw, ivory | | | | | | |
| 4. Flute | 1 brass | Canandaigua, N.Y., Ontario County Hist. Soc. | | | | boxw, ivory | | | | | | |

[1] Robert Eliason has labelled this distinctive flap shape (seen on several makers ca. 1800-1820 who worked in Hartford, Conn.) the "Hartford spade." It is illustrated in a drawing on the Catlin page.

PLATES

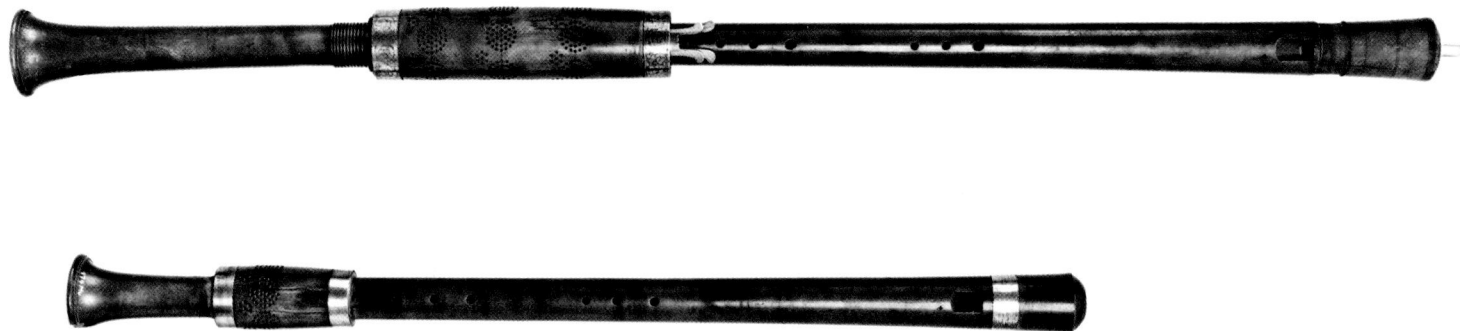

Plate I: Two bass recorders by Hans Rauch von Schratt (...1535...) from the Bayerisches Nationalmuseum, Munich. Top: Great bass, No. Mu 180 Bottom: Quintbass, No. 174. Reproduced with the kind permission of Dr. Georg Himmelheber, Direktor.

Plate II: Three details of the instruments in Plate I. Same credit. In the left close-up, note the two trefoils below the fipple hole.

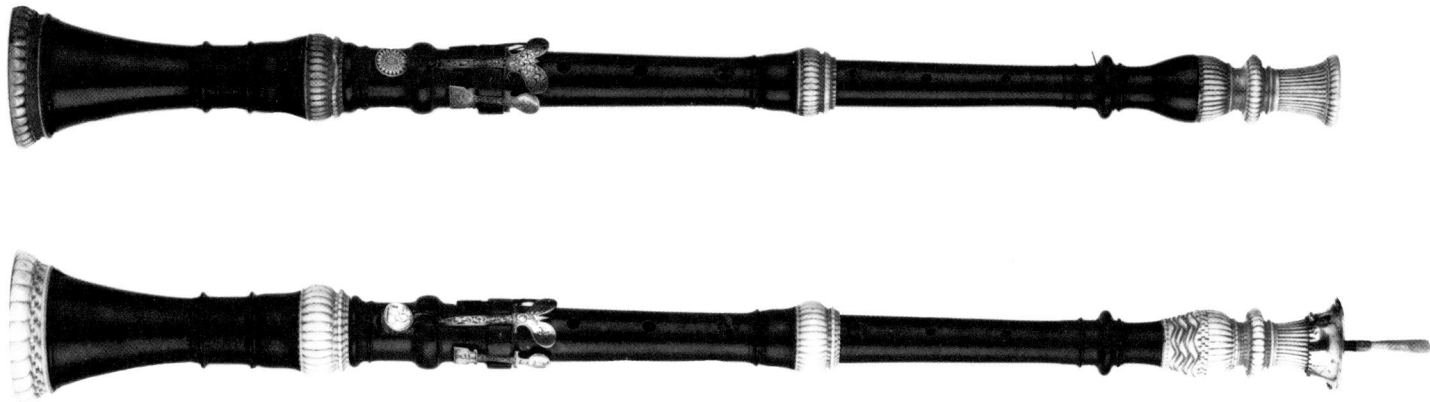

Plate III: Two oboes by Hendrik Richters from the Gemeente Museum, The Hague. Top: No. Ea 7-x1952. Bottom: No. Ea 584-1933. Reproduced with the kind permission of Dr. C.C.J. von Gleich, Director of the Music Department.

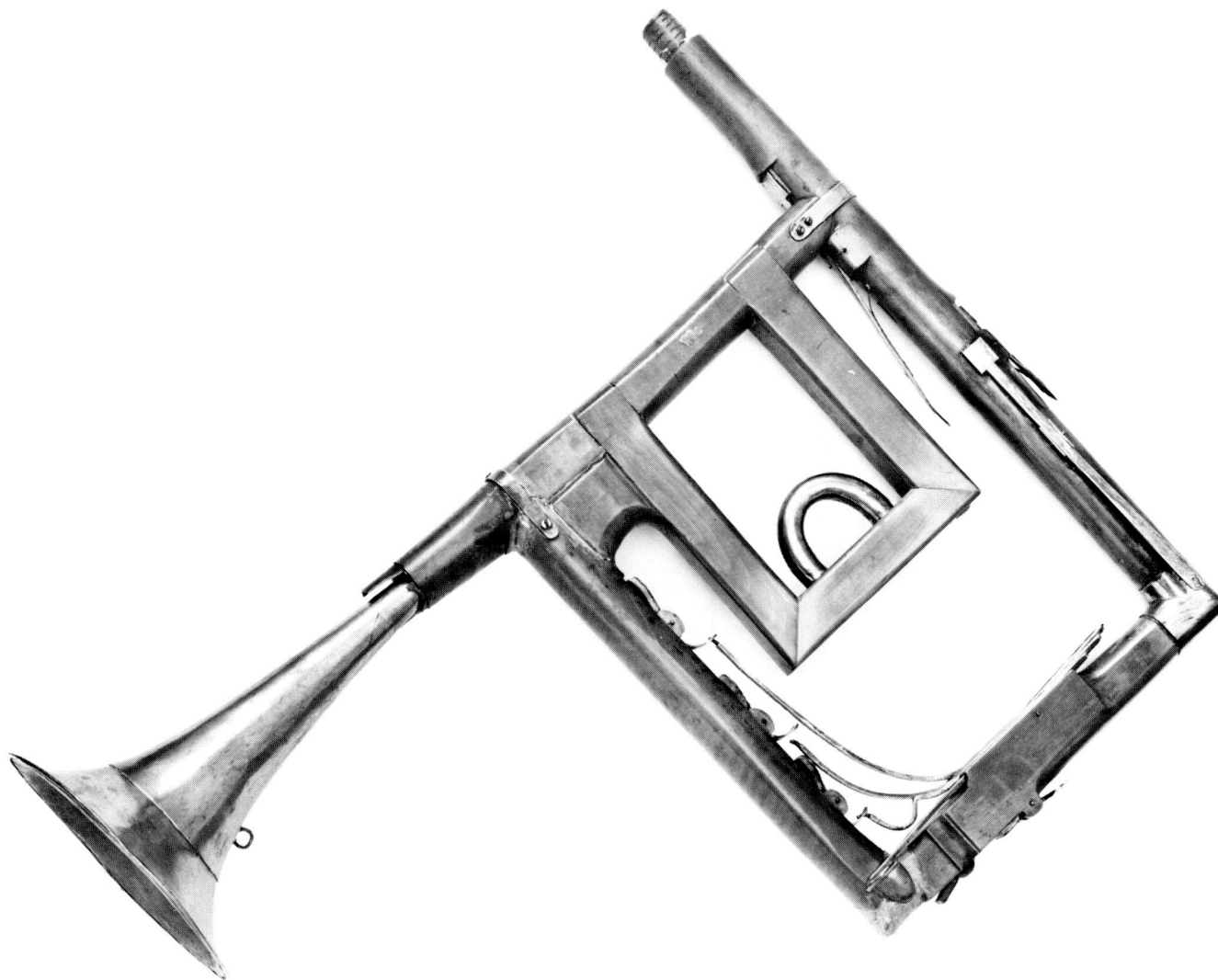

Plate IV (also frontispiece): Basset horn, by Johann Georg Eisen-
menger, Mannheim, No. Mu. 128, Bayerisches Nationalmuseum, Munich. Reproduced with the kind permission of Dr. Georg Himmelheber, Direktor.

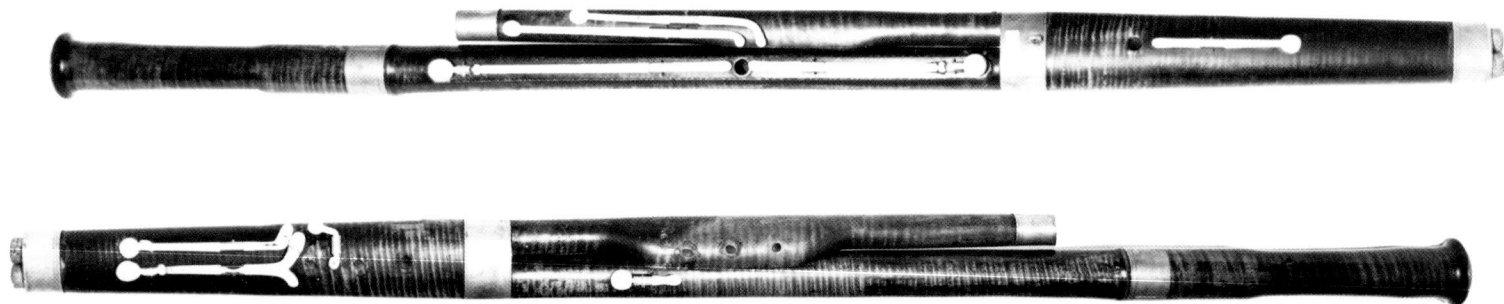

Ea 61-x-1952

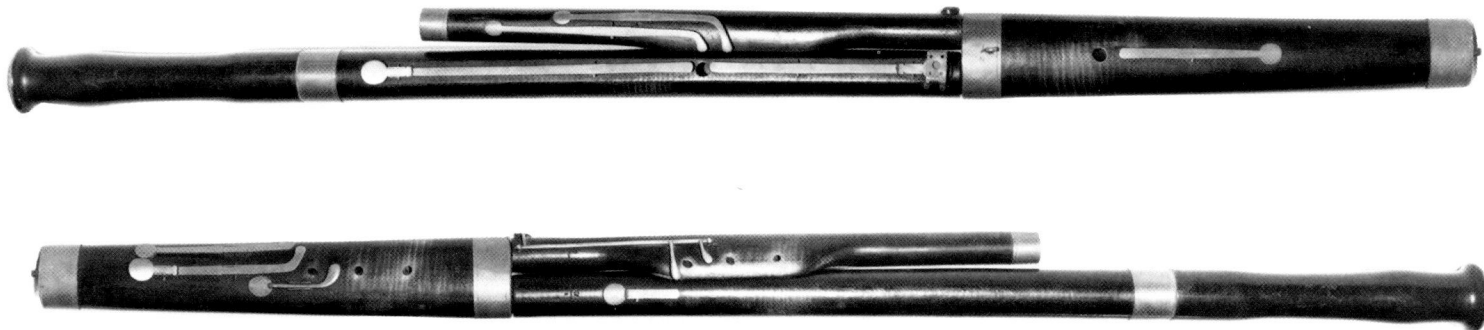

Ea 148-1950

Plate V: Four bassoons by Heinrich Grenser, Dresden, from the Gemeente Museum, The Hague. Each instrument is pictured with the front view on the top and rear view on the bottom. Reproduced with the kind permission of Dr. C.C.J. von Gleich, Director of the Music Department.

Ea 418-1933

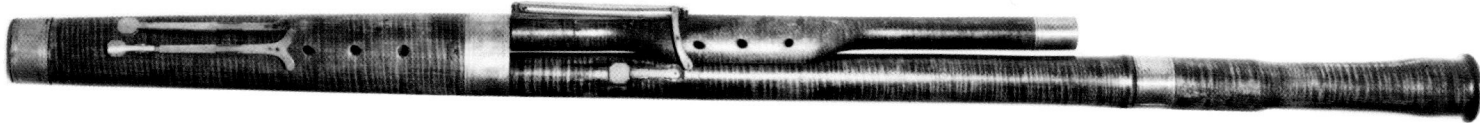

Ea 570-1933

Plate V *(cont.)*

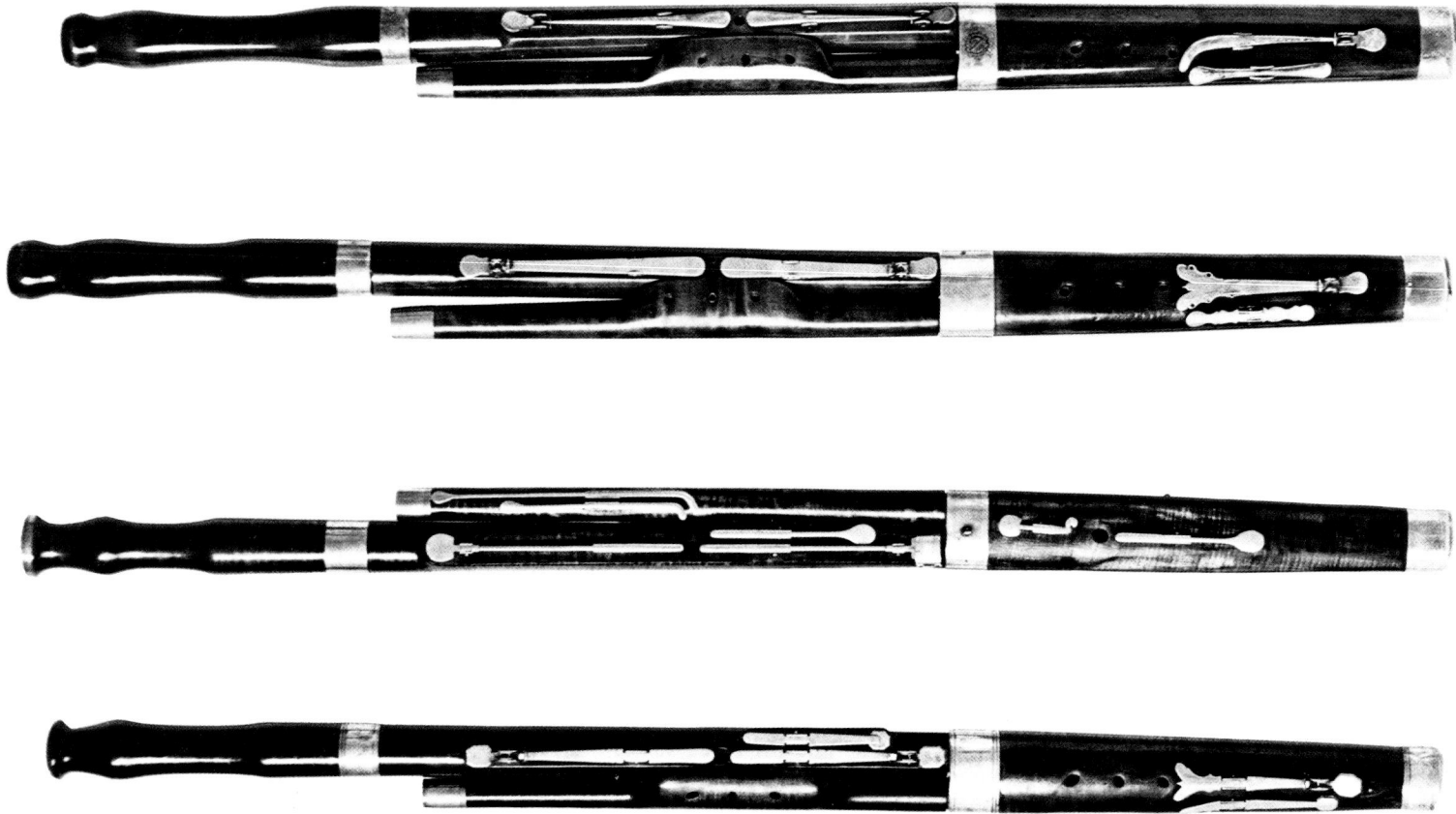

Plate VI: Four bassoons from the collection of William Waterhouse, London. The makers are (1) F.G.A. Kirst, (2) Kaspar Tauber, Vienna, (3) Thomas Stanesby, Sr., except wing joint by Stanesby, Jr. and (4) Stanesby, Jr., dated 1747. Three of the bass joints are intentionally reversed to show keys. This photograph is reproduced with the kind permission of Mr. Waterhouse and was made by John Cuerden, Grays, Essex, who retains its copyright and to whom the thanks of the author are expressed.

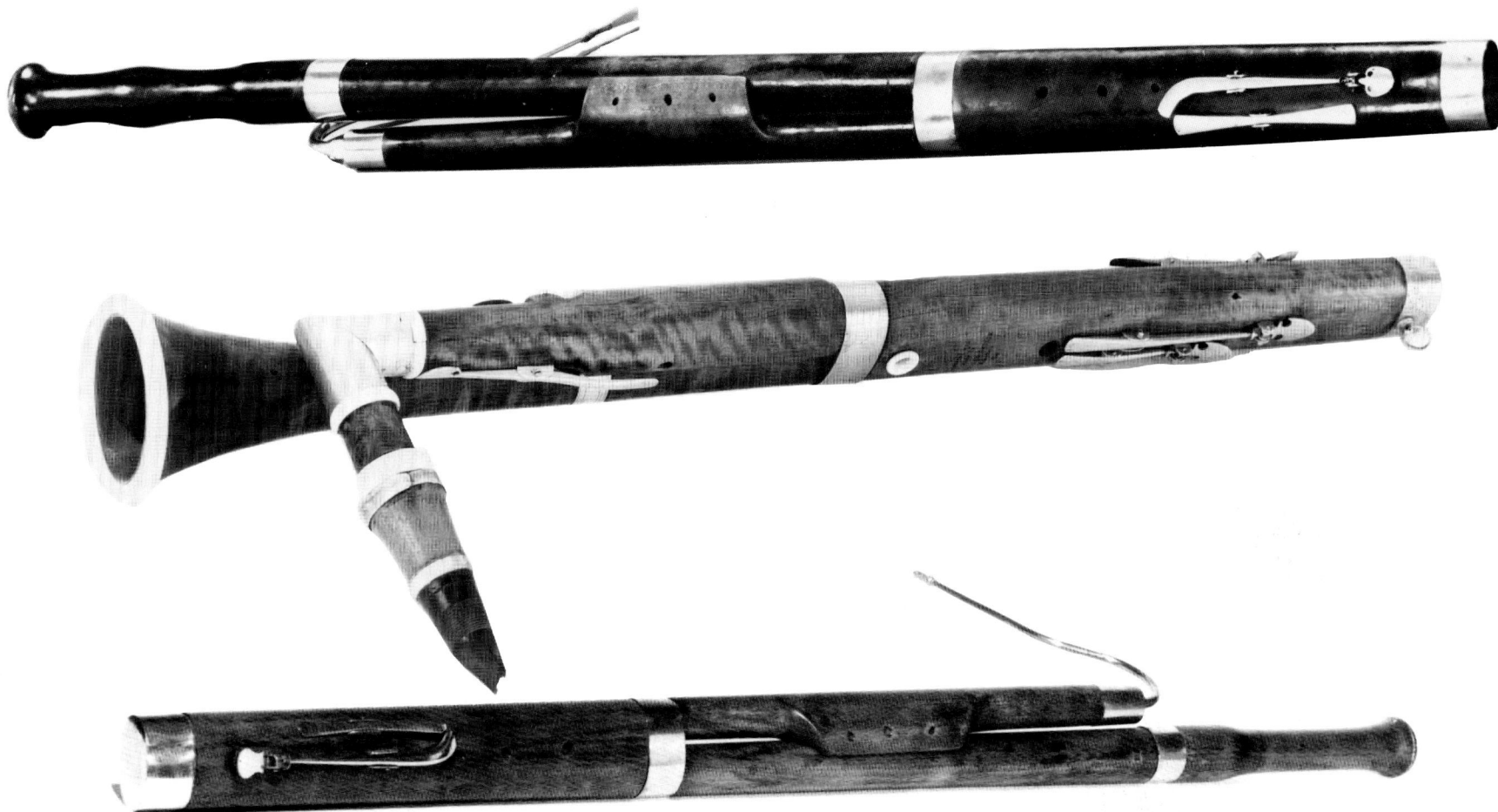

Plate VII: Three early American instruments, ca. 1810. Top: bassoon, John Meacham, Jr., Hartford, from the Collection of Prof. Richard Lottridge, Madison, Wisconsin, and used with his permission. 4 brass keys. Middle: bass clarinet, "Invented and Made by George Catlin, Hartford, Con." from the Henry Ford Museum, Dearborn, Michigan, No. 77.68.1, 6 brass keys. Used with permission. Bottom: bassoon, Catlin Bliss, Hartford, from the Collection of Greenfield Village and the Henry Ford Museum, Dearborn, Michigan, No. 77.68.2, 6 brass keys. Used with permission.

Plate VIII: Two Hotteterre instruments from the Collection of Frans Brüggen, Amsterdam and reproduced with his kind permission. Oboe: 2 silver keys, boxwood, ivory mounts. Tenor recorder: (anchor) 1 silver key, grenadilla, ivory mounts.

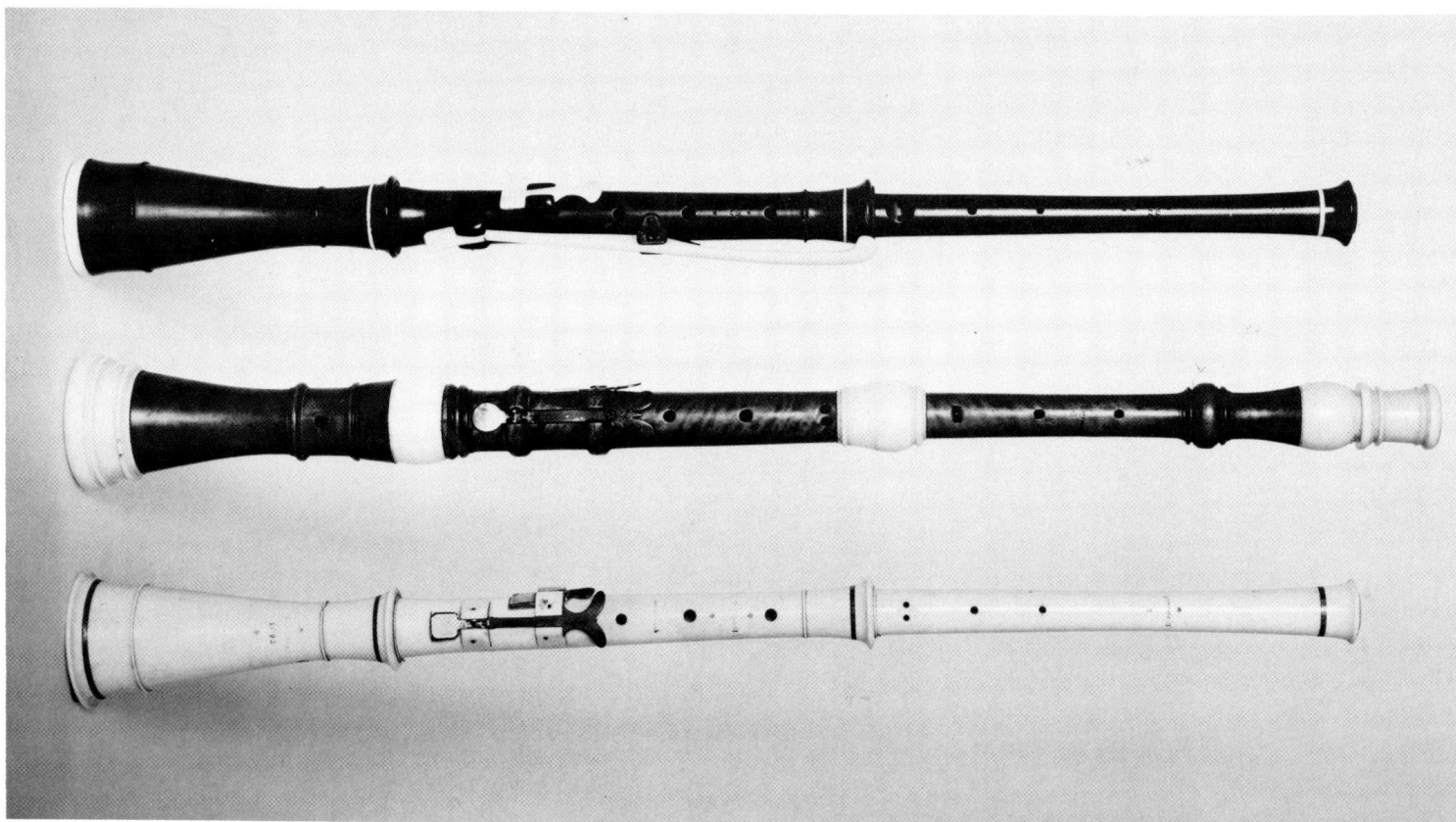

Plate IX: Three oboes from the Musikinstrumenten Museum, Leipzig. Top: No. 1327, Fornari, Venice (undated), ivory keys, one a long c' for LH 4. Middle: No. 1312, Rippert (undated), 2 silver keys, boxwood with ivory mounts. Bottom: No. 1328, Fornari, Venice (dated 1792), 2 brass keys, ivory with brass mounts. Reproduced with the kind permission of Dr. Hubert Henkel, Direktor.

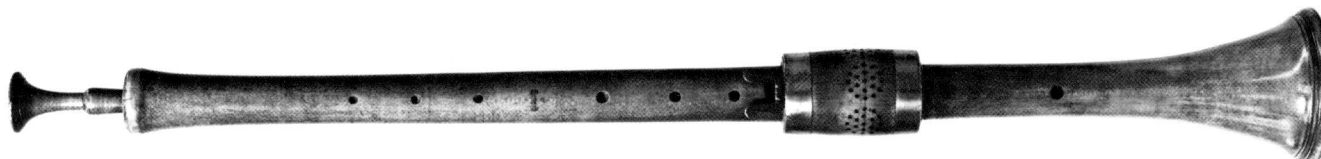

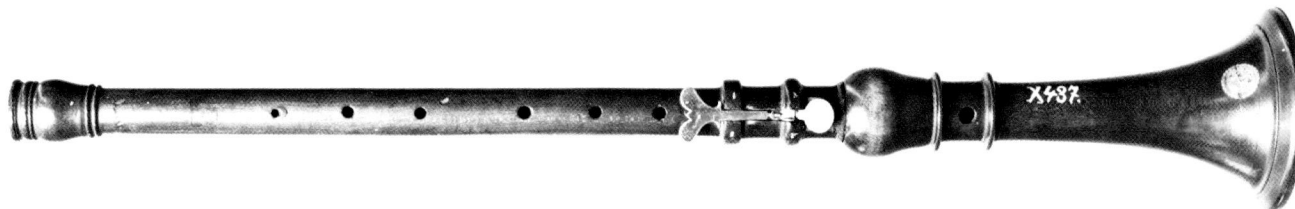

Plate X: Two pommers from the Historisches Museum, Frankfurt am Main. Top: Alto pommer, Johann Christoph Denner, No. X436, 1 brass key . Bottom: Discant pommer, Jacob Denner, No. x437, 1 brass key (the entire key is exposed to view). Reproduced with the kind permission of the Director.

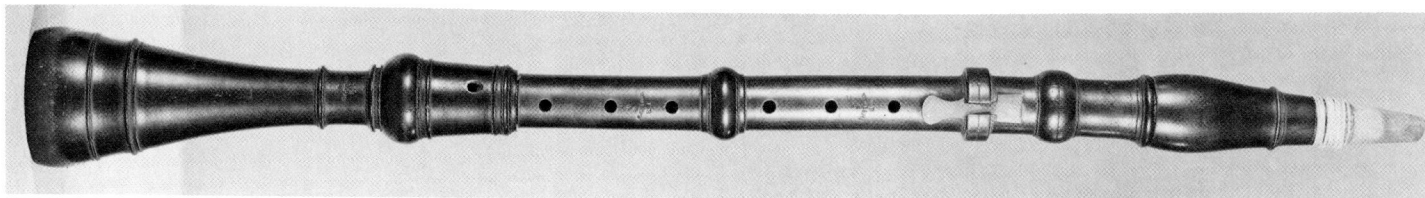

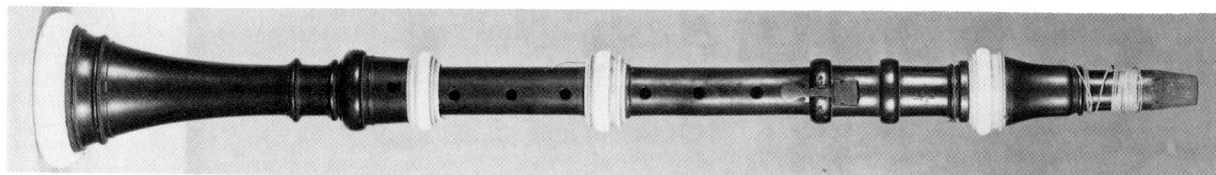

Plate XI: Two clarinets from the Musée Instrumental, Brussels. Top: J.B. Willems, No. 2573. Bottom: Thomas Boekhout, No. 2561. Reproduced with the kind permission of René de Maeyer, Directeur.

Plate XII: Bass flute by Joannes Maria Anciutti, Milan, dated 1739, Kunsthistorisches Museum, Vienna, No. GdM 371. Reproduced with the kind permission of Dr. Kurt Wegerer, Direktor of the Musikinstrumenten Sammlung.

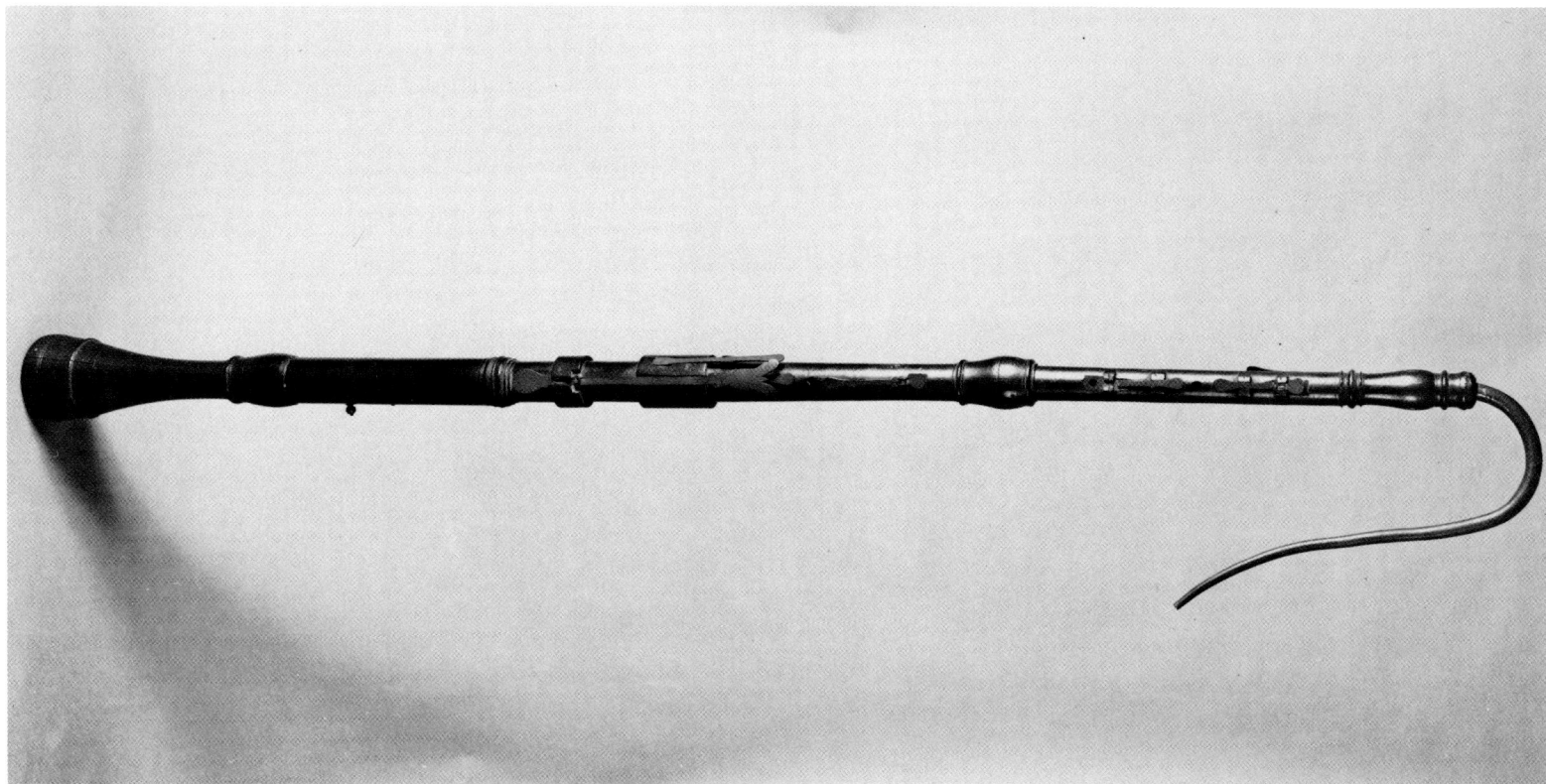

Plate XIII: Contrebasse oboe, Christoph Delusse, from the Musée Instrumental, Conservatoire National Superieur de Musique, Paris, Nos. E.150 and C. 459, over 6' high!. Reproduced with the kind permission of the Conservateur, Mme. J. Bran-Ricci.

| Young No. | No. Keys and Metal | City, Owner, No. | PITCH | No. Pcs. | Length | Body, Mounts | Flaps | SAT | Holes Dbld. | Tuning Holes | Additional Data | Ill. Source |
|---|---|---|---|---|---|---|---|---|---|---|---|---|
| **MEACHAM (all)** *(cont.)* | | | | | | | | | | | | |
| **J. & H. MEACHAM, ALBANY** *(cont.)* | | | | | | | | | | | | |
| 1. Piccolo | 1 brass | Washington: DCM 346 | A♭ | 3 | | boxw, ivory | | | | | Lower jt and ft jt 1-pc. | Ill. AMIS V-VI, fig. 5 |
| 1. Drum | | Baltimore: Md. Hist. Soc. | | | | | | | | | | |
| **MEACHAM & POND, ALBANY** | | | | | | | | | | | | |
| 1. Flute | 1 brass | Washington: DCM 568 | C | 4 | 60.4 | boxw, unmt | trap | SATK | | | No register. | |
| 2. Flute | 1 brass | Washington: Smithsonian 65.2700 | C | 4 | 60.2 | boxw, ivory | sq | SATK | | | | |
| 3. Flute | 1 brass | New York: Frederick Selch | | | | boxw, ivory | | | | | | |
| 4. Flute | 4 silver | New York: the late Josef Marx | C | 4 | 60.3 | boxw, ivory | sq(F) | SATK | | | Keys mtd in blocks. | |
| 5. Flute | 6 silver | Washington: DCM 923 | C | 5 | 61.2 | rosew, ivory | dome | SATK | | | No register. | |
| 6. Flute | 6 silver | Interlochen, Mich., Greenleaf Coll. | C | | | boxw, ivory | | | | | Foot to c'. Pewter plugs for c' and c♯'. | |
| 7. Flute | 8 silver | Washington: DCM 1162 | C | 5 | 66.3 | rosew, silver | dome | SATK | | | No register. Pewter plug for c' and c♯'. | |
| 8. Flute | 8 silver | Dearborn: Henry Ford Museum 78.64 | C | 5 | | cocus | dome | | | | Keys mtd in blocks. Plug flaps c' and c♯'. | Ill. AMIS V-VI, fig. 7. |
| 1. Clarinet | 5 brass | Oxford: Bate 404 | C | 5 | 59.5 | boxw, ivory | sq | | | | | |
| 2. Clarinet | 5 brass | New Haven: Yale | C | 5 | 58.4 | boxw, ivory | sq | | | | | |
| 3. Keyed Bugle | 8 brass | Dearborn: Henry Ford Museum 77.68.5 | B♭ | | | copper, brass | flat ro | | | | Also stamped "made for J.D. Sheppard, Buffalo" | Ill. AMIS V-VI, fig. 8 |
| **MEACHAM & CO., ALBANY** | | | | | | | | | | | | |
| 1. Flute | 1 brass | Philadelphia: Hans Moennig | C | | | boxw, ivory | sq | | | | | |
| 2. Flute | 1 silver | Delmar, N.Y.: C. Allanson | G | 3 | 39.7 | rosew, ivory | sq | | | | | |
| 3. Flute | 1 brass | New Haven: Yale 460 | C | 4 | 61.4 | boxw, ivory | sq(F) | | | | | |
| 1. Clarinet | 5 brass | Delmar, N.Y.: C. Allanson | C | 5 | 59.4 | boxw, ivory | sq | | | | | |
| 2. Clarinet | 5 brass | Milwaukee: F. Benkovic | B♭ | | | boxw, ivory | flat, ro | | | | | Ill. AMIS V-VI, fig. 6. |
| 3. Clarinet | 5 brass | Interlochen, Mich., Greenleaf, Coll. | C | | | boxw, ivory | | | | | | |
| 4. Clarinet | 5 brass | Three Oaks, Mich., R. Hunerjager | C | | | boxw, ivory | | | | | | |

# MILHOUSE, NEWARK

## FLUTES

| Young No. | No. Keys and Metal | City, Owner, No. | PITCH | No. Pcs. | Length | Body, Mounts Flaps | SAT | Holes Dbld. | Tuning Holes | Additional Data | Ill. Source |
|---|---|---|---|---|---|---|---|---|---|---|---|
| 1. | 1 silver | Washington: DCM 1073 | | 4 pc | 59.7 | ivory, unmtd sq | | | | | |
| 2. | | Keighley: Cliffe Castle Museum | | | | ivory | | | | | |

## OBOES

| Young No. | No. Keys and Metal | City, Owner, No. | PITCH | No. Pcs. | Length | Body, Mounts Flaps | SAT | Holes Dbld. | Tuning Holes | Additional Data | Ill. Source |
|---|---|---|---|---|---|---|---|---|---|---|---|
| 1. | 2 silver | London: C. Bradshaw | | | | st. boxw, ivory | | | | GS Exhib' 51, no. 74 | |
| 2. | 2 brass | Oxford: Bate 25 | | | 57.7 | maple? unmtd | | 3 dbl. | | Straight top. | Ill. Bate Oboe, Pl. III |
| 3. | 2 brass | Oxford: Bate 26 | | | 58.1 | pear? ivory ro | SATW | 3 dbl. | 2 | Straight top. | LOM 169 |
| 4. | | Birmingham | | | | | | | | | |
| 5. | | Chesham Bois: Hunt | | | | | | | | | |
| 6. | 2 brass | Vermillion: Univ. of S.D. 2503 | | | 57.15 | boxw, unmtd ro | SATW | 3 dbl. | | Brass bell rim! | |

## VOX HUMANA[1]

| Young No. | No. Keys and Metal | City, Owner, No. | PITCH | No. Pcs. | Length | Body, Mounts Flaps | SAT | Holes Dbld. | Tuning Holes | Additional Data | Ill. Source |
|---|---|---|---|---|---|---|---|---|---|---|---|
| 1. | 2 brass | Edinburgh: Royal Scottish Mus. | F | | 72.2 | boxw, ivory flat sq | | | | GS '68 Exhib, no. 121 | |
| 2. | 2 brass | Witenham Church, Lincs | | | | wood, brass, ivory | | | | | |

## TENOR OBOE[1]

| Young No. | No. Keys and Metal | City, Owner, No. | PITCH | No. Pcs. | Length | Body, Mounts Flaps | SAT | Holes Dbld. | Tuning Holes | Additional Data | Ill. Source |
|---|---|---|---|---|---|---|---|---|---|---|---|
| 1. | 2 brass | Boston: MFA 17.1911; B. 139 F | F | | 72.5 | boxw, ivory | | 0 dbl. | 0 | "Short model". RME 203 (1890) flared bell, no inner rim. | |
| 2. | 2 | Newark Municipal Mus. | | | | | | | | | |

## BASSOONS

| Young No. | No. Keys and Metal | City, Owner, No. | PITCH | No. Pcs. | Length | Body, Mounts Flaps | SAT | Holes Dbld. | Tuning Holes | Additional Data | Ill. Source |
|---|---|---|---|---|---|---|---|---|---|---|---|
| 1. | 4 brass | Sheffield City Museum | | | | wood, brass long (U) | | | | d. 1783 | Details & ill. GSJ X, Half-penny bassoon, opp. p 38 |
| 2. | 4 brass | Scarsdale: D. & R. Rosenbaum | | | 123.5 | wood, brass long (U) | SATW | | | ex-Halfpenny. Bell old shape. | Details & ill. GSJ X, Half-penny bassoon, opp. p 38 |
| 3. | 4 brass | London: Cave Collection | | | | wood, brass long (U) | | | | Ill. Baines, WITH, pl XXV. Details & ill. GSJ X, opp. p. 38 |
| 4. | 4 | Cambridge: Balsham Church | | | | | | | | | |
| 5. | 4 brass | Washington: Smith-sonian 66.14 | | | 123.3 | maple, brass | SATW | | | 4 pc + crook. Nice case. | |
| 6. | 4 brass | London: W. Waterhouse | | | 125.2 | maple, brass | | | | Millhouse (with two 'L's) | |
| 7. | 5 | Peterborough: Museum | | | | | | | | | |
| 8. | 5 brass | Boston: MFA 17.1925; B. 148 | | | 122.8 | maple, brass | | | | 5 keys: Bb, D, Eb L th, F, G#. All in saddles. Brass crook. | |

[1] These designations are used by the sources that list them but are usually considered synonymous. I have examined only the Boston specimen.

| Young No. | No. Keys and Metal | City, Owner, No. | Pitch | No. Pcs. | Length | Body, Mounts Flaps | SAT | Holes Dbld. | Tuning Holes | Additional Data | Ill. Source |
|---|---|---|---|---|---|---|---|---|---|---|---|
| **MILHOUSE, NEWARK** *(cont.)* | | | | | | | | | | | **MILHOUSE, NEWARK** *(cont.)* |
| **BASSOONS** *(cont.)* | | | | | | | | | | | |
| 9. | 6 | London: Horniman 1969. 679(G) | | | 123.5 | dk st w, brass | | | | | |
| 10. | 6 | York: Castle Museum | | | | | | | | | |
| 11. | 6 | Oxford: Bate 34 | | | 122.7 | fruitw | | | | | |
| 12. | 6 | Keighley Museum 24.55 | | | | | | | | | |
| 13. | 6 | Nantwich: David E. Owen | | | | | | | | | |
| 14. | ? | Newark Municipal Museum | | | | | | | | | |
| 15. | | Bassingham Church, Lincs. | | | | | | | | | |
| 16. | | London: Reuben Greene | | | | | | | | | |
| 17. | | London: Kneller Hall | | | | | | | d. 1788 | | |
| 18. | | Yorks | | | | | | | | | |
| 19. | | ex-John Isaacs, sold to American via Sotheby's | | | | | | | 2 keys added, both stamped IH. | | |

**SERPENT**

| | | | | | | | | | | | |
|---|---|---|---|---|---|---|---|---|---|---|---|
| 1. | | London: sold by Sotheby to Becott & Company, 1968. | | | | | | | | | |

# MILHOUSE, LONDON

| Young No. | No. Keys and Metal | City, Owner, No. | Pitch | No. Pcs. | Length | Body, Mounts Flaps | SAT | Keys mtd. in | Address | Additional Data | Ill. Source |
|---|---|---|---|---|---|---|---|---|---|---|---|
| **FLUTES** | | | | | | | | | | | **MILHOUSE, LONDON** |
| 1. | 1 brass | Vermillion: Univ. of SD 2650 | C | | 61.0 | boxw, ivory flat sq(C) | SATK | block | 337 Oxford St. | 3 keys added. | |
| 2. | 1 brass | Washington: DCM 1146 | A | 3 pc | 36.5 | boxw, ivory flat sq | | knob | 337 Oxford St. | No separate ft jt. 3 pc = head, upper jt, lower jt. | |
| 3. | 1 brass | Washington: DCM 936 | C | 4 pc | 60.8 | boxw, ivory flat sq | | knob | 337 Oxford St. | 4 pc = head, upper, lower, foot. | |
| 4. | 1 silver | New Haven: Yale 433 | C | 4 pc | 60.7 | boxw, ivory flat sq | SATK | knob | | 4 pc = head, upper, lower, foot. | |
| 5. | 1 silver | London: RCM 325 | C | 4 pc | 60.2 | boxw, ivory flat sq | | block | 337 Oxford St. | 1 upper jt. 4 pc. | |
| 6. | 1 silver | Meopham: Nicholas Benn | C | | 61.4 | boxw, ivory | | | 337 Oxford St. | Head cap not original, adds slightly to given length. | |
| 7. | 5 | London: Jeremy Montagu IV 130 | | | | boxw, ivory | | | | | Ill. Montagu RM, Pl. X |
| 8. | 5 | New Paltz, N.Y.: M. Zadro | C | | | boxw | | | | | |
| 9. | 6 silver | Oxford: Bate 121 | C | | (58.8) | boxw, ivory flat sq | | blocks & knob | 337 Oxford St. | Length given is from embouchure. | Ill. Bate Flute, pl 6-h |
| 10. | 7 silver | London: RCM 326 | C | 4 pc | 66.7 | dk st w, silver flat sq | | blocks | 337 Oxford St. | 2Xtouches for B♭. | |

| Young No. | No. Keys and Metal | City, Owner, No. | Pitch | No. Pcs. | Length | Body, Mounts | Flaps | SAT | Holes Dbld. | Tuning Holes | Additional Data | Ill. Source |
|---|---|---|---|---|---|---|---|---|---|---|---|---|

## MILHOUSE, LONDON *(cont.)*

### FLUTES *(cont.)*

| Young No. | No. Keys and Metal | City, Owner, No. | Pitch | No. Pcs. | Length | Body, Mounts | Flaps | SAT | Holes Dbld. | Tuning Holes | Additional Data | Ill. Source |
|---|---|---|---|---|---|---|---|---|---|---|---|---|
| 11. | 7 silver | Washington: DCM 1192 | C | 4 pc | 68.0 | ebony, ivory | flat sq(F) | SATK | blocks | | Foot to C. | |
| 12. | 7 | Dorking: R. Glenton | | | | | | | | | | |
| 13. | 7 silver | Vermillion: Univ. of SD 2651 | C | 5 pc | 67.3 | boxw, ivory | round cupped | | blocks | 337 Oxford St. | Metal-lined head, 5 pc = head, bbl, upper, lower, foot | |
| 14. | 7 silver | Aachen: Dr. W. Willms | C | 4 pc | 67.1 | boxw, ivory | flat sq | | | 337 Oxford St. | 2 upper jts. 4 pc. | |
| 15. | 7 silver | New Haven: Yale 459 | C | 4 pc | 69.07 | boxw, ivory | | SATK | blocks & knob | | Ft to C. Had 6 upper jts, now 3. | |
| 16. | 8 silver | Washington: DCM 464 | C | 5 pc | 67.2 | rosew, silver | dome | | | 337 Oxford St. | has bbl. Reduced head diameter | |
| 17. | 8 silver | Washington: DCM 1102 | C | 5 pc | 66.7 | "curly" w, ivory | dome[1] | | | 337 Oxford St., | | |
| 18. | 8 silver | Edgware: Boosey & Hawkes | | | | ebony, silver | dome | | | 337 Oxford St. | | |
| 19. | 8 | Louisville: S-M Vance 17 | | | | rosew? | dome[1] | | | 337 Oxford St. | Ft to C. | |
| 20. | 8 silver | Cambridge, Mass.: Eddy | | 5 pc | 67.0 | grena, nick. silv | dome | | | | Ft to C. | |
| 21. | ? | Washington: DCM 1100 | C | | | boxw, ivory | | | | | Ft to C. FOOTJOINT ONLY. | |
| 22. | ? | New York: MMA 53.56.25 | | | (20.5) | boxw | | | | | The two uppermost jts only: head and upper. 3 fingerholes, 2 keys. | |
| 23. | | Lincs: Witenham Church | | | | | | | | 337 Oxford St. | | |
| 24. | | Manchester: H. Watson Library | | | | | | | | | | |
| 25. | | Bethersden: C.F. Colt | | | | | | | | | | |
| 26. | | Peebles: F.E. Dodman | | | | | | | | | | |
| 27. | | Dorking: Lady Jeans | | | | | | | | | | |
| 28. | | Dorking: Lady Jeans | | | | | | | | | | |
| 29. | | Dorking: Lady Jeans | | | | | | | | | | |
| 30. | | Dorking: Lady Jeans | | | | | | | | | | |
| 31. | | Dorking: Lady Jeans | | | | | | | | | | |
| 32. | | Dorking: Lady Jeans | | | | | | | | | | |
| 33. | | Royal Mil. Exhib. No. 87 | | | | | | | | | | |

### CLARINETS

| Young No. | No. Keys and Metal | City, Owner, No. | Pitch | No. Pcs. | Length | Body, Mounts | Flaps | SAT | Holes Dbld. | Tuning Holes | Additional Data | Ill. Source |
|---|---|---|---|---|---|---|---|---|---|---|---|---|
| 1. | 5 brass | London: Jeremy Montagu III 170 | | | | | | | | | | Ill. Montagu RM, Pl. X |
| 2. | 5 brass | Leipzig 1483 | A | | 59.7+ | boxw, ivory | sq | SATK | | | Mthpc missing so given length is short. | |
| 3. | 5 brass | Cambridge: N. Shackleton | C | | 59.9 | boxw, ivory | sq | SATK | | | | |

[1]Except two plug keys.

| Young No. | No. Keys and Metal | City, Owner, No. | PITCH | No. Pcs. | Length | Body, Mounts | Flaps | SAT | Holes Dbld. | Tuning Holes | Additional Data | Ill. Source |
|---|---|---|---|---|---|---|---|---|---|---|---|---|

**CLARINETS** *(cont.)*

| | | | | | | | | | | | | |
|---|---|---|---|---|---|---|---|---|---|---|---|---|
| 4. | 6 brass | Cambridge: N. Shackleton | B♭ | | 60.0 | boxw, ivory | sq | SATK | | | 6th key is trill key. | |
| 5. | 6 | Brighton: Municipal Museum | C | | 59.5 | boxw, ivory | sq | | | | | Ill. EAMI 627 |
| 6. | 8 | London: Horniman 260 | C | | 58.7 | boxw, ivory | | | | | "Fixed barrel & unflared bell." | |
| 7. | 8 brass | Oxford: Bate 4001, loan from Bourne | C | | | boxw, ivory | | | | | 337 Oxford St. | |
| 8. | 10 brass | Edgware: Boosey & Hawkes 313 | A | | | boxw, ivory | | | | | 337 Oxford St. 2 keys in saddles. Perhaps 8 keys originally? | |
| 9. | | Birmingham & Midland Inst. | | | | | | | | | | |
| 10. | | York: Castle Museum | | | | | | | | | | |

| | | | Halfpenny type | | | | | | Holes Dbld. | Tuning Holes | | |
|---|---|---|---|---|---|---|---|---|---|---|---|---|

**OBOES**

| | | | | | | | | | | | | |
|---|---|---|---|---|---|---|---|---|---|---|---|---|
| 1. | 2 silver | London: J.P.S. Montagu I 188 | D | | 57.5 | boxw, unmtd | oct | SATK | 3&4 | 2 | No. 21, X-rays, Eric Halfpenny, GSJ II | Ill. Montagu RM, Pl. X |
| 2. | 2 silver | Boston: MFA 17.1925, B. 135 | D | | 56.8 | boxw, unmtd | ro? | SATK | 3&4 | 2 | | RME 186 (1890) |
| 3. | 2 silver | Washington: Smithsonian 74.8 | | | 57.1 | boxw, unmtd | oct | SATK | 3&4 | | | |
| 4. | 2 silver | Oxford: Bate 203 | D | | 57.4 | boxw, unmtd | | | 3&4 | | | |
| 5. | 2 silver | Oxford: Bate 27 | D | | 56.8 | boxw, ivory | oct | SATK | 3&4 | | | EAMI 566 |
| 6. | 2 silver | University of Victoria, Canada | D | | 56.8 | boxw, unmtd | oct(R) | SATK | 3&4 | 2 | | LOM 170 |
| 7. | 2 brass | Haslemere: Dolmetsch 73 | C? | | 58.0 | plumw, ivory | ro | | 3 | 2 | 1 upper jt. "Plain top." Meaning straight? | |
| 8. | 2 | xBerlin 2939 | | | 56.0 | boxw | | | | | | |
| 9. | 2 silver | Scarsdale: D & R Rosenbaum 61 | D | | 56.9 | boxw, ivory | flat ro | SATK | 3 | 2 | 5 added keys have now been removed. | |
| 10. | 3 silver | London: V&A 45-1884 | D | | 57.0 | boxw, unmtd | ro | | 3&4 | 2 | 3rd of orig. keys is g♯, 3 other added keys. Ill[1] | |
| 11. | 3 | Florence 127 | D | | 56.5 | | oct | | 3&4 | 2 | | Drawing, Gai cat., p 204 |
| 12. | 6 | Cobham: the late R. Morley-Pegge[2] | | | | | | | | | | |
| 13. | 7 silver | Scarsdale: D & R Rosenbaum | D | | 56.45 | boxw, unmtd | sq-cors[2] | SATK | 3&4 | 2 | | |
| 14. | 7 silver | Edgware: Boosey & Hawkes | D | | 57.0 | boxw, unmtd | both ro & oct | | | | | |

[1] Error in Baines V&A catalogue. This instrument is on the *left* in Fig. 127, not on the right as captioned.

[2] The C', C♯', E♭', and G♯' cps are sq-cors; the B♭' and oct key cps are round; the F' key cp is square. It may well have been originally a four-keyed oboe.

**MILHOUSE, LONDON** (*cont.*)　　　　　　　　　　　　　　　　　　　　　　**MILHOUSE, LONDON** (*cont.*)

OBOES (*cont.*)

| Young No. | No. Keys and Metal | City, Owner, No. | Pitch | No. Pcs. | Length | Body, Mounts | Flaps | SAT | Holes Dbld. | Tuning Holes | Additional Data | Ill. Source |
|---|---|---|---|---|---|---|---|---|---|---|---|---|
| 15. | 8 silver | Edinburgh: Melville-Mason? | | | 55.3 | | ro | | | | | |
| 16. | 8 | York: Castle Museum | | | | | | | | | | |
| 17. | | Snowhill Manor, Glos. acc. to Langwill | | | | | | | | | | |
| 18. | | Snowhill Manor, Glos. acc. to Langwill | | | | | | | | | | |
| 19. | | Snowhill Manor, Glos. acc. to Langwill | | | | | | | | | | |
| 20. | | Royal Mil. Exhib. 177 [1] | | | | | | | | | | |
| 21. | | Royal Mil. Exhib. 181 [1] | | | | | | | | | | |

ENGLISH HORNS

| Young No. | No. Keys and Metal | City, Owner, No. | Pitch | No. Pcs. | Length | Body, Mounts | Flaps | SAT | Holes Dbld. | Tuning Holes | Additional Data | Ill. Source |
|---|---|---|---|---|---|---|---|---|---|---|---|---|
| 1. | 2 silver | Edgware: Boosey & Hawkes 231 | | | | boxw, ivory | sq | | | | Bulb bell. Unusual position for dbl 4th hole. Angular. | |
| 2. | | London, Tower of | | | | | | | | | Bulb bell. Referred to in Bate Oboe, note 12, pg 117. Angular | |

BASSOONS

| Young No. | No. Keys and Metal | City, Owner, No. | Pitch | No. Pcs. | Length | Body, Mounts | Flaps | SAT | Holes Dbld. | Tuning Holes | Additional Data | Ill. Source |
|---|---|---|---|---|---|---|---|---|---|---|---|---|
| 1. | 5 brass | Sheffield City Museum, ex J. Parr | | | | | | | | | | |
| 2. | 6 brass | Sheffield City Museum, ex J. Parr, J1955 7j | | | 124.2 | | | | | | | |
| 3. | 6 | Sheffield City Museum | | | | | | | | | | |
| 4. | 6 | Bradford: Bolling Hall Museum | | | | | | | | | | |
| 5. | 6 | London: Kneller Hall 44 | | | | | | | | | | |
| 6. | 6 brass | Oxford: Baines, loan to Bate Coll.x3 | | | | fruitw, brass | | | | | | |
| 7. | 6 | Hants: Yately Church, per Langwill | | | | | | | | | | |
| 8. | 6 | Leeds, University of: Perkins Coll. | | | | | | | | | | |
| 9. | 6 | Ilford: the late E. Half-penny's coll. | | | | | | | | | | Ill. GSJ X, pl I, II, III, & IV, F. |
| 10. | 6 brass | London: W. Waterhouse | | | 121.1 | maple, brass | | | | | | |

[1] Where is it now? One of those above?

| Young No. | No. Keys and Metal | City, Owner, No. | Pitch | No. Pcs. | Length | Body, Mounts Flaps | SAT | Holes Dbld. | Tuning Holes | Additional Data | Ill. Source |
|---|---|---|---|---|---|---|---|---|---|---|---|

**MILHOUSE, LONDON** *(cont.)*

**BASSOONS** *(cont.)*

**MILHOUSE, LONDON** *(cont.)*

| Young No. | No. Keys and Metal | City, Owner, No. | Pitch | No. Pcs. | Length | Body, Mounts Flaps | SAT | Holes Dbld. | Tuning Holes | Additional Data | Ill. Source |
|---|---|---|---|---|---|---|---|---|---|---|---|
| 11. | 6 brass | London: W. Waterhouse | | | — — | maple, brass | | | | Bell missing. Length not determinable. | |
| 12. | 7 | Edinburgh: Melville-Mason? (ex Rendall) | | | | | | | | | |
| 13. | 7 | Leeds, University of, Perkins Coll. | | | | | | | | | |
| 14. | 7 brass | Scarsdale: D & R Rosenbaum 110 | | | 123.0 | maple, brass (U) | SATW | | | ex E. Parr. | |
| 15. | 8 brass | London: Horniman 152 | | | 116.4 | dk st w, brass | | | | Brass bell! | |
| 16. | 8 | Tarring: West Tarring Church | | | | | | | | | |
| 17. | 8 | Edinburgh: L. G. Langwill | | | 123.0 | | | | | | |
| 18. | 8 brass | Oxford: Bate 37 | | | 121.3 | | | | | | |
| 19. | 8 brass | Meopham: Nicholas Benn | | | | | | | | | |
| 20. | 8 | Lincolnshire: Winterton Church | | | | | | | | Only 2 joints survive. | |
| 21. | 8 brass | Biebrich: Heckel 7-D | | | 123.4 | pearw, brass (U) | | | | Keys B♭, D, E♭ L Th,[1] G♯, F, F♯, 2 wing keys. | |
| 22. | 8 brass | New Haven: Yale 448 | | | 124.3 | maple, brass (U) | SATW[2] | | | Keys B♭, D, E♭ L Th,[1] G♯, F, F♯, 2 wing keys. | |
| 23. | 8 | Bussum: Carol van Leeuwen Boomkamp | | | | | | | | per Langwill, but perhaps quite recent. Not in 1971 catalogue. | |
| 24. | 9 | London: RCM 197 | | | 122.5 | maple, brass | | | | Keys in saddles. | |
| 25. | 9 | Lewis: Lewis Museum, per Langwill | | | | | | | | ex Sidlesham Church | |
| 26. | 10 brass | Cambridge: N. J. Shackleton | | | 124.0 | maple, brass ro | SATK | | | | |
| 27. | 10 | Royal Society of Musicians | | | | | | | | | |
| 28. | 13 | Glasgow, University of, ex B. Hague | | | | | | | | | |
| 29. | 15 modern | Glasgow, University of (same instr?) | | | | maple | | | | | |
| 30. | | Amsterdam: Henk de Wit, jr. | | | 121.6 | maple, brass | | | | | |
| 31. | | York per Langwill | | | | | | | | | |
| 32. | | Wigan per Langwill | | | | | | | | | |

[1] This E♭ key is to *left* of D key.  [2] Except for two wings keys, which are SATK.

| Young No. | No. Keys and Metal | City, Owner, No. | Pitch | No. Pcs. | Length | Body, Mounts Flaps | | SAT | Holes Dbld. | Tuning Holes | Additional Data | Ill. Source |
|---|---|---|---|---|---|---|---|---|---|---|---|---|

**MILHOUSE, LONDON** (*cont.*)

BASSOONS (*cont.*)

| | | | | | | | | | | | | |
|---|---|---|---|---|---|---|---|---|---|---|---|---|
| 33. | | Wigan: Haigh Hall per Langwill | | | | | | | | | | |
| 34. | | St. Albans | | | | | | | | | | |
| 35. | | Sussex: Hove Art Museum per Langwill | | | | | | | | | | |

SMALL BASSOON

| | | | | | | | | | | | | |
|---|---|---|---|---|---|---|---|---|---|---|---|---|
| 1. | 8 brass | Vermillion: U. of SD 2671 | | | 83.5 | maple, brass | flat sq | SATW | | | Tenoroon | |

# NAUST

FLUTES

| | | | | | | | | | | | | |
|---|---|---|---|---|---|---|---|---|---|---|---|---|
| 1. | 1 silver | Copenhagen E. 135 | | 4 pc | 63.0+ | ivory, unmtd | sq | SATK | | | Head cap missing. Engraved key. Sachs said c. 1700[1] | Ill. Bowers, AMIS 3, p 23 |
| 2. | 1 brass | Berlin 2667 | | 3 pc | 68.0 | boxw, unmtd | sq | SATW | | | | |

FLUTE D'AMOUR

| | | | | | | | | | | | | |
|---|---|---|---|---|---|---|---|---|---|---|---|---|
| 1 | 1 silver | Paris C. 441 | | 3 pc | 77.25 | boxw, ivory | sq | SATW | | | | Ill. Bowers, AMIS 3, p 24. EAMI 467 |

FLUTET

| | | | | | | | | | | | | |
|---|---|---|---|---|---|---|---|---|---|---|---|---|
| 1. | | xBerlin 2732 | | 3 pc | 26.5 | ebony, ivory | | | | | Sachs says c. 1700.[1] | |

FRENCH FLAGEOLET

| | | | | | | | | | | | | |
|---|---|---|---|---|---|---|---|---|---|---|---|---|
| 1. | 0 keys | Washington: DCM 624 | | | 19.8 | ebony, ivory | | | | | Checklist says early 19C.[1] | EAMI 436 |

OBOE

| | | | | | | | | | | | | |
|---|---|---|---|---|---|---|---|---|---|---|---|---|
| 1. | 3 silver | London: RCM 97 | | 3 pc | now 48.3 | ivory, unmtd | sq[2] | SATW | | | 2 th. Badly altered.[2] | |

CLARINETS

| | | | | | | | | | | | | |
|---|---|---|---|---|---|---|---|---|---|---|---|---|
| 1. | | Puttick & Simpson Sale, per Langwill | | | | | | | | | | |
| 2. | | Clarinet in C reported by N.J. Shackleton | | | | | | | | | | |

[1] Was there more than one maker of this name or is the flageolet a facetious forgery? More likely, the Checklist errs.

[2] E♭ LH key is a replacement with round flap. The Museum believes that even the C' and RH E♭' keys may be later replacements. Perhaps the entire oboe is a composite. Only the lower jt is stamped. The upper jt has been cut down, rebored, and drilled with new finger holes. The bell has also been cut down at its top with new tuning holes drilled.

| Young No. | No. Keys and Metal | City, Owner, No. | PITCH | No. Pcs. | Length | Body, Mounts Flaps | SAT | Holes Dbld. | Tuning Holes | Additional Data | Ill. Source |
|---|---|---|---|---|---|---|---|---|---|---|---|

# J. W. OBERLENDER I

*Nickel's "number"*

## SOPRANINO RECORDER

| | | | | | | | | | | | |
|---|---|---|---|---|---|---|---|---|---|---|---|
| 1. | | Hague Ea 277-1933 | | 3 | 26.0 | ivory | | a | | | |

## ALTO RECORDERS

| | | | | | | | | | | | |
|---|---|---|---|---|---|---|---|---|---|---|---|
| 1. | | Rome: Galleria del Lazio 2211 | | | 50.0 | boxw | | ss | | | |
| 2. | | Vienna GdM 110 | | 3 | 50.0 | boxw, ivory | | tt | | | |
| 3. | | Paris C. 398, E. 192 | | 3 | 50.1 | boxw, unmtd | | pp | | | |
| 4. | | Paris C. 400, E. 193 | | 3 | 50.4 | boxw, unmtd[1] | | | | | |
| 5. | | Paris C. 397, E. 373 | F | 3 | 49.1 | boxw, horn | | oo | | | |
| 6. | | Paris: the late Comtesse de Chambure | | 3 | 50.5 | boxw | | rr | | | |
| 7. | | Paris: the late Comtesse de Chambure | | 3 | 48.5 | ivory | | qq | | | |
| 8. | | Hague Ea 276-1933 | | 3 | 49.5 | ivory | | dd | | | |
| 9. | | Copenhagen 418 | | 3 | 44.5 | boxw, unmtd | | ff | | | |
| 10. | | Copenhagen E. 101 | F | 3 | 50.0 | ivory, unmtd | | gg | | Bad crack, nicely pinned and filled. | |
| 11. | | Munich BNM Mu 162 | F | 3 | 45.0 | ivory, unmtd | | mm | | | |
| 12. | | Nürnberg MIR 201 | E | 3 | 50.0 | boxw, unmtd | | nn | | | |
| 13. | | Bonn BH Zimmermann 11) | F♯ | 3 | 44.1 | ivory | | ee | | | |
| 14. | | Bavaria: anonymous | F | 3 | 49.9 | boxw, unmtd | | | | Middle jt has illegible, different maker's stamp. | Ill. GSJ XXXV |
| 15. | | London: RCM 96 | | 3 | 50.0 | carved boxw, unmtd | | kk | | | |
| 16. | | Leipzig 1123 | | 3 | 49.6 | carved boxw, unmtd | | hh | | | Ill. color, Paganelli; Ill., Heyde Leipzig, tafel 6 |
| 17. | | Leipzig 1131 | E♭ | 3 | 52.0 | boxw, unmtd | | ii | | | Ill. Heyde Leipzig, tafel 6 |
| 18. | | xBerlin 2788 | F♯ | 3 | 44.0 | ivory | | aa | | | |
| 19. | | xBerlin 2797 | | | 51.5 | boxw | | bb | | | |
| 20. | | xBerlin 2808 | E | | 50.0 | ivory | | cc | | | |
| 21. | | Stockholm Nordiska 39.218 | | | | boxw | | | | | |
| 22. | | Budapest Natl. Museum 1860.3 | | 3 | 50.0 | boxw, unmtd | | | | | |
| 23. | | Modena: Museum Civico 15 | | | 50.0 | boxw, unmtd[2] | | ll | | | |
| 24. | | Meopham: Nicholas Benn | | 3 | 49.6 | carved boxw, unmtd | | | | | |
| 25. | | New York: MMA 89.4.2208 | G | 3 | 43.8 | boxw, horn | | | | | |

[1] A horn ring is added at the top of the foot joint as a repair.  [2] A brass ring is added as a repair.

| Young No. | No. Keys and Metal | City, Owner, No. | Pitch | No. Pcs. | Length | Body, Mounts Flaps | SAT | Holes Dbld. | Tuning Holes | Additional Data | Ill. Source |
|---|---|---|---|---|---|---|---|---|---|---|---|

Nickel's "number"

### BASS RECORDERS [1]

| No. | Keys/Metal | City, Owner | Pitch | Pcs | Length | Body, Mounts | SAT | Dbld | Additional Data |
|---|---|---|---|---|---|---|---|---|---|
| 1. | 1 brass | Paris E. 2316 | | 3 | 101.0 | maple, unmtd | SATW | bb | Crook into top. |
| 2. | 1 brass | Nürnberg MI 96 | E | 3 | 102.0 | plum, brass | SATW | aa | Crook into top. |
| 3. | 1 | Salzburg 3/14 | E | 3 | 102.0 | apple | | cc | Stamp ill. Birsak catalogue, taf XV-23 |

### FLUTES

| No. | Keys/Metal | City, Owner | Pitch | Pcs | Length | Body, Mounts Flaps | SAT | Dbld | Additional Data | Ill. Source |
|---|---|---|---|---|---|---|---|---|---|---|
| 1. | 1 brass | Washingt : DCM 1343 | E♭ | 4 pc | 53.0 | ivory, unmtd sq(G) | SATK | | | |
| 2. | 1 | Rome: Galleria del Lazio 623 | | | | ivory | | bb | Which Oberlender is very uncertain. | |
| 3. | 1 | Modena 4 | | | 63.0 | nutw, horn | | aa | | |
| 4. | 1 silver | Zurich: Willi Burger | D' | 4 pc | 60.74 | ivory, unmtd trap | | | 3 upper jts. | |

### FLUTE D'AMOUR

| Keys/Metal | City, Owner | Pitch | Pcs | Length | Body, Mounts Flaps | Dbld | Additional Data |
|---|---|---|---|---|---|---|---|
| 1 brass | Boston: MFA 17.1855; B. 47 | A | 4 pc | 73.0 | boxw, unmtd sq | b | Said to have belonged to the celebrated Krafft.[2] |

### CLARINETS

| No. | Keys/Metal | City, Owner | Pitch | Pcs | Length | Body, Mounts | Dbld | Additional Data | Ill. Source |
|---|---|---|---|---|---|---|---|---|---|
| 1. | 2 brass | Berlin 2870 | D | 3 pc | 54.0 | boxw, unmtd | a | Only the middle joint survived WW2. | Ill. Kroll Clarinet, pl 5. |
| 2. | 2 brass | Leningrad 486 | C | 3 pc | 55.2 | boxw, unmtd | b | Oct/speaker key missing, but hole is higher than A' hole. | |

### OBOE D'AMORE

| Keys/Metal | City, Owner | Pitch | Length | Body, Mounts Flaps | Additional Data |
|---|---|---|---|---|---|
| 3 brass | Nürnberg MI 92a | A | 61.9 | boxw, unmtd trap-cors E♭ | Stamp all but illegible. O-below is clear. No tree. |

### OBOE

| No. | Keys/Metal | City, Owner | Length | Body, Mounts Flaps | Additional Data |
|---|---|---|---|---|---|
| 1. | 3 brass | Sotheby auction, Nov. 1979 | 56.9 | boxw, unmtd E♭s sq, C ro | Stamp: name in scroll, fleur de lys above. 3 dbl.[3] |

# J. W. OBERLENDER II
# J. W. OBERLENDER II

### FLUTE

Nickel no.

| No. | Keys/Metal | City, Owner | Pitch | Pcs | Length | Body, Mounts Flaps | Nickel no. | Ill. Source |
|---|---|---|---|---|---|---|---|---|
| 1. | 1 silver | Leipzig 1245 | C | 4 pc | 63.5 | ivory, unmtd sqC | 1 | Ill. Heyde Leipzig, taf 9 |

### ALTO RECORDER

| No. | City, Owner | Pcs | Length | Body, Mounts | Ill. Source |
|---|---|---|---|---|---|
| 1. | Scarsdale: D & R Rosenbaum | 3 pc | 50.0 | carved boxw, unmtd | LOM 64 |

---

[1] The tenor recorder listed by Nickel is now said to be by G.A. Rottenburgh, this per H. Heyde, Leipzig.

[2] A cellist and member of Haydn's orchestra at Esterhazy. The inside of the head cap is signed in ink "KRAFFT."

[3] Ill. in Sotheby catalogue, pg 15.

| Young No. | No. Keys and Metal | City, Owner, No. | Pitch | No. Pcs. | Length | Body, Mounts | Flaps | SAT | Holes Dbld. | Tuning Holes | Additional Data | Ill. Source |
|---|---|---|---|---|---|---|---|---|---|---|---|---|
| **J. W. OBERLENDER II** *(cont.)* | | | | | | | | | | | | |
| CLARINET | | | | | | | | | | *Nickel no.* | | |
| 1. | 2 brass | Leipzig 1470 | | 3 pc. | 54.6 | boxw, ivory | trap | SATW | | 2 | | |

| | | | | | | | | | | | | |
|---|---|---|---|---|---|---|---|---|---|---|---|---|
| **F. OBERLENDER** | | | | | | | | | | | | |
| PICCOLO | | | | | | | | | | | | |
| 1. | 1 brass | Stockholm Nordiska 77216 | | | 33.5 | boxw, horn | | | | 1 | | |
| ALTO CLARINET | | | | | | | | | | | | |
| 1. | 5 brass | Stockholm Nordiska 81435 | | | – – | plumw, bone | trap | SATK | | 2 | All flaps have ⚒ or ⊕ in middle, upper surface.[1] | |

| | | | | | | | | | | | | |
|---|---|---|---|---|---|---|---|---|---|---|---|---|
| **J. G. OTTO[2]** | | | | | | | | | | | | |
| FLUTES | | | | | | | | | | *Dated* | | |
| 1. | 1 brass | Washington: DCM 386 | C | 4 pc | 61.3 | boxw, ivory | trap[3] | SATW | | 1797 | | |
| 2. | 1 brass | Leipzig 1252 | C | 4 pc | 62.7 | boxw, ivory | sq | SATW | | 1791 | | Ill. Heyde Leipzig, taf 10 |
| 3. | 1 brass | Zurich: Museum Belle-rive 142 | F | | 51.2 | boxw, horn | | | | | 3 upper jts. | |
| 4. | 1 brass | Vermillion, S. D., U. of S.D. 2668 | C | 4 pc | 62.7 | boxw, ivory | sq | SATW | | 1800 | | |
| OBOES | | | | | | | | | | | | |
| 1. | 2 brass | Markneukirchen 1040 | | | 57.8 | boxw, unmtd | sq eb?, oct C | SATW | 3 dbl. | 1785 | 2 th. | Ill. color Hanna Jordan: Markneukirchen guidebook p. 34 |
| 2. | 2 brass | Zurich: Museum Belle-rive 115 | | | 55.8 | boxw, unmtd | | | | 1799 | | |
| CLARINETS | | | | | | | | | | | | |
| 1. | 5 brass | Nürnberg MIR 429 | C | 5 pc | 59.8 | boxw, horn | | | 3 dbl. | 1802 | | |
| 2. | | Peine: Gunter Hart | | | incomplete | | | | | 1809 | | |

---

[1] There is a mouthpiece of horn that (now, at least) accompanies this instrument, as well as a brass crook. The mouthpiece is without the usual tenon and slips over the brass neck. Otherwise, the instrument is made up of 3 pieces: upper jt, lower jt, and bell. The A' key is missing.

[2] This relatively obscure maker first attracted my attention because of the extraordinary similarity in many details of his instruments to Jakob Grundmann's, e.g. the Markneukirchen oboe. In addition, Otto uses the crossed swords motive as a device above his name and dates his instruments, both points reminiscent of Grundmann and, to a lesser extent, the Grensers. So strong is the apparent influence, I will offer the guess that Otto apprenticed in Dresden. Heyde in his Leipzig catalogue gives Otto's dates as 1762-1821 and has told me that he doubts the Dresden connection.

[3] Inverse trapezoid.

| Young No. | No. Keys and Metal | City, Owner, No. | Pitch | No. Pcs. | Length | Body, Mounts Flaps | SAT | Holes Dbld. | Tuning Holes | Additional Data | Ill. Source |
|---|---|---|---|---|---|---|---|---|---|---|---|
| **J. G. OTTO** *(cont.)* | | | | | | | | | | | **J. G. OTTO** *(cont.)* |
| **BASSET HORN** | | | | | | | | | | | |
| 1. | 8 brass | Munich BNM Mu 116 | | | 94.0 | boxw, horn, brass | SATW[1] | | 1801 | Angular form. Brass bell & mthpc missing. Brass mts either end of knee. | |
| **BASSOON** | | | | | | | | | | | |
| 1. | 6 | Stuttgart: G. Hase[2] | | | | | | | | | |
| **HERALD'S TRUMPET** | | | | | | | | | | | |
| 1. | | Markneukirchen 990, per Langwill[2] | | | | | | | | | |

# PAPALINI

PAPALINI

**BASS CLARINETS**

| Young No. | No. Keys and Metal | City, Owner, No. | Pitch | No. Pcs. | Length | Body, Mounts Flaps | SAT | Holes Dbld. | Additional Data | Ill. Source |
|---|---|---|---|---|---|---|---|---|---|---|
| 1. | 5 brass | Brussels 940 | C | 5 pcs | 67.2 | maple, horn sq | SATK | All keys mtd in blocks | Wood pins 1&6 dbl. Neck-coil all horn Horn ring, non-detachable. Holes not numbered (stamped). F♯ key touch is straight. Bore 1.97. Bell diameter 14.0. | Drawing, Mahillon II, p 221; ill. Rendall Clarinet, pl 7b. LOM 246. |
| 2. | 5 brass | Boston: MFA 17.1879; B. 119 | C | 5 pcs | 68.0 | pearw, horn sq | SATK | All keys mtd in blocks | Metal pins 1&6 dbl. Neck-coil wood. Ivory mini-bbl. Holes not numbered. F♯ key touch angled. Bore 2.0. Bell diameter 10.0. | Ill, Remnant, pl 112; EAMI 649. LOM 247 |
| 3. | 5 | Leipzig 1538 | C | | | | | | | |
| 4. | 8[3] | Paris C. 550 | | | | | | | | From the collection of Adolphe Sax. |
| 5. | 5 brass | New York MMA 2545 | C | 5 pcs | 68.5 | cocus & olive sq unmtd | | All keys mtd in blocks | No pins 1&6 dbl. Neck-coil wood. Wood bbl. Holes not numbered. F key touch angled. | Ill. Musical Instruments in the Metropolitan Museum, X-ray photo. |

# POERSCHMAN

POERSCHMAN

**ALTO RECORDER**

| Young No. | No. Keys and Metal | City, Owner, No. | Pitch | No. Pcs. | Length | Body, Mounts Flaps | SAT | Additional Data | Ill. Source |
|---|---|---|---|---|---|---|---|---|---|
| 1. | | Copenhagen: Claudius Collection 417 | | | 49.0 | boxw, unmtd | | | LOM 84 |

**FLUTES**

| Young No. | No. Keys and Metal | City, Owner, No. | Pitch | No. Pcs. | Length | Body, Mounts Flaps | SAT | Additional Data | Ill. Source |
|---|---|---|---|---|---|---|---|---|---|
| 1. | 1 silver | Leningrad 453 | E♭? | 4 pc | 50.8 | boxw, ivory sq | SATK | | LOM 85 |
| 2. | 1 | Zurich: Willi Burger | A? | 4 pc | 75.0 | boxw, ivory — — — | — — — | Originally 1 key; that replaced later and 4 other silver keys added. | |
| 3. | x1 | xBerlin 107 | F | | 46.0[4] | | | | |
| 4. | | Berlin: Dr. Walter Thoene | | | | | | Headjoint only. Rest of flute by Scherer | |

[1] 'A' and speaker key are SATK.  [2] Langwill lists the maker as "Franz Otto."  [3] Of the 8 keys, 3 "marchant a l'aide de 3 boutons en brass."  [4] Incorrectly given in GSJ XXXI as 64.0 cm.

| Young No. | No. Keys and Metal | City, Owner, No. | Pitch | No. Pcs. | Length | Body, Mounts Flaps | | SAT | Holes Dbld. | Tuning Holes | Additional Data | Ill. Source |
|---|---|---|---|---|---|---|---|---|---|---|---|---|

**POERSCHMAN** *(cont.)*

**OBOE**

| | | | | | | | | | | | | |
|---|---|---|---|---|---|---|---|---|---|---|---|---|
| 1. | | Poznan | | | | | | | | | Fragment only, not specified which: letter, 1978. | |

**OBOE D'AMORE**

| | | | | | | | | | | | | |
|---|---|---|---|---|---|---|---|---|---|---|---|---|
| 1. | 2 brass | New York: MMA 2041 | | | 62.9 | blk st maple, unmtd | ro | SATW | | 3&4 dbl. | | Ill. Hailperin GSJ XXVIII. LOM 82. |

**BASSOON**

| | | | | | | | | | | | | |
|---|---|---|---|---|---|---|---|---|---|---|---|---|
| 1. | 8 brass[1] | Leipzig 1384 | | | 120.4 | box or maple?[2](U) brass | | SATK | | | Decorative bell band. Flat table on bass joint.[3] | |

# PRUDENT

**FRENCH FLAGEOLET**

| | | | | | | | | | | | | |
|---|---|---|---|---|---|---|---|---|---|---|---|---|
| 1. | x5 silver | xBerlin 2752 | C | | 34.5 | ebony, ivory | | | | | | |
| 2. | 3 silver | Oxford: Bate 09 | A | 3 pc | 38.2 | cocus, ivory | | | | | | |
| 3. | | Sax Sale 1877, no. 7. | | | | | | | | | | |
| 4. | | Sax Sale 1877, no. 7. | | | | | | | | | | |
| 5. | | Sax Sale 1877, no. 7 | | | | | | | | | | |
| | | (These above 3 per Langwill) | | | | | | | | | | |
| 6. | 1 silver | Leningrad 419 | | 4 pc | 36.0 | ebony, bone? | | | | | | |

**PITCH PIPE**

| | | | | | | | | | | | | |
|---|---|---|---|---|---|---|---|---|---|---|---|---|
| 1. | | Paris C. 746, E. 661 | | | | boxw, unmtd. | | | | | | |

**FLUTES**

| | | | | | | | | | | | | |
|---|---|---|---|---|---|---|---|---|---|---|---|---|
| 1. | 1 brass | Munich Stadtmuseum 42/15 | C | 4 pc | 63.0 | ebony, ivory | oval(Y) | SATW | | | 2 keys added later in saddles. | |
| 2. | 1 | Basel: Michel Piguet | | | | | | | | | | |
| 3. | 9 | Leningrad 1148 | | 5 pc | 66.5 | ivory, silver? | | | | | | |

**OBOES**

| | | | | | | | | | | | | |
|---|---|---|---|---|---|---|---|---|---|---|---|---|
| 1. | 3 | Vienna: R. Clemencic | | | | | | | | | Stamp includes fleur de lys. | |
| 2. | 2 | Stockholm F. 280 | | | | boxw, ivory | ro | | 3&4 | 2 th. | | Ill. Halsingborg catalogue, pl. XI |
| 3. | 2 brass | Leningrad 515 | | | 57.5 | boxw, unmtd | | | 3&4 | | | |
| 4. | 2 brass | Leningrad 516 | | | 59.9 | boxw, horn? | | | | | 3 added keys. | |
| 5. | 2 | Brussels 3116 | | | 57.2 | ebony, ivory | | SATW | 3 | 2 th. | | |

---

[1] All its keys are replacements, the change made c. 1800, the Museum believes. The later keys are Bb, D, Eb L Th, F, F♯, G♯, and two wing keys.

[2] Because the instruments is very heavy in weight, it may be boxwood. A boxwood bassoon by Eichentopf, now in Linz, is easily the heaviest bassoon I have ever held.

[3] I am unable to recall seeing this on any other bassoon this early, but for two of the six known bassoons by Scherer. Poerschman's student, August Grenser, is the next one known to me to have used this advance in key mounting.

| Young No. | No. Keys and Metal | City, Owner, No. | Pitch | No. Pcs. | Length | Body, Mounts | Flaps | SAT | Holes Dbld. | Tuning Holes | Additional Data | Ill. Source |
|---|---|---|---|---|---|---|---|---|---|---|---|---|
| **PRUDENT** *(cont.)* | | | | | | | | | | | | **PRUDENT** *(cont.)* |
| CLARINETS | | | | | | | | | | | | |
| 1. | x5 | xBerlin 2879 | C | | 60.5 | boxw, ivory | | | | | | |
| 2. | | Loup Sale 194, per Langwill | | | | | | | | | | |
| BASSOONS | | | | | | | | | | | | |
| 1. | 5 brass | Paris C. 503 | | | 130.5 | maple, brass | (V) | SATW | | | Keys in saddles. Made for Poirier Lataille.[1] | Ill. JJ-GT-BR, no. 102. |
| 2. | 5 | Basel: Michel Piguet | | | | | | | | | | |
| 3. | 6 brass | Paris C. 1121 | | | 126.8 | maple, brass | | | | | | |
| 4. | 6 gilt | Neuchatel: Kunst & Hist. Museum. | | | 126.0 | | flaps[2] | | | | Keys recessed into wood. | EAMI 608. |
| **QUANTZ** | | | | | | | | | | | | **QUANTZ** |
| FLUTES | | | | | | | | | | | | |
| 1. | 2 silver | Washington: DCM 916 | C | | 67.2 | ebony, ivory | sq | | | | 6 upper jts. | EAM 471; ill. Gilliam-Lichtenwanger checklist. |
| 2. | 2 silver | Berlin 5076 [3] | C | | 66.0 | ebony, ivory | sq | SATK | | | 5 upper jts. Register. No stamp. | LOM 70. |
| 3. | 1 silver | Berlin 4229 | C | | 63.6 | ebony, ivory | | | | | 2 upper jts. No register. No maker's stamp. | |
| 4. | 2 brass | Scarsdale: D & R Rosenbaum | C | | 73.6 | ebony, ivory | | | | | 5 upper jts. Register. No maker's stamp. "XV" on each tenon. | |

**RAFI** [4]

FLUTES

| | City, Owner, No. | Length | Body | | pitch | stamp | | Ill. Source |
|---|---|---|---|---|---|---|---|---|
| 1. | Biblioteca Capitolare, Verona, no. 4. | 54.9[5] | Boxwood? | | Tenor-altus | C ✚ RAFI | | Inst. ill. & stamp, GSJ XXXII, pl V & VI |
| 2. | Museo degli Strumenti Musicali, Rome, no. 2789 | 57.7[5] | | | Tenor-altus | C ✚ RAFI | | |
| 3. | Accademia Filarmonica, Verona, no. 13287 | 64.8 | Boxwood? | | Tenor | G ● RAFI | | |

---

[1] (1754-1841), musician in the King's Chapel. One key with lateral movement.

[2] "Open work, in fan pattern."

[3] Berlin 5076

| | |
|---|---|
| Head joint (1 of 2) | 23.6 |
| Head joint (1 of 2) | 23.65 |
| Upper joint no. 1 | 18.8 |
| Upper joint no. 2 | 18.1 |
| Upper joint no. 3 | 17.4 |
| Upper joint no. 4 | 16.7 |
| Upper joint no. 5 | 16.0 |
| Lower jt + foot | 25.15 |
| Overall | 66.0 with upper joint no. 3. |

Notches on the end of each tenon to distinguish one upper joint from another. No numbers on exterior.

[4] This inventory of Rafi instruments owes a special debt to the article, in GSJ XXXII, by Filadelfio Puglisi. The groundwork has now begun, to lead us toward a fresh appreciation of the importance of the Rafi family.

[5] These are sounding lengths, not overall lengths.

| Young No. | No. Keys and Metal | City, Owner, No. | Pitch | No. Pcs. | Length | Body, Mounts Flaps | SAT | Holes Dbld. | Tuning Holes | Additional Data | Ill. Source |
|---|---|---|---|---|---|---|---|---|---|---|---|
| **RAFI** (cont.) | | | | | | | | | | | |
| **FLUTES** (cont.) | | | | | | | | | | | |
| 4. | | Eisenach: Bachaus I-100 | | | 70.75 cm. | Plumwood, brass mts | Tenor | C | • | RAFI | | |
| 5. | | Brussels 1066 | | | 71.7 cm. | Boxwood? Maple? | Tenor | C | • | RAFI | Bore: head 1.8; ft 1.78-1.8. pl. III-14. LOM 5 | Color Ill. Bragard-deHen |
| 6. | | Museo degli Strumenti Musicali, Rome, no. 2788 | | | 86.05[1] cm. | | Bass | M | • | RAFI | | |
| 7. | | xLeipzig 1274 (lost WW2) | | | x95.5 cm. | Boxwood, horn mounts | Bass | | | RAFI[2] | | Ill. Kinsky Kleiner |
| **TENOR RECORDER** | | | | | | | | | | | |
| 1. | | Accademia Filarmonica, Bologna, no. 8. | | | 49.75[3] | | | C | | RAFI | | |
| **BASSET RECORDER** | | | | | | | | | | | |
| 1. | | Accademia Filarmonica, Bologna, no. 9. | | | 77.5[1] cm. | | | C | | RAFI | | |
| **"RECORDERS AND FIFES"** (from Langwill, 5th edition) | | | | | | | | | | | |
| 1. | | Museo Settala, no. 10. | | | | | | | | | | |
| 2. | | Museo Settala, no. 19. | | | | | | | | | | |
| 3. | | Museo Settala, no. 20. | | | | | | | | | | |
| 4. | | Museo Settala, no. 21. | | | | | | | | | | |
| 5. | | Museo Settala, no. 22. | | | | | | | | | | |

# RAUCH VON SCHRATT [4]

| Young No. | No. Keys and Metal | City, Owner, No. | Pitch | No. Pcs. | Length | Body, Mounts Flaps | SAT | Holes Dbld. | Tuning Holes | Additional Data | Ill. Source |
|---|---|---|---|---|---|---|---|---|---|---|---|
| **SOPRANO RECORDER** | | | | | | *dated:* | | | | | |
| 1. | | Brussels 189 | | | 50.8 | maple, brass | undated | | | | Columnar form. Swallowtail key is a second-class lever, covered by perforated brass box. | Ill. color, Bragard-deHen, pl III-13. LOM 2. |
| **TENOR RECORDER** | | | | | | | | | | | |
| 1. | | Celle: Dr. Herman Moeck | | | 61.4 | | undated | | | | Edge-blown. | |

[1] These are sounding lengths, not overall lengths.

[2] Dr. Heyde seems to suggest in his Leipzig flute catalogue that the full name "Claude Rafi" was stamped on this instrument, but I doubt this very much. Georg Kinsky is no more specific on this point in the Kleiner Heyer. For now, then, I omit an initial for this instrument.

[3] This is not the original length, but its present speaking length.

[4] Note: The above is simply a list of instruments I have learned are attributed to or known to be by Caspar or Hans Rauch von Schratt or von Schrattenbach. Two instruments—Salzburg 3/12 and Munich's Bayerisches Nationalmuseum Mu 180—actually have the name Hans Rauch von Schratt engraved on metal. The presence of one or more ♣ trefoil devices "stamped" or burned into the wood body of the instruments, seems to have convinced other museums that any c. 16th century woodwind instrument bearing a similar trefoil ♣ may be by one or another member of the Rauch family. This is a perfectly reasonable assumption, temporarily, but a great deal more work needs to be done on this topic.

| Young No. | No. Keys and Metal | City, Owner, No. | Pitch | No. Pcs. | Length | Body, Mounts Flaps | SAT | Holes Dbld. | Tuning Holes | Additional Data | Ill. Source |
|---|---|---|---|---|---|---|---|---|---|---|---|
| **RAUCH VON SCHRATT** *(cont.)* | | | | | | | *dated:* | | | | **RAUCH VON SCHRATT** *(cont.)* |
| BASS RECORDERS | | | | | | | | | | | |
| 1. | | Salzburg 3/12 | | | 84.0 | boxwood | d. 1535[1] | | | Engraved name-band. | Ill. Birsak catalogue, pl 30. |
| 2. | | Nürnberg MIR 212 | | | 85.5 | maple, brass | undated | | | | |
| QUINTBASS RECORDER | | | | | | | | | | | |
| 1. | | Munich BNM Mu 174 | | | 126.0 | maple, brass | undated | | | Key & crook missing. Fontanelle crushed but repaired. Crook went into top. 1 pc body. | Ill. this book, Pl. I |
| GREAT BASS RECORDER | | | | | | | | | | | |
| 1. | | Munich BNM Mu 180 [2] | | | 179.0 | maple, brass | undated | | | 1 brass, swallowtail key. Crook goes into top. 2 pc body. Engraved name ca. same as Salzburg. | Ill. this book, Pl. I |
| DOUBLE BASS RECORDER | | | | | | | | | | | |
| 1. | | Antwerp: Vleeshuis V.44 [3] | | | 262.0 | | undated | | | | Ill. Hunt, pl V (replacement parts removed for photo); ill. EAMI 414 (replacement parts are shown). |
| QUARTFLOTE [4] | | | | | | | | | | | |
| 1. | | Frankfurt X-2460 | | | | | | | | | |
| **F. RICHTERS** | | | | | | | | | | | **F. RICHTERS** |
| OBOES | | | | | | | | | | | |
| 1. | 3 silver | Hague Ea 439-1933 | | | 58.0 | ebony, silver | | | | | |
| 2. | 3 silver | Hague Ea 284-1933 [5] | | | 57.5 | ebony, ivory | | | | | ill. 1974 booklet, ill. top finial, frontespiece, right; ill. instrument, p 52, top right. |
| 3. | 3 silver, engraved | Hague Ea 624-1933 | | | 57.8 | ebony, silver | | | | | |

[1] This date appears on the brass band of the fontanelle.

[2] There is a copy in Brussels Musee Instrumental.

[3] This instrument is attributed to Caspar Rauch von Schrattenbach on the basis of Charles Burney's account in *Present State of Music . . .*, 1773. The Brussels Musee Instrumental and the New York Metropolitan have copies.

[4] I have not seen this instrument. It may be a quartbass recorder, a hochquart recorder, or a hochquart transverse flute.

[5] The Museum inventory lists this instrument as by "RICHTERS" with no initial specified, but the 1974 exhibition catalogue, *Historische Blaasinstrumenten, Kasteel Ehrenstein Kerkrade* lists it as made by Frederik. See following note. The booklet may still be available from the Gemeente Museum, The Hague.

Note: The booklet referred to above includes an important study of early Dutch woodwind makers, unfortunately written in uncompromising Dutch. The authors, S.A.C. Dudok van Heel and Marieke Teutscher, have concluded that Richter oboes without initial may be assigned to Hendrik if the trefoil trademark's stem curves to the *left* and to Frederik if the trefoil stem curves to the right. Thus,

Hendrik Richters

Frederik Richters

| Young No. | No. Keys and Metal | City, Owner, No. | Pitch | No. Pcs. | Length | Body, Mounts | Flaps | SAT | Holes Dbld. | Tuning Holes | Additional Data | Ill. Source |
|---|---|---|---|---|---|---|---|---|---|---|---|---|

## H. RICHTERS

## H. RICHTERS

### OBOES

| Young No. | No. Keys and Metal | City, Owner, No. | Pitch | No. Pcs. | Length | Body, Mounts | Flaps | SAT | Holes Dbld. | Tuning Holes | Additional Data | Ill. Source |
|---|---|---|---|---|---|---|---|---|---|---|---|---|
| 1. | 3 silver | Hague Ea 286-1933 | | | 57.5 | ebony, ivory | | | 3&4 | | Keys engraved. | |
| 2. | 3 silver | Hague Ea 436-1933 | | | 57.0 | ebony, ivory | | | 3&4 | | Keys engraved. | |
| 3. | 3 silver | Hague Ea 548-1933 | | | 56.7 | ebony, ivory | ro C, trap (L)e♭ | SATW | 3&4 | | Keys engraved. | Ill. '74 exhib catalogue: keys, p 3; instrument, p. 52. LOM 74. ill. this book, Pl. III |
| 4. | 3 silver | Hague Ea 7-X-1952 | | | 57.3 | ebony, ivory | | | 3&4 | | Keys engraved. | Keys ill. 1974 exhib catalogue, p 3. ill. this book. Pl. III |
| 5. | 3 silver | Hague Ea 8-X-1952 | | | 56.6 | ebony, ivory | | | 3&4 | | | |
| 6. | 3 silver | Hague Ea 15-X-1952 | | | 56.5 | ebony, ivory | | | 3&4 | | Kéys engraved. | |
| 7. | 3 silver | Hague Ea 17-X-1952 | | | 57.2 | ebony, ivory | ro C, sq e♭ | | 3&4 | 2 th. | Keys engraved. | |
| 8. | 3 silver | Washington: DCM 158 | | | 57.2 | ebony, ivory | ro C, (L) e♭ | SATW | 3&4 | 2 th. | Keys engraved. | |
| 9. | 3 silver | Bonn BH (Zimmer-mann 93) | | | 58.25 | ebony, ivory | ro C, (L) e♭. | SATW | 3&4 | 2 th. | Keys engraved. | |
| 10. | 3 silver | Vienna 653 | | | 57.1 | ebony, ivory | ro C, (L) e♭. | SATW | 3&4 | 2 th. | Keys engraved. | |
| 11. | 3 silver | New York: MMA 53.56.11 | | | 57.2 | ebony, ivory | ro C, (L) e♭. | SATW | 3&4 | 2 th. | Keys engraved. | LOM 75. |
| 12. | 3 brass | London: Horniman 210 | | | (58.2) | boxw, unmtd | | | | | Bell by P. Borkens | |
| 13. | 3 silver | London: T. Bingham cat. 7 | | | 57.2 | ebony, ivory | | | | | | |
| 14. | 3 | Basel: M. Piguet | | | | | | | | | | |
| 15. | middle jt only | New Paltz, N.Y.: Zadro | | | | | | | | | | |

### TAILLE - TENOR OBOE

| Young No. | No. Keys and Metal | City, Owner, No. | Pitch | No. Pcs. | Length | Body, Mounts | Flaps | SAT | Holes Dbld. | Tuning Holes | Additional Data | Ill. Source |
|---|---|---|---|---|---|---|---|---|---|---|---|---|
| 1. | 3 brass | Paris C.1116, E.1185 | | | 84.5 | boxw? maple? ivory | (S) C, (G) e♭ | SATW | 3&4 | 2 th. | | LOM 77. |

### "RICHTERS" (NO INITIAL) OBOES

| Young No. | No. Keys and Metal | City, Owner, No. | Pitch | No. Pcs. | Length | Body, Mounts | Flaps | SAT | Holes Dbld. | Tuning Holes | Additional Data | Ill. Source |
|---|---|---|---|---|---|---|---|---|---|---|---|---|
| 1. | 3 silver | Hague Ea 442-1933 | | | 57.0 | ebony, silver engraving | | | 3&4 | | Keys engraved. | |
| 2. | 3 modern brass | Brussels 1981 | | | | ebony, carved ivory | | | 3&4 | 2 th | | |

### ATTRIBUTED TO "H. RICHTERS" (unmarked or no initial, trefoil stem direction undetermined) OBOES

| Young No. | No. Keys and Metal | City, Owner, No. | Pitch | No. Pcs. | Length | Body, Mounts | Flaps | SAT | Holes Dbld. | Tuning Holes | Additional Data | Ill. Source |
|---|---|---|---|---|---|---|---|---|---|---|---|---|
| 1. | 3 silver | Hague Ea 4-X-1952 | | | 57.3 | ebony, silver | ro C, sq e♭. | | | | Keys engraved. 1 flap dated 1744! | |
| 2. | 3 silver | Hague ea 5-X-1952 | | | 56.5 | ebony | ro C, sq e♭. | | 3&4 | | Keys engraved | |
| 3. | | Loup Sale 199, per Langwill | | | | | | | | | | |

**H. RICHTERS** *(cont.)*
**H. RICHTERS** *(cont.)*
ATTRIBUTED TO "H. RICHTERS" *(cont.)*

| Young No. | No. Keys and Metal | City, Owner, No. | Pitch | No. Pcs. | Length | Body, Mounts | Flaps | SAT | Holes Dbld. | Tuning Holes | Additional Data | Ill. Source |
|---|---|---|---|---|---|---|---|---|---|---|---|---|
| 4. | | Loup Sale 204, per Langwill | | | | | | | | | | |
| 5. | | Samary Sale 101, per Langwill | | | | | | | | | | |
| 6. | | Weiskaupt Sale 28, now Guy Oldham | | | | | | | | | | |
| 7. | | Col. Myddleton, Galpin Exhib. '59. | | | | | | | | | | |
| 8. | | E. van Tright | | | | | | | | | | |
| 9. | | Langwill 4th & 5th editions also list Hague Ea 707 | | | | | | | | | | |
| 10. | | Langwill 4th & 5th editions also list Hague Ea 717 | | | | | | | | | | |

# RIJKEL
RIJKEL

## ALTO RECORDERS

| Young No. | No. Keys and Metal | City, Owner, No. | Pitch | No. Pcs. | Length | Body, Mounts | Flaps | SAT | Holes Dbld. | Tuning Holes | Additional Data | Ill. Source |
|---|---|---|---|---|---|---|---|---|---|---|---|---|
| 1. | | Paris C. 399 | F | 3 pc | 49.0 | boxw, ivory | | | | | Main joint and foot have Jacob Denner's [1] stamp. "RYKEL" with "T T" below, on head jt. (Headjoint, only, by Rijkel.) | |
| 2. | | xBerlin 2809 | E♭ | | 50.5 | ivory | | | | | | |
| 3. | | Stockholm 21.979 | F | | | ivory | | | | | | |
| 4. | | Sigmaringen 304 | | | | | | | | | Foot jt is stamped "Rijkel & Haka," only known instance. Main jt "Rijkel" alone.[1] | |

## OBOES

| Young No. | No. Keys and Metal | City, Owner, No. | Pitch | No. Pcs. | Length | Body, Mounts | Flaps | SAT | Holes Dbld. | Tuning Holes | Additional Data | Ill. Source |
|---|---|---|---|---|---|---|---|---|---|---|---|---|
| 1. | 3 brass | Hague Ea 6-X-1952 | | | 53.85 | boxw, ivory | ro C, sq (L) e♭ | SATW | 3&4 | 2 th. | Brass bell rim. | Ill. Langwill 5th ed., p 80[2] |
| 2. | 3 silver | Hague Ea 440-1933 | | | 56.8 | ebony, ivory | ro C, sq (L) e♭. | | 3&4 | 2 th. | | Ill. Langwill 5th ed., p 80[3] |

# RIPPERT
RIPPERT

## SOPRANINO RECORDERS

| Young No. | No. Keys and Metal | City, Owner, No. | Pitch | No. Pcs. | Length | Body, Mounts | Flaps | SAT | Holes Dbld. | Tuning Holes | Additional Data | Ill. Source |
|---|---|---|---|---|---|---|---|---|---|---|---|---|
| 1. | | Munich: BNM Mu 151 (Bierdimpfl no. 4)[4] | | 2 pc | 24.5 | ivory, unmtd | | | | | Hole 7 dbl. in foot joint. | One of these two is ill. Hunt, pl. VIII. |
| 2. | | Munich: BNM Mu 164 (Bierdimpfl no. 17) | | 2 pc | 24.5 | ivory, unmtd | | | | | Hole 7 dbl. in foot joint. | One of these two is ill. Hunt, pl. VIII |

[1] The head joint is by Jacob Denner and carries his usual stamp with fir tree and I D.
[2] 4th from left.
[3] 2nd from right, even though not so labeled. Also ill. Hague 1974 Exhibition catalogue, no. 103.
[4] K.A. Bierdimpfl: *Die Sammlung . . .*, Munich 1883. Full title is given in the bibliography.

| Young No. | No. Keys and Metal | City, Owner, No. | Pitch | No. Pcs. | Length | Body, Mounts | Flaps | SAT | Holes Dbld. | Tuning Holes | Additional Data | Ill. Source |
|---|---|---|---|---|---|---|---|---|---|---|---|---|
| **RIPPERT** *(cont.)* | | | | | | | | | | | | **RIPPERT** *(cont.)* |
| **ALTO RECORDERS** | | | | | | | | | | | | |
| 1. | | Munich: BNM Mu 160 (Bierdimpfl no. 13) | | | 45.0 | ivory, unmtd | | | | | | One of these two is (also) ill. Hunt, pl. VIII. |
| 2. | | xMunich BNM x(Bierdimpfl, no. 14) | | | 44.0 | | | | | | | One of these two is (also) ill. Hunt, pl. VIII. |
| 3. | | Paris C.1387 | | | 46.05 | boxw, ivory | | | | | | |
| **TENOR RECORDERS** | | | | | | | | | | | | |
| 1. | | xMunich: BNM x(Bierdimpfl no. 11) | | | 60.0 | | | | | | | |
| 2. | 1 key | xMunich: BNM x(Bierdimpfl no. 9) | | | 60.0 | ivory | | | | | | |
| 3. | no key | Basel 1956.633 | D | | 58.0 | boxw, unmtd | | | | | | Ill. Hunt, pl XIV-11 |
| 4. | | Celle: Dr. H. Moeck | | | | ebony, ivory | | | | | | |
| 5. | | Glasgow: Glen Collection[1] | | | | | | | | | | |
| **BASS RECORDERS** | | | | | | | | | | | | |
| 1. | | xMunich: BNM x(Bierdimpfl no. 10) | | | 96.0 | ivory | | | | | | |
| 2. | 1 brass | Washington: DCM 800 | | | 113.0 | red-brn wood, ro ivory | | | | | | Brass crook goes into top. | Ill. Gilliam-Lichtenwanger checklist. |
| 3. | 1 brass | Paris C.412, E.247 | | | 113.0 | fruitw, ivory, ro horn | | SATW | | | Brass crook goes into top. |
| 4. | 1 brass | Paris C.411, E.185 | | | 109.0 | maple? brass ro | | SATW | | | Brass crook goes into top. Has floor peg-crutch-strut. |
| 5. | | Glasgow: Glen Collection[1] | | | | | | | | | | |
| **FLUTES** | | | | | | | | | | | | |
| 1. | 1 silver | Glasgow: Glen Collection | | | c. 57.5 | pear, ivory | trap | | | | | See GSJ IV, p 42 for detailed descrip. & photo. |
| 2. | | Saint Moritz: Museum Engadin | | | | wood, ivory | | | | | | |
| **OBOES** | | | | | | | | | | | | |
| 1. | 2 silver | Leipzig 1312 | | | 59.3 | boxw, ivory (wide) | ro C. sq e♭. | SATW | 3&4 | 2 th. | | Ill. Rubardt Führer, taf XIII ill. this book, PL IX |
| 2. | | Lery Sale no. 66, per Langwill | | | | | | | | | | |

[1] The presence of these two recorders in the Glen Collection was reported too late for verification. Let us hope they exist and are there.

# G. A. ROTTENBURGH

# G. A. ROTTENBURGH

## TENOR RECORDER

| Young No. | No. Keys and Metal | City, Owner, No. | Pitch | No. Pcs. | Length | Body, Mounts | Flaps | SAT | Holes Dbld. | Tuning Holes | Additional Data | Ill. Source |
|---|---|---|---|---|---|---|---|---|---|---|---|---|
| 1. | | Leipzig 1132 | | 3 pc | 57.5 | boxw | | | | | | |

## FLUTES

| Young No. | No. Keys and Metal | City, Owner, No. | Pitch | No. Pcs. | Length | Body, Mounts | Flaps | SAT | Holes Dbld. | Tuning Holes | Additional Data | Ill. Source |
|---|---|---|---|---|---|---|---|---|---|---|---|---|
| 1. | 1 silver | Washington: DCM 1128 | C | 4 pc | 60.2 | boxw, ivory | sq | SATK | | | | |
| 2. | 1 silver | Brussels 2682 | C | 4 pc | 60.3 | boxw, ivory | | | | | 3 more keys added later. | |
| 3. | 1 silver | Munich Stadtmuseum 42/16 | C | 4 pc | 61.7 | ebony, ivory, horn | sq(F) | SATK | | | Ebony cap & screw. | |
| 4. | 1 silver | Amsterdam: F. Brüggen | | 4 pc | 64.8 | boxw, ivory | sq | SATW | | | In contemporary double case. | |
| 5. | 1 silver | Amsterdam: F. Brüggen | | 4 pc | 64.8 | boxw, ivory | sq | SATW | | | In contemporary double case. | |
| 6. | 1 silver | Brussels 3570 | | 4 pc | 61.75 | boxw, ivory | sq | SATK | | | | |
| 7. | 1 silver | Brussels 3784 | | 4 pc | 62.2+ | boxw, ivory | sq | SATW | | | | |
| 8. | 1 brass | Brussels 2683 | | 4 pc | 63.4 | boxw, ivory | ——— | ——— | | | Headjoint only, rest by I.H. Rottenburgh. No ivory on head jt. | |
| 9. | 1 brass | Washington: DCM 507 | | 4 pc | 65.0[1] | boxw, ivory | sq | SATW | | | 2 upper joints. | |
| 10. | upper jt only | Meopham: Nicholas Benn | | | | | | | | | Rest is by I.B. Willems. | |
| 11. | | Bruges: B. Kuijken | | | | | | | | | | |
| 12. | | Bruges: B. Kuijken | | | | | | | | | | |

## ALTO FLUTES

| Young No. | No. Keys and Metal | City, Owner, No. | Pitch | No. Pcs. | Length | Body, Mounts | Flaps | SAT | Holes Dbld. | Tuning Holes | Additional Data | Ill. Source |
|---|---|---|---|---|---|---|---|---|---|---|---|---|
| 1. | | Bruges: B. Kuijken | | | | | | | | | | |
| 2. | | Bruges: B. Kuijken | | | | | | | | | | |

## OBOES

| Young No. | No. Keys and Metal | City, Owner, No. | Pitch | No. Pcs. | Length | Body, Mounts | Flaps | SAT | Holes Dbld. | Tuning Holes | Additional Data | Ill. Source |
|---|---|---|---|---|---|---|---|---|---|---|---|---|
| 1. | 2 | Stockholm F. 278 | | | | boxw, ivory | | | | | | Ill. Halsingborg catalogue, pl XI |
| 2. | 3 silver | Brussels 2610 | | 3 pc | 57.8 | boxw, ivory | sq-cors | SATW | 3&4 | 2 th. | | |

## TAILLE

| Young No. | No. Keys and Metal | City, Owner, No. | Pitch | No. Pcs. | Length | Body, Mounts | Flaps | SAT | Holes Dbld. | Tuning Holes | Additional Data | Ill. Source |
|---|---|---|---|---|---|---|---|---|---|---|---|---|
| 1. | 2 brass | Paris C.184, E.2184 | | 3 pc | 84.2 | boxw, brass | | | 3 | | Military model, like Brussels, Bate, & Stockholm specimens by I.H. Rottenburgh. | |

## CLARINETS

| Young No. | No. Keys and Metal | City, Owner, No. | Pitch | No. Pcs. | Length | Body, Mounts | Flaps | SAT | Holes Dbld. | Tuning Holes | Additional Data | Ill. Source |
|---|---|---|---|---|---|---|---|---|---|---|---|---|
| 1. | 2 brass | Brussels 915 | E♭ | 4 pc | 53.8 | boxw, ivory | | | 0 dbl. | | | |
| 2. | 2 brass | Brussels 2571 | C | 3 pc | 53.7 | ebony, ivory | sq | SATW | 0 dbl. | | Bore 1.32-1.38 cm. Horn sleeve over bell. | |
| 3. | 2 | Brussels 2517 | C | | | | | | | | Not in 197? checklist by M. Tilmans. Others are. | |
| 4. | 4 brass | Brussels 2572 | B♭ | 3 pc | 54.55 | boxw, ivory | sq | SATW | | | Mthpc missing. Bore 1.46. | |

[1] 61.3 cm. to top tenon.

| Young No. | No. Keys and Metal | City, Owner, No. | Pitch | No. Pcs. | Length | Body, Mounts | Flaps | SAT | Holes Dbld. | Tuning Holes | Additional Data | Ill. Source |
|---|---|---|---|---|---|---|---|---|---|---|---|---|

**G. A. ROTTENBURGH** *(cont.)*

**G. A. ROTTENBURGH** *(cont.)*
**CLARINETS** *(cont.)*

| | | | | | | | | | | | | |
|---|---|---|---|---|---|---|---|---|---|---|---|---|
| 5. | 4 brass | Cambridge: N. Shackleton | A | 4 pc | 74.1[1] | boxw, ivory | sq | SATW | | | Bbl. missing. No f♯ key. Lower jt & bell = 1 pc. | |
| 6. | 5 brass | Brussels 168 | B♭ | 4 pc | 63.0? | boxw, ivory | sq | SATW | 0 dbl. | | Bad warp. Bore 1.24. | |
| 7. | 5 brass | Brussels 4363 | A? | | 68.0 | boxw, ivory | | | 0 dbl. | | | |
| 8. | x5 brass | xBerlin 2876 | B♭ | | 70.5 | boxw | | | | | All keys in blocks. | |
| 9. | 5 brass | Paris | | | 56.0 | boxw | | | | | ex A. Sax | |
| 10. | 5 brass | Zurich: H.R. Stalder | A | | | | | | | | | |

**CLARINET D'AMOUR**

| | | | | | | | | | | | | |
|---|---|---|---|---|---|---|---|---|---|---|---|---|
| 1. | 6 brass | Brussels 2595 | G | 6 pc | 89.5 | boxw, ivory | sq | SATW | | | Bore 1.59. 6th key is beside g♯ & is for usual open hole. | |

# I. H. ROTTENBURGH

**I. H. ROTTENBURGH**

**ALTO RECORDERS IN F**

| | | | | | | | | | | | | |
|---|---|---|---|---|---|---|---|---|---|---|---|---|
| 1. | | Berlin 2799 | | 3 pc | 50.5 | boxw, ivory | | | | | | |
| 2. | | Brussels 1036 | | 3 pc | 50.2 | boxw, ivory | | | | | | |
| 3. | | Brussels 1027 | | 3 pc | 50.2 | boxw, ivory | | | | | | Ill. Mahillon II, p 287 |
| 4. | | Brussels 2643a | | 3 pc | 50.0 | pearw, unmtd | | | | | identical pair | LOM 65 |
| 5. | | Brussels 2643b | | 3 pc | 50.0 | pearw, unmtd | | | | | identical pair | |
| 6. | | Brussels 2644 | | 3 pc | 51.0 | pear? boxw? unmtd | | | | | | |

**TENOR RECORDER IN C**

| | | | | | | | | | | | | |
|---|---|---|---|---|---|---|---|---|---|---|---|---|
| 1. | | Berlin 2814 | C' | 3 pc | 59.5 | boxw, unmtd | | | | | | Ill. Sachs catalogue, taf 25 |

**BASS RECORDER**

| | | | | | | | | | | | | |
|---|---|---|---|---|---|---|---|---|---|---|---|---|
| 1. | 2 brass | Hague Ea 401-1933 | | 4 pc | 98.5 | boxw, ivory | trap | | | | Crook missing, but goes into top. | |

**FLUTES**

| | | | | | | | | | | | | |
|---|---|---|---|---|---|---|---|---|---|---|---|---|
| 1. | 1 | Stockholm F. 186 | | | | ebony, ivory embouch & bushing | | | | | | |
| 2. | 1 brass | Brussels 1077 | | 4 pc | 63.5 | boxw, ivory | sq | SATK | | | | |
| 3. | 1 brass | Brussels 2384 | | 4 pc | 62.2 | boxw, unmtd | sq | SATW | | | | |
| 4. | 1 brass | Brussels 2679 | | 4 pc | 63.8+ | boxw, ivory | sq | SATW | | | End cap missing. | |
| 5. | 1 brass | Brussels 2680 | | 4 pc | 60.1 | boxw, ivory | sq | SATW | | | End cap missing. | |
| 6. | 1 silver | Brussels 2681 | | 4 pc | 58.8 | boxw, silver | long sq | SATW | | | End cap missing. | |
| 7. | 1 silver | Brussels 2001 | | 4 pc | 64.9 | ebony, silver | sq | SATW | | | | |
| 8. | 1 brass | Brussels 2683 | | 4 pc | 63.4 | boxw, ivory | sq | SATW | | | Head joint by GAR. | |

[1] 61.3 cm. to top tenon.

| Young No. | No. Keys and Metal | City, Owner, No. | Pitch | No. Pcs. | Length | Body, Mounts | Flaps | SAT | Holes Dbld. | Tuning Holes | Additional Data | Ill. Source |
|---|---|---|---|---|---|---|---|---|---|---|---|---|
| **I. H. ROTTENBURGH** *(cont.)* | | | | | | | | | | | | |
| **FLUTES** *(cont.)* | | | | | | | | | | | | |
| 9. | x1 silver | xBerlin 2654 | 8ᵛᵉ flute | 3 pc | 32.0 | boxw, ivory | sq | | | | End cap missing. | |
| 10. | x1 silver | xBerlin 2668 | B | | 64.5 | boxw, ivory | sq | | | | | |
| 11. | 1 silver | Berlin (seen '79) | | 3 pc | | cocus, ivory | sq | | | | | |
| **OBOES** | | | | | | | | | | | | |
| 1. | 3 brass | Brussels 4360 | | | 59.3 | boxw, ivory | | | 3 | | | |
| 2. | 3 brass | Brussels 965 | A ? | | 64.0 | boxw, ivory | | SATW | 4 | | 1 pc missing. | |
| 3. | 2 brass | Brussels 966 | | | 58.1 | boxw, ivory | | SATW | 3&4 | | Bell by GAR, rest by I.H. Rottenburgh | |
| 4. | 3 brass | Brussels 2608 | | | 59.9 | boxw, ivory | sq eb, ro C. | SATW | 3 | | | LOM 91 |
| 5. | 3 silver | Brussels 2609 | | | 59.4 | boxw, unmtd | sq eb, ro C | SATW | 3&4 | | | |
| 6. | 3 | Basel: M. Piguet Michigan 667 | | | | | | | 3 | | | |
| 7. | 2 brass | Ann Arbor: U. of Michigan 667 | | | 58.2 | boxw, ivory | | | 3&4 | 2 th. | Stanley cat. says 3 keys. | |
| 8. | 3 brass | xBerlin 2944 | | | 60.0 | boxw | ro | | | | | |
| **TENOR OBOES** (all 'Military model') | | | | | | | | | | | | |
| 1. | 3 brass | Brussels 2618 | | | 74.8 | boxw, brass | ro | SATW | 3&4 | | | |
| 2. | 3 brass | Brussels 2619 | | | 74.6 | boxw, brass | ro | SATW | 3&4 | | | |
| 3. | 3 brass | Brussels 180 | | | (73.05) | boxw, brass | ro | SATW | 3 | | 2 pc by IHR, 1 by GAR | Ill. Bragard-deHen, pl IV-14 |
| 4. | 3 brass | Stockholm F. 288 | | | 74.5 | boxw, brass | | | 3 | | | |
| 5. | 3 brass | Oxford: Bate 248 | | | 72.6 | boxw, brass | ro | SATW | 3 | | | LOM 95 |
| **BASSOONS** | | | | | | | | | | | | |
| 1. | 4 brass | Leipzig 1374 | | | 125.0 | maple, brass | (V) | SATW | | | Keys in brass saddles. B♭, D, F, G♯. | |
| 2. | 4 brass | Bruges-Gruuthouse | | | | | | | | | | |

| Young No. | No. Keys and Metal | City, Owner, No. | Pitch | No. Pcs. | Length | Body, Mounts Flaps | | SAT | Holes Dbld. | Tuning Holes | Additional Data | Ill. Source |
|---|---|---|---|---|---|---|---|---|---|---|---|---|

# J. C. E. SATTLER

Actual stamp:

**J. C. E. SATTLER**

## RECORDERS

| Young No. | No. Keys and Metal | City, Owner, No. | Pitch | No. Pcs. | Length | Body, Mounts Flaps | | SAT | Holes Dbld. | Tuning Holes | Additional Data | Ill. Source |
|---|---|---|---|---|---|---|---|---|---|---|---|---|
| 1. | Soprano | Stockholm 159 | | | | boxw | | | | | Stamp 'A' | |
| 2. | Alto | Stockholm 161 | | | | boxw | | | | | Stamp 'A' | |
| 3. | Alto | Stockholm 162 | | | | boxw | | | | | Stamp 'A' | |
| 4. | Alto | Ann Arbor: Univ. of Michigan 505 | | 3 pc | 49.5 | boxw | | | | | Stamp 'A' | See GSJ XXIII, Warner & von Huene, detailed drawing. |

## OBOES

| Young No. | No. Keys and Metal | City, Owner, No. | Pitch | No. Pcs. | Length | Body, Mounts Flaps | | SAT | Holes Dbld. | Tuning Holes | Additional Data | Ill. Source |
|---|---|---|---|---|---|---|---|---|---|---|---|---|
| 1. | 2 brass | Stockholm 157 | | | 56.6 | boxw, unmtd | ro C, sq eb | SATW | 3&4 | 2 th. | Stamp 'B' | |
| 2. | 2 brass | Leningrad 506 | | | 57.7 | boxw, brass | | | 3&4 | | Probably stamp 'A' | |
| 3. | 3 brass | Oxford: Bate 204 | | | 52.6 | boxw, ivory | ro C, sq eb | | | | Stamp 'B'. Upper jt unmarked. Bell not original. | |
| 4. | 3 | Stockholm: Hammer Coll. auction 1477, per Langwill | | | | | | | | | | |
| 5. | 3 | Stockholm: Hammer Coll. auction 1485, per Langwill | | | | | | | | | | |

## OBOES D'AMORE

| Young No. | No. Keys and Metal | City, Owner, No. | Pitch | No. Pcs. | Length | Body, Mounts Flaps | | SAT | Holes Dbld. | Tuning Holes | Additional Data | Ill. Source |
|---|---|---|---|---|---|---|---|---|---|---|---|---|
| 1. | 3 brass | Stockholm 148 | | | 60.6 | boxw, unmtd | ro | SATW | 3&4 | 0 th. | Stamp 'A' | |
| 2. | 3 brass | Munich: DM 18868 | | | 61.6 | boxw, horn | | | 3&4 | | Stamp 'B' | |
| 3. | 2 brass | Copenhagen E.70 | | | 60.6 | boxw, unmtd | ro C, trap eb | SATW | 3&4 | | Stamp 'A' | |
| 4. | 3 brass | Nürnberg MIR 392 | | | 60.65 | boxw, unmtd | ro eb[1] | SATW | 3&4 | 0 th. | Stamp 'A' *without* initials.[2] | |
| 5. | | Prague 1701E | | | | | | | | | | |

## BASSOON

| Young No. | No. Keys and Metal | City, Owner, No. | Pitch | No. Pcs. | Length | Body, Mounts Flaps | | SAT | Holes Dbld. | Tuning Holes | Additional Data | Ill. Source |
|---|---|---|---|---|---|---|---|---|---|---|---|---|
| 1. | 4 brass | Trondheim: Ringve Museum 75/2 | | | | | | | | | Stamp 'B' | |

# CARL SATTLER

**CARL SATTLER**

## FIFE

| Young No. | No. Keys and Metal | City, Owner, No. | Pitch | No. Pcs. | Length | Body, Mounts Flaps | | SAT | Holes Dbld. | Tuning Holes | Additional Data | Ill. Source |
|---|---|---|---|---|---|---|---|---|---|---|---|---|
| 1. | x0 keys | xBerlin 2714 | F | | 44.25 | | | | | | Stamp 'CARL / SATTLER / G' | |

## FLUTES

| Young No. | No. Keys and Metal | City, Owner, No. | Pitch | No. Pcs. | Length | Body, Mounts Flaps | | SAT | Holes Dbld. | Tuning Holes | Additional Data | Ill. Source |
|---|---|---|---|---|---|---|---|---|---|---|---|---|
| 1. | 1 brass | Stockholm F.737 | | | 63.3 | boxw, horn | | | | | Dated 1732 but suspicious. Much repaired. | |
| 2. | | Prague 604E | | | | | | | | | | |

Note: as I pointed out in GSJ XXXI, Carl Sattler, a woodwind maker c. 1770 who may also have worked in Leipzig, used (or used as well?) the stamp 'CARL SATTLER.' Thus 'SATTLER / S' may be an alternate stamp of either J.C.E. Sattler or Carl Sattler. The recurring 'S' below the name would seem to favor the former, earlier maker.

Stamp 'A'    J·C·E·SATTLER / S

Stamp 'B'    SATTLER / S

[1] The C flap is a replacement.
[2] But with 'S' below and crown above. This is on all three joints.

| Young No. | No. Keys and Metal | City, Owner, No. | PITCH | No. Pcs. | Length | Body, Mounts | Flaps | SAT | Holes Dbld. | Tuning Holes | Additional Data | Ill. Source |
|---|---|---|---|---|---|---|---|---|---|---|---|---|

**CARL SATTLER** (*cont.*)

OBOES

| | | | | | | | | | | | | |
|---|---|---|---|---|---|---|---|---|---|---|---|---|
| 1. | x2 | xBerlin 72 | | | 57.0 | boxw, ivory | | | | | Stamp 'CARL / SATTLER' An octave key was added to the original 2 keys. | |
| 2. | 2 brass | Bonn BH (Zimmermann 94) | | | 57.3 | boxw, ivory | sq-cors C, sq e♭ | SATW | 3 dbl. | 2 th. | Stamp 'CARL SATTLER' (on same line).[1] There are 2 upper joints. The height given is with the larger. With the shorter it's 56.84 cm. | Ill. Zimmermann cat., p 27. |
| 3. | 2 | Prague 1334E | | | | | | | | | | |
| 4. | | Prague 1705E | | | | | | | | | | |
| 5. | | Stockholm 153 | | | | | | | | | | |
| 6. | | Prague 326E | | | | | | | | | | |

BASSOON

| | | | | | | | | | | | | |
|---|---|---|---|---|---|---|---|---|---|---|---|---|
| 1. | 5 brass | Leipzig 1023 | | | | | | | | | The 5 keys are B♭, D, E♭ L4, F, G♯. | |

# SAVARY PERE

FLUTE

| | | | | | | | | | | | | |
|---|---|---|---|---|---|---|---|---|---|---|---|---|
| 1. | | Paris C.426 | B | | | | | | | | | |

OBOES

| | | | | | | | | | | | | |
|---|---|---|---|---|---|---|---|---|---|---|---|---|
| 1. | 4 | Milan 382 | F ! | | 43.0 | boxw | | | | | Stamped 'SAVARI / A PARIS' | |
| 2. | 11 brass | Hague Ea 443-1933 | | | 57.5 | palisander | | | 3 dbl. | | | Ill. Hague 1974 Exhib., p 26, no. 37 |

CLARINET

| | | | | | | | | | | | | |
|---|---|---|---|---|---|---|---|---|---|---|---|---|
| 1. | 5 brass | Milan reported by N.J. Shackleton | F | | | boxw | | | | | Stamp 'SAVARI' | |

BASSOON[2]

| | | | | | | | | | | | | |
|---|---|---|---|---|---|---|---|---|---|---|---|---|
| 1. | 9 brass | Brussels 3120 | | | 129.5 | maple, brass | ro | SATK | | | B♭, D, E♭ L Th, F, F♯, G♯, B♭ RH3, 2 wing keys. Keys in unusual saddles. | |

TENOROON

| | | | | | | | | | | | | |
|---|---|---|---|---|---|---|---|---|---|---|---|---|
| 1. | 5 brass | Paris E. 0282 | | | | | | | | | Stamp 'SAVARY' | |

[1]with a fleur de lys below. The stamp is clear and on all three joints.     [2]Stamped

*Savary PERE A PARIS*

| Young No. | No. Keys and Metal | City, Owner, No. | Pitch | No. Pcs. | Length | Body, Mounts | Flaps | SAT | Holes Dbld. (date) | Tuning Holes (stamp) | Additional Data | Ill. Source |
|---|---|---|---|---|---|---|---|---|---|---|---|---|

# SAVARY JEUNE

## BASSOONS

| Young No. | No. Keys and Metal | City, Owner, No. | Pitch | No. Pcs. | Length | Body, Mounts | Flaps | SAT | Holes Dbld. (date) | Tuning Holes (stamp) | Additional Data | Ill. Source |
|---|---|---|---|---|---|---|---|---|---|---|---|---|
| 1. | modern | Oxford: Bate 313 | | | 125.0 | maple | | | d. 1820 | "jeune" | 2 original wing keys in saddles; all other keys are replacements, now 16 in all. | |
| 2. | 8 brass | Antwerp 61 | | | 127.0 | | | | d. 1823 | jeune | Keys in saddles. | |
| 3. | 10 brass | London: Waterhouse | | | 127.2 | maple | | | d. 1823 | jeune | F & G keys have large rollers | |
| 4. | 11 brass | Vermillion, S.D., U of SD 2418 | | | 125.1 | maple | | | d. 1823 | jeune | 2 wing joints, tuning extensions, tip-up butt, octagonal wooden case. SATW!! | |
| 5. | 10 brass | Oxford: Bate 325 | | | 128.5 | maple | ro flat | | d. 1825 | jeune | Keys in saddles. See key details in catal. | LOM 254 |
| 6. | 10 | Paris C.509, E. 360 | | | | | | | d. 1826 | | Now added keys, put there by Eugene Jancourt, owner, user, donor, and great player. | |
| 7. | 12 | Oxford: Bate 314 | | | 125.0 | maple | dome | | d. 1828 | jeune | In saddles. See key details in catalogue. | |
| 8. | 11 | London; Horniman 110 | | | 125.8 | maple | | | d. 1829 | jeune | Wing jt a replacement. See note below. | Ill. front & back, Horniman WIEAM, pl VII & VIII. |
| 9. | 10 | Brussels 3406 | | | | | | | d. 1832 | | | |
| 10. | 16 brass | Oxford: Bate 315 | | | 127.0 | maple | dome | | d. 1833 | jeune | Keys in saddles. | LOM 255 |
| 11. | 15 | Oxford: Bate 316 | | | 126.4 | maple | dome | | d. 1840 | jeune | Keys in saddles. See key details in cat. | |
| 12. | 14 brass | Victoria, U. of | | | | maple | dome | | d. 1845 | jeune | Keys in saddles. Wing jt by Gallander, Paris. | |
| 13. | 9 brass | Oxford: Bate 324 | | | 126.0 | maple | flat ro | | | jeune | Keys in saddles. Ivory bell ring. "c. 1835" | |
| 14. | 10 brass | Antwerp 64 | | | | | | | | jeune | Part by Adler, Paris | |
| 15. | 8 brass | Nürnberg MI 472 | | | 127.4 | maple | | | | jeune | See note below. Gold leaf(?) on carved, sculpted bell. Loaned by Karl Ventzke. | Ill. Jansen, fig. 226. |
| 16. | 13 | Paris C.1123 | | | | | | | | jeune | | |
| 17. | 15 | Brussels 3565 | | | | | | | | | | |
| 18. | | Brussels 4351 | | | | | | | | jeune | Incomplete | |
| 19. | 16 brass | Oxford: Bate 317 | | | 126.5 | maple | dome | | | jeune | Keys in saddles. See key details in catal. "c. 1840" | |
| 20. | 18 brass | Paris E.1674 | | | | | dome | | d. 1852 | jeune | All keys in saddles except Bb & D flaps in post & axles. Rue Dauphine | |
| 21. | | Paris C.1515 | | | | | | | | | 2 wing joints. | |
| 22. | | Paris C.506, E.645 | | | | | | | | | Belonged to Cokken, prof of bassoon at Conservatoire, virtuoso. Given 9 keys by Trieber. | |
| 23. | 11 brass | Boston: Casadesus 67 | | | 126.4 | maple | dome | | d. 1829 | jeune | Brass stud above each stamp, all four pieces. Ivory bushed boot holes, but not thumb hole. | |
| 24. | | Darmstadt, per W. Jansen | | | | | | | | | | |

Note: Inscribed on Horniman-Carse bassoon no. 110 is "Savary fils je., 1829, Ar^te Fac^r d'ins^ms., élève du Conservatoire de Musique, rue de Bussy, No. 16, Fb. St. Gm. a Paris"
On Nürnberg MI 472 is incribed "Savary fils jne/élève du Conservatoire/Royale de Musique rue/de Bussi St Gain/a Paris" Jansen also illustrates (fig. 661 and 662) a second Savary jeune bassoon, which he says is in the Musée Instrumental, Paris, and which has a sculpted bell design. The same photographs are instead identified as a bassoon by Winnen in Langwill's *The Bassoon and Contrabassoon*, plate 16. I do not know who is right.

| Young No. | No. Keys and Metal | City, Owner, No. | Pitch | No. Pcs. | Length | Body, Mounts | Flaps | SAT | Holes Dbld. | Tuning Holes | Additional Data | Ill. Source |
|---|---|---|---|---|---|---|---|---|---|---|---|---|
| **SAVARY JEUNE** *(cont.)* | | | | | | | | | *dated:* | | | |
| **SMALL BASSOONS** | | | | | | | | | | | | |
| 1. | 11 brass | Paris C.500, E.646 | octave bsn | | | maple | dome | | d. 1827 | jeune | Keys in saddles. Lower 3 finger holes now ivory bushed. | |
| 2. | 11 brass | Biebrich: Heckel Museum PF-1 | "QUART-FAGOTT" | | | | | | d. 1832 | jeune | | Ill. Heckel, *Der Fagott*, Seite 16 |
| 3. | 13 brass | Edinburgh, Univ. of | | | 96.5 | maple | dome | | d. 1840 | jeune | Extra wing joint. | Ill. GS 1968 Exhib. cat., no. 235 |
| 4. | 14 brass | Oxford: Bate 336 | "TENOR-OON in F" | | 97.3 | maple | | | | jeune | | Ill. GS 1968 Exhib. cat. no. 236. EAMI 603. Ill. Montagu RM, Pl. 54. |
| 5. | 15 brass | Oxford: Bate ? [1] | | | 97.5 | maple | dome | | | jeune | | Ill. GS 1968 Exhib. cat., no. 237 |
| 6. | | USA private collection, per Will Jansen | | | | | | | | | | |
| 7. | 15 brass | Paris E.2329 | "QUINT" | | | | | | d. 1841 | jeune | Keys on posts and axles. | |
| 8. | | Boston: Casadesus per Bessaraboff | | | | | | | | | | |
| 9. | 11 brass | London: William Waterhouse [2] | "TENOR-OON" | | 98.8 | maple | | | n.d. | jeune | | |
| 10. | | Perth, Australia | "TENOR-OON" | | | | | | | jeune | | |

# A. SAX

| | City, Owner, Number | Pitch | Height | Body Metal | No. of keys and metal | Ser. No. | Ca. Date | Additional details | Where illustrated |
|---|---|---|---|---|---|---|---|---|---|
| **FLUTE** | | | | | | | | | |
| 1. | Paris C. 1101, E. 0264 | | | metal | 1 key | 12158 | 1854 | | |
| **CLARINET** | | | | | | | | | |
| 1. | present location unknown | | | | 13 keys | | | No. 251, Royal Military Exhibition, London, 1890. Then in the W. Hugh Spottiswoode collection. | |
| **BASS CLARINETS** | | | | | | | | | |
| 1. | Brussels 175 (S10) | B♭ | 131.2 | grena | 21 G. silver keys | –– | ca.1840 | Charles-Joseph Sax's stamp, but known to be by Adolphe | Ill. Haine-Keyser, p 75 |
| 2. | Brussels 2625 (S11) | B♭ | 132.0 | boxw | 21 brass keys | –– | ca. 1840 | Charles-Joseph Sax's stamp, but known to be by Adolphe | Ill. Haine-Keyser, p 77 |
| 3. | Hague 691 | | 133.0 | maple | 20 brass keys | –– | ca. 1840? | Adolphe Sax & Cie | EAMI 650 |
| 4. | Paris C. 1137, E. 1223 | | | | | | | Adolphe Sax & Cie | |
| 5. | Paris C. 552, E. 759 | | | | | | | | |

---

[1] Probably the same instrument immediately preceding it above, but listed separately here because of the supposed different number of keys and slight difference in height. This 15-keyed "tenoroon" was loaned by Philip Bate to the Galpin Society 1968 Edinburgh exhibition and is described in that catalogue. [2]Formerly in the collection of James MacGillivray and before that of R. Morley-Pegge.

| Young No. | City, Owner, Number | Pitch | Height | Body Metal | No. of keys and metal | Ser. No. | Ca. Date | Additional details | Where illustrated |
|---|---|---|---|---|---|---|---|---|---|
| **A. SAX** *(cont.)* | | | | | | | | | |
| **BASS CLARINETS** *(cont.)* | | | | | | | | | |
| 6. | xBerlin 2901 | | | | 19 keys | | | attributed to A. Sax; not stamped | Ill. Sachs, tafel 29 |
| 7. | Paris C. 551, E. 713 | | | metal | | | | attributed to A. Sax; not stamped | |
| 8. | Scarsdale: D & R Rosenbaum 144 | | | | 21 keys | | | attributed to A. Sax; not stamped | |
| **BASSOON** | | | | | | | | | |
| 1. | Paris C. 1401, E. 1465 | | | metal | 23 keys | | | | |
| **SOPRANINO SAXOPHONE** | | | | | | | | | |
| 1. | London: Horniman 83 | E♭ | 54.0 | silver | 15 silv keys and body | 10183 | 1844-53 | | Ill. Horniman WIEAM, Pl. 13. EAMI 658 |
| **SOPRANO SAXOPHONES** | | | | | | | | | |
| 1. | Bruges: Wijsberg | B♭ | | | | 12345 | 1854-55? | | |
| 2. | Linköpings Stads Mus. 7783 | B♭ | | | | 17077 | 1856-57? | | |
| 3. | Amsterdam: van Oostrom | B♭ | | | | 19575 | 1859 | | |
| 4. | Brussels 3111 (S63) | B♭ | 62.5 | brass | 18 | 20432 | 1860 | | Ill. Haine-Keyser, p 197 |
| 5. | Paris: Vignon | B♭ | | | | 21202 | 1860-63 | | |
| 6. | Muncie: BSU | B♭ | | | | 22627 | 1860-63 | | |
| 7. | Binningen: Buser | B♭ | | | 18 | 23969 | 1860-63 | | |
| 8. | Amsterdam': van Oostrom | B♭ | | | | 24662 | 1860-63 | | |
| 9. | Brussels: Sebille | B♭ | | | | 28251 | 1865-66 | | |
| 10. | Muncie: BSU | B♭ | | | | 31699 | 1867 | | |
| 11. | Paris E. 1684 | B♭ | | | | 32131 | 1867 | | |
| 12. | New York: MMA 89.4.2138 | B♭ | | brass | 17 | 41121 | 1878-87 | | Ill. 1904 Crosby Brown catalogue, p 141 |
| 13. | xBerlin 2909 | C | 57.5 | brass | 15 | | | Sachs: "Supposedly the first C saxophone of Sax, ca 1840" | |
| **ALTO SAXOPHONES** | | | | | | | | | |
| 1. | Boston: MFA 17.1889 (B. 122) | E♭ | 58.0 | brass | 18 | 5828 | 1844-46? | | Ill. Bessaraborff, Pl. III |
| 2. | Paris C. 553, E. 714 | | | | | 6497 | 1844-46? | | |
| 3. | Brussels JT 191 (S67) | E♭ | 62.0 | silv | 20 | 9935 | 1851 | | Ill. Haine-Keyser, p 206 |
| 4. | Bern: K. Burri | | | | | 10228 | 1851-54 | | |
| 5. | Nürnberg MIR 486 | E♭ | 68.9 | brass | | 11658 | 1854 | | |
| 6. | Paris: Selmer | E♭ | | | | 15511 | 1856 | | |
| 7. | Linköpings Stads Mus. 7782 | E♭ | | | | 17650 | 1856-59 | | |
| 8. | New York: Rascher | E♭ | | | | 18046 | 1859 | | |

| | | | | | | | | | |
|---|---|---|---|---|---|---|---|---|---|

**A. SAX** *(cont.)* **A. SAX** *(cont.)*

ALTO SAXOPHONES *(cont.)*

| Young No. | City, Owner, Number | Pitch | Height | Body Metal | No. of keys and metal | Ser. No. | Ca. Date | Additional details | Where illustrated |
|---|---|---|---|---|---|---|---|---|---|
| 9. | Interlochen, Mich. Green- leaf | E♭ | | | | 18838 | 1859 | | |
| 10. | London: Montagu VII 150 | E♭ | | | 19 | 19804 | 1859 | | Ill. Montagu RM, Pl. XII |
| 11. | Muncie: BSU | E♭ | | | | 20139 | 1860 | | |
| 12. | Chatou, France: Pareille | E♭ | | | | 20200 | 1860 | | |
| 13. | Amsterdam: van Oostrom | E♭ | | | | 21 . . 3 | 1860-63 | | |
| 14. | Paris: Vignon | E♭ | | | | 23307 | 1860-63 | | |
| 15. | Brussels 3769 (S64) | E♭ | 61.5 | brass | 20 | 25307 | 1862-63 | | Ill. Haine-Keyser, p 198 |
| 16. | Paris E. 1085 | E♭ | | | | 27403 | 1863-66 | | |
| 17. | Munich: DM 16809 | E♭ | 62.0 | brass | | 27870 | 1863-66 | | |
| 18. | Brussels 3769 (S68) | E♭ | 61.0 | G. silv | 20 | 28 . . . | 1865 | | Ill. Haine-Keyser, p 209 |
| 19. | Bern: K. Burri | E♭ | | | | 31215 | 1867 | | |
| 20. | Düren: K. Ventzke 54 | E♭ | | | | 32063 | 1867 | | |
| 21. | Bordeaux: Londeix | E♭ | | | | 32089 | 1867 | | |
| 22. | Paris E. 1890 | E♭ | | | | 33451 | 1868 | Highly engraved | |
| 23. | Paris: Losse | E♭ | | | | 33467 | 1868 | | |
| 24. | Paris C. 554, E. 715 | E♭ | | | | 35557 | 1869? | | |
| 25. | Begles: Thymel | E♭ | | | | 37338 | 1870 | | |
| 26. | Markneukirchen 3475 | E♭ | | | | 37637 | 1870-75 | | |
| 27. | Mimizan: Claverie | E♭ | | | | 39557 | 1876 | | |
| 28. | Dinant: Raulin | E♭ | | | | 39561 | 1876 | | |

TENOR SAXOPHONES

| Young No. | City, Owner, Number | Pitch | Height | Body Metal | No. of keys and metal | Ser. No. | Ca. Date | Additional details | Where illustrated |
|---|---|---|---|---|---|---|---|---|---|
| 1. | Paris C. 555, E. 716 | B♭ | | | | 15353 | 1854-55 | | |
| 2. | Paris E. 013 | B♭ | | | | 16872 | 1856 | | |
| 3. | Brussels 3765 (S65) | B♭ | 78.1 | G silv | 20 | 17059 | 1856 | | Ill. Haine-Keyser, p 201; LOM 252 |
| 4. | Interlochen, Mich.: Greenleaf | C | | | 20 | 17401 | 1856-58 | | |
| 5. | Ann Arbor: U. Mich. 641 | E♭ | 117.0[1] | | 20 | 20669 | 1860 | | |
| 6. | Brussels JT 200 (S69) | B♭ | 80.0 | brass | 20 | 21401 | 1861 | | Ill. Haine-Keyser, p 211 |
| 7. | Düren: Ventzke 56 | B♭ | | | | 25827 | 1861-62 | | |
| 8. | Bordeaux: Londeix | B♭ | | | | 27741 | 1863 | | |
| 9. | Schiltigheim, France | B♭ | | | | 28155 | 1863 | | |
| 10. | Amsterdam: van Oostrom | B♭ | | | | 30037 | 1866-67 | | |
| 11. | Evanston: Northwestern University | B♭ | | | | 32269 | 1867 | | |
| 12. | Paris E. 1686 | B♭ | | | | 33886 | 1868 | | |

[1] overall length of air column

| Young No. | City,Owner, Number | Pitch | Height | Body Metal | No. of keys and metal | Ser. No. | Ca. Date | Additional details | Where illustrated |
|---|---|---|---|---|---|---|---|---|---|
| **A. SAX** *(cont.)* | | | | | | | | | **A. SAX** *(cont.)* |
| **TENOR SAXOPHONES** *(cont.)* | | | | | | | | | |
| 13. | Muncie: BSU | B♭ | | | | 36458 | 1868-69 | | |
| 14. | Vienna GdM 143 | B♭ | | | 20 | 37870 | 1870-75 | | |
| 15. | Leningrad 53 | C | 81.5 | brass | nick pl keys & body | 40623 | 1878-86 | | |
| 16. | Leipzig 1545 | B♭ | | | 20 nick pl keys & body | ––– | ? | | |
| 17. | Evanston, Ill.: Hemke | | | | | ––– | ? | | |
| 18. | Frankfurt am Oder | C | 82.5 | brass | 19 | | ? | | |
| **BARITONE SAXOPHONES** | | | | | | | | | |
| 1. | Paris E. 556, C. 717 | E♭ | | | | 17609 | 1856-58 | | |
| 2. | Brussels 3663 (S66) | E♭ | 103.3 | brass | 18 silv pl keys & body | 20449 | 1860 | | Ill. Haine-Keyser p 204; LOM 253 |
| 3. | Amsterdam: van Oostrom | E♭ | | | | 20461 | 1860 | | |
| 4. | (listed by Haine-Keyser) | | | | | 26638 | 1860-65 | Present whearabouts unknown. | |
| 5. | Düren: Ventzke 60 | E♭ | | | | 26688 | 1860-65 | | |
| 6. | xBerlin 1346 | E♭ | 101.0 | brass | 18 | 26695 | 1865 | | Ill. Sachs, Tafel 29 |
| 7. | Düren: Ventzke 53 | E♭ | | | | 31207 | 1867 | | |
| 8. | Stockholm 425 | E♭ | | | | 32849 | 1867 | | |
| 9. | Paris E. 1687 | E♭ | | | | 34463 | 1868-69 | | |
| 10. | Muncie: BSU | E♭ | | | | 40415 | 1878-86 | | |
| **BASS SAXOPHONES** | | | | | | | | | |
| 1. | Munich: DM 40107 | B♭ | 112.5 | brass | | 34285 | 1868 | | |
| 1  2. | Paris: Selmer | B♭ | | | | 34289 | 1868 | | |

Note: For further details of Adolphe Sax and his instruments, the reader
is of course referred to the recent monumental studies by Malou Haine
and Ignace de Keyser, listed in the bibliography, Appendix B of this book.

| Young No. | No. Keys and Metal | City, Owner, No. | Pitch | No. Pcs. | Length | Body, Mounts | Flaps | SAT | Holes Dbld. | Tuning Holes | Additional Data | Ill. Source |
|---|---|---|---|---|---|---|---|---|---|---|---|---|

# SCHELL

## ALTO RECORDERS

| Young No. | No. Keys and Metal | City, Owner, No. | Pitch | No. Pcs. | Length | Body, Mounts | Flaps | SAT | Holes Dbld. | Tuning Holes | Additional Data | Ill. Source |
|---|---|---|---|---|---|---|---|---|---|---|---|---|
| 1. | | Basel 1956/632 | F | 3 pc | | boxw, unmtd | | | | | | Ill. Hunt, pl XIV |
| 2. | | Washington: DCM 658 | F | | 50.3 | boxw, unmtd | | | | | | |
| 3. | | Linz 152 | | 3 pc | 50.0 | boxw, unmtd | | | | | | |
| 4. | | London: Guy Oldham | | | | | | | | | | |
| 5. | | Salzburg: Mozarteum | | | 51.1 | | | | | | | |
| 6. | | Rome Galleria del Lazio 2203[1] | | | | | | | | | | |

## TENOR RECORDERS

| Young No. | No. Keys and Metal | City, Owner, No. | Pitch | No. Pcs. | Length | Body, Mounts | Flaps | SAT | Holes Dbld. | Tuning Holes | Additional Data | Ill. Source |
|---|---|---|---|---|---|---|---|---|---|---|---|---|
| 1. | | Innsbruck 2, 85 | | 3 pc | 64.9 | boxw | | | | | | |
| 2. | | Bologna 1769 | | 3 pc | | boxw, ivory | | | | | | |

## BASS RECORDERS

| Young No. | No. Keys and Metal | City, Owner, No. | Pitch | No. Pcs. | Length | Body, Mounts | Flaps | SAT | Holes Dbld. | Tuning Holes | Additional Data | Ill. Source |
|---|---|---|---|---|---|---|---|---|---|---|---|---|
| 1. | 1 brass | Linz 159 | | 3 pc | 99.0 | maple, unmtd | | | | | | Crook goes into top. |
| 2. | 1 brass | Linz 160 | | 3 pc | 99.0 | maple, unmtd | | | | | | Crook goes into top. |
| 3. | 1 brass | Nürnberg MI 95 | | | 99.0 | boxw | sq | SATW | | | | Crook goes into top. Also stamped "J. DENNER CORRIGIERT" |

## RECORDER: PITCH UNDETERMINED

| Young No. | No. Keys and Metal | City, Owner, No. | Pitch | No. Pcs. | Length | Body, Mounts | Flaps | SAT | Holes Dbld. | Tuning Holes | Additional Data | Ill. Source |
|---|---|---|---|---|---|---|---|---|---|---|---|---|
| 1. | | Innsbruck | | | | boxw | | | | | | Perhaps same as the tenor above. |

## FLUTE

| Young No. | No. Keys and Metal | City, Owner, No. | Pitch | No. Pcs. | Length | Body, Mounts | Flaps | SAT | Holes Dbld. | Tuning Holes | Additional Data | Ill. Source |
|---|---|---|---|---|---|---|---|---|---|---|---|---|
| 1. | | Celle: Dr. Hermann Moeck | | | | ivory | | | | | | At least 2 upper joints. |

## OBOE

| Young No. | No. Keys and Metal | City, Owner, No. | Pitch | No. Pcs. | Length | Body, Mounts | Flaps | SAT | Holes Dbld. | Tuning Holes | Additional Data | Ill. Source |
|---|---|---|---|---|---|---|---|---|---|---|---|---|
| 1. | 3 brass | Leningrad 1146 | | | 50.4 | | | | 3 dbl. | | | Blagodatov says 50.4cm H. In D? |

[1] Per Nickel.

# SCHERER

# SCHERER

## BASSET RECORDER[1]

| Young No. | No. Keys and Metal | City, Owner, No. | Pitch | No. Pcs. | Length | Body, Mounts | Flaps | SAT | Holes Dbld. | Tuning Holes | Additional Data | Ill. Source |
|---|---|---|---|---|---|---|---|---|---|---|---|---|
| 1. | 1 brass | Leipzig 1145 | F♯ | | 104.1 | walnut | ro | | | | Brass crook goes into top. | Ill. Heyde Leipzig, taf 4 |

## WALKING STICK FLUTE

| Young No. | No. Keys and Metal | City, Owner, No. | Pitch | No. Pcs. | Length | Body, Mounts | Flaps | SAT | Holes Dbld. | Tuning Holes | Additional Data | Ill. Source |
|---|---|---|---|---|---|---|---|---|---|---|---|---|
| 1. | | Darmstadt | | | | | | | | | | |

## FLUTES

| Young No. | No. Keys and Metal | City, Owner, No. | Pitch | No. Pcs. | Length | Body, Mounts | Flaps | SAT | Holes Dbld. | Tuning Holes | Additional Data | Ill. Source |
|---|---|---|---|---|---|---|---|---|---|---|---|---|
| 1. | 1 silver | Washington: DCM 330 | C | 4 pc | 63.4 | ivory | long sq | | | | | |
| 2. | 1 silver | Washington: DCM 440 | C | 4 pc | 60.3 | ivory | | | | | 2 upper joints. Headjt socket unscrews! Repair? | |
| 3. | 1 silver | Amsterdam: Frans Brüggen [2] | | 4 pc | 62.0+ | ivory | | SATK | | | | |
| 4. | 1 silver | London: RCM 102 | C | 4 pc | 61.3 | ivory, unmtd | oval | | | | 1 upper joint. | |
| 5. | 1 | Berlin: Dr. Walter Thoene | | | | ivory | | | | | Headjoint by Poerschman. | |
| 6. | 1 silver | Berlin 1531 | A/C | 4 pc | 63.0[3] | ivory | ro | | | | 1 head jt, 8 upper, 2 lower, 2 ft jts. Belonged to Frederick the Great. | |
| 7. | 1 silver | Paris: late Comtesse de Chambure | F | 4 pc | 52.4 | ivory | sq | | | | | Ill. JJ-GT-BR, no. 86; EAMI 470 |
| 8. | 1 silver | Zurich: Walter Thut | F | 4 pc | 53.0+ | ivory | | | | | 53.0 cm is embouchure to end of foot. 3 keys added. | |
| 9. | 1 silver | Brussels 3130 | C | 4 pc | 62.0 | ivory | trap | SATK | | | | |
| 10. | 1 silver | Basel 1956/374 | F | 4 pc | 51.15 | ivory | sq | | | | | |
| 11. | 1 silver | Hague Ea 291-1933 | C | 4 pc | 61.0 | ivory | sq | | | | | |
| 12. | 1 silver | Nürnberg MI 284 | C | 4 pc | 61.7 | boxw, ivory | trap | SATK | | | | |
| 13. | 1 silver | Zurich: Willi Burger | C | 4 pc | 63.5 | ivory | sq | SATI | | | | |
| 14. | 1 silver | Cambridge: N. J. Shackleton | C | 4 pc | 64.8 | ivory, unmtd | sq | SATI | | | | |
| 15. | 1 silver | Aachen: Dr. W. Willms | C | | 63.7 | ivory | sq | | | | | |
| 16. | 1 | Bruges: B. Kuijken | | | | ivory | | | | | | |
| 17. | 1 | Arnhem (priv. coll.) | | | | boxw, ivory | | | | | | |
| 18. | 1 brass | Zurich: Museum Belle-rive 132 | C | 4 pc | 64.5 | ivory | sq | | | | Key is later replacement on axle, posts, mounting plate. | |
| 19. | 1 brass | Copenhagen E. 62 | | 4 pc | 74.7! | ivory, unmtd | | SATK | | | | |
| 20. | 1 brass | Aachen: Dr. W. Willms | C | | 64.0 | ivory | sq | | | | Cap missing, so length is slightly more than given. | |

[1] Dr. Heyde so labels this instrument in his 1978 Leipzig flute catalogue.    [2] Formerly in the collection of the late Eric Halfpenny. Key not original.    [3] with longest upper and longer lower and ft. jts.

| Young No. | No. Keys and Metal | City, Owner, No. | Pitch | No. Pcs. | Length | Body, Mounts | Flaps | SAT | Holes Dbld. | Tuning Holes | Additional Data | Ill. Source |
|---|---|---|---|---|---|---|---|---|---|---|---|---|

**SCHERER** *(cont.)*
FLUTES *(cont.)*

| | | | | | | | | | | | | |
|---|---|---|---|---|---|---|---|---|---|---|---|---|
| ⁻21. | 1 brass | Cologne Stadtmuseum I/12 | | 4 pc | 74.6! | boxw, ivory | sq | SATK | | | | |
| 22. | 1 brass | Frankfurt: Dr. R. Menger | | | | ivory | | | | | | |
| 23. | x1 | xBerlin 97 | | | 63.0 | ivory | ro | | | | | |
| 24. | | Neuwied am Rhein: Giesbert | | | | ivory | | | | | | |
| 25. | | Hammer Sale 1445, per Langwill | | | | | | | | | | |
| 26. | 3 silver | Markneukirchen 1068 | | | 60.70 | ivory, unmtd | sq | SATK | | | 3 upper joints. Keys are all later replacements. | |
| 27. | 7 silver | Berlin, loan by Dr. Bruno Dohme | | 4 pc | 60.9¹ | ivory, unmtd | | SATK | | | In vertical case w no. 1531. Said to be Frederick the Great's. | |
| 28. | x7 white met. | xBerlin 100² | A♭ | 4 pc | 78.5 | ivory | ro | | | | Foot to c'. | |

FLUTES D'AMOUR

| | | | | | | | | | | | | |
|---|---|---|---|---|---|---|---|---|---|---|---|---|
| 1. | 1 silver | Oxford: Bate 1011 | A | 4 pc | 77.1 | ivory | trap | | | | | Ill. Bate Flute, pl 11 |
| 2. | 1 | Leipzig 1272 | A | 4 pc | 68.4 | ivory | | | | | Foot to b. All keys later replacements. | |

OBOES

| | | | | | | | | | | | | |
|---|---|---|---|---|---|---|---|---|---|---|---|---|
| 1. | 2 brass | Paris C.477 | | | (57.7) | boxw, unmtd | | | | | Belonged to A. Sax. Lower jt stamped "Clapisson, Lyons" | |
| 2. | 2 silver | Berlin 71 | | | 59.0 | ivory | | | 3 | 2 | | |
| 3. | 2 silver | Munich Stadtmuseum 66-88 | | | 59.3 | ivory | trap | SATI | 3 | 2 | Both knobs are *round*. | |
| 4. | | Coburg | | | | ivory | | | | | | |

OBOE D'AMORE

| | | | | | | | | | | | | |
|---|---|---|---|---|---|---|---|---|---|---|---|---|
| 1. | 2 brass | Zurich: Museum Belle- rive 116 | | | 65.0 | boxw, ivory | trap e♭, ro c. | | 3 | | | |

TENOR OBOE

| | | | | | | | | | | | | |
|---|---|---|---|---|---|---|---|---|---|---|---|---|
| 1. | 3 brass | Berlin 2959 | | 4 | 76.2 | boxw, horn | trap eb, (Y) c | SATW | 3&4 | | Bulb bell. Top finial-baluster separate, = 4 pcs. Straight form. | |
| 2. | 2 brass | Brussels 978³ | | 3 | 89.0 | plum? maple? unmtd | trap eb, ro c. | SATW | 3&4 | | Bulb bell. Straight form. | |

---

¹With upper joint no. 2.
²Listed here as Dr. Sachs lists it, a 'flute' rather than 'flute d'amour' but it must have been a (one keyed, originally) flute d'amour.

³From its length this instrument might be a baritone oboe, but Mahillon says it is in F. Perhaps this is analagous to the disparate lengths of the several J.C. Denner tenor oboes.

| Young No. | No. Keys and Metal | City, Owner, No. | Pitch | No. Pcs. | Length | Body, Mounts | Flaps | SAT | Holes Dbld. | Tuning Holes | Additional Data | Ill. Source |
|---|---|---|---|---|---|---|---|---|---|---|---|---|
| **SCHERER** (*cont.*) | | | | | | | | | | | | |
| **CLARINETS** | | | | | | | | | | | | |
| 1. | 2 silver | London: RCM 101 | D | 4 | 52.5 | ivory, unmtd | sq | SATI | 0 | | Bore 1.6. 4 pc (mthpc&bbl=1 pc[1]) | Ill. Rendall Clarinet, pl I-c |
| 2. | 2 silver | Paris C.529, E.697 | D | 4 | 54.0 | ivory, unmtd | sq (C) | SATI | | | Bore 1.3. 4 pc | LOM 99 |
| 3. | 3 silver | Brussels 924 | D | 4 | 56.5 | boxw, ivory | trap | SATW | 0 | | Bore 1.22. 4 pc (mthpc&bbl=2 pc) | Ill. Rendall Clarinet, pl I-g |
| 4. | 2 brass | Eisenach L-4 | E | 3 | 47.4 | boxw, ivory | trap | | 0 | | Bore 1.3. 3 pc (mthpc&bbl=1 pc[2]) | Ill. color, Heyde Eisenach, p 228 |
| 5. | 2 | Haren, Holland (priv.) | D | | | boxw, ivory | | | | | | |
| 6. | 2 | London: Sotheby auction 1980 | D | | | boxw, ivory | | | | | | |
| **FAGOTTINI** | | | | | | | | | | | | |
| 1. | 4 brass | Brussels 426 | C | | 64.5 | maple, brass | | SATW | | | Decorative bell ring. Keys mtd in blocks. | |
| 2. | 4 brass | Leipzig 1548 | C | | 64.2 | maple, brass | | SATW | | | Decorative bell ring.[3] Keys mtd in blocks and knobs. | |
| 3. | 4 brass[4] | Paris C.498, E.186 | C | | 63.9 | maple, brass | | | | | Decorative bell ring. | |
| 4. | 5 brass | Zurich: Museum Belle-rive 102 | | | note 5 | maple, brass | | | | | Keys mounted in blocks. | |
| **BASSOONS** | | | | | | | | | | | | |
| 1. | 4 brass | Hague Ea 62-X-1952 | | | 125.0 | maple, brass | ro | | | | | |
| 2. | 4 brass | New York MMA 89.4.886 | | | 126.5 | maple, brass | ro | SATW | | | Decorative bell ring. Boot stamped "Butzbach"[1]. Keys mtd in blocks. | |
| 3. | 4 brass | Eisenach I-159 | | | | boxw, brass | sq | | | | Decorative bell ring. Flat table. Keys mounted in blocks. | Ill. color[3] |
| 4. | 4 | Zurich: Kunstgewerbe Museum[7] | | | | | | | | | | |
| 5. | 5 | Zurich: Kunstgewerbe Museum[7] | | | | | | | | | | |
| 6. | 5 brass[4] | Zurich: Museum Belle-rive 106 | | | note 8 | maple, brass | ro | SATW | | | Decorative bell ring. Flat table. Keys mounted in blocks. | |

[1] Upper and lower jts separate, bell, one-piece mouthpiece & barrel = 4 pcs.

[2] One integral main joint, rather than separate upper & lower = 3 pcs.

[3] Heyde Eisenach, p 240. I cannot agree with Dr. Heyde that these instruments should be called 'd'amore' because the bulge in their bells is hollowed out slightly.

[4] These two instruments have a duplicate G key for LH4 if played with the left hand lowermost. The only other bassoon known to me with this feature is the J.C. Denner-Salzburg fragment. Unfortunately, this Zurich bassoon has lost its G key, but it is clearly broken off, and the remains of its (integral) block are very much in evidence.

[5] Air column length 110.0 cm.

[6] Butzbach is north of Frankfurt. Is this where Scherer worked before going to Paris? (It would seem likely.) Was Butzbach also his birthplace?

[7] Per Will Jansen.

[8] Air column length 215.0 cm.

| Young No. | No. Keys and Metal | City, Owner, No. | Pitch | No. Pcs. | Length | Body, Mounts Flaps | SAT | Holes Dbld. | Tuning Holes | Additional Data | Ill. Source |
|---|---|---|---|---|---|---|---|---|---|---|---|

# J. SCHLEGEL

## RECORDERS

| | | | | | | | | | | | |
|---|---|---|---|---|---|---|---|---|---|---|---|
| 1. | Sopranino | Paris C.392, E.683 | | 3 pc | 25.43[1] | ivory, unmtd | | | | | EAMI 423 LOM 61 |
| 2. | Sopranino | Paris C.392, E.683 | | 3 pc | 25.43[1] | ivory, unmtd | | | | | EAMI 423 LOM 61 |
| 3. | Alto | Paris C.392, E.683 | | 3 pc | 49.5[1] | ivory, unmtd | | | | | EAMI 423 LOM 61 |
| 4. | Alto | Paris C.392, E.683 | | 3 pc | 49.6[1] | ivory, unmtd | | | | | EAMI 423 LOM 61 |

## FLUTES

| | | | | | | | | | | | |
|---|---|---|---|---|---|---|---|---|---|---|---|
| 1. | 1 silver | Washington: DCM 801 | C | 4 pc | 63.7 | boxw, ivory | | | | 3 upper jts. With other 2, lengths are 63.0 and 62.1 | |
| 2. | 1 silver | Washington: DCM 810 | C | 4 pc | 61.9 | boxw, ivory | | | | Finger holes not in line. Slanted outward for left, inward for right. | |
| 3. | 1 brass | Washington: DCM 997 | C | 4 pc | (64.2) | boxw, ivory | | | | Head joint by A. Grenser. | |
| 4. | 1 silver | Paris C.440 | | 4 pc | 71.0 | | | | | Extendable key. | |
| 5. | 1 silver | Munich Stadtmuseum 53/24 | | 4 pc | 63.5 | ebony, ivory | sq(F) | SATK | | 2 upper joints, 15.93 & 14.8 cm. | |
| 6. | 1 brass | Basel 1879.10 | | | 65.0 | | | | | 3 upper joints. With other 2, length is 63.0 & 62.0 | |
| 7. | | Basel 1923.364 | | | | ivory | | | | | |
| 8. | | Cobham: late R. Morley Pegge | | | | | | | | | |
| 9. | | Berne 16875 | | | | | | | | | |

## OBOES

| | | | | | | | | | | | |
|---|---|---|---|---|---|---|---|---|---|---|---|
| 1. | 2 brass | Oxford: Bate x21 (loan, A.C. Baines) | | | 57.1 | boxw, unmtd sq | | 3 dbl. | | | |
| 2. | 2 brass | Leipzig 1322 | | | 58.4 | boxw, ivory | sq(B) | SATK 3 dbl. | 2th | ivory-bushed. | |
| 3. | 2 | Basel 74 (1878.16) | | | 60.0 | boxw? ivory | | | | | |
| 4. | 2 | Basel 1908.122 | | | | | | | | | |
| 5. | 2 | Basel: M. Piguet | | | | | | | | | |
| 6. | 2 | Lucerne: late Otto Dreyer | | | | | | | | | |
| 7. | 3 | Lucerne: Tribschen Wagner Museum | | | | | | | | | |

## CLARINET

| | | | | | | | | | | | |
|---|---|---|---|---|---|---|---|---|---|---|---|
| 1. | 5 brass | Markneukirchen 1041 | C | 6 pcs | | ivory, horn | | | | | Ill. color, 1975 guidebook, p 34 |
| 2. | 5 silver | Bonn BH (Zimmermann 137) | B♭ | 5 pcs | 68.0 | ebony, ivory | | | | | Ill. Zimmermann catalogue, p 51 |
| 3. | 5 silver | Copenhagen | B♭ | 6 pcs | 67.4 | ivory | | SATK | | Bore 1.47. Grenadilla mthpc. | |

Note: The two Schlegels, supposedly father and son, are more often confused than any other family, notwithstanding the distinction made between their respective stamps by Karl Nef as long ago as 1906. The above list almost certainly contains errors, but corrects some of those in Langwill.

[1] These four are in a single case, as a set.

| Young No. | No. Keys and Metal | City, Owner, No. | Pitch | No. Pcs. | Length | Body, Mounts | Flaps | SAT | Holes Dbld. | Tuning Holes | Additional Data | Ill. Source |
|---|---|---|---|---|---|---|---|---|---|---|---|---|

## J. SCHLEGEL (cont.)

J. SCHLEGEL (cont.)

### CLARINETS D'AMOUR

| 1. | 5 | Paris C.1135 | | | | | | | | | | |
| 2. | 4 brass | Brussels 931 | G | | 80.0 | ebony, ivory | | | | | 4th key is g♯. | |

### DISCANT BASSOON

| 1. | 4 brass | Copenhagen E.132 | | | 61.7 | boxw, brass | (U) | | | | wide shanks, all keys in saddles. | |

# C. SCHLEGEL

C. SCHLEGEL

### RECORDERS

| 1. | Alto | Basel 1950.89 | F | | 47.4 | boxw, unmtd | | | | | | Ill. Hunt, pl XIV-5 |
| 2. | Alto | Paris: late Comtesse de Chambure F3LC4 | F | | | | | | | | | |
| 3. | Basset | Basel 56 (1879.100) | G | | 84.0 | walnut, unmtd | ro | | | | Has beak, no crook | Ill. Hunt, pl XIV-13 |
| 4. | Basset | Basel 57 (1879.101) | F | | 89.0 | walnut, unmtd | trap[1] | | | | Has crook at 90° angle | Ill. Hunt, pl XIV-14 |

### FLUTE D'ACCORD

| 1. | | Basel 58 (1902.36) | | | 31.0 | fruitw | | | | | | Ill. Hunt, pl XIV-1 |

### OBOE

| 1. | 2 | Lucerne Tribschen 125 | | | | | | | | | | |

### OBOES D'AMORE

| 1. | 2 brass | Zurich: Allgemein 2687 | | | | boxw | trap(L) eb, ro c. | | | | 3&4 dbl. 2 th. d. 1717. | Ill. Jakob, opp p 32 |
| 2. | 2 brass | Basel 75 (1882.14) | | | 59.0 | boxw, unmtd | | | | | 3&4 dbl. | |

### SCHALMEI

| 1. | no keys | Basel 71 (1879.98) | | | 61.5 | fruitw? brass | | | | | | |
| 2. | no keys | Zurich: Willi Burger | | | 61.1 | fruitw | | | | | | |

# B. SCHOTT FILS

B. SCHOTT FILS

### CANNE FLUTE (recorder)

| 1. | 6 | Brussels 2346 | | | 84.0 | | | | | | | |

### OBOES

| 1. | 12 brass | Brussels 2332 | | | | boxw, ivory | | | | | | |
| 2. | 12 | Brussels 3579 | | | | | | | | | | |
| 3. | | Hague 1438 | | | | | | | | | | |

[1] one brass ring on head joint, likely a repair.　　See note at bottom of J. SCHLEGEL page.

| Young No. | No. Keys and Metal | City, Owner, No. | Pitch | No. Pcs. | Length | Body, Mounts | Flaps | SAT | Holes Dbld. | Tuning Holes | Additional Data | Ill. Source |
|---|---|---|---|---|---|---|---|---|---|---|---|---|

**B. SCHOTT FILS** (cont.)

ENGLISH HORN

| | | | | | | | | | | | | |
|---|---|---|---|---|---|---|---|---|---|---|---|---|
| 1. | x11 | xBerlin 2965 | | | 76.0 | boxw, ivory | | | | | | Ill. Sachs, tafel 26 |
| 2. | 10 | Zurich: Willi Burger | | | | | | | | | | |
| 3. | 13 brass | Brussels 2620 | | | | boxw, ivory | | | | | "Les Fils de . . ." | |

BASSET HORN

| | | | | | | | | | | | | |
|---|---|---|---|---|---|---|---|---|---|---|---|---|
| 1. | 15 brass | Brussels 174 | F | | | boxw, ivory | | | | | brass bell; angular form. ivory knee. | Ill. Mahillon, Vol I, p 222 |

BASSOONS [1]

| | | | | | | | | | | | | |
|---|---|---|---|---|---|---|---|---|---|---|---|---|
| 1. | 16 brass | London: Horniman 52 | | | 129.1 | maple, brass | ro | | | | Keys in saddles. Bb, B♮, D, Eb L4, E♮, F, F♯, etc. | Ill. Horniman WIEAM, pl 7, no. 36. |
| 2. | 10 brass | Biebrich: Heckel Museum F-10 | | | 131.7 | maple, brass | ro | | | | Keys in saddles. Bb, D, Eb L4, F, F♯, G♯, 3 wing keys, dome C. | LOM 257 |
| 3. | 10 brass | Brussels 4354 | | | | maple, brass | ro | | | | Keys in saddles. Bb, D, Eb L4, F, F♯, G♯, 3 wing keys, dome C. | |

CONTRABASSOONS

| | | | | | | | | | | | | |
|---|---|---|---|---|---|---|---|---|---|---|---|---|
| 1. | 6 brass | Brussels 1001 | | | c. 170.0 | maple, brass | sq-cors | | | | Keys in saddles. Ivory bell ring. | |
| 2. | 8 brass | Berlin 2974 | | | 164.5 | maple, brass | | | | | "Les Fils/de B. Schott/a Anvers" | |

# SCHUCHART

SCHUCHART

RECORDERS

| | | | | | | | | | | | | |
|---|---|---|---|---|---|---|---|---|---|---|---|---|
| 1. | Discant | ? ex-Taphouse Collection | | | | | | | Mark (i) [2] | GSJ no. 4. | | |
| 2. | Alto | Brighton: Spencer Collection | | | | boxw, ivory | | | Mark (i) | GSJ no. 1. | | |
| 3. | Alto | London: Horniman 274 | | | 50.2 | boxw, unmtd | | | Mark (i) | GSJ no. 2. | Description GSJ IX, p 82; | ill. Hunt, pl XII-4 |
| 4. | Alto | London: V&A 287-1882 | | | 48.6 [3] | boxw, ivory | | | Mark (ii) | GSJ no. 3. | Middle jt shortened c. 1.6 cm. | Ill. Baines V&A cat., Fig. 117 |

FLUTES

| | | | | | | | | | | | | |
|---|---|---|---|---|---|---|---|---|---|---|---|---|
| 1. | 1 silver | Oxford: Bate 101 | C | 4 pc | 63.6 | ivory, silver | sq | SATK | Mark (iii) | GSJ no. 5. | Has monogram DCM | LOM 69 |
| 2. | 1 silver | Washington: DCM 1233 | C | 4 pc | 64.2 | ivory, unmtd | | | Mark (iii) | GSJ no. 6. | 3 upper jts, producing other lengths 61.2 & 60.4 | |

[1] Note: It is only the bassoons that are of much interest or importance, the first two above (Horniman 52 and Biebrich F-10) presumably being made by Carl Almenraeder (1786-1843) and young Johann Adam Heckel (1812-1877) in the Schott workshop, where they first met. There do not seem to be preserved other specimens from this early collaboration, a sad loss. The Horniman example is the more important, being in fine condition and unaltered, while the Heckel specimen is in a rather sad, unfortunate state, frequently altered and its bell, at least, shattered and crudely stuck back together. It arrived in Vancouver in October 1980 for *The Look of Music* exhibition newly restored in part, and quite handsome, contradicting the catalogue description.

[2] Note: Schuchart's marks are differentiated by Dr. Maurice Byrne in GSJ XVIII.

[3] Its length is now 47.0 cm.

| Young No. | No. Keys and Metal | City, Owner, No. | Pitch | No. Pcs. | Length | Body, Mounts Flaps | SAT | Holes Dbld. | Tuning Holes | Additional Data | Ill. Source |
|---|---|---|---|---|---|---|---|---|---|---|---|
| **SCHUCHART** *(cont.)* <br> *(cont.)* | | | | | | | | | | | **SCHUCHART** *(cont.)* |
| 3. | 1 silver | Cobham: late R. Morley Pegge[2] | | | | ivory | | | | Mark (iii) | GSJ no. 7. Cap a replacement. |
| 4. | 1 | Lucerne: Tribschen 121 | | | | ivory | | | | Mark (iii) | GSJ no. 8. |
| 5. | 1 silver | Edinburgh: Melville-Mason?[3] | | | | ivory | | | | Mark (iii) or (iv). | GSJ no. 9. |
| 6. | 1 | Sevenoaks: Champion Collection[2] | | | | dark w, ivory | | | | | GSJ no. 10. |
| 7. | 1 missing | Washington: DCM 1183 | C | | | light w, ivory — — — — — — | | | | Mark (iii) | GSJ no. 11. Cap missing. |
| 8. | 1 — — — | London: Kneller Hall 3 | | | | boxw, ivory — — — — — — | | | | Mark (iv) | GSJ no. 12. Foot joint missing. |
| 9. | 1 brass | Peebles: F.E. Dodman | | | | boxw, unmtd | | | | Mark (iv) | GSJ no. 13. Also on headjoint, WOODWARD in small letters. |
| 10. | 1 silver | London: Horniman 135 | C | | 60.6 | ivory, silver | | | | Mark (iii) | GSJ no. 14. |
| 11. | 1 replacemt | Bristol: Blaize Castle House | | | | ivory | | | | Mark (iii) | GSJ no. 15. |
| 12. | 1 | ex-Nettlefold Collection[2] | | | | | | | | | GSJ no. 16. |
| 13. | 1 silver | Oxford: Bate x11, loaned Baines | | | 53.9+[4] | boxw, ivory | | | | | GSJ no. 20. |
| 14. | 1 missing | Wrexham: H.D. Jones | | | | boxw | | | | | GSJ no. 21. |
| 15. | 1 | London: Horniman 412 | C | | 60.4 | ivory | | | | | |
| 16. | 1 silver | Haslemere: Dolmetsch 69a | C | 4 pc | 59.0 | ivory, silver | sq | | | | |
| 17. | 6 silver | New York City: Straus | | | | boxw, ivory | sq | | | | |
| **OBOES** | | | | | | | | | | | |
| 1. | 3 brass | Berlin 2951, only charred remains | | | — — — | boxw, ivory | ro | SATW | 4dbl | Mark (iii) | GSJ no. 17. Top joint destroyed WW2; rest preserved, poor state. |
| 2. | 3 brass | Glasgow: Glen Collection 209 | | | | boxw, ivory | | | | Mark (iii) | GSJ no. 18. Ill. and full measurements, GSJ II, p 10; pl III, middle. |
| **TENOR OBOE** | | | | | | | | | | | |
| 1. | 2 brass | Swindon Museum | | | | boxw, ivory | | | | Mark (iii) | GSJ no. 19. Single touch, not a swallowtail. |
| **BASSOON** | | | | | | | | | | | |
| 1. | | Sotheby's auction, May 1980 | | | | | | | | | |

[2]Present whereabouts unknown.    [3]Formerly in the Rendall Collection.    [4]This is the speaking length, from center of embouchure to foot end.

| Young No. | No. Keys and Metal | City, Owner, No. | Pitch | No. Pcs. | Length | Body, Mounts Flaps | SAT | Holes Dbld. | Tuning Holes | Additional Data | Ill. Source |
|---|---|---|---|---|---|---|---|---|---|---|---|

## T. STANESBY, SR.

### RECORDERS

| Young No. | No. Keys and Metal | City, Owner, No. | Pitch | No. Pcs. | Length | Body, Mounts Flaps | SAT | Holes Dbld. | Tuning Holes | Additional Data | Ill. Source |
|---|---|---|---|---|---|---|---|---|---|---|---|
| 1. | 6th flute | Washington: DCM 1214 | D | | 30.4 | ivory, unmtd | | | | GSJ No. 1. "Sixth flute" | |
| 2. | Alto | Haslemere: Dolmetsch | F | | | boxw, ivory | | | | GSJ No. 4. Retuned. | Ill. Hunt, pl XI-d |
| 3. | Alto | London: Horniman 319 | Eb | | 51.1 | ebony, ivory | | | | GSJ No. 3. | Ill. JJ-GT-BR, no. 71 |
| 4. | Alto | London: late Eric Half-penny | | | | pearw, unmtd | | | | GSJ No. 5. | Ill. Baines MITA, pl 21d; ill. Galpin OEIM, pl 29; Details & Ill. GSJ IX, pl VIII |
| 5. | Alto | London: Mrs. Ruth Liebrecht | | | | ivory | | | | GSJ No. 13. Headjt and ft by TS, body by Harris. | |
| 6. | xAlto | xBerlin 2806 | | | 50.0 | boxw | | | | GSJ No. 2. | |
| 7. | Voice flute | Upper Bourne End: L. Lefkovitch | D | | | unmtd | | | | GSJ No. 6. | |
| 8. | Tenor | New Zealand: Ronald Castle | | | | | | | | GSJ No. 7. | |
| 9. | Bass; 1 brass key | Ilford: late Eric Half-penny | | | 89.75 | pearw, brass | | | | GSJ No. 8. Attributed to Thomas Stanesby. "TS" only mark. | Full details & ill. GSJ XV, p 49 |
| 10. | Alto | Amsterdam: Frans Brüggen | | | 51.8 | boxw, unmtd | | | | | |

### FLUTE

| Young No. | No. Keys and Metal | City, Owner, No. | Pitch | No. Pcs. | Length | Body, Mounts Flaps | SAT | Holes Dbld. | Tuning Holes | Additional Data | Ill. Source |
|---|---|---|---|---|---|---|---|---|---|---|---|
| 1. | 1 silver | Washington: DCM 1177 | C | | 60.0 | boxw, ivory | | | | Now 4 keys. Head jt has socket, not tenon, latter Stanesby usual. Head jt "STANESBY LONDON" | |

### OBOES

| Young No. | No. Keys and Metal | City, Owner, No. | Pitch | No. Pcs. | Length | Body, Mounts Flaps | SAT | Holes Dbld. | Tuning Holes | Additional Data | Ill. Source |
|---|---|---|---|---|---|---|---|---|---|---|---|
| 1. | 3 silver | Scarsdale: D & R Rosen-baum | | | 58.9 | pearw, ivory  ro | SATW | 3&4 | 2 | GSJ No. 9. Type A. | LOM 90 |
| 2. | 3 brass | London: Horniman 232 | | | 59.6 | boxw, unmtd  ro | SATW | 3&4 | 2 | GSJ No. 10. Type A.[1] | EAMI 551 |
| 3. | 3 silver | London: Horniman 277 | | | 59.6 | boxw, ivory  ro | SATW | 3&4 | 2 | GSJ No. 11. Type A.[1] | Ill. JJ-GT-BR, no. 96 |
| 4. | 3 silver | Edinburgh: Melville-Mason? | | | 59.0 | boxw, unmtd  ro | SATW | 3&4 | 2 | GSJ No. 12. Type A.[1] | Ill. GSJ II, pl II & III. |
| 5. | 3 | London: J. MacGillivray | | | | wood, ivory  ro (massive!) | | 3&4 | | Type A. | |
| 6. | 2 | Wolverhampton: E. M. Shaw-Hellier | | | | boxw, unmtd  ro | | | | GSJ No. 14. Type A. No duplicate eb' key. | |

### BASSOON

| Young No. | No. Keys and Metal | City, Owner, No. | Pitch | No. Pcs. | Length | Body, Mounts Flaps | SAT | Holes Dbld. | Tuning Holes | Additional Data | Ill. Source |
|---|---|---|---|---|---|---|---|---|---|---|---|
| 1. | 4 brass | London: William Water-house | | | 126.3 | maple, brass | SATW | | | Wing is by Stanesby Jr.[2] | Ill. this book, Pl. VI |

[1] These three oboes are described in detail in Eric Halfpenny's important study of the English two- and three-keyed oboe, which appeared in GSJ II. "Type A," "B", "C" & "D" are defined therein.

[2] This important instrument was acquired by Mr. Waterhouse in November 1979 and is the only known bassoon by Thomas Stanesby Sr. The wing joint by Thomas Stanesby Jr. is only the second (piece of) bassoon to survive made by the son. While the bass joint is not stamped, its wood and key design are identical to the other joints by Stanesby Sr. The boot and bell are stamped precisely as the Rosenbaum oboe, among von-Huene's drawings illustrated by Langwill.

# STANESBY, JR.                                                                          STANESBY, JR.

## RECORDERS

| Young No. | No. Keys and Metal | City, Owner, No. | Pitch | No. Pcs. | Length | Body, Mounts Flaps | SAT | Holes Dbld. | Tuning Holes | Additional Data | Ill. Source |
|---|---|---|---|---|---|---|---|---|---|---|---|
| 1. | Sixth flute | Amsterdam: Frans Brüggen, ex Hunt | D | 3 pc | 30.0 | carved ivory, unmtd | | | | GSJ No. 1. Cherub's head on mouthpiece, grapevine on body. | |
| 2. | Fifth flute | Vienna: R. Clemencic, ex Baines | | | | ivory | | | | GSJ No. 2. | |
| 3. | Alto | Shipston-on-Stour: Mrs. I. Bennett | | | | | | | | GSJ No. 3. Stamp 3. | |
| 4. | Alto | London: Horniman 275 | | 3 pc | 50.0 | boxw, unmtd | | | | GSJ No. 4. Full dimensions, GSJ IX, p 84 (no. 8.) | |
| 5. | Alto | Paris: late Comtesse de Chambure | | | | | | | | GSJ No. 5. Stamp 1. | |
| 6. | Alto | ? Capt. R.G. Gerry, USN | | | | | | | | GSJ No. 6. Marked 'F' | |
| 7. | Alto | Ilford: late Eric Halfpenny | | | | | | | | GSJ No. 7. Stamp 1. Full dimensions & photos, GSJ IX, p 84 (no. 5) | Ill. GSJ IX |
| 8. | Alto | Peebles: F.E. Dodman | | | | wood, ivory | | | | GSJ No. 34. | |
| 9. | Tenor | Amsterdam: F. Brüggen, ex Bergmann | B♭ | 3 pc | 73.0 | boxw, unmtd | | | | GSJ No. 8. Stamp 2. 1 brass key. Marked '4' = fourth flute. | |
| 10. | Tenor | Paris: late Comtesse de Chambure | | 4 pc | | boxw | | | | GSJ No. 9. With flute-type ft jt. Marked 'C' | |
| 11. | Tenor | Royston: Dr. R. Harding | B♭ | | | | | | | GSJ No. 10. | |
| 12. | Tenor | Cambridge: Dr. M. Lobban | | | | | | | | GSJ No. 11. | |

## FLUTES

| Young No. | No. Keys and Metal | City, Owner, No. | Pitch | No. Pcs. | Length | Body, Mounts Flaps | SAT | Holes Dbld. | Tuning Holes | Additional Data | Ill. Source |
|---|---|---|---|---|---|---|---|---|---|---|---|
| 1. | 1 silver | London: Philip Bate | | | | ivory, silver | | | | GSJ No. 12. Engraved head plate. | |
| 2. | 1 silver | London: Horniman 281 | C | | 60.8 | ivory, silver | | | | GSJ No. 13. Engraved head plate. | |
| 3. | 1 silver | London: Horniman 264 | | | 61.3 | ivory, silver | | | | GSJ No. 14. Engraved head plate. 3 added keys. | |
| 4. | 1 silver | London: Horniman 241 | | 4 pc | 61.6 | boxw, ivory | | | | GSJ No. 15. | Ill. Carse MWI, Pl. I-A |
| 5. | 1 | Sevenoaks: C.M. Champion | | | | wood, ivory | | | | GSJ No. 16. 3 keys added but now removed. | |
| 6. | 1 | Sevenoaks: C.M. Champion | F | | | ivory, unmtd | | | | GSJ No. 17. | |
| 7. | 1 missing | Meopham: Nicholas Benn, ex Greene | C | 6 pc | 59.2 | ivory, silver | — — — | — — — | | GSJ No. 18. Engraved head plate. Head-joint has tenon. | |
| 8. | 1 silver | Scarsdale: D & R Rosenbaum 16[1] | C | 4 pc | 61.6 | ebony, ivory sq | SATK | | | GSJ No. 19. Engraved head plate. | |
| 9. | 1 silver | Washington: DCM 269 | | 4 pc | 61.6 | ivory, silver sq | | | | GSJ No. 20, a&b. Engraved head plate. Made up of parts of 2 TS Jr flutes. | |
| 10. | 1 silver | Washington: DCM 388 | | 4 pc | 59.6 | ivory, silver sq | | | | GSJ No. 21. Engraved head plate. 5 added keys. | |

Note: Stanesby Jr.'s marks are differentiated by the late Eric Halfpenny in GSJ XIII.          [1]ex-Halfpenny

**STANESBY JR.** *(cont.)*

FLUTES | *(cont.)*

| Young No. | No. Keys and Metal | City, Owner, No. | Pitch | No. Pcs. | Length | Body, Mounts | Flaps | SAT | Holes Dbld. | Tuning Holes | Additional Data | Ill. Source |
|---|---|---|---|---|---|---|---|---|---|---|---|---|
| 11. | 1 silver | Washington: DCM 1030 | C | 4 pc | 60.5 | ivory, silver | sq | | | | GSJ No. 22. Added silver mounts. Much repaired. | |
| 12. | 1 silver | Washington: DCM 1125 | C | 4 pc | 60.9 | ivory, unmtd | sq | | | | GSJ No. 23. Silver head plate. | |
| 13. | 1 silver | Washington: DCM 1177 | C | 4 pc | 60.0 | boxw, ivory | | | | | GSJ No. 24. Now 4 keys. Headjoint has Stamp 5 and has socket, not tenon. Rest unmarked. | |
| 14. | 1 brass | London: RCM 326 | C | 4 pc | 60.35 | boxw, unmtd | sq | | | | GSJ No. 25. Head joint has socket. | Ill. Ridley Luton cat., Fl. I |
| 15. | 1 brass | Newcastle upon Tyne: Mrs. C. Ring | | | | boxw, brass | | | | | GSJ No. 26. Head joint has socket. | |
| 16. | 1 gold plated | Paris E.979.2.33, ex Chambure | C | 4 pc | 61.0 | ivory, gold pl. | sq | SATK | | | GSJ No. 33. Engraved key. | |
| 17. | 1 silver | Meopham: N. Benn, ex Greene | | 6 pc | 57.95 | ivory, silver | rect. | SATK | | | GSJ No. 35. Head joint has tenon. | |
| 18. | 1 silver | London: RCM 292 | | | | violetw, ivory | sq | | | | GSJ No. 37. Head joint has tenon. Head and lower jt unstamped. | |
| 19. | 1 silver | London: J.P.S. Montagu III 154 | | 4 pc | 61.44 | ivory, silver | sq | SATK | | | GSJ No. 38. Cut down in past. | |
| 20. | 1 silver | Edinburgh: Rendall Collection | C | 4 pc | 61.0 | ivory, silver | sq | | | | GSJ No. 39. | |
| 21. | FIFE | Sutton Coldfield: Miss J. Beat | C | 1 pc | 39.0 | boxw, brass | | | | | GSJ No. 40. Stamp 5. | |
| 22. | 1 silver | Newcastle upon Tyne: Mrs. C. Ring | | | | ivory, silver | | | | | GSJ No. 41. | |
| 23. | 1 silver | Beverley: H.S. Woledge | | | | boxw, ivory | | | | | GSJ No. 42. Stamp 7. | |
| 24. | FIFE | Keighley Museum 40/55 | | | | boxw, brass | | | | | GSJ No. 43. | |
| 25. | 1 silver | Amsterdam: F. Brüggen | C | | 60.9 | wood, ivory | sq | SATK | | | GSJ No. 44. | |
| 26. | 1 | London: Guy Oldham | | | | ivory, silver | | | | | GSJ No. 45. Stamp 4. | |
| 27. | 1 | Leningrad 483 | | 4 pc | 63.7 | silver | | | | | GSJ No. 46. Now 6 keys. Mother-of-pearl head or mouthplate? | |
| 28. | 1 silver | Leningrad 2360 | | 4 pc | 59.5 | ivory, silver | | | | | GSJ No. 47. Now has 6 keys. | |
| 29. | 1 brass | Gloucester: City Museum | | | | boxw, ivory | | | | | GSJ No. 48. Head joint has tenon. | |
| 30. | 1 brass | New York City: Strauss | | | | boxw | | | | | | |
| 31. | 1 silver | Washington: DCM 1504 | | 4 pc | 61.3 | ivory, silver | | | | | Flap missing, but sq cut-out. Silver bands at D' and G' holes. Repair? | |
| 32. | | Ipswich Museum 1935/249 | | | | | | | | | | |
| 33. | 1 | Amersfoort: J. van der Grinten | | | | | | | | | | |
| 34. | 1 silver | Leipzig 1246 | C | 4 pc | 60.9 | ivory, silver | sq | SATK | | | Heyde says originally was SATW. | Ill. Heyde Leipzig, tafel 9 |

| Young No. | No. Keys and Metal | City, Owner, No. | Pitch | No. Pcs. | Length | Body, Mounts | Flaps | SAT | Holes Dbld. | Tuning Holes | Additional Data | Ill. Source |
|---|---|---|---|---|---|---|---|---|---|---|---|---|
| **BASS FLUTES** | | | | | | | | | | | | |
| 1. | 1 | Modena Museo Civico | | | | wood, unmtd | | | | | GSJ No. 36. | |
| 2. | 1 silver | Edgware: Boosey & Hawkes | G | | | violetw, ivory | | | | | Attributed to TS jr. No stamp. Headjoint has tenon, Stanesby-style | |
| **OBOES** | | | | | | | | | | | | |
| 1. | 2 silver | Oxford: Bate 29 | | | 56.8 | maple, silver | ro | | | | GSJ No. 27. Type B. Full details, GSJ II. Nearly "straight," but bulges | Ill. 1968 Exhib, no. 83; Ill. Bate Oboe, pl III |
| 2. | 3 silver | London: Horniman 1969.683 | | | 59.6 | boxw, unmtd | ro | | | | GSJ No. 28. Type A. Heavy turnings. | Ill. Horniman WIEAM, pl V, no. 27; Ill. JJ-GT-BR no. 97. |
| 3. | 2 silver | Scarsdale: D & R Rosenbaum 60 | | | 61.0 | boxw, ivory | ro | SATK | 3 dbl | 2 th | Straight model. | |
| **TENOR OBOE** | | | | | | | | | | | | |
| 1. | 2 brass | London: V & A 291-1882 | | | 76.5 | cedar, unmtd | | | | | GSJ No. 29. "Vox humana" | Ill. JJ-GT-BR, no. 100. Ill. Baines V&A cat., 23/5. LOM 89 |
| **CLARINET** | | | | | | | | | | | | |
| 1. | Barrel only | Washington: DCM 275 | | | | boxw, ivory | | | | | GSJ No. 32. Found as part of a clarinet by Wrede. Only clue that TS Jr. made clarinets, too. | |
| **BASSOON** | | | | | | | | | | | | |
| 1. | 4 brass | London: William Waterhouse, ex Sharp | | | 122.5 | maple, brass | | | | | GSJ No. 30. d. 1747. | Ill. Galpin Old English Instruments of Music, pl 34-8. Ill. this book, Pl. |
| 2. | 4 brass | London: William Waterhouse | | | | maple, brass | | | | | Wing joint only, goes with Stanesby Sr. instrument | Ill. this book, Pl.)0 |
| **CONTRABASSOON** | | | | | | | | | | | | |
| 1. | 4 brass | Dublin: National Museum no. 2-1907 | | | 253.0 | maple, brass | ro | | | | GSJ No. 31. d. 1739. | Ill. 1968 GS Exhib. cat., pl XII; ill. Jansen, fig. 262 |

## STEENBERGEN

### RECORDERS

| | | | | | | | | | | | | |
|---|---|---|---|---|---|---|---|---|---|---|---|---|
| 1. | xQuartflöte | xBerlin 2785 | | | | | | | | | | |
| 1. | xQuartflöte | xBerlin 2785 | B | 2 pc | 35.0 | boxw | | | | | | |
| 2. | xDiskant-flöte | xBerlin 2787 | G' | 3 pc | 42.5 | boxw, ivory | | | | | | |
| 3. | Soprano | Stockholm 160 | | | | boxw | | | | | | |
| 4. | Alto | Amsterdam: Frans Brüggen | F | 2 pc | 50.5 | boxw, ivory | | | | | | |

### OBOES

| | | | | | | | | | | | | |
|---|---|---|---|---|---|---|---|---|---|---|---|---|
| 1. | 3 silver | Hague Ea 3-X-1952 | | | 57.2 | boxw | | | 3&4 | | | Ill 1974 Hague Exhib. cat, p 52(107) |
| 2. | x3 | xBerlin 2940 | | | 57.5 | ebony | | | | | | |
| 3. | x3 | xBerlin 2949 | | | 57.5 | boxw | | | | | | |
| 4. | 3 brass | Brussels 967 | | | 62.0[1] | boxw, ivory | (D) Eb (Y) C | SATW | 3&4 | 2 | | |
| 5. | 3 silver | Brussels 968 | | | 62.0[1] | boxw, ivory | (D) Eb (Y) C | SATW | 3&4 | 2 | | |
| 6. | 3 brass | Brussels 2611 | | | | boxw | | | | | | |

## STENGEL

### FRENCH FLAGEOLET

| | | | | | | | | | | | | |
|---|---|---|---|---|---|---|---|---|---|---|---|---|
| 1. | x 4 brass | xLeipzig 1157 | C | | 42.0 | boxw, ivory | | | | | lost WW2 | |

### PICCOLOS

| | | | | | | | | | | | | |
|---|---|---|---|---|---|---|---|---|---|---|---|---|
| 1. | 1 brass | Munich: Deutsches Museum 5488 | C | | 32.0 | boxw, black hrn | sq | | | | | key in block |
| 2. | 1 brass | Washington: DCM 664 | C | 4 pc | 32.0 | boxw, horn | sq | SATK | | | | |
| 3. | 1 | Florence 112 | C | | | | | | | | | |

### FLUTES

| | | | | | | | | | | | | |
|---|---|---|---|---|---|---|---|---|---|---|---|---|
| 1. | 1 brass | Munich Stadtmuseum 60/84 | C | 4 pc | 51.2 | boxw, horn | sq | | | | "STENGEL / + F + ". No register. | |
| 2. | 1 brass | Munich Stadtmuseum 42/155 | C | 4 pc | 51.8 | boxw, ivory | sq | SATK | | | "STENGEL / + F +". | |
| 3. | 5 brass | Nürnberg MI 332 | D | 5 pc | 63.0 | boxw, brass | | | | | | |
| 4. | 6 brass | Washington: DCM 971 | C | 5 pc | 61.8 | boxw, ivory | ro | | | | | |
| 5. | 8 brass | Leipzig 1268 | C | 4 pc | 67.0 | boxw, ivory, brass | | | | | Changed to Boehm system. | |

[1] perhaps an error? Too long?

| Young No. | No. Keys and Metal | City, Owner, No. | Pitch | No. Pcs. | Length | Body, Mounts | Flaps | SAT | Holes Dbld. | Tuning Holes | Additional Data | Ill. Source |
|---|---|---|---|---|---|---|---|---|---|---|---|---|

**STENGEL** *(cont.)*

**FLUTES** *(cont.)*

| | | | | | | | | | | | | |
|---|---|---|---|---|---|---|---|---|---|---|---|---|
| 6. | 9 brass | Berlin 2691 | C | 5 pc | 70.5 | boxw, ivory | ro | | | | Only charred remains left from WW2. Foot to b. | |
| 7. | 9 | Milan Museo Civico | | 5 pc | 71.0 | boxw, ivory | | | | | | |
| 8. | 10 brass | Washington: DCM 354 | C | 4 pc | 70.5 | boxw, ivory | dome | | | | Flaps riveted to keys. Supplementary stamp[1] | |
| 9. | | Stuttgart: G. Hase | | | | | | | | | | |

**OBOES**

| | | | | | | | | | | | | |
|---|---|---|---|---|---|---|---|---|---|---|---|---|
| 1. | 9 Germ. silver | Berkeley: U. of Cal. 16 | | | 55.9 | boxw,[2] ivory | | | | | Keys b, c', c#', eb', f', f#', g#', bb' X2, c#', oct. Supplementary stamp.[1] | |
| 2. | 9 brass | Oxford: Bate x22, loan from Baines | | | 55.5 | boxw, ivory | dome | | | | Flaps riveted to keys. Supplementary stamp[1] Ill.[3] | |
| 3. | 10 brass | Munich Stadtmuseum 65/29 | | | 57.3 | boxw, ivory | | | | | Keys on axles & posts: b', c', c#', d#', f', g#', b' w 2 touches, C'', 2 oct keys. | |
| 4. | 10 | Milan Sci & Techn Mus. L. da Vinci | | | | | | | | | Most keys on pillars, but lower ones in knobs. | |
| 5. | | Florence 131 | | | | | | | | | | |
| 6. | 14 silver | New Haven: Yale 400 | | | 56.0 | ebony, ivory | dome | | | | Keys on posts & axles. 13 touches & 2 rings. | |

**ENGLISH HORNS**

| | | | | | | | | | | | | |
|---|---|---|---|---|---|---|---|---|---|---|---|---|
| 1. | 12 | xBerlin 1393 | | | 81.0 | rosew, G. silver | | | | | Straight form. | Ill. Sachs cat., taf 26 |
| 2. | 6 | Milan: Sci & Techn Mus., L. da Vinci | | | | | | | | | Angular form. Ivory knee. | |

**BASSOONS**

| | | | | | | | | | | | | |
|---|---|---|---|---|---|---|---|---|---|---|---|---|
| 1. | 6+ brass | Frankfurt am Oder | | | 122.9 | maple, brass | | | | | 1 key added. | |
| 2. | 8 brass | Oxford: Bate x31, loan from Baines | | | 126.2 | maple, brass | | | | | Keys recessed into body. Extendable wing jt. Brass-tipped tenons. Ivory crook socket | |
| 3. | 9 brass | Munich: Deutsches Museum 17906 | | | 130.4 | maple, brass | ro | | | | Decorative ivory band on bell. | |
| 4. | 12 brass | Nürnberg MI 340 | | | 130.0 | maple, brass | dome | | | | | |
| 5. | 14 brass | New Haven: Yale 431 | | | 132.87 | maple, brass | dome | | | | | |
| 6. | 16 brass | Hamburg: MHG 1926.411 | | | 130.0 | maple, brass | dome | | | | Keys recessed into body. | EAMI 605. Ill. Schröder cat., abb. 18 |

**CLARINETS**

| | | | | | | | | | | | | |
|---|---|---|---|---|---|---|---|---|---|---|---|---|
| 1. | 5 brass | Munich Deutsches Museum 1974/7 | Bb | 6 pc | 66.5 | boxw, horn | a' & oct sq, rest ro | | | | In knobs & blocks. Integral bell ring. | |
| 2. | 5 | Markneukirchen 119 | | | | | | | | | | |
| 3. | 7 brass | London: RCM 83 | C | 6 pc | | boxw, ivory | 6 sq, 1 ro | | | | 5 keys in blocks, 1 in added block, 1 in saddle. | |
| 4. | 9 G/silver | New York: MMA 89.4.2174 | A | 4 pc | 34.9 | boxw, silver | dome | | | | Keys on pillars. Monogram "JS" | |

[1] STENGEL / BAIREUTH / crown / Deposito Brizzi a Niccolai / Firenze, Brevattato sa S.M. il Re  [2] In my opinion, boxwood, although the catalogue says maple.  [3] Illustrated, Baines: *Woodwind Instruments & Their History* Pl. 31

| | | | | | | | | | | | | |
|---|---|---|---|---|---|---|---|---|---|---|---|---|
| **STENGEL** *(cont.)* | | | | | | | | | | | | **STENGEL** *(cont.)* |

## CLARINETS *(cont.)*

| Young No. | No. Keys and Metal | City, Owner, No. | Pitch | No. Pcs. | Length | Body, Mounts | Flaps | SAT | Holes Dbld. | Tuning Holes | Additional Data | Ill. Source |
|---|---|---|---|---|---|---|---|---|---|---|---|---|
| 5. | 9 brass | Edinburgh: Rendall Collection | B♭/A | | 58.4 | boxw, ivory | dome | | | | Bore 1.42. | |
| 6. | 9 brass | Nürnberg MI 336 | A | 4 pc | 72.0 | boxw, brass | dome | | | | | |
| 7. | 12 brass | Leipzig 1495 | B♭ | 5 pc | 57.95 | boxw, ivory | sq | | | | Ivory mouthpiece. | EAMI 631 |
| 8. | 12 brass | Göttingen, U of, 301 | | | 69.5 | boxw, brass | | | | | Joh. Christoph & Joh. Simon: "STENGEL/BAYREUTH/INHABER/ etc.[1] | |
| 9. | 13 brass | Oxford: Bate x44, loan from Baines | A | 5 pc | 63.0 | boxw, ivory | dome | | | | Brass tuning slide, ivory thumb rest. | Ill. Baines WITH, pl 31 |
| 10. | 14 brass | Nürnberg MI 335 | B♭ | 4 pc | 67.5 | boxw, horn | dome | | | | Serial no. 33309. | |
| 11. | 12 brass | Nürnberg MIR 456 | A | 5 pc | 67.5 | boxw, brass | | | | | | |
| 12. | | Leipzig 1464 | G | | | | | | | | | |
| 13. | | Leipzig 1489 | | | | | | | | | | |
| 14. | 11 brass | Cambridge: N.J. Shackleton | D | 5 pc | | boxw, brass | | | | | Has original mouthpiece with maker's stamp. Stengel/Baireuth. | |
| 15. | 12 brass | Cambridge: N.J. Shackleton | B♭ | 5 pc | | boxw, ivory | | | | | Stengel/Stuttgart | |
| 16. | 7 brass | Göttingen, Univ. of, 306 | | | 64.5 | boxw, horn | | | | | Johann Samuel ("STENGEL / BAIREUTH") | |

## BASSET HORNS

| Young No. | No. Keys and Metal | City, Owner, No. | Pitch | No. Pcs. | Length | Body, Mounts | Flaps | SAT | Holes Dbld. | Tuning Holes | Additional Data | Ill. Source |
|---|---|---|---|---|---|---|---|---|---|---|---|---|
| 1. | 9 brass | Leipzig 1531 | | | 100.3 | maple? ivory | sq | | | | ivory mouthpiece with maker's stamp. Angular form. | |
| 2. | 9? | Florence 159 | | | | | | | | | | |
| 3. | | Zumikon, Schweiz: Hans Rudolf Stalder | | | | | | | | | | |

## ALTO CLARINETS

| Young No. | No. Keys and Metal | City, Owner, No. | Pitch | No. Pcs. | Length | Body, Mounts | Flaps | SAT | Holes Dbld. | Tuning Holes | Additional Data | Ill. Source |
|---|---|---|---|---|---|---|---|---|---|---|---|---|
| 1. | 7 | Leipzig 1523 | | | | | | | | | | |
| 2. | 13 brass | Munich Stadtmuseum 67/48 | | 5 pc | 84.2 | boxw, ivory | | | | | I. Muller system. Some rollers. 5 pc: bell, long lower jt, upper jt, barrel, mouthpiece | |

## TENOR CLARINET

| Young No. | No. Keys and Metal | City, Owner, No. | Pitch | No. Pcs. | Length | Body, Mounts | Flaps | SAT | Holes Dbld. | Tuning Holes | Additional Data | Ill. Source |
|---|---|---|---|---|---|---|---|---|---|---|---|---|
| 1. | 10 brass | Washington: Smithsonian 95.296 | | 6 pc (7?) | (83.8) | boxw, ivory | | | | | Mouthpiece missing. 3 keys post & axles, 3 saddles, rest knobs! | |

## BASS CLARINETS

| Young No. | No. Keys and Metal | City, Owner, No. | Pitch | No. Pcs. | Length | Body, Mounts | Flaps | SAT | Holes Dbld. | Tuning Holes | Additional Data | Ill. Source |
|---|---|---|---|---|---|---|---|---|---|---|---|---|
| 1. | | Brussels 943 | B♭ | | 75.0 | | | | | | Bassoon form. Metal bell. | |
| 2. | | Florence 161 | | | | | | | | | Bassoon form. Metal bell. | |
| 3. | 18 brass | Halle: Handelhaus MS 404 | | | 123.5 | grena, brass | | | | | | |

[1] (Rest of stamp) "Zweyer/Preiss/Medaillen"

# STREITWOLF STREITWOLF

## FLAGEOLET

| Young No. | No. Keys and Metal | City, Owner, No. | Pitch | No. Pcs. | Length | Body, Mounts | Flaps | SAT | Holes Dbld. | Tuning Holes | Additional Data | Ill. Source |
|---|---|---|---|---|---|---|---|---|---|---|---|---|
| 1. | 2 silver | Berlin 109 | E♭ | | 33.0 | ebony, ivory | sq | | | | Clarinet-shaped bell. | |

## FLUTES

| Young No. | No. Keys and Metal | City, Owner, No. | Pitch | No. Pcs. | Length | Body, Mounts | Flaps | SAT | Holes Dbld. | Tuning Holes | Additional Data | Ill. Source |
|---|---|---|---|---|---|---|---|---|---|---|---|---|
| 1. | 7 brass | Oxford: Bate 1026 | | | 59.8[1] | boxw, ivory | ro | | | | Foot to c. | |
| 2. | 8 silver | Oxford: Bate 135 | | | 61.9[1] | ebony, ivory | ro | | | | Foot to b. Lapped brass tenons. | Ill. Bate Flute, pl 7 |
| 3. | 8 brass | Berlin 4010 | | 4 pc | | boxw, ivory | ro | SATK | | | Foot to c. Flaps carved to body. Horn ring at end of head jt. 4 pc. | |
| 4. | 8 silver | Bonn BH (Zimmermann 67) | | 4 pc | 72.0 | ebony, ivory | ro | | | | Foot to b. 4 pc. | |
| 5. | 8 brass | Leningrad 2302 | | 4 pc | 70.2 | boxw, bone? | | | | | 4 pc. | |
| 6. | 8 | Zurich: Museum Bellerive | | | | | | | | | | |
| 7. | | Hague 62 | | | | | | | | | | |
| 8. | | Hague 71 | | | | | | | | | | |
| 9. | 8 silver | Vermillion: U. of S.D. 2669 | | | 69.5 | ebony, ivory | ro | SATK | | | Lapped tenons. Keys mtd in blocks. Foot to b. | |
| 10. | | Stuttgart: G. Hase | | | | | | | | | | |

## OBOES

| Young No. | No. Keys and Metal | City, Owner, No. | Pitch | No. Pcs. | Length | Body, Mounts | Flaps | SAT | Holes Dbld. | Tuning Holes | Additional Data | Ill. Source |
|---|---|---|---|---|---|---|---|---|---|---|---|---|
| 1. | 13 brass | Halle Handelhaus MS 423 | | | 57.7 | boxw, ivory | | | 0 dbl | | | |
| 2. | 12 brass | Eisenach Bachhaus I-154 | | | 56.9 | boxw, ivory | dome | | 3 dbl | | 2 upper joints. 14 touches. Keys in integral blocks. | |

## ENGLISH HORNS

| Young No. | No. Keys and Metal | City, Owner, No. | Pitch | No. Pcs. | Length | Body, Mounts | Flaps | SAT | Holes Dbld. | Tuning Holes | Additional Data | Ill. Source |
|---|---|---|---|---|---|---|---|---|---|---|---|---|
| 1. | 14 | Leipzig 1351 | | | | | | | | | | |
| 2. | 18 brass | Leningrad 783 | | 5 pc | 76.5 | boxw, metal | | | | | "pipe shape" (straight, but upturned wooden bell). 5 pc. | LOM 239[2] |
| 3. | | Biebrich: Heckel Museum | | 5 pc | | wood, ivory | | | | | "pipe shape" (Same). 5 pc. | Ill. Heckel Der Fagott, p 10-d. |
| 4. | | Zurich: Museum Bellerive | | | | | | | | | | |
| 5. | 16 brass | Nürnberg MI 468, loan by Ventzke | | | c78.0 | boxw, ivory, | ro | | 0 dbl | 1 th | 1 brass saddle, rest of keys in integral blocks. [3] | |

## CLARINETS

| Young No. | No. Keys and Metal | City, Owner, No. | Pitch | No. Pcs. | Length | Body, Mounts | Flaps | SAT | Holes Dbld. | Tuning Holes | Additional Data | Ill. Source |
|---|---|---|---|---|---|---|---|---|---|---|---|---|
| 1. | 13 | Peine: Günter Hart | | | | | | | | | | |
| 2. | | Biebrich: Heckel Museum | E♭ | | | | | | | | | Ill. Heckel Der Fagott, p 23-p |
| 3. | | Berwick-on-Tweed: Brackenbury | | | | | | | | | | |

[1] Speaking length rather than overall length.
[2] Ill. Blagodatov catalogue, the only English horn or instrument with "pipe shape" that is illustrated. (There are neither page nor plate numbers).
[3] U-shape section at bottom is of wood with brass U-bend. This is true of all English horns said to be pipe-shape, as far as I know.

| --- | --- | --- | --- | --- | --- | --- | --- | --- | --- | --- | --- | --- |

**STREITWOLF** *(cont.)* **STREITWOLF** *(cont.)*

### BASSET HORN

| 1. | x16 brass | xBerlin 91 | F | | 69.5 | boxw, ivory, brass | | | | | Bore 1.8 | |

### BASS CLARINETS

| 1. | 16 brass | Munich: Deutsches Museum 68079 | C | | 85.5 | boxw, brass | | | | | Bassoon form. Ivory mouthpiece. Keys given in cat. | Ill. Seifers, p 101 |
| 2. | 18 brass | Leipzig 1539 | | | 83.1 | boxw, brass | ro | | | | Bassoon form. 1 key missing. | |
| 3. | 19 brass | Hague Ea 135-1959 | | | 90.6 | rosew, brass | ro | SATK | | | Bassoon form. Brass neck and bell. | Ill. Hague 1974 Exhib. cat. LOM 248 |
| 4. | x19 | xBerlin 87 | E♭ | | 95.0 | maple, brass, ivory | ro | | | | Bassoon form. | |
| 5. | | Hague 1617 or 697? | | | | | | | | | | |
| 6. | | Zurich: Museum Belle-rive | C | | | | | | | | Goes chromatically to Bb, uses both thumbs. | |

### BASSOONS

| 1. | 14 brass | Hamburg MHG 1912.1546 | | | 128.5 | maple, brass | ro | | | | Keys in blocks and saddles. | |
| 2. | 15 brass | Markneukirchen 2252 | | | | maple, brass | | | | | Keys on posts and axles. | |
| 3. | 10 brass | Göttingen City Museum | | | 128.5 | maple, brass | | | | | Wood U-bend at bottom of boot jt. | Ill. Jansen, fig. 397 |

### CHROMATIC BASS HORNS

| 1. | 10 brass | Munich: Deutsches Museum 10223 | C | | 126.5 | maple, brass | | | | | Also stamped "R. Haaken". Round cps. | Ill. Seifers cat., p 108 |
| 2. | 10 brass | Markneukirchen 102 | | | | maple, brass | | | | | | |
| 3. | 10 brass | Hague Ea 69-X-1952 | | | 126.5 | maple, brass | | | | | | Ill. Hague 1974 exhib. cat. p 42 |
| 4. | 11 brass | Hamburg MHG 1898.124 | B♭ | | 125.0 | maple, brass | | | | | Ivory mouthpiece. | Ill. Schröder cat., pl 16. LOM 283 |
| 5. | | xBerlin 57 | | | | | | | | | | |
| 6. | | Brunswick Stadtmuseum 68 | | | | | | | | | | |
| 7. | | Stockholm 119 | | | | | | | | | | |

# TAUBER **TAUBER**

### FLUTES

| 1. | 1 brass | Zell-Riedichen: Paul Hailperin | C | 3 pc | 60.7 | boxw, horn | sq | | | | Key mtd in knob | |
| 2. | 1 | Markneukirchen 109 | | | | | | | | | | |
| 3. | 4 brass | Halle: Handelhaus MS 339 | C | 5 pc | 61.0 | boxw, ivory | | | | | 1 upper joint. | |

| Young No. | No. Keys and Metal | City, Owner, No. | Pitch | No. Pcs. | Length | Body, Mounts | Flaps | SAT | Holes Dbld. | Tuning Holes | Additional Data | Ill. Source |
|---|---|---|---|---|---|---|---|---|---|---|---|---|
| **TAUBER** *(cont.)* | | | | | | | | | | | | |
| **FLUTES** *(cont.)* | | | | | | | | | | | | |
| 4. | 4 silver | Leipzig 1254 | C | | 59.2 | ivory, G silver | sq | | | | | Ill. Heyde Leipzig, taf 9 |
| 5. | x8 | xBerlin 1425 | | | 71.5 | ebony, silver | | | | | Foot to b. Keys b', c', c♯-d♯', f' with 2 touches, g♯', b♭' with 2 touches, c" | |
| 6. | | Rome, per Pail Hailperin | | | | | | | | | | |
| **OBOES** | | | | | | | | | | | | |
| 1. | 2 brass | Munich Stadtmuseum 64/22 | | | 56.5 | boxw, ivory | sq-cors (N) | SATW | 3 dbl | 2 th | 3 dbl. 2 th. 2 upper joints. | |
| 2. | 9 brass | Basel 1956.339 | | | | boxw | sq-cors (N) | | 3 dbl | 2 th | 3 dbl. 2 th. | |
| **ENGLISH HORNS** | | | | | | | | | | | | |
| 1. | 5 | London: Horniman 177 | | | 76.7 | dark w, ivory | | | | | curved form. "Mostly covered with leather." | |
| 2. | 8 brass | Quito, Ecuador 3452 | | | 80.3 | dk boxw | | | 3 dbl | | 3 dbl. 3 joints covered with leather (?). | |
| **CLARINETS** | | | | | | | | | | | | |
| 1. | 6 brass | Cambridge: N.J. Shackelton | A | | 62.9 | boxw, ivory | sq | SATW | | | Owner thinks this may be the ex Boomkamp instrument.[1] | |
| 2. | 6 | Bussum: Boomkamp (perhaps same instr.?) | A | | | | | | | | Gemeente Museum does not have it. | |
| 3. | 6 | London: Sotheby auction, early 1979 | B♭ | | | | | | | | 6th key is C♯ in saddle. | |
| 4. | | London: Sotheby auction, early 1979 | C | | | | | | | | Mthpc, upper and middle joints missing Consists of bbl, lower jt, bell. | |
| 5. | | ? Horace Fitzpatrick has partly-Tauber clarinet | | | | | | | | | | |
| **HIGH BASSOONS** | | | | | | | | | | | | |
| 1. | 9 brass | Salzburg 15/8 | | | 96.5 | pearw, brass | | | | | "Hochterz" | |
| 2. | 12 brass | Berlin 1873 | | | 96.45 | maple, brass | (X) & (Y) | | | | "Hochquart". 1 key now missing. | |
| **BASSOONS** | | | | | | | | | | | | |
| 1. | 7 | Florence 137 | | | 125.0 | maple, brass | | | | | | |
| 2. | 8 brass | Nürnberg MIR 411 | | | 122.35 | maple, brass | | | | | Ornate silver wire inlay all over body. | |
| 3. | 8 brass | Quito, Ecuador 3453 | +1 | | 123.2 | maple, brass | | | | | | |
| 4. | 9 brass | Biebrich: Heckel Museum F-8c | | | 126.7 | maple, brass | (X) | SATK | | | Has brass bell rim ring. Flat table. | |
| 5. | 9 brass | London: William Waterhouse | | | 125.7 | maple, brass | (X) | SATK | | | | |

[1] 6th key is C♯ in saddle.

**TAUBER** *(cont.)*  **TAUBER** *(cont.)*

BASSOONS *(cont.)*

| | | | | | | | | | | | | |
|---|---|---|---|---|---|---|---|---|---|---|---|---|
| 6. | | Celle: Dr. Hermann Moeck | | | | | | | | | | |
| 7. | | Vienna: Nikolaus Harnoncourt | | | | | | | | | | |
| 8. | | Vienna: Nikolaus Harnoncourt | | | | | | | | | | |
| 9. | | Munich: Jürgen Eppelsheim | | | | | | | | | | |

CONTRABASSOONS

| | | | | | | | | | | | | |
|---|---|---|---|---|---|---|---|---|---|---|---|---|
| 1. | 5. brass | Oxford: Bate 344 | | | 166.5 | maple, brass | U-shape | SATK | | | 2nd boot jt inverted at top. | EAM 611 & 612; LOM 194 |
| 2. | 6 brass | Stockholm 380 | | | | | U-shape | | | | 2nd boot jt inverted at top. | |
| 3. | 7 brass | Nieuw Loosdrecht: Will Jansen | | | | | | | | | Hairpin brass tube in place of 2nd boot jt. | |
| 4. | 7 brass | Naples 540, per Will Jansen | | | 194.0[1] | | | | | | Lost in 1973 fire. Descends to low E (not sure whether EE or EEE.) | Ill. E. Santagata cat. |
| 5. | 6 brass | Zurich: Willi Burger | | | 166.0 | maple, brass | | | | | | |
| 6. | | Amsterdam: Henk de Wit, Jr. | | | | | | | | | | Ill. Jansen, fig. 299 |
| 7. | | Zofingen, Schweiz: Hist. Mus. per Will Jansen | | | | | | | | | | Ill. Jansen, fig. 298, 342, 343, 347. |

# TERTON  # TERTON

RECORDERS

| | | | | | | | | | | | | |
|---|---|---|---|---|---|---|---|---|---|---|---|---|
| 1. | Alto | Brussels 1038 | | 3 pcs | 50.0 | boxw, ivory | | | | | | |
| 2. | Alto | Washington : DCM 871 | F | 3 pcs | 44.8 | boxw, ivory | | | | | | |
| 3. | Alto | Hague: Ea 31-X-1952 | | 3 pcs | 49.6 | boxw | | | | | | |
| 4. | | Hague 50 | | | | | | | | | | |
| 5. | | Hague 621 | | | | | | | | | | |
| 6. | | Hague 626 | | | | | | | | | | |

FLUTE

| | | | | | | | | | | | | |
|---|---|---|---|---|---|---|---|---|---|---|---|---|
| 1. | 1 | Hague 66 | | | | | | | | | | |

OBOES

| | | | | | | | | | | | | |
|---|---|---|---|---|---|---|---|---|---|---|---|---|
| 1. | x3 silver | xBerlin 2941 | | | 57.5 | ebony, ivory | | | | | | |
| 2. | x3 silver | xBerlin 2945 | D | | 47.25 | ebony, ivory | | | | | | |
| 3. | 3 brass | Washington: Smithsonian 208.185 | | | 57.0 | dk boxw, unmt | ro C, (L) Eb | SATW | 3 &4 dbl | 2 th | | |
| 4. | | Hague 720 | | | | | | | | | | |
| 5. | 3 | London: Roy. Mil. Exhib. 183 | | | | | | | | | | |

[1] acc to catalogue.

| Young No. | No. Keys and Metal | City, Owner, No. | Pitch | No. Pcs. | Length | Body, Mounts | Flaps | SAT | Holes Dbld. | Tuning Holes | Additional Data | Ill. Source |
|---|---|---|---|---|---|---|---|---|---|---|---|---|

# TRIEBERT

TRIEBERT

## FLUTES

| | | | | | | | | | | | | |
|---|---|---|---|---|---|---|---|---|---|---|---|---|
| 1. | 5 silver | Washington: DCM 617 | | | 61.8 | ebony, ivory | flat ro | | Stamp TaP T3[1] | | Silver saddles. Stamp uses taller letters than oboe stamp. | |
| 2. | 5 silver | Washington: DCM 605 | | | 61.3 | rosew, silver | dome | | TaP T3 | | Post & axles on crescent plates. Taller letters than oboe stamp. | |
| 3. | 6 silver | Washington: DCM 1121 | | | 61.5 | rosew, silver | dome | | TaP T | | Post & axles on crescent plates. Taller letters than oboe stamp. | |

## OBOES (without rings and not stamped BREVETE)

| | | | | | | | | | | | | |
|---|---|---|---|---|---|---|---|---|---|---|---|---|
| 1. | 7 brass | Copenhagen E. 155 | | | 56.3 | ? ivory | | | TaP T3[1] | | | |
| 2. | 8 brass | Oxford: Bate 212 | | | 56.2 | boxw, ivory | flat ro | | TaP T3 | | On blocks or saddles. 3&4 dbl. | EAMI 571 |
| 3. | 8 brass | Oxford: Bate 219 | | | 56.2 | boxw, ivory | | | TaP T3 | | Catalogue says "similar" to preceding. | LOM 231 |
| 4. | 8 brass | Oxford: Bate 220 | | | 56.2 | boxw, ivory | | | TaP T3 | | "Similar" but more keys added. | |
| 5. | 9 brass | London: Bate | | | 56.5 | boxw, ivory | | | | | C & D♯ in blocks, rest saddles. | |
| 6. | 9 brass | Leningrad 519 | | | 56.5 | boxw | | | TaP T3 | | 3 dbl. | |
| 7. | 10 brass | Leningrad 522 | | | 56.5 | | | | TaP T3 | | 3 dbl. | |
| 8. | 10 G. silver | London: Horniman 216 | | | 56.5 | boxw, ivory | | | TaP T3 | | 3 & 4 dbl. Keys in saddles. | |
| 9. | 10 silver | Nürnberg MI 458 | | | 56.5 | rosew, silver | | | | | 3 dbl. Systeme 3, no rings, 10 keys. Loaned by Karl Ventzke. | |
| 10. | 11 | Stockholm F. 258 | | | 52.55 | boxw, silver | dome | | TaP T3 | | All keys on posts & axles with one exception. | |
| 11. | 12 silver | Edgware: Boosey & Hawkes 210 | | | 54.5 | rosew | | | | | "Ordinary simple system," according to catalogue by A. C. Baines. | |
| 12. | 13 silver | Scarsdale: D & R Rosenbaum 70 | | | 56.1 | boxw, ivory | dome | | TaP T3 | | 3 dbl. 0 th. Modified Sellner system. | |

## OBOES (with rings and not stamped BREVETE)

| | | | | | | | | | | | | |
|---|---|---|---|---|---|---|---|---|---|---|---|---|
| 1. | 9 silver | Oxford: Bate 235 | | | 56.1 | boxw, silver | | | TaP T3 | | "Cup keys on screwed-in pillars." To low B. Brille with very fine rings. | LOM 232 |
| 2. | 12 silver | Brussels 939 | | | 62.5! | boxw, silver | | | TaP T3 | | | |
| 3. | 12 brass | Brussels 2318 | | | 56.2 | boxw, ivory | | | TaP T3 | | 2 rings. | |
| 4. | 12 silver | Brussels 2319 | | | 56.3 | rosew, silver | | | TaP T3 | | 2 rings. | |
| 5. | | Oxford: Bate 236 | | | | boxw, brass | | | | | "Early version of systeme 4." Bell a replacement made by Philip Bate | Ill. Bate Oboe, Pl. 5; Ill. Montagu, RM, Pl. 37 |

[1] This abbreviation signifies that the usual Triebert stamp shown at right is used, the tower trademark with either 3 or 4 crenellations. I am indebted to Karl Ventzke for first pointing out this change in the tower, which he believes occurred by a certain year, the discovery of which would assist us greatly in dating Triebert instruments. He believes that BREVETE indicates an instrument made after 1848. There are no known instances of the stamp "G. TRIEBERT" or "F. TRIEBERT."

TRIEBERT
A PARIS

| Young No. | No. Keys and Metal | City, Owner, No. | Pitch | No. Pcs. | Length | Body, Mounts Flaps | SAT | Holes Dbld. (Stamp) | Tuning Holes | Additional Data | Ill. Source |
|---|---|---|---|---|---|---|---|---|---|---|---|

**OBOES (with rings and not stamped BREVETE)** *(cont.)*

| Young No. | No. Keys and Metal | City, Owner, No. | Pitch | No. Pcs. | Length | Body, Mounts Flaps | SAT | Stamp | Tuning Holes | Additional Data | Ill. Source |
|---|---|---|---|---|---|---|---|---|---|---|---|
| 6. | 13 G. silver | London: Horniman 149 | | | 56.3 | cocus, G. silv. | | TaP T3 | | 3 rings. | |
| 7. | 13 silver | Edinburgh: Rendall Coll. | | | 55.5 | rosew, silver | | | | 3 rings. | |
| 8. | 13 G. silver | Scarsdale: D & R Rosenbaum 78 | | | 55.8 | rosew, silver | | TaP T3 | | 3 rings, posts & axles. | |
| 9. | | Nürnberg MI 459 | | | 55.6 | rosew, silver | | TaP T3 | | Systeme 4, 3 dbl. | |
| 10. | | London: Muffet | | | | | | | | | |
| 11. | 15 G. silver | London: Horniman 20 | | | 54.0 | cocus | | TaP T | | 2 rings. Lowest note B. 2 octave keys, shake key. | |
| 12. | 15 G. silver | London: Horniman 1970.19 | | | 59.3 | cocus | | TaP T | | | |
| 13. | 15 G. silver | Edgware: Bossey & Hawkes 209 | | | 58.5 | rosew, G. silver | | | | Simple system with brille, low B, no half-hole plate. | |
| 14. | 15 G. silver | Edgware: Boosey & Hawkes 211 | | | 58.0 | rosew | | | | Combined thumb-plate and Conservatory system, to low B. | |
| 15. | 15 | Edgware: Boosey & Hawkes 212 | | | 57.0 | rosew, silver | | | | Combined thumb-plate and Conservatory system. | |
| 16. | 15 G. silver | Edgware: Boosey & Hawkes 213 | | | 66.0 | rosew | | | | In B♭! An experimental "military model," a whole-tone lower than usual. | |
| 17. | | New York City: late Josef Marx | | | | | | | | | |
| 18. | | New York City: late Josef Marx | | | | | | | | | |
| 20. | | Halifax: Bankville Museum, per Langwill | | | | | | | | | |

**OBOES (known to be BREVETE, which began c. 1849)**

| Young No. | No. Keys and Metal | City, Owner, No. | Pitch | No. Pcs. | Length | Body, Mounts Flaps | SAT | Stamp | Tuning Holes | Additional Data | Ill. Source |
|---|---|---|---|---|---|---|---|---|---|---|---|
| 1. | | London: Horniman 21 | | | 58.4 | wood, G. silver | | TaP T | | Full key system with Barrett action and thumbplate, 2 shakes keys, 3 rings. | |
| 2. | 12 silver | London: RCM 326 0/4 | | | 55.9 | boxw, silver | | TaP T | | Keys on pillars. 3 dbl! To B. No serial number. | |
| 3. | 13 silver | London: RCM 323 | | | 59.75 | rosew, silver | | TaP T | | Thumbplate, rings, no serial number. | |
| 4. | | Stockholm 1964-65/13 | | | 56.78 | rosew, silver | | TaP T4 | | | |
| 5. | | Stockholm 1964-65/14 | | | 56.76 | rosew, silver | | TaP T3 | | | |
| 6. | | Stockholm 1964-65/9 | | | 56.85 | rosew, silver | | TaP T3 | | | |
| 7. | | Aachen: Dr. W. Willms | | | 55.6 | rosew, silver | | TaP T | | | |
| 8. | | Aachen: Dr. W. Willms | | | 60.3 | rosew | | TaP T | | Serial number 5714. | |
| 9. | | Hague or Bussum (Boomkamp?) | | | 56.9 | rosew, silver | | TaP T | | System 4, pillars with footplate. Needle springs. | |
| 10. | | Scarsdale: D & R Rosenbaum 71 | | | 56.8 | cocus, G. silver | | TaP T3 | | Barrett's first model of 1850. | |

| Young No. | No. Keys and Metal | City, Owner, No. | Pitch | No. Pcs. | Length | Body, Mounts Flaps | SAT | Holes Dbld. | Tuning Holes | Additional Data | Ill. Source |
|---|---|---|---|---|---|---|---|---|---|---|---|

**TRIEBERT** *(cont.)*

OBOES (known to be BREVETE, which began c. 1849) *(cont.)*

| | | | | | | | | | | | |
|---|---|---|---|---|---|---|---|---|---|---|---|
| 11. | | Nürnberg MI 417 | | | 62.9 | rosew, silver | | TaP T | | Loaned by Karl Ventzke. | |
| 12. | | Nürnberg MI 460 | | | 56.1 | ebony, silver | | TaP T3 | | Loaned by Karl Ventzke. | |
| 13. | | Nürnberg MI 461 | | | 56.8 | rosew, silver | | TaP T3 | | Loaned by Karl Ventzke. | |
| 14. | | Düren: K. Ventzke 10 | | | | | | | | Boehm system, 1867 | |
| 15. | | Düren: K. Ventzke 52 | | | | | | | | Conservatory system, ca 1885, serial no. 1185 | |
| 16. | | Düren: K. Ventzke 50 | | | | | | | | Boehm system. ca. 1860 | |

## UNCLASSIFIED OBOES[1]

| | | | | | | | | | | | |
|---|---|---|---|---|---|---|---|---|---|---|---|
| 1. | | Oxford: Bate 239 | | | 57.5 | rosew, silver | | | | Barrett model. Thumbplate, automatic octave key. | |
| 2. | | London: Bate | | | 57.0 | blackw | | | | | EAMI 575 |
| 3. | 8 silver | Paris C. 482 | | | 57.4 | boxw, ivory | | TaP T3 | | 3 & 4 dbl. Were 2 th, one now B. Keys in knobs, saddles, and a few posts & axles. | |
| 4. | 10 silver | Biebrich: Heckel Museum 0-11 | | | 56.7 | boxw, silver | | TaP | | | Ill. Heckel *Der Fagott*, K, seite 10. |
| 5. | 13 silver | Birbrich: Heckel Museum 0-28 | | | 55.8 | boxw, silver | | TaP | | | |
| 6. | 14 G. silver | Biebrich: Heckel Museum 0-32 | | | 54.7 | rosew, G. silver | | TaP | | 3 dbl. | Ill. Heckel *Der Fagott*, 1, seite 10. |
| 7. | 15 G. silver | Biebrich: Heckel Museum 0-31 | | | 56.3 | rosew, G. silver | | TaP | | 3 dbl. | |
| 8. | 17 silver | Paris C. 484 | | | | violetw | | | | Gift of Frederic Triebert; belonged to his brother, the virtuoso Charles Triebert. | |
| 9. | | Basel: Michel Piguet | | | | | | | | System 3. | |
| 10. | | Oxford: Bate 237 | | 59.2 | rosew, | | | | | One-pc. body. Boehm system. To low B , 3 dbl. | Ill. Montagu, RM. Pl. 37 |
| 11. | | Oxford: Bate 238 | | 56.6 | rosew, | | | | | System 3 with half-hole plate. To low B , 3 dbl. | Ill. Montagu, RM, Pl. 37 |
| 12. | | London: Montagu V 232 | | | | | | | | Military band oboe. | Ill. Montagu, RM, Pl. XI |

## CHALUMEAU DE CHASSE

| | | | | | | | | | | | |
|---|---|---|---|---|---|---|---|---|---|---|---|
| 1. | | Geneva Musée d'Art & d'Hist 831, per Langwill | | | | | | | | | |

## BASSOONS

| | | | | | | | | | | | |
|---|---|---|---|---|---|---|---|---|---|---|---|
| 1. | 15? keys | Amsterdam: Henk de Wit, Jr. | | | | | | TaP T | | 2 rings. | |
| 2. | 15? | Amsterdam: Henk de Wit, Jr. | | | | | | TaP T | | 2 rings. BREVETE. | |
| 3. | | Aachen: Dr. W. Willms | | | | | | TaP T | | In perhaps the most beautiful leather bassoon case I have ever seen! BREVETE | |

[1] All of these will fit into the other classifications upon closer examination.

**TRIEBERT** *(cont.)*
BASSOONS *(cont.)*
**TRIEBERT** *(cont.)*

| Young No. | No. Keys and Metal | City, Owner, No. | Pitch | No. Pcs. | Length | Body, Mounts Flaps | SAT | Holes Dbld. | Tuning Holes | Additional Data | Ill. Source |
|---|---|---|---|---|---|---|---|---|---|---|---|
| 4. | 17 | Bologna Museo Civico 1820 | | | | rosew | | | | | |
| 5. | | Brussels 3119 | | | 132.5 | rosew | | TaP T4 | | BREVETE | Ill. Bragard-dHen, pl VI-9; EAMI 614 |
| 6. | 19 G. silver | Boston: MFA 17.1927 | | | 132.7 | rosew, G. silv. | | | | "A. Marzoli, a Paris, Brevete. 92" | Ill. Bessaraboff, pl IV-151 |
| 7. | | Paris C. 510 | | | | | | | | | |
| 8. | 17 G. silver | Oxford: Bate 328 | | | 127.8 | rosew | | | | | |
| 9. | | Chesham Bois: E. Hunt | | | | | | | | | |
| 10. | 17 G. silver | Stockholm 1963-64/17 | | | 130.5 | rosew/maple | | TaP T3 | | BREVETE. O rings. | |
| 11. | | Stockholm 1963-65/18 | | | | | | | | | |
| 12. | | Stockholm 1964-65/10 | | | | | | | | | |

ENGLISH HORNS

| Young No. | No. Keys and Metal | City, Owner, No. | Pitch | No. Pcs. | Length | Body, Mounts Flaps | SAT | Holes Dbld. | Form Tuning Holes | Additional Data | Ill. Source |
|---|---|---|---|---|---|---|---|---|---|---|---|
| 1. | 2 brass | Eisenach Bachhaus 156 | | | 74.5 | brown leath, maple, horn | | | Curved | CPs octagonal. 3 dbl. | B&W x-ray & color photo, Heyde, Eisenach, p 232 |
| 2. | 9 brass | Brussels 974 | | | 87.0 | leath, ivory | TaP T3 | | Curved | CPs dome. 3 dbl. 2 th. | |
| 3. | 9 brass | Brussels 2321 | | | c80.0 | leath, ivory | TaP T3 | | Curved | CPs dome. 2 th. | Ill. Mahillon, Vol. IV |
| 4. | 10 brass | Oxford: Bate 262 | | | 76.2 | leath, ivory, horn | TaP | | Curved | CPs dome. 3 dbl. 2 th. 6 keys in saddles, 4 posts & axles. | |
| 5. | 10 brass | Oxford: Bate 259 | | | 74.8 | leath, maple, ivory, ebony | | | only upper joint curved | | |
| 6. | 10 brass | London: Horniman 234 | | | 80.0 | leath, ivory | TaP T | | Curved | 3 dbl. 0 th. | |
| 7. | 10 brass | London: Horniman 425 | | | 78.0 | leath, ivory | TaP T | | Curved | | |
| 8. | 10 brass | Zurich: Willi Burger | | | 78.0 | leath, ivory | TaP T | | | Keys on posts & axles. | |
| 9 | 10 | Basel: Michel Piguet | | | | | | | | | |
| 10. | 10 | Ann Arbor: U. of Mich. 674 | | | 79.0 | leath, ivory | | | Curved | | |
| 11. | 10 G. silver | Oxford: Bate 252 | | | 77.0 | leath, horn, G. silv. | TaP4 | | Curved | 1 ring?. 3 dbl. | LOM 234; ill. Montagu, RM, Pl. 40 |
| 12. | 10 silver | Copenhagen-Claudius 463 | | | 79.5 | leath, horn, silver | TaP | | Curved | 3 dbl. | |
| 13. | 12 G. silver | Edinburgh: Rendall | | | 78.9 | violetw, G. silver | | | Straight | 4 rings. | |
| 14. | 12 G. silver | Oxford: Bate 253 | | | 79.0 | maple, G. silver | | | Upper jt. curved | 3 dbl. | |
| 15. | 13 brass | Zurich: Willi Burger | | | | black leath | TaP T4 | | Curved | 2 ½-moon, partial rings. | |
| 16. | 14 silver | Edgware: Boosev & Hawkes no. 235 | | | | cocus | TaP | | Only upper joint curved | 2 rings. | |
| 17. | | Basel: Michel Piguet, another | | | | | | | | | |
| 18. | 10 brass | Boston Casadesus 94 | | | 79.0 | maple, brass, leath | TaP T4 | | Curved | 3 dbl, 2 th. No crook. | |
| 19. | | Geneva Musee d'Art & Hist 831 | | | | | | | | | |
| 20. | | Paris 493 | | | | | | | | | |

| Young No. | No. Keys and Metal | City, Owner, No. | Pitch | No. Pcs. | Length | Body, Mounts Flaps | SAT | Holes Dbld. | Tuning Holes | Additional Data | Ill. Source |
|---|---|---|---|---|---|---|---|---|---|---|---|
| **TRIEBERT** *(cont.)* | | | | | | | | | *Form* | | |
| **ENGLISH HORNS** *(cont.)* | | | | | | | | | | | |
| 21. | | Zurich: Museum Bellerive | | | | | | | Curved | 3 dbl. | |
| 22. | Silv pl | Scarsdale: D & R Rosenbaum 97 | | | 79.2 | | TaP T3 | | | | LOM 234 |
| **BARITONE OBOES** | | | | | | | | | | | |
| 1. | 7 brass | London: RCM 79 | | | 73.2 | boxw, ivory | | | | | CPs dome. 3 & 4 dbl. Posts & axles | EAMI 580 |
| 2. | 8 brass | Paris C. 495, E. 388 | | | 71.8 | maple, ivory | TaP T3 | | | | CPs round flat. 3 & 4 dbl. Keys on brass saddles. Belonged to Vogt, celebrated player. | |
| 3. | 9 | Oxford: Bate 260 | | | 73.7 | boxw, G. silver | TaP T3 | | | | 9 CPs dome, screwed-in pillars. | Ill. Bate Oboe. LOM 235; ill. Montague, RM, Pl. 41 |
| 4. | 9 | Oxford: Bate 261[1] | | | 73.6 | rosew, silver | TaP T3 | | | | | |
| 5. | 10 brass | Paris E. 2186 | | | 73.4 | cherry? maple? brass, ivory | | | | | CPs dome. All keys in saddles. 3 & 4 dbl. 0 th. | |
| 6. | 10 brass | New Haven: Yale | | | | maple, ivory, brass | TaP T3 | | | | CPs dome. All keys on posts & axles on crescent plates. Incomplete. | |
| 7. | 13 | Ann Arbor: U. of Mich. | | | | dark w, ivory | | | | | | |
| 8. | | Edgware: Boosey & Hawkes | | | 73.5 | rosew, silver | TaP | | | | | |
| **MUSETTES** | | | | | | | | | | | |
| 1. | 9 silver | Oxford: Bate 273 | | | 32.5 | rosew, G. silver | | | | | CPs dome + brille. | |
| 2. | keyless | London: Horniman 179 | | | 46.5 | dark w, ivory | | | | | | |

# TRUSCHKA

| Young No. | No. Keys and Metal | City, Owner, No. | Pitch | No. Pcs. | Length | Body, Mounts Flaps | SAT | Holes Dbld. | Tuning Holes | Additional Data | Ill. Source |
|---|---|---|---|---|---|---|---|---|---|---|---|
| **BASSOONS** | | | | | | | | | | | |
| 1. | 5 wooden | Salzburg 15/6[2] | | | 124.5 | boxw, brass | | | | | Brass decorative bell rim ring. | Ill. Birsak, taf IX & 31 |
| **CONTRABASSOON** | | | | | | | | | | | |
| 1. | 5 brass | Prague 183E | | | 172.0 | | | | | | Extraordinary. Inlaid with bone, both black & white, and mother-of-pearl | Ill. GSJ XXIV, pl XVI |
| 2. | 6 | Hague[3] | | | | | | | | | | Ill. drawing, Jansen, fig. 264 |

[1] or "possibly successors" to Triebert made this instrument, according to the Bate collection catalogue, written by Anthony Baines.
[2] Birsak lists the instrument as made by "RUSCHKA, PRAG," and includes a photograph of the actual stamp that confirms this version on this instrument at least. On the other hand, the maker has been thoroughly studied and the name *is* Simon Josef Truschka (1734-1809). An especially interesting, brief biography is to be found in GSJ XXIV, p 101, as well as a photo of his contrabasson, Prague 183E.
[3] Museum number unknown. It is not that given by Langwill.

| Young No. | No. Keys and Metal | City, Owner, No. | Pitch | No. Pcs. | Length | Body, Mounts | Flaps | SAT | Holes Dbld. | Tuning Holes | Additional Data | Ill. Source |
|---|---|---|---|---|---|---|---|---|---|---|---|---|

## I. S. W. (Johann Stefan Walch, or I. S. W. Trifftern?)

## I. S. W. (Johann Stefan Walch, or I. S. W. Trifftern?)

### FLUTE

| | | | | | | | | | | | | |
|---|---|---|---|---|---|---|---|---|---|---|---|---|
| 1. | 1 | Lucerne: Tribschen Museum 117 | | | | | | | | | | |

### OBOES

| | | | | | | | | | | | | |
|---|---|---|---|---|---|---|---|---|---|---|---|---|
| 1. | 3 brass | Munich: Deutsches Mus. 18867 | | | 51.8 | maple, horn | sq | | 3 | 2 | "I. ST. W." | |
| 2. | 3 brass | Nurnberg MIR 372 | | | 57.0 | boxw, horn | c'ro Eb sq | | 3 & 4 | 2 | Middle jt & bell by ISW, upper jt by J. Denner | |

### ENGLISH HORN

| | | | | | | | | | | | | |
|---|---|---|---|---|---|---|---|---|---|---|---|---|
| 1. | 3 | Salzburg 13/6 | | | 78.0 | maple, horn, black leather | | | | | | |

### CLARINETS

| | | | | | | | | | | | | |
|---|---|---|---|---|---|---|---|---|---|---|---|---|
| 1. | 3 brass | Salzburg 18/4[1] | A | 4 pc | 76.0 | | sq | | 7 | | "Ioseph/SW/Trifftern." Note 1. | Instr & stamp ill. Birsak cat., taf XI & 42. |
| 2. | 3 brass | Linz W. 146 | A | 5 pc | 64.0 | boxw, horn | | | 7 | | "ISW" | |
| 3. | 4 brass | London: Horniman 243 | B♭ | | 67.6 | boxw, horn | trap | | | | "I. S. W." Swallowtail G♯. | Ill. Carse MWI, pl VII-A |
| 4. | 4 brass | Salzburg 18/6[1] | A | 4 pc | 70.0 | | sq | | 7 | | "I. S. W." Swallowtail G . | |
| 5. | 4 brass | Salzburg 18/7[1] | A | 4 pc | 70.0 | | sq | | | | "I. S. W." | |
| 6. | 3? brass | Salzburg 18/5[1] | A♭ | 4 pc | 70.0 | | | | 7 | | "I. S. W." | |

### CLARINETS D'AMOUR

| | | | | | | | | | | | | |
|---|---|---|---|---|---|---|---|---|---|---|---|---|
| 1. | 3 brass | Berlin 2892 | | | 74.0 | pearw, horn | trap a' & 8$^{ve}$ | | | | Bore 1.25-1.3. Neck & mthpc missing. Note 1. | |
| 2. | 3 brass | Bonn BH (Zimmermann 152) | | 4 pc | 75.5 | pearw, horn | sq | | | | | |
| 3. | 3 brass | Nürnberg MIR 462 | | 6 pc | 77.0 | plumw, horn | sq | | | | Wooden bulb, not hollow, between neck & mouthpiece. | |
| 4. | 4 brass | Munich BNM Mu 115 | | 5 pc | 89.0 | horn, brass | sq | SATW | | | 4th key swallowtail for G♯. Bore 1.42 | LOM 102 |

### BASSET HORN

| | | | | | | | | | | | | |
|---|---|---|---|---|---|---|---|---|---|---|---|---|
| 1. | 7 | Salzburg 18/31 | | | 118.0 | boxw, black leather, horn | sq & trap | | | | "I. S. W." but also "MACHT FRANZ SCHOFFTLMAYR IN BASSAU" on brass bell.[2] | |

---

[1] These four Salzburg clarinets by I. S. W. are unusual in that they have a brass neck that curves slightly, on the end of which the wood mouthpiece is placed. The appearance, then, is somewhat like a clarinet d'amour but without the globular bell, that last assumption based on Birsak's photo of 18/4, but note that some of the "clarinets d'amour" listed are of similar length. It might prove that only Horniman-Carse is a true clarinet, having neither metal neck nor globular bell. I have not been able to see Linz W. 146.

[2] instrument and stamp both ill. in Birsak catalogue, taf XII and 33.

| Young No. | No. Keys and Metal | City, Owner, No. | Pitch | No. Pcs. | Length | Body, Mounts | Flaps | SAT | Holes Dbld. | Tuning Holes | Additional Data | Ill. Source |
|---|---|---|---|---|---|---|---|---|---|---|---|---|

**I. S. W. (Johann Stefan Walch, or I. S. W. Trifftern?)** *(cont.)*

**I. S. W. (Johann Stefan Walch, or I. S. W. Trifftern?)** *(cont.)*

BASSOON

| | | | | | | | | | | | | |
|---|---|---|---|---|---|---|---|---|---|---|---|---|
| 1. | 5 brass | Salzburg 15/3 | | | 114.0 | maple, brass | | | | | F swallowtail; crook missing. | |

RACKETT

| | | | | | | | | | | | | |
|---|---|---|---|---|---|---|---|---|---|---|---|---|
| 1. | 0? keys | Munich BNM Mu 125 | | | | wood body, brass band at end | | | | | | |

# ANDRÉ WALCH

ANDRÉ WALCH

CLARINET

| | | | | | | | | | | | | |
|---|---|---|---|---|---|---|---|---|---|---|---|---|
| 1. | 5 brass | Nürnberg MIR 434 | | | 48.5 | boxw, horn | sq | | | | | |

# A. (AUGUSTIN - 17 C) WALCH

A. (AUGUSTIN - 17 C) WALCH

OCTAVE RECORDER

| | | | | | | | | | | | | |
|---|---|---|---|---|---|---|---|---|---|---|---|---|
| 1. | | Bonn BH (Zimmermann 6) | E | | 26.5 | ivory | | | | | "2nd half, 17 C" | Stamp ill. Zimmermann cat., p 16, instr. ill. p 17. |

ALTO RECORDER

| | | | | | | | | | | | | |
|---|---|---|---|---|---|---|---|---|---|---|---|---|
| 1. | | London: A. Lumsden | F | | | | | | | | | |

# F. WALCH

F. WALCH

QUERPFEIFE

| | | | | | | | | | | | | |
|---|---|---|---|---|---|---|---|---|---|---|---|---|
| 1. | | xBerlin 2707 | G | | 40.5 | | | | | | "Bavaria 17th or 18th century?" | |

# WALCH (No Initial)

WALCH (No Initial)

FLUTE HARMONIQUE

| | | | | | | | | | | | | |
|---|---|---|---|---|---|---|---|---|---|---|---|---|
| 1. | | Paris | | | | made of wood | | | | | | |

| Young No. | No. Keys and Metal | City, Owner, No. | Pitch | No. Pcs. | Length | Body, Mounts | Flaps | SAT | Holes Dbld. | Tuning Holes | Additional Data | Ill. Source |
|---|---|---|---|---|---|---|---|---|---|---|---|---|

## I. G. WALCH

I. G. WALCH

### TENOR OBOES

| | | | | | | | | | | | | |
|---|---|---|---|---|---|---|---|---|---|---|---|---|
| 1. | 3 brass | Salzburg 13/4 | F | 3 pc | 75.0 | plum | ro C, sq eb | | 3 & 4 dbl. | | | Ill. Birsak cat., taf VII & stamp 41 |
| 2. | | Salzburg 13/4a | | | 34.0 | plum | | | | | Lower jt only. | |

### RECORDERS

| | | | | | | | | | | | | |
|---|---|---|---|---|---|---|---|---|---|---|---|---|
| 1. | | Hamburg 1924.217 | soprano in G | 3 pc | 41.0 | maple, unmtd | | | | | | LOM 61 |
| 2. | | Paris: late Comtesse de Chambure | soprano in B | | | fruitw | | | | | | |

## G. WALCH

G. WALCH

### SCHWEGEL IN B

| | | | | | | | | | | | | |
|---|---|---|---|---|---|---|---|---|---|---|---|---|
| 1. | | New York MMA 89.4.2397 | | 1 pc. | 38.1 | maple | | | | | Knob on each end of straight tube. | Ill. MMA Checklist Flutes, p 14 |

### DOUBLE FLAGEOLET

| | | | | | | | | | | | | |
|---|---|---|---|---|---|---|---|---|---|---|---|---|
| 1. | | Hague 149, per Langwill | | | | | | | | | Dated 1662. | |

### DOUBLE FLUTE

| | | | | | | | | | | | | |
|---|---|---|---|---|---|---|---|---|---|---|---|---|
| 1. | | Markneukirchen 963, per Langwill | | | | | | | | | | |

### HIGH FLUTES

| | | | | | | | | | | | | |
|---|---|---|---|---|---|---|---|---|---|---|---|---|
| 1. | | Nürnberg MIR 281 | | | | maple, horn | | | | | "Diskant-querpfeife". 2 pc: head jt & main jt. | |

### FLUTES

| | | | | | | | | | | | | |
|---|---|---|---|---|---|---|---|---|---|---|---|---|
| 1. | 1 silver | Salzburg 6/4 | C | 4 pc | 62.0 | boxw, ivory | sq(F) | | | | 2 upper jts, given length is with longer. | Ill. Birsak cat., taf II & stamp 40. |
| 2. | | Zurich: Hiestand-Schnellman | | | | | | | | | | |

### TENOR RECORDERS

| | | | | | | | | | | | | |
|---|---|---|---|---|---|---|---|---|---|---|---|---|
| 1. | | Nürnberg MIR 209 | | 3 pc | 65.0 | plum, unmtd | | | | | | |
| 2. | 1 brass | Salzburg 3/9 | B♭ | 1 pc | 72.5 | cherry | ro | | | | Swallowtail touch. | Ill. Birsak cat., taf 3/9 & stamp 40 |
| 3. | 1 key | Salzburg 3/10 | B♭ | 3 pc | 71.0 | cherry, horn | sq | | | | Brass crook. | Ill. Birsak cat., taf 3/10 & stamp 40 |
| 4. | | Salzburg 3/11 | B♭ | 3 pc | 71.0 | cherry, horn | sq | | | | Brass crook | Stamp ill. Birsak cat. stamp 40 |

| Young No. | No. Keys and Metal | City, Owner, No. | Pitch | No. Pcs. | Length | Body, Mounts Flaps | | SAT | Holes Dbld. | Tuning Holes | Additional Data | Ill. Source |
|---|---|---|---|---|---|---|---|---|---|---|---|---|

## G. WALCH (cont.)

G. WALCH (cont.)

### CLARINETS

| Young No. | No. Keys and Metal | City, Owner, No. | Pitch | No. Pcs. | Length | Body, Mounts | Flaps | SAT | Holes Dbld. | Tuning Holes | Additional Data | Ill. Source |
|---|---|---|---|---|---|---|---|---|---|---|---|---|
| 1. | 2 brass | Salzburg 18/1 | D | 3 pc | 53.0 | plum, brass | sq | | | | Decorative brass band on bbl & bell rim. | Ill. Birsak cat., taf XI & stamp 40 |
| 2. | 3 brass | Salzburg 18/2 | D | 3 pc | 57.0 | pear | sq | | | | F-hole double. | Ill. Birsak cat., taf XI & stamp 40 |
| 3. | | Salzburg 18/2a FRAGMENT | Bb | | | plum | | | | | | |
| 4. | | Salzburg 18/2b FRAGMENT | A | | | pear | | | | | | |
| 5. | 5 brass | New Haven: Goldie's Music | D | 6 pc | 57.8 | boxw, horn | trap | | | | Integral bell ring. Typical 5-key clar. Stamp like Birsak 40. | |
| 6. | 2 brass | Bonn BH (Zimmermann 122) | Eb | 6 pc | 57.8 | boxw, horn lt wood | trap | | | | Certainly a different G. Walch than made preceding.[1] | Ill. Zimmermann. p 51 |
| 7. | 5 brass | Bonn BH (Zimmermann 123) | D | 6 pc | 51.0 | lt wood, horn lt w, horn | sq sq | | | | Dr. Zimmermann says last half 18C vs. preceding's 1st qy quarter 18C. | |
| 8. | 5 brass | Nürnberg MIR 430 | C | | 60.5 | plum, horn | gq | | | | "Top two sections not original;" which ones not known. | |

## L. WALCH (I)

L. WALCH (I)

### RECORDERS

| Young No. | No. Keys and Metal | City, Owner, No. | Pitch | No. Pcs. | Length | Body, Mounts Flaps | SAT | Holes Dbld. | Tuning Holes | Additional Data | Ill. Source |
|---|---|---|---|---|---|---|---|---|---|---|---|
| 1. | | Salzburg 3/4 | G' | 3 pc | 42.0 | plum, horn | | | | | Stamp (only) ill. Birsak, no. 43. |

### DOUBLE RECORDERS

| Young No. | No. Keys and Metal | City, Owner, No. | Pitch | No. Pcs. | Length | Body, Mounts Flaps | SAT | Holes Dbld. | Tuning Holes | Additional Data | Ill. Source |
|---|---|---|---|---|---|---|---|---|---|---|---|
| 1. | | Salzburg 3/17 | A & C | 1 pc | 35.5 | plum, unmtd | | | | | Stamp & instr. ill. Birsak, taf II & 43 |
| 2. | | Salzburg 3/18 | G♯ & B | 1 pc | 40.0 | plum | | | | | Stamp (only) ill. Birsak, no. 43 |
| 3. | | Munich: BNM Mu 141 | F & Ab | 1 pc | 32.0 | plum, unmtd | | | | | |
| 4. | | Munich: DM 19855 | | 1 pc | 39.8 | plum, unmtd | | | | | |
| 5. | | Nürnberg MIR 193 | | | | wood, unmtd | | | | | |

### FLUTES

| Young No. | No. Keys and Metal | City, Owner, No. | Pitch | No. Pcs. | Length | Body, Mounts Flaps | SAT | Holes Dbld. | Tuning Holes | Additional Data | Ill. Source |
|---|---|---|---|---|---|---|---|---|---|---|---|
| 1. | 0 keys | Salzburg 7/3 | G | 1 pc | 40.8 | elderw | | | | | Stamp ill. Birsak no. 43 |
| 2. | 0 keys | Nürnberg MIR 259 | | 1 pc | 35.0 | maple, unmtd | | | | | |
| 3. | 1 silver | Munich DM 5481 | C | 4 pc | 62.0 | ebony, ivory, 1 horn band | | | | | |

[1]this one being much like Jacob Denner's or J.W. Kenigsperger's clarinets.

## L. WALCH (I) *(cont.)*

L. WALCH (I) *(cont.)*

### SCHALMEI

| No. | No. Keys and Metal | City, Owner, No. | Pitch | No. Pcs. | Length | Body, Mounts Flaps | Ill. Source |
|---|---|---|---|---|---|---|---|
| 1. | 0 keys | Salzburg 12/1 | D | 2 pc | 50.8 | cherry, horn | Ill. Birsak cat., taf VI & no. 43. EAMI 544 |
| 2. | 0 keys | Salzburg 12/5 | G | 2 pc? | 68.0 | plum, brass | Ill. Birsak cat., taf VI & no. 43 |
| 3. | 0 keys? | Berlin 2931[1] | C | 2 pc | 57.0 | wood, brass | |

# L. WALCH (III)

# L. WALCH (III)

### RECORDERS

| No. | No. Keys and Metal | City, Owner, No. | Pitch | No. Pcs. | Length | Body, Mounts Flaps | Ill. Source |
|---|---|---|---|---|---|---|---|
| 1. | | Munich DM 25961 | D | 3 pc | 30.0 | plum, unmtd | |
| 2. | | Salzburg 3/3 | C | 3 pc | 33.5 | boxw, horn | Stamp ill. Birsak cat. "LORENZ WALCH, BERCHTESGADEN" EAMI 432 |
| 3. | | Washington: DCM 663 | C | 3 pc | 34.0 | lt wood, horn | |
| 4. | | Bonn GH (Zimmermann 8) | C | 3 pc | 30.0 | plum | Drawing of stamp in Zimmermann catalogue |
| 5. | | Berchtesgaden Heimat Museum | | | | | |
| 6. | | Berchtesgaden Heimat Museum | | | | | |
| 7. | | Berchtesgaden Heimat Museum | | | | | |
| 8. | "piccolo" | Stuttgart: G. Hase | | | | | |

### DOUBLE RECORDER

| No. | City, Owner, No. | Pitch | No. Pcs. | Length | Body, Mounts Flaps |
|---|---|---|---|---|---|
| 1. | Linz W. 162 | D & F | 1 pc | 32.0 | unmtd |

### FLUTES

| No. | No. Keys and Metal | City, Owner, No. | Pitch | No. Pcs. | Length | Body, Mounts Flaps | Additional Data |
|---|---|---|---|---|---|---|---|
| 1. | 0 keys | Linz W. 164[2] | | 1 pc | 36.0 | unmtd | |
| 2. | | Copenhagen E. 85 | G | 1 pc | 33.5 | | Stamp "L. WALCH / BERCHTESGADEN" |
| 3. | | Copenhagen E. 83 | D | | 43.0 | | Stamp "L. WALCH" |
| 4. | | Copenhagen E. 84 | F | | 37.5 | | Stamp "L. WALCH" |
| 5. | | Berchtesgaden Heimat Museum | | | | | |

### STOCKFLOTE

| No. | City, Owner, No. | Length | Ill. Source |
|---|---|---|---|
| 1. | Copehangen E. 26 | 82.0 | Ill. Hammerich cat., p 24 |

[1] But Sachs says it is stamped "WALCH" without initial.    [2] stamped only "WALCH" apparently.

## L. WALCH (III) *(cont.)*

L. WALCH (III) *(cont.)*

### FRENCH FLAGEOLET

| | | | | | | | | | | | |
|---|---|---|---|---|---|---|---|---|---|---|---|
| 1. | | Munich DM 5501 | F | 2 pc | 23.2 | plum | | | | | |
| 2. | | Berchtesgaden Heimat Museum | | | | | | | | | |

## UNCERTAIN WHICH "L. WALCH"  OR UNCERTAIN IF "WALCH"  UNCERTAIN WHICH "L. WALCH"

| | | | | | | | | | | | |
|---|---|---|---|---|---|---|---|---|---|---|---|
| 1. | double flageolet | Vienna GdM 112 | | | | | | | | | |
| 2. | | Geneva | | | | | | | | | |
| 3. | | Paris 419 | | | | | | | | | |
| 4. | | Berchtesgaden | | | | | | | | | |
| 5. | | Howard de Walden | | | | | | | | | |
| 6. | double flageolet | Savoye coll. | | | | | | | | | |
| 7. | oboe | Savoye coll. | | | | | | | | | |
| 8. | double recorder | xLeipzig 1151, lost in WW2 | | | | | boxw | | | | Was stamped "—LCH" |

## P. WALCH

P. WALCH

### FLUTES (ALL SMALL?)

| | | | | | | | | | | | |
|---|---|---|---|---|---|---|---|---|---|---|---|
| 1. | Schweizer flute | Ann Arbor: U. of Michigan 581 | B♭ | | 37.7 | wood, horn | | | | 6 finger holes. "C. PAUL WALCH/ BERCHTESGADEN" |
| 2. | Piccolo | Berchtegaden Heimat Museum | | | | | | | | |
| 3. | Piccolo | Berchtesgaden Heimat Museum | | | | | | | | |
| 4. | | Berchtesgaden Heimat , Museum | | | | | | | | |
| 5. | | Berchtesgaden Heimat Museum | | | | | | | | |
| 6. | | Berlin 2707 | G | | | | | | | (also listed under "F. WALCH," which is how Sachs reads the stamp.) |

### WALKING STICK FLUTES

| | | | | | | | | | | | |
|---|---|---|---|---|---|---|---|---|---|---|---|
| 1. | 1 brass | London: Sotheby's auction 1974 | | | | | | | | "PAUL WALCH/BERCHTESGADEN/ C" |
| 2. | 1 brass | Washington: DCM 1391 | | | 90.4 | | | | | |
| 3. | 1 | Salzburg 6/12 | C | | 89.0 | brass, mother-of-pearl | | | | |

### RECORDERS

| | | | | | | | | | | | |
|---|---|---|---|---|---|---|---|---|---|---|---|
| 1. | Soprano | Salzburg 3/1 | D | | 30.0 | rosew, ivory | | | | 3 pc |
| 2. | | Nürnberg per Langwill | | | | | | | | |

| Young No. | No. Keys and Metal | City, Owner, No. | PITCH | No. Pcs. | Length | Body, Mounts Flaps | | SAT | Holes Dbld. | Tuning Holes | Additional Data | Ill. Source |
|---|---|---|---|---|---|---|---|---|---|---|---|---|

## FLAGEOLETS

| | | | | | | | | | | | | |
|---|---|---|---|---|---|---|---|---|---|---|---|---|
| 1. | | Berchtesgaden Heimat Museum, per Langwill | | | | | | | | | | |
| 2. | | Munich: DM, per Langwill | | | | | | | | | probably the one listed under L. WALCH III | |

## CLARINETS

| | | | | | | | | | | | | |
|---|---|---|---|---|---|---|---|---|---|---|---|---|
| 1. | 5 | Salzburg 18/12 | A | | 66.0 | boxw | sq | | | | "PAUL WALCH/BERCHTESGADEN" | |
| 2. | 9 | Salzburg 18/19 | B♭ | | 64.5 | boxw | sq | | | | "PAUL WALCH/BERCHTESGADEN" | |
| 3. | 9 brass | Munich Stadtmuseum | E♭ | | as is,42.4 | boxw, horn | ro | SATK | | | 5 pc + missing mthpc. Integral bell ring. "PAUL WALCH" | |
| 4. | 3 silver+ | Bonn BH (Zimmermann 125) | F | | 42.5 | boxw, metal | sq | | | | 2 German silver keys added later. "PAUL WALCH/BERCHTESGADEN/F*" | |
| 5. | 5 brass | Bonn BH (Zimmermann 128) | E♭ | | 47.5 | boxw, horn | sq | | | | "PAUL WALCH/ BERCHTESGADEN/**" | |
| 6. | 5 brass | Bonn BH (Zimmermann 143) | C | | 58.0 | boxw, horn | sq | | | | "PAUL WALCH/BERCHTESGADEN/ **" | Ill. Zimmermann catalogue, p. 51 |

# WHITELEY

## FIFE

| | | | | | | | | | | | | |
|---|---|---|---|---|---|---|---|---|---|---|---|---|
| 1. | | Deansboro, N.Y.: Music Museum | B | | 44.2 | boxw, ivory | | | | | | |

## FLUTES

| | | | | | | | | | | | | |
|---|---|---|---|---|---|---|---|---|---|---|---|---|
| 1. | 1 silver | Washington: DCM 1204 | C | 4 | 59.8 | boxw, ivory | sq(F) | SATK | | | | |
| 2. | 1 brass | Washingtin: DCM 932 | C | 4 | 60.3 | apple or pear? ivory | ro | SATK | | | | |
| 3. | 1 brass | Dearborn: Henry Ford Mus | C | 4 | 58.5 | boxw, ivory | sq(F) | | | | | |
| 4. | | New York City: Frederick Selch | D? | | | | | | | | | |
| 5. | 4 silver | Washington: DCM 397 | C | 5 | 61.5 | rosew, ivory | dome | SATK | | | | |
| 6. | 8 silver | Dearborn: Henry Ford Mus 71-70-25 | C | | 66.4 | | | | | | | |

## CLARINETS

| | | | | | | | | | | | | |
|---|---|---|---|---|---|---|---|---|---|---|---|---|
| 1. | 5 brass | Deansboro, N.Y. Music Museum | C | | 59.8 | boxw, ivory | sq | | | | | |
| 2. | 5 brass | Washington: Smithsonian 65.729 | C | 5 | 59.8 | boxw, ivory | sq | SATW? | | | | |

|---|---|---|---|---|---|---|---|---|---|---|---|---|

**WHITELEY** *(cont.)* **WHITELEY** *(cont.)*

CLARINETS *(cont.)*

| Young No. | No. Keys and Metal | City, Owner, No. | Pitch | No. Pcs. | Length | Body, Mounts | Flaps | SAT | Holes Dbld. | Tuning Holes | Additional Data | Ill. Source |
|---|---|---|---|---|---|---|---|---|---|---|---|---|
| 3. | 5 brass | Washington: Smithsonian 65.729a | C | 5 | 54.2[1] | boxw, ivory | sq | SATK | | | 5 pc + missing mthpc | |
| 4. | 5 brass | Dearborn: Henry Ford Mus 71-70-30 | B♭ | 5 | 60.6[1] | boxw, ivory | ro | | | | 5 pc + missing mthpc, so given length is without it | |
| 5. | | Windsor, N.Y.: Derwood Crocker | | | | boxw | | | | | | |
| 6. | 5 | Buffalo & Erie Historical Socity | | | | boxw | | | | | | |
| 7. | 5 | New York City: Frederick Selch | | | | | | | | C | | |
| 8. | 9 brass | Deansboro, N.Y. Music Museum | C | | 58.6 | boxw, ivory | ro | | | | | |
| 9. | | Minneapolis: H.C. Peterson | C | | | | | | | | | |
| 10. | | Rhode Island Historical Society | | | | | | | | | | |

# WIESNER **WIESNER**

BASSOONS

| Young No. | No. Keys and Metal | City, Owner, No. | Pitch | No. Pcs. | Length | Body, Mounts | Flaps | SAT | Holes Dbld. | Tuning Holes | Additional Data | Ill. Source |
|---|---|---|---|---|---|---|---|---|---|---|---|---|
| 1. | 10 brass | Stockholm 1954-55/25 | | | | | | | | | | |
| 2. | 10 brass | Copenhagen E. 24 | | | 127.0 | | | | | | | |
| 3. | 13 | Amsterdam: Henk de Wit, Jr. | | | | | | | | | | |
| 4. | 13 silver | Biebrich: Heckel Museum F-14 | | | 129.2 | | | | | | | |
| 5. | 14 brass | London: William Waterhouse | | | 127.2 | maple, brass | | | | | | |
| 6. | 16 silver | London: William Waterhouse | | | 126.8 | maple, silver | | | | | | |
| 7. | 17 brass | Washington: DCM 1119-B | | | 126.0 | maple, brass | | | | | | |
| 8. | | Basel | | | | | | | | | | |
| 9. | | Bella Coola, B.C. Canada | | | | | | | | | | |
| 10. | | Nieuw Loosdrecht: Will Jansen | | | | | | | | | | |
| 11. | | England: in an anon private collection, acc. to W. Waterhouse | | | | | | | | | | |

[1] without (missing) mouthpiece

# WILLEMS

| Young No. | No. Keys and Metal | City, Owner, No. | Pitch | No. Pcs. | Length | Body, Mounts | Flaps | SAT | Holes Dbld. | Tuning Holes | Additional Data | Ill. Source |
|---|---|---|---|---|---|---|---|---|---|---|---|---|
| **FLUTES** | | | | | | | | | | *Stamp* | | |
| 1. | 1 brass | Washington: DCM 508 | G | 4 pc | 83.1 | boxw, unmt | sq | SATK | | "J.B."[1] | | |
| 2. | x1 silver | xBerlin 2669 | | | 60.0 | boxw, ivory | sq | | | "I.B." | | |
| 3. | 1 silver | Washington: DCM 509 | C | 4 pc | 63.0 | boxw, ivory | oval | SATK | | "J." | | |
| 4. | 1 silver | Brussels 1060 | C | | 33.0 | boxw, ivory | | | | "J." | | |
| 5. | 1 silver | Brussels 2663 | G | | | boxw, ivory | | | | "J." | | |
| 6. | 1 silver | Brussels 2689 | C | 4 pc | 61.5 | boxw, ivory | sq | SATW | | "I.B." | | |
| 7. | 1 silver | Brussels 2690 | C | 4 pc | 62.4+ | boxw, ivory | sq | SATW | | "I.B." | | |
| 8. | 1 silver | Brussels 2691 | C | 4 pc | 64.3 | boxw, ivory | sq | SATW | | "I.B." | | |
| 9. | 1 brass | Brussels 2692 | B | 4 pc | 66.5 | boxw, unmt | sq | SATW | | "I.B." | | |
| 10. | 1 brass | Brussels 2664 | C | | | ebony, ivory | | | | "J." | | |
| **OBOES** | | | | | | | | | | | | |
| 1. | 2 brass | Brussels 2607 | | | 60.5 | ivory, unmt | ro | SATW | | "I.B." | 3 dbl. 2 th. E♭ key is dumbell shape. | |
| 2. | 2 brass | Brussels 2317 | | | 56.9 | boxw, ivory | sq-cors | SATK | | "I.B." | 3 & 4 dbl. 2 th. | |
| 3. | 3 brass | Brussels 2606 | | | 59.4 | boxw, unmt | ro | | | "I.B." | 3 dbl. 2 th. E♭ key is dumbell shape. | |
| 4. | 2 | Chirk Castle, England | | | | | | | | | | |
| **CLARINETS** | | | | | | | | | | | | |
| 1. | 2 brass | Brussels 916 | G | | 41.5 | boxw, unmt | sq | SATW | | "I.B." | Bore 1.17. | Ill. this book, Pl. 00 |
| 2. | 2 brass | Brussels 2573 | B♭ | 4 pc | 65.8 | boxw, unmt | sq | SATW | | "J.B." | Bore 1.29-1.42. mthpc-bbl, upper jt, lower.jt, bell. | Ill. this book, Pl. 00 |
| 3. | 4 brass | Brussels 919 | A♭ | 5 pc | 74.0 | boxw, unmt | sq | SATW | | "I.B." | Bore 1.43. | Ill. Rendall, pl I |
| 4. | 5 brass | Brussels 920 | A | | 70.0 | | | | | "I.B." | | |
| 5. | 5 brass | Brussels 921 | B♭ | | 70.0 | | | | | "I.B." | | |
| 6. | 4 brass | Brussels 2560 | C | 3? pc | | boxw, unmt | sq [2] | | | "I.B." | | |

[1] not known whether the difference in "I.B." and "J." signifies two different makers or not

[2] but low E is round. Added?

# APPENDIX A
## MUSEUMS AND COLLECTIONS REPRESENTED

Aachen: Dr. Wolfgang Willms
Assen, Netherlands: Drents Museum
Amersfoort: Joost van der Grinten
Amsterdam: Frans Brüggen
Amsterdam: Henk de Wit, Jr.
Amsterdam: Jaap Frank
Amsterdam: Mrs. Misset-Oudheusden
Amsterdam: L. van Oostrom
Amsterdam: Han de Vries
Ann Arbor: University of Michigan School of
   Music, Stearns Collection
Ann Arbor: Glennis Stout
Ann Arbor: Helen de. Kornfeld
Antwerp: Vleehuis Museum

Baltimore: Maryland Historical Society
Baltimore: Sidney Forrest
Basel: Historisches Museum, Sammlung alter
   Musikinstrumente
Basel: Michel Piguet
Basel: Renate Hildebrand
Bassingham, Lincs.: Bassingham Church
Bath: Mrs. Robin Eden
Begles: Ch. Thymel Collection
Berchtesgaden: Heimat Museum
Berkeley: University of California Department
   of Music
Berlicum, Netherlands: E. van Tright
Berlin: Musikinstrumenten Museum, Staatlichen
   Institüt für Musikforschung
Berlin: Dr. Walter Thoene
Bern: Karl Burri
Bern: Historisches Museum
Berwick-on-Tweed: C. Brackenbury
Betherden, Kent: C.F. Colt
Beverly: H.S. Woledge
Biebrich: Heckel Museum, Wilhelm Heckel KG
Binningen, Switzerland: Ernst W. Buser
Birmingham: Museum of the Birmingham &
   Midlands Institute

Bochum: Städtlisches Musikinstrumentensamm-
   lung Grumbt bei der Städtbucherei Bochum
Bologna: Accademia Filarmonica
Bologna: Museo Civico
Bonn: Beethovenhaus
Boston Museum of Fine Arts
Boston: Casadesus Collection of the Boston
   Symphony Orchestra
Bordeaux: J.M. Londeix
Bradford: Bolling Hall Museum
Bremen: Focke Museum
Bremen: Richard Müller
Breslau: Schlesisches Museum (instruments now
   all or mainly transferred to Poznan)
Brighton: Royal Pavilion Museum
Brighton: Municipal Museum
Bristol: Blaize Castle Museum
Bristol: The Mickleburgh Collection
Broadway: Snowhill Manor
Bruges: Gruuthouse Museum
Bruges: Barthold Kuijken
Bruges: Wijsberg Collection
Brunswick Städtisches Museum
Brussels: J. Sebille
Brussels: Musée Instrumental
Budapest National Museum
Buffalo & Erie Historical Society
Burgdorf: Schloss Burgdorf, Switzerland
Bury St. Edmonds: Moyse's Hall Museum
Bussum: Carel van Leeuwen Boomkamp Col-
   lection (partly transferred to The Hague)

Cambridge: Cambridge University
Cambridge: N.J. Shackleton
Cambridge: Dr. M. Lobban
Cambridge: Vivian Law
Cambridge: C.R.F. Maunder
Cambridge: Balsham Church
Cambridge, Mass.: Mr. & Mrs. G.N. Eddy

Canandaigua, N.Y.: Ontario County Historical
   Society
Carmel, California: Rosario Mazzeo
Celle: Dr. Hermann Moeck
Chesham Bois: Edgar Hunt
Chester: Grosvenor Museum
Chirk Castle
Cincinnati Art Museum
Claremont, California: Janssen Collection
Cobham: the late R. Morley Pegge
Coburg: Kunst Sammlung der Veste
Colchester & Essex Museum
Cologne Stadtmuseum
Cologne: Prof. E. Schamberger
Cologne: Bernard von Hünerbein
Concord, Massachusetts, Antiquarian Society
La Couture-Boussey, France: Musée Communal
   d'Instruments de Musique à Vent
Copenhagen: Musikhistorisk Museum & Carl
   Claudius Collection
Cuxton: W.A. Marshall

Darmstadt: Hessisches Landesmuseum
Deansboro, N.Y. Music Museum
Dearborn: Greenfield Village & Henry Ford
   Museum
Dearborn: Robert E. Eliason
Deerfield, Massachusetts: Historical Deerfield, inc.
Delmar, N.Y.: Clifford Allanson
DeWitt, N.Y.: Ralph D'Mello
Dinant: Collection Raulin
Dorking: Lady Jeans
Dorking: R. Glenton
Dublin National Museum
Düren: Karl Ventzke

Edgware: Boosey & Hawkes, Ltd.
Edinburgh: The Rendall Collection
Edinburgh: University of Edinburgh & Galpin
   Society Collection

Edinburgh: Royal Scottish Museum
Edinburgh: Lyndesay G. Langwill
Eisenach: Bachhaus
Evanston: Northwestern University
Evanston: Fred Henke

Florence: Museo degli Strumenti Musicali del
    Conservatorio "L. Cherubini"
Forest Hills, N.Y.: the late Harry Moskovitz
Frankfurt am Main: Historisches Museum
Frankfurt am Oder: Museum Viadrina

Gavle Museum, Sweden
Geneva: Musée d'Art & d'Histoire
Geneva: Musée des Instruments anciens de
    Musique
Geneva: Mme. Teyssere-Vuilleumier
Glasgow: University of Glasgow
Glasgow: Art Gallery & Museum, including
    much of the Glen Collection
Gloucester: Folk Life & Regimental Museum
Goteborg: Historisk Museet
Göttingen, University of, Musikinstrumenten
    Sammlung des Musikwissenschaftlichen
    Institüt
Gottweig Abbey
Graz Landesmuseum Joanneum
Greifensee, Switzerland: Bernoulli Collection

Haarlem: Piet Honingh
Hague: Gemeente Museum
Hague: Rob van Acht
Halifax: Bankville Museum
Halle: Handelhaus
Halsingborg Museum (instruments largely trans-
    ferred to Stockholm Musik Museet)
Hamburg: Museum für Hamburgische Geschichte
Hanover, New Hampshire: Dartmouth College
Harburg über Donauwörth: Furstliche Oettingen-
    Wallerstein'sche Bibliothek und Kunst-
    sammlung, Schloss Harburg
Haslemere: The Dolmetsch Collection
Haywood, California: D.L. Parker

Helsinki: Museum Virasto
Huddersfield: Tolson Memorial Museum

Ilford: the late Eric Halfpenny
Innsbruck: Tiroler Landesmuseum Ferdinandeum
Ingolstadt: Stadtarchiv & Stadtmuseum
Interlochen, Michigan: National Music Camp.
    Leland B. Greenleaf Collection
Iowa City, Iowa: Prof. Himie Voxman
Ipswich Museum

Kalmar Slott Och Museum, Sweden
Kassel: Littmann-Gutbier
Keighley: Cliffe Castle Museum
Kilmarnock: Howard de Walden
Kremsmünster, Austria: Kremsmünster Abbey

Lancaster, Pennsylvania: Historical Society
Lahr/Schwatzwald: Johannes Hammig
Leamington Spa: Maurice Byrne
Leeds, University of
Letchworth State Park, New York
Leipzig: Musikinstrumenten Museum, Karl Marx
    Universität
Leningrad: Institute of Theatre, Music, and
    Cinematography
Lewis: Lewis Museum
Lilienfeld, Austria: Meimatmuseum
Lincolnshire:Winterton Church
Linköping: Ostergötlands och Linköpings stads
    Museum, Sweden
Linz: Oberösterreichisches Landesmuseum
Lisbon: Museu Instrumental de Conservatorio
    Nacional
Litchfield, Connecticut. Historical Museum
Liverpool City Museum
London, Tower of
London: Royal College of Music Museum of
    Instruments
London: Victoria & Albert Museum
London: Horniman Museum
London: Philip Bate
London: A. Lumsden

London: Guy Oldham
London: James MacGillvray
London: Muffet Collection
London: Walter Avery
London: Reuben Greene Collection (although
    supposedly dispersed)
London: Cave Collection
London: Michael Oridge
London: Kneller Hall
London: William Waterhouse
Louisville, Kentucky: Stuart-Morgan Vance
Lucerne: Tribschen Museum
Lucerne: the late Otto Dreyer
Lund, Sweden: Musikhistoriska Museet

Madison, Wisconsin: Robert S. Cole
Madison, Wisconsin: Prof. Richard Lottridge
Manchester: Henry Watson Collection in the
    Central and also Wilbraham Libraries
Markneukirchen Musikinstrumenten Museum
Markneujirchen: Fritz Berndt
Massapequa Park, N.Y.: William J. Maynard
Meopham, Kent: Nicholas Benn
Meran, Tirol, Italy: Landesfürstliche Burg
Middlebury, Connecticut: Gordon Somers
Milan: Museo degli Strumenti Musicali Castello
    Sforzesco
Milan: Museo Nazionale della Scienza e della
    Technica "Leonardo da Vonci"
Milwaukee: Fred Benkovic
Milwaukee: Judy Plant
Mimizan: Marceau Claverie
Modena: Museo Civico di Storia e di Arte
    Medievale e Moderna
Mount Vernon, Virginia: Mount Vernon Estates
Muncie: Ball State University
Munich: Bayerisches Nationalmuseum
Munich: Musikinstrumentenmuseum im
    Stadtmuseum
Munich: Deutsches Museum
Munich: Dr. Manfred Hermann Schmid

Munich: Albert Müller
Munich: Ludwig Böhm
Munich: Otto Eckart

Nantwich: David E. Owen
Nazareth, Pennsylvania: Moravian Historical Society
Neuchatel: Musée d'Histoire de la Ville
Neuwied am Rhein: Giesbert Collection
Newark Municipal Museum
Newcastle-upon-Tyne: Mrs. C. Ring
New Orleans: Dr. James Swain
New Paltz, N.Y.: Michael Zadro
New Rochelle: James B. Hosmer
New York: Metropolitan Museum of Art
New York: the late Josef Marx
New Yrok: Frederick Selch
New York: Robert A. Lehman
New York: Straus Collection
New York: Sigurd M. Rascher
Niederalteich, BRD: Dr. Konrad Ruhland
Nieuw Loosdrecht: the late Will Jansen

Nordenham: Hansheiner Ritz
Northampton, Massachusetts, Historical Society
Norwich: St. Peter Hungate Museum
Nürnberg: Germanisches Nationalmuseum
Nürnberg: Friedemann Hellwig

Oettingen: Heimatmuseum
Offenbach am Main: Stadtmuseum (collection sold, partly/mainly? to Göttingen)
Oklahoma City: Dr. Richard W. Payne
Oslo: Norsk Folkemuseum
Oxford: The Bate Collection, Faculty of Music
Oxford: Dr. A.C. Baines
Oxford: Pitt Rivers Museum
Oxford: Jeremy Montagu

Paris: Musée Instrumental
Paris: Philippe Suzanne
Paris: Selmer Collection
Paris: J.P. Vignon

Paris: Marcel Josse
Peebles: F.E. Dodman
Peine, BRD: Pastor Günter Hart
Perrysburg, Ohio: David Karstaedt
Philadelphia: Hans Moennig
Pittsfield, Massachusetts. Berkshire Museum
Poznan: Museum Nardowe w Poznaniu-Muzeum Instrumentow Muzycznych
Prague: Hudebni Oddeleni Narodniho Muzea
Providence, Rhode Island Historical Society

Qualicum Beach, B.C., Canada: the late Edward Eames
Quito, Ecuador: Pedro Traversari Collection

Regensburg: Museum der Stadt Regensburg
Rheinfelden, Schweiz: Fricktaler Museums
Richmond: E.C. Murray
Rochester, N.Y.: Martin Lessen
Rockport, Maine: John Shortridge
Rome: Galleria del Lazio
Rome: Raccolta statale de strumenti musicali/ same as Museo degli Strumenti Musicali
Rothenburg ob Tauber: Reichstadt Museum
Royston: Dr. R. Harding

San Diego: Miss C. Hall
St. Albans City Museum
San Diego: Miss C. Hall
St. Albans City Museum
St. Johnsbury, Vermont: Arthur L. Graves
St. Moritz: Musée Engadin
Salisbury, North Carolina: Dale Higbee
Salzburg: Museum Carolino Augusteum
Scarsdale, N.Y.: Dorothy & Robert Rosenbaum
Schiltigheim: Fanfare de Schiltigheim
Seattle: Jerome Kohl
Seattle: Jack Peters
Sevenoaks: C.M. Champion
Sheffield City Museum
Shipston-on-Stour: Mrs. I. Bennett

Sigmaringen: Fürstlich Hohenzollernisches Museum
Sollentuna, Sweden: Johannes Brinkmann
Springfield: Kenneth C. Parker (now living elsewhere, collection dispersed)
Stockholm: Musik Museet
Stockholm: Nordiska Museum (instruments transferred/loaned to Musik Museet)
Sturbridge, Massachusetts: Old Sturbridge Village
Stuttgart: Gerhard Häse
Stuttgart: H. Böhm
Stuttgart: Gerhard Braun
Sussex: Hove Art Museum
Swindon Museum

Tarring: West Tarring Church
Tettnang: Helmut Steinkrauss
Three Oaks, Michigan: Robert Hunerjager
Torrington, Connecticut, Historical Society
Trondheim: Ringve Museum

Upper Bourne End: Leonard Lefkovitch
Urbana: University of Illinois

Vermillion, South Dakota: University of S.D.
Vernon, B.C.: Walter Karen
Verona: Accademia Filarmonica
Verona: Biblioteca Capitolare
Versailles: Bricqueville Collection
Victoria, B.C., Canada: University of Victoria
Victoria, B.C., Canada: Phillip T. Young
Vienna: Kunsthistorisches Museum (Sammlung alter Musikinstrumente: Neue Burg)
Vienna: Prof. Gerhard Stradner
Vienna: Rene Clemencic
Vienna: Nikolaus Harnoncourt
Vienna: Klose
Vienna: Hans Ulrich Staeps
Vienna: Technisches Museum

Waiblingen: Peter Thalheimer
Warrensburg, Missouri: Central Missouri State
   University
Washington, D.C.: Smithsonian Institution
Washington, D.C.: Library of Congress, Dayton
   C. Miller Collection
Washington, D.C.: United States Marine Band
Washington, D.C.: Robert Sheldon
West Caldwell, New Jersey: Robert Helmacy
Wigan: Haigh Hall

Witenham Church, Linc.
Winchester, New Hampshire: Wheeler Collection
Williamstown, Massachusetts: Williams College
Windsor, Vermont: Constitution House
Wolverhampton: E.M. Shaw-Hellier
Windsor, N.Y.: Derwood Crocker
Wrexham: H.D. Jones

York: York Castle Museum

Zell-Riedichen: Paul Hailperin
Zofingen, Switzerland: Historisches Museum
Zumikon: Hans Rudolf Stalder
Zurich: Museum Bellerive
Zurich: Hiestand-Schnellman Collection
Zurich: Allgemein Musikgesellschaft
Zurich: Walter Thut
Zurich: Schweizer Landesmuseum
Zurich: Willi Burger

# BIBLIOGRAPHY & SOURCES OF ILLUSTRATIONS OF SPECIFIC INSTRUMENTS

*Abbreviation used in text, always at far right*

AMIS — American Musical Instrument Society *Journal*, New York 1974 -

Baines V&A — Anthony Baines, *Musical Instruments, Vol. II, Non-Keyboard, Catalogue of the Victoria & Albert Museum*, London 1968

Baines MITA — Anthony Baines, editor, *Musical Instruments through the Ages*, 2nd edition, London 1966

Baines WITH — Anthony Baines, *Woodwind Instruments and Their History*, 3rd edition, London 1967

Bate catalogue — Anthony Baines, *The Bate Collection of Historical Wind Instruments*, Oxford 1976

Bate Flute — Philip Bate, *The Flute*, London 1969

Bate Oboe — Philip Bate, *The Oboe*, 3rd edition, London 1975

Bessaraboff — Nicholas Bessaraboff, *Ancient European Musical Instruments*, Boston, 1941

Birsak Woodwinds — Kurt Birsak, *Die Holzblasinstrumente im Salzburger Museum Carolino Augusteum*, Salzburg 1973

Birsak Brass — Kurt Birsak, *Jahresschrift 22-1976, Die Blechblasinstrumente im Salzburger Museum Carolino Augusteum*, Salzburg 1977

Blagodatov — G.I. Blagodatov, *Katalog Sobraniya Muzykalnych Instrumentov*, Leningrad, 1972

Bowers AMIS 3 — Jane Bowers, "New Light on the Development of the Transverse Flute . . .," American Musical Instrument Society *Journal*, Vol. II, New York 1977

Bragard-deHen — Roger Bragard and Ferdinand de Hen, *Musical Instruments in Art and History*, New York, 1968

Buchner — Alexander Buchner, *Musical Instruments through the Ages*, London 1961

Carse MWI — Adam Carse, *Musical Wind Instruments*, New York (reprint) 1965

Crosby Brown — *Catalogue of the Crosby Brown Collection of Musical Instruments*, New York 1901-1907

DCM Flute — Dayton C. Miller, *The Flute and Flute Playing*, New York, 1960;

EAMI — Anthony Baines, *European and American Musical Instruments*, New York 1966

Eliason Graves — Robert E. Eliason, *Graves & Company, Musical Instrument Makers*, Dearborn 1975

Eppelsheim — Jürgen Eppelsheim, *Die Instrumente*, booklet to accompany the phonograph album no. 2722 013 (Chamber Music II) in Archiv's recordings of the complete works of J.S. Bach.

Epstein — P. Epstein, *Sammlung alter Musikinstrumente*, Frankfurt 1927

Gai — Vinicio Gai, *Gli Strumente Musicali della Corte Medicea*, Licosa-Firenze 1969

Gallini 1863 — N. & F. Gallini, *Museo degli Strumenti Musicali*, Firenze 1963 (not to be confused with earlier catalogues of the same collection, in each of which the identification numbers for each instrument are changed without even references to other numbers.)

Galpin OEIM — Francis W. Galpin, *Old English Instruments of Music*, 4th edition, London 1965

GSJ — Galpin Society *Journal*, 1948-

GS Exhib 1968 — The Galpin Society: *European Musical Instruments, Edinburgh 1968*. The catalogue of an extensive loan exhibition.

Gilliam & Lichtenwanger — Laura E. Gilliam & William Lichtenwanger, *The Dayton C. Miller Flute Collection: A Checklist of the Instruments*, Washington 1961

Girard — Girard, *La Flute*, 1953

Grove 6 — Stanley Sadie, editor, *The New Grove's Dictionary of Music & Musicians*, sixth edition. New York 1980

Haine-de Keyser — Malou Haine and Ignace de Keyser, *Catalogue des Instruments Sax au Musée Instrumental de Bruxelles*, Brussels, 1980

Halsingborg — UTSTÄLLNING AV MUSKINSTRUMENT UR DANIEL FRYKLUNDS SAMLING I HALSINBORG, Halsingborg 1945

Hammerich — A. Hammerich, *Das Musikhistorische Museum zu Kopenhagen . . .*, Copenhagen 1911

Hague 1974 Exhib — *Historische Blaasinstrumenten: Kasteel Ehrenstein Kerkrade,* The Hague 1974. The important catalogue of a loan exhibition.

Heyde Eisenach — Herbert Heyde, *Historische Musikinstrumente im Bach-haus, Eisenach,* Eisenach 1976

Heyde Leipzig — Herbert Heyde, *Flöten Musikinstrumenten Museum der Karl-Marx-Universität, Leipzig, Katalog, Band I,* Leipzig 1978

Heckel Der Fagott — Wilhelm Heckel, *Der Fagott,* Leipzig 1931

Harrison-Rimmer — Harrison & Rimmer, *European Musical Instruments,* New York 1964

Horniman WIEAM — Horniman Museum, *Woodwind Instruments of European Art Music,* London 1974

Hunt — Edgar Hunt, *The Recorder,* New York 1962

Jakob Allgemein — Friedrich Jakob, *Die Instrumente der Zürcher Musikkollegien und der Allgemeinen Musikgesellschaft Zürich,* Zurich 1973

Jansen — Will Jansen, *The Bassoon,* Buren, Netherlands 1978

Jenkins ICOM — Jean Jenkins, editor, *International Directory of Musical Instrument Collections,* Buren, Netherlands 1977

JJ-GT-BR — Jean Jenkins, Gertrude Thibault, and Josiane Bran-Ricci, *Eighteenth Century Musical Instruments: France & Britain,* London 1973

Jordan — Hanna Jordan, *Führer durch das Musikinstrumenten-Museum Markneukirchen,* Markneukirchen 1975

Kinsky Kleiner — Georg Kinsky, *Kleiner Katalog der Sammlung alter Musikinstrumenten,* Cologne 1913

Kroll — Oskar Kroll, *The Clarinet,* New York 1968

Langwill — Lyndesay G. Langwill, *Index of Wind Instrument Makers,* 6th edition, Edinburgh 1980

Lichtenwanger — William Lichtenwanger, Dale Higbee, Cynthia Hoover and Phillip Young, *A Survey of Musical Instrument Collections in the United States and Canada,* Ann Arbor 1974

Linz — Othmar Wessely, *Die Musikinstrumenten-sammlung des Oberosterreichischen Landesmuseum,* Linz n.d.

LOM — Phillip T. Young, *The Look of Music, Catalogue of the Loan Exhibition 1980-81, Vancouver Centennial Museum,* Canada 1980

Lübeck booklet — *Alte Musikinstrumente,* n.d. (c1970), published by the St. Annen Museum, Lübeck

Mahillon — V.C. Mahillon, *Catalogue descriptif et analytique du Musée . . .,* vol. 1-5, Brussels 1893-1912; reprint, Brussels, 1978

MMA Checklist R — Laurence Libin et al, *A Checklist of Western European Flageolets, Recorders and Tabor Pipes* (in the Metropolitan Museum of Art, New York City), New York 1976

MMA Checklist F — Laurence Libin et al, *A Checklist of Western European Fifes, Piccolos and Transverse Flutes* (in the Metropolitan Museum of Art, New York City), New York 1977

MGG — *Die Musik in Geschichte und Gegenwart,* Kassel 1949

Montagu MR — Jeremy Montagu, *The World of Medieval and Renaissance Musical Instruments,* London 1976

Montagu BC — Jeremy Montagu, *The World of Baroque and Classical Musical Instruments,* London 1979

Montagu RM — Jeremy Montagu: *The World of Romantic and Modern Musical Instruments,* London 1981

Nickel — Ekkehart Nickel, *Der Holzblasinstrumentenbau in der Freien Reichsstadt Nürnberg,* Munich 1971

Ott — Alfons Ott, *Tausend JahreMusikleben 800-1800,* Munich 1963

Otto — Irmgard Otto, *Musikinstrumenten Museum, Berlin,* Berlin 1965

Paganelli — Sergio Paganelli, *Musical Instruments from the Renaissance to the 19th century,* London 1970

Remnant — Mary Remnant, *Musical Instruments of the West,* London 1978

Rendall — F. Geoffrey Rendall, *The Clarinet,* 3rd edition revised by Philip Bate, London 1971

Rephann — Richard Rephann, *A Catalogue of the Pedro Traversari Collection of Musical Instruments,* New Haven 1978

Ridley Luton — *The Ridley Collection of Musical Wind Instruments in Luton Museum,* Luton 1957. (Instruments now in the Museum of Instruments, Royal College of Music, London)

Roth — Richard Roth, *Die Musikinstrumente des Fricktaler Museums . . .,* Rheinfelden 1976

Rubardt Führer — Paul Rubardt, *Führer durch das Musikinstrumenten-Museum der Karl-Marx-Universität, Leipzig,* Leipzig 1964

Saam — Josef Saam, *Das Bassetthorn, seine Erfindung und Weiterbildung,* Mainz 1971

Sachs — Curt Sachs, *Sammlung alter Musikinstrumente dei der Staatliche Hochschule für Musik zu Berlin,* Berlin 1922

Sachs Handbuch — Curt Sachs, *Handbuch für Musikinstrumentenkunde,* Leipzig 1920

Schlosser — J. Schlosser, *Die Sammlung alter Musikinstrumente, Kunsthistorisches Museum in Wien,* Vienna 1920

Schröder Hamburg — Hans Schröder, *Verzeichnis der Sammlung alter Musikinstrumente Museum für Hamburgische Geschichte,* Hamburg 1930

Schröder Brunswick — Hans Schröder, *Verzeichnis der Sammlung alter Musikinstrumente Stadtischen Museum Braunschweig,* Brunswick 1928

Seifers — Heinrich Seifers, *Die Blasinstrumente im Deutsches Museum,* Munich 1976

Stanley-Stearns — Albert A. Stanley, *Catalogue of the Stearns Collection of Musical Instruments,* Ann Arbor 1918

Stauder — Wilhelm Stauder, *Alte Musikinstrumente,* Brunswick 1973

Szulc Poznan — Zdzislaw Szulc, *Katalog Instrumentow Muzycznych, Muzeum Wielkopolskie,* Poznan 1949

Vancouver LOM — Phillip T. Young, *The Look of Music, Catalogue of the Loan Exhibition at the Vancouver Centennial Museum, 1980-81,* Vancouver 1980

van der Meer Wegweiser — John Henry van der Meer, *Wegweiser durch die Sammlung Historischer Musikinstrumente, Germanisches Nationalmuseum Nürnberg,* Nürnberg n.d. (c1970?)

van der Meer HT — John Henry van der Meer, *Verzeichnis der Europäischen Musikinstrumente in Germanischen Nationalmuseum Nürnberg, Band I, Hörner und Trompeten, Membranophone, Idiophone,* Wilhelmshaven 1979

Ventzke — Karl Ventzke, *Die Boehmflöte,* Frankfurt 1966

Vleeshuis catalogue — *Stad Antwerpen Oudheidkundige Musea Vleeshuis, Vol. 5, Muziekinstrumenten,* Antwerp n.d.

Winternitz MIWW — Emanuel Winternitz, *Musical Instruments of the Western World,* London 1966

Zimmermann — Josef Zimmermann, *Katalog Einer Sammlung Historischer Holzblasinstrumente,* Düren 1967. The late Dr. Zimmermann's important collection has been acquired by the Beethoven Haus, Bonn.

# ABBREVIATIONS

*All measurements are in centimeters*

| | |
|---|---|
| attrib | attributed |
| bbl | barrel, e.g. the barrel joint of the clarinet (German: Birn) |
| c | circa |
| cor, cors | corner(s), e.g. key flaps are often sq-cors (square minus corners) |
| CPs | coverplate(s), that portion of the key that closes a hole |
| cyl | cylindrical |
| d. | dated, e.g. d.1800 |
| dec. | decorative, ornamental |
| dbl | double or doubled |
| ft | foot, as in foot joint |
| G. silv. | German silver (German: Neusilber) |
| Ill. | Illustrated in, usually by photograph |
| jt | joint, synonymous with piece or section |
| L | left |
| lac | lacquer or lacquered |
| leath | leather |
| mthpc | mouthpiece |
| p | page |
| pl | plate, as in photographic plate |
| pl | plated, as in gold plated |
| pc | piece, synonymous with joint or section |
| R | right |
| ro | round |
| SATI | Springs attached to ivory body |
| SATW | Springs attached to wood body |
| SATK | Springs attached to underside of key |
| sq | square |
| sq-cors | square flap with its corners removed but not enough to produce an octagon with equal-length sides. |
| st | stained, as with oil stain |
| Th | thumb, used when giving bassoon keys, e.g. L Th or R. Th. |
| trap | trapezoid |
| up | upper, as in upper joint |
| W or WW | wing key or indicating two wing keys, used when giving bassoon keys |
| w | with |
| x | the instrument no longer exists |

# APPENDIX D
## SOME COMMON FLAP DESIGNS

*These will be referred to by letter in the inventories.*

A　　　B　　　C　　　D　　　E　　　F　　　G　　　H

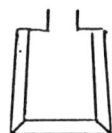
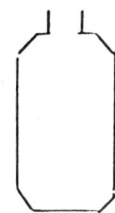
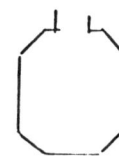
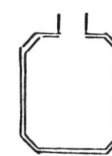

I　　　J　　　K　　　L　　　M　　　N　　　O　　　P

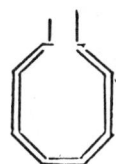
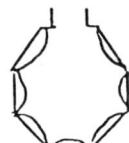
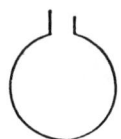
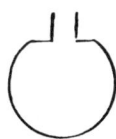

Q　　　R　　　S　　　T　　　U　　　V　　　X　　　Y

155